PRAISE FOR MARY-ANNE O'CONNOR

'Meticulously researched, thought-provoking and utterly compelling, *Sisters of Freedom* is yet another marvellous Australian historical from Mary-Anne O'Connor, cementing her place at the top of this genre. I highly recommend this to readers of rich, transportive historical fiction with empowering, female characters.'

—*Better Reading*

'A wonderful tale of love, adventure and bushrangers in colonial Australia...gripping and compelling.'

—*Canberra Times* on *Where Fortune Lies*

'A mix of history and escapism, and a strong sense of place, makes this novel an enjoyable read for lovers of Australian stories.'

—*R.M. Williams Outback* on *Where Fortune Lies*

'Mary-Anne always weaves multiple layers to her tales, and here is no different. A cast of complex and truly compelling characters reels you in and takes you on an absolutely riveting adventure. I was completely sold on this story from the start.'

—*Better Reading* on *Where Fortune Lies*

'...an epic, panoramic, historic tour-de-force...here is an author who knows how to craft an historical drama in prose as clear and cascading as an Irish mountain stream.'

—*Irish Scene* on *In a Great Southern Land*

'Wins over the reader with the clarity of her characters and a strong plot...beautiful, engaging storytelling'

—*Daily Telegra*

T0359686

'...from oppression overseas to the gold rush and horror of the Eureka Stockade, [this] is historical escapism in epic, sweeping form.'

'An epic, sweeping tale revolving around a clever, spirited woman and a fiery, charismatic Irishman. Dramatic, gripping and colourful, it's historical fiction of a quality that will take you on a beguiling roller-coaster ride, skilfully written by an author inspired by her own family history.'

'...vivid, authentic and historically well informed...*In a Great Southern Land* is another highly regarded novel from Mary-Anne O'Connor, a superior voice in Australian historical fiction.'

'...vivid and enthralling *War Flower* is a roller-coaster of emotions. One minute it'll have you laughing; the next you'll be heartbroken. It's that good.'

'O'Connor has written an insightful and well-researched novel that explores the lives of the young men who were conscripted into service as well as what life was like in the sixties for those left behind.'

'As we reflect on the lasting impact of a war that occurred a hundred years ago, Mary-Anne O'Connor brings us a story celebrating the good that can spring from war – love, hope and courage. In the heart-warming and heart-wrenching *Gallipoli Street*, the lives of three families will be irrevocably altered...from one Great War to the next, family and faith provides the ultimate reminder of what it truly means to be human.'

—Meredith Jaffe, *The Hoopla*

'Through her sensitivity, beautiful writing and gift as a storyteller, O'Connor's readers come to know and love her characters.'

—*The Weekly Times* on *Gallipoli Street*

'Ultimately *Worth Fighting For* is a tale of love, of hanging on and holding out hope when all seems lost. A tale of enduring through hardship and learning to live with the nightmares; a tale of hope, of loss, of friendship, betrayal and resilience.'

—*Beauty and Lace*

Mary-Anne O'Connor has a combined arts education degree with specialities in environment, music and literature. She worked in marketing and lecturing and co-wrote/edited *A Brush with Light* and *Secrets of the Brush* with artist Kevin Best, her late father.

Mary-Anne lives in a house overlooking her beloved bushland in northern Sydney with her husband Anthony, their two sons Jimmy and Jack, and their very spoilt dog Saxon. This is her seventh major novel. Her previous novels, *Gallipoli Street*, *Worth Fighting For*, *War Flower*, *In a Great Southern Land*, *Where Fortune Lies* and *Sisters of Freedom* have all been bestsellers.

Also by Mary-Anne O'Connor

Sisters *of* Freedom

Mary-Anne
O'CONNOR

AUTHOR'S NOTE

Sisters of Freedom is a work of fiction and, although it has been based on some true events in history, artistic licence has been employed at times to ensure cohesion is maintained.

First Published 2021
Second Australian Paperback Edition 2022
ISBN 9781867244493

SISTERS OF FREEDOM
© 2021 by Mary-Anne O'Connor
Australian Copyright 2021
New Zealand Copyright 2021

Published by
HQ Fiction
An imprint of Harlequin Enterprises (Australia) Pty Limited (ABN 47 001 180 918),
a subsidiary of HarperCollins Publishers Australia Pty Limited (ABN 36 009 913 517)
Level 13, 201 Elizabeth St
SYDNEY NSW 2000
AUSTRALIA

® and TM (apart from those relating to FSC®) are trademarks of Harlequin Enterprises (Australia) Pty Limited or its corporate affiliates. Trademarks indicated with ® are registered in Australia, New Zealand and in other countries.

A catalogue record for this book is available from the National Library of Australia
www.librariesaustralia.nla.gov.au

Printed and bound in Australia by McPherson's Printing Group

For my gentle mother Dorn who epitomises the dignity of true feminism

The best protection any woman can have … is courage.

—Elizabeth Cady Stanton

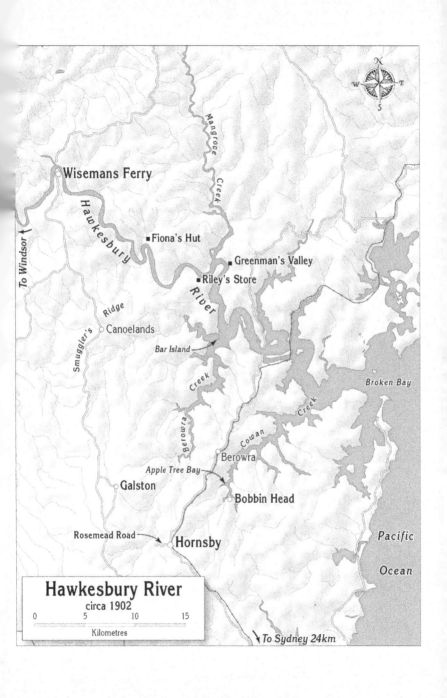

Hawkesbury River
circa 1902

Wisemans Ferry

Hawkesbury

To Windsor

Mangrove Creek

■Fiona's Hut

■Greenman's Valley

■Riley's Store

River

Smuggler's Ridge

○ Canoelands

Bar Island

Creek

Berowra

Broken Bay

Cowan Creek

Berowra

Apple Tree Bay

○ Galston

○ Bobbin Head

Rosemead Road

Hornsby

Pacific

Ocean

0   5   10   15
Kilometres

To Sydney 24km

Part One

To follow water

Part One

To follow water

One

'Don't look much like sisters to me.'

Ten-year-old Eddie Bryant said it and the irony of the comment wasn't lost on the trio of young women who gazed out at the Three Sisters that clear summer morning. The famous monolithic spears of rock before them were beautiful in their own crumbling, craggy way, yet different from one another indeed, despite being hewn from a singular giant cliff of sandstone.

The Merriweather sisters perusing them were much the same, so unalike no-one ever assumed them to be related, yet it could never be argued that they weren't derived from the same firm rock of their parents. In fact, argument was one of the unifying traits that proved their common parentage; 'healthy debate' their mother, Harriet, termed it. But the impassioned conversation that sparked endlessly between them all often drove their quiet father Albert to smoke his pipe in the garden.

Brown-haired Agatha, Aggie, was the eldest, and a more pleasant countenance would be hard to find, as her father had once remarked. Some thought her open features reflected a meek or compliant disposition, a misconception swiftly rectified in most cases.

Middle sister Frances stood beside her, tall and robust with long blonde hair that she characteristically plaited into a thick rope that swung about as she strode through life. Frankie often shrugged away compliments about its bright golden sheen, deeming it her only nod to beauty, but the others disagreed.

Ivy was the last, redheaded like her mother, and a world of colour next to Aggie, who was dressed in her usual practical grey. Ivy wore a bright green dress coupled with an orange hat, an outfit that would scream disaster on anyone else but she somehow managed to carry it off, as always. Besides, as her sisters well knew, Ivy didn't care about convention and enjoyed clashing bright tones together. 'God has coloured me brightly so I may as well join the party,' she'd often say.

Yet, as flamboyantly dressed as she was, she could also be a dreamy soul, and the natural monuments before them entranced her as she stared across the great valley. The Three Sisters were gold, brown and red hued too, she noted, pleased with the similarity, their myriad shades compressed into thousands of layers of time, weathering away. She supposed one day she and her siblings would weather away too before disintegrating back into the earth, then she shook such sombre musings away. It was far too lovely a day for such melancholy.

'Would you like to see the rainforest?' Frankie asked their young charge. It was a welcome diversion and Eddie grinned and ran ahead with the other children as the sisters followed, glad to be given the chance to be by themselves and chat. Not that it would be easy. It was no mean feat trying to talk and walk when Frankie set the pace.

'Slow down, Frankie,' Ivy soon complained, holding on to her hat. Why her sister needed to march along like a determined soldier she'd never understand.

'Nonsense. A good brisk walk is just what the doctor ordered – it's excellent for the constitution,' Frankie said over her shoulder.

'Women's suffrage is what's good for the Constitution,' Aggie returned.

'Too true,' Frankie agreed as Aggie almost tripped over a rock in her haste to keep up. 'Watch out,' she added cheerfully.

'What's that doing lying there?' Aggie grumbled, glancing back at the rock in a confused way.

'Think of it as a metaphor for overcoming obstacles in your path,' Frankie told her.

'We'll fall for sure at this pace,' Ivy complained, panting behind. 'Why do you have to walk so ridiculously fast all the time?'

'Not my fault you're as slow as a wet week. Look alive,' Frankie declared as she bounced along, her long plait swinging, 'there's adventures to be had and plans to be made.'

'Ankles to be broken and knees to be grazed, more like,' Aggie said. 'Slow down Frankie, for pity's sake.'

'Oh, quit your belly-aching,' Frankie said taking in a deep breath and letting it out with a whoosh. 'So invigorating up here in the mountain air, isn't it? Gives one a wonderful sense of clear-headedness.'

'Pig-headedness, more like,' Aggie muttered and Ivy giggled.

'Nothing wrong with that. If every woman a little more pig-headed we'd have secured the vote years ago,' Frankie said.

'I tell you who is pig-headed is that Father Brown—' Aggie was interrupted as Frankie came to a sudden halt and pointed across her into the bushes.

'Hold your horses — is that … a lyrebird?' Sure enough one went scuttling through the undergrowth. 'After it!'

She was off at a run, skirts held high, and the children came racing back after her as Aggie tried to stop the commotion, following more carefully and calling out warnings.

'There'll be snakes in there. Get back on the path! Frankie! Frankie, come back here right now.'

Ivy found herself alone and grinning. Frankie was so tomboyish and impulsive compared to Aggie who was very much the elder sister, often cast in the role of parent when the three of them were together. She showed great responsibility in her volunteer role at the local orphanage with the Sisters of Mercy too *and* she'd been married to Robert Stapleton for three years. At twenty-one years old, Aggie was as reliable as her grey day dress and sturdy walking boots conveyed.

A loud screech followed by a splash sounded and Frankie could be heard blustering. 'Blast and double blast.' Children's laughter echoed too and Ivy could well imagine the scene as Aggie's admonishment rang clear.

'Serves you right for running across such a slippery log. Honestly, of all the silly … careful now and grab my hand. Don't pull too … ah … ah … argh!'

The sound of her second sister falling into the creek had Ivy laughing hard and Frankie could be heard swearing well before they eventually reappeared, muddy, wet and with a gang of excited boys and girls at their heels.

'For goodness' sake, stop using that language in front of them,' Aggie exclaimed, wiping mud from her hem in disgust as they landed back on the path and the children ran on ahead once more.

'Oh, blast isn't a swearword.'

'Bugger is,' Eddie pointed out, turning back with a gap-toothed grin, and Frankie looked a bit guilty as Aggie wrung her skirt and the water dripped onto the ground.

'It's quite rare to see a lyrebird,' Frankie said, a distinct pout forming as Aggie fumed.

'My favourite boots soaking wet and now mud stains all over my good new dress ...'

'Quite a story to tell at least,' Ivy said, trying to break the tension and not make it worse by laughing as Aggie wiped her face on her sleeve, unwittingly smearing mud across her cheek. 'At least you can say you had that adventure Frankie promised.'

'I've more than enough adventures on my hands as it is, dealing with that fool of a man Father Brown,' Aggie said, pulling a handkerchief from her bag and attempting to clean herself up as Frankie emptied and banged her boots.

'You really shouldn't call a priest a fool,' Ivy said, a little scandalised. If it had come from Frankie she wouldn't have commented but Aggie was usually more respectful.

'I don't care who he is – the man's a fool. Besides, he doesn't deserve to call himself a priest, there isn't a compassionate bone in his body. Gave me a severe telling off again this week for trying to intervene when anyone ... with half a heart would see ... ugh,' she interspersed her tirade with swift swipes at the muddy cloth, 'it was the only Christian thing to do.'

'Another poor woman in trouble then?' Frankie asked as she relaced her boots and shook out her plait.

'Child, more like. Not yet fifteen and some man attacked her down by the railway. How can he expect me to leave a girl in her condition out on the street when there's a clean bed inside the orphanage? And at Christmas time too. I'll never understand it.'

Ivy shook her head, sorry for the girl, as Aggie continued.

'I gave her my milk money but that would hardly last a day – she'll probably end up having the baby in the bush or in gaol. No-one should go have to go through that,' she added, a catch in her voice now. 'Least of all a helpless, tiny newborn.'

'Why would anyone want to have a baby in gaol?' Ivy asked, horrified.

'Better than starving on the streets; half the women in city prisons are pregnant on arrival, committing crimes just to get in,' Frankie said, angry now too, and she twisted her hair back roughly. 'Three meals a day and a bed to give birth in is a fate better than that. Look at that poor wretch Maggie Heffernan.'

Ivy had heard the basics of the awful story but had so far avoided any discussion as to why the woman was arrested for drowning her newborn in the Yarra River. Fortunately Aggie didn't pursue the diversion.

'It's a disgusting state of affairs,' Aggie declared with a sniff as she shoved her soiled handkerchief away. 'A poor woman has no rights in this country and a wealthy one not many more. There's change coming, mark my words.'

She sounded exactly like Frankie's writing when she got all fired up, especially when she penned pieces for popular feminist bulletins such as *The Dawn* and *The Woman's Sphere*, which Aggie revered. Such passionate declarations were made by her sisters with religious fervour but Ivy found the whole 'Cause' argument over injustice and women's rights, or lack of them, depressing. It was just altogether too big and too sad to deal with.

'Anyway, it's a lovely day up here in mountains,' she ventured, changing the subject. 'Let's not let a little mud and thoughts of a horrid man spoil things; those children haven't got much to smile about and this outing is all about giving them a Christmas treat, remember?'

Aggie sighed. 'Yes, I suppose you're right, but I just can't stop thinking about that poor wee baby, and the girl herself, walking away with her almost empty bag; skin and bone save her round tummy. Julia, her name was.'

'Pretty name,' Ivy said.

'Ugly fate,' Frankie added darkly.

'Someone will take her in, I'm sure of it,' Ivy reassured Aggie as brightly as she could as they set back off.

Aggie gave her a wary glance. 'I know you like to believe the best, Ivy, but careful you don't just stick your head in the sand and expect problems to go away or be someone else's responsibility. We won't get anywhere collectively unless we take action as individuals.'

Ivy felt a bit put out at being lectured but she didn't respond, wanting to end the conversation. She chose to lag behind instead as Frankie strode on and Aggie tried to keep up, nagging her to slow her pace lest another incident occur.

It soon became peaceful without her sisters and Ivy stared up at the treetops and drew the fresh alpine air deep into her lungs as Frankie had done before, pushing thoughts of unwed teenage girls and prison cells far from her mind. It wasn't sticking one's head in the sand exactly, just one's face in the sunshine. She lowered her gaze and found herself smiling at the sight of her sisters up ahead, mud-splattered skirts flapping as they gathered up children and laughed. Sometimes the problems of the world had to be faced, she supposed, but other times, like right now in a beautiful rainforest? In Ivy's opinion they were best ignored.

Two

'Kuranda', Hornsby, New South Wales,
24 December 1901

The sun beat down on the red roof of Kuranda in brilliant Sydney fashion but the clever design of the modern bungalow and her shadowed verandah wings kept the house cool, even on such a day. The house on Rosemead Road was built for summer comfort, as well as for warmth in the chilly winters, with numerous fireplaces throughout. However, as much as her mother loved the artistically styled new home they'd built after moving from their previous, rather uninteresting, house around the corner, her father loved the gardens more, Ivy knew.

After much cultivation, the extensive grounds were now filled with fruit trees and roses among the native bushland, and it also boasted a brand-new tennis court, which the girls enjoyed immensely, especially Frankie. But it was the ponds and the dragonflies that hovered around them that Professor Albert Merriweather enjoyed the most since he'd retired from full-time teaching. They always followed water, he'd reminded his daughters often enough when they were children.

11

'If ever you find yourself lost in the bush, look for the dragonflies,' he'd say. 'They'll show you the way to the nearest creek, the lifeblood of the Australian bush – not just for the insects and the animals, mind, for we humans too – and you can follow it down to a river and passing boats. It's instinctual with these creatures, you see,' he'd add fondly, his voice always infectiously warm when he spoke of his beloved dragonflies. 'Most species spend the first few years as water nymphs; the majority of their life cycle, in fact.'

Ivy loved water and she loved that fact. It always made her feel safe and connected to Mother Nature, who would send these ethereal creatures to guide her should she ever need them, like they were tiny fairies, made just for her rescue should such a thing ever occur. This was a lovely thought to a child raised with a healthy fear of being lost in the Australian wilderness. Unfortunately her intellectual father liked to stick to the facts and tended to interrupt such whimsical ponderings with less beatific scientific reality. 'Once they emerge, they metamorphose from larvae by splitting their heads to shed their exoskeleton,' she remembered him adding once. 'Fascinating moulting process, the ecdysis.'

Her mother had teased him for turning something comforting into a horror story at the time, and indeed Ivy had been rather repulsed by the image, but now she smiled at the recollection, looking over at him fondly.

'What a beauty,' Albert was mumbling as he squinted at a waterfall redspot hovering above the main pool. He'd been pleased to see their numbers increasing this season after the installation of a small fountain, and Ivy studied the iridescent imprints and red spots on its wings, trying to ascertain the exact colours so she could capture them for him accurately. She'd been enjoying her art immensely this past year and her father had encouraged her, especially since she'd begun painting these whimsical, delicate creatures, the subject of his life's work.

'Ah, the fates have been kind today, Ivy girl,' he observed with contentment as he took out his spectacles and made notes in his pocket book. 'A marvellous turnout.'

'Have you decided on a name yet?'

Albert had retired from lecturing and was now a full-time entomologist and scholar. He was soon to release yet another book, but so far the titles he'd entertained were yawningly dreary, from her point of view. Then again they usually were. The study of insectivorous *Odonata* was hardly a poetic theme. However Albert found great joy in his dragonfly world and the fact that there was room for these life-giving pools scattered across Kuranda made their new home his very own paradise on earth. His wife and daughters didn't share in his enthusiasm for the actual recorded science but Ivy enjoyed watching them hover about in the sunshine nevertheless.

'How about *South Eastern Dragonflies: a Biological Classification and Seasonal Recorded Study*.' Ivy harrumphed and the professor's bushy eyebrows rose up to his wide-brimmed hat in surprise. 'What's wrong with that?'

'It's boring, that's what.'

'Boring?' he said, as if considering the word for the first time. 'Well, what would you suggest then?' he asked as he followed the dragonfly across the lawn at a stroll, notebook at the ready.

'I don't know, maybe something a little more romantic,' she said, following him.

'Romantic?' he said with a wry chuckle. 'I hardly think a scientific study falls into that category.'

'It could work. You could make it about their colours or their behaviour. Or something about the ponds perhaps.' She paused to stare out at the sky as she considered it. 'How about *To Follow Water*. You've often mentioned them doing that.'

'Have I?' Albert said as he looked across at her, amused. 'Well, it's a lovely name but more suited to a book filled with your artwork, my dear. Most dusty old scientists such as myself lack a fondness for romanticism, I'm afraid.'

'And ditzy young women like me are silly enough to look at the pretty pictures and learn little else, I suppose.'

She was miffed now and Albert's keen blue eyes recognised it at once.

'Truly seeing the beauty in nature surpasses mere observation,' he said, coming to a standstill to face her fully. 'Those who deeply appreciate it practise the highest form of intelligence, in my humble opinion. Never underestimate that about yourself, Ivy,' he added gently. 'I know I certainly don't.'

A lump began to form in her throat at his words, and she was surprised how deeply they affected her. Ivy was accustomed to being complimented on her appearance or her charm but rarely for her intelligence.

'I … I just like to soak it all in, especially since I've spent more time on my painting and sketching. Details have become, well, more detailed to me, I suppose …' She faltered, wishing she'd left things at 'intelligent'.

Albert seemed unperturbed. 'Precisely,' he said, turning back to study the dragonfly. 'It's become your purpose, I think. The water you follow, if you'll forgive my own clumsy attempt at romanticism.'

Ivy considered the concept as the dragonfly hovered. 'I've never thought of it that way. I suppose it is developing into more than just a habit or a hobby, perhaps even a purpose, as you say. I … I was thinking I might take classes and develop it somewhat. Maybe even teach the children at the orphanage, if the nuns would allow it.'

'Your mother always enjoys art,' the professor said, squinting at the insect and scribbling in his book. 'Why not discuss it with her and see what you two can come up with?'

'Oh, I don't know,' Ivy said, frowning now. 'I don't think she would take it very seriously. I mean it's not like politics or journalism or something, you know, important.'

Her father merely smiled as he worked. 'Human beings are complicated creatures, Ivy girl, flying along so fast,' he added as the dragonfly came to rest on a reed, its wings in gentle pause. 'Without the humanities how would we ever remember to stop and enjoy it?' Ivy looked at him and he met her gaze over his spectacles. 'Seems rather an important thing to me.'

He said it with such understanding Ivy felt the lump in her throat return but then Frankie's strong voice sailed from the balcony window above, interrupting the moment.

Daughters of freedom, the truth marches on,
Yield not the battle till ye have won!

Albert and Ivy both began to laugh. 'And what form of intelligence do you suppose that is?' Ivy was prompted to ask.

'That, my dear, is pure enthusiasm coupled with determination, something all of my daughters possess in spades. Although I don't suppose I could have expected anything less when I married your mother.'

'Yes, I guess you knew what you were getting into,' Ivy said with a giggle as Frankie's voice continued to ring out and they made their way back to the house.

'I'd like to say that was true, Ivy girl, but nothing and no-one could have prepared me for the three of you.'

His smile was indulgent as Harriet's voice carried across the lawn, instructing them to pick some lemons on their way in. The request only further emphasised just how different her parents were, aside from a shared love of the sciences.

Harriet loved lemon in her tea whereas Albert preferred milk and sugar. She also loved brass bands, modern architecture, full-blown roses and her pet talking parrot Pretty Boy. Albert preferred orchestra music, hadn't the foggiest idea about architecture, got the sneezes around roses and as for Pretty Boy, well, he was prone to pecking Albert's fingers on occasion, especially when he clipped the poor chap's wings.

The clipping was a recent necessity and seemed a cruel thing to do but Ivy had made her peace with it. She'd hated that he was confined to the house and never able to fly, so much so that last year she'd let him out, thinking he'd have a lovely time then head back home. Instead, the big pink cockatoo had flown up a gum tree and sat there for three days, at a loss how to survive on his own after a lifetime of being in captivity – firstly in an aviary on their Uncle Frank's farm and then in the Merriweather's living room.

When he grew weak and fell out and had to be nursed back to health the vet had advised that Albert clip him regularly to prevent such a drama occurring again but the professor hated doing it. He'd dedicated his life to observing wildlife in flight and the simple freedom that afforded and besides, he'd developed a soft spot for the funny fellow. They all had. Still, on the positive side of things, Pretty Boy was allowed outside now that he couldn't fly away and Harriet rather outrageously enjoyed parading about town with the bird on her shoulder. It wasn't just his startling and unexpected appearance as an accessory that appealed either, Ivy knew. His lack of censorship wickedly amused her mother too.

Albert and Ivy paused at the lemon tree to grab a few pieces of fruit before retiring inside to find Harriet serving tea and scones, Pretty Boy watching with interest from his perch on her shoulder.

'Watcha doin', lovey?' the bird enquired in his comical way.

'Be a dear and put him on his tree, Bertie,' Harriet instructed. Albert did as she asked, although Pretty Boy looked at him warily as he was transferred to the 'tree'. It was really just an old branch Albert had anchored in a tin when the bird had arrived one day as a gift from Harriet's uncle. The story went that the cockatoo had fallen out of his nest as a chick but Albert said he'd always suspected that Uncle Frank had climbed up and robbed him from his nest. At seventy-two, old Frank was still a daredevil and not entirely on the straight and narrow. Maybe that was why Pretty Boy was such a character himself – he was literally stolen property. The branch had a seed box attached and Albert added some to it, which seemed to mollify him.

'Pretty Boy,' the bird cooed. He was fond of saying his own name, and he really was pretty, being a rare Major Mitchell cockatoo, mostly pink and white with glorious orange, yellow and red markings above his beak and in his crest. That he seemed aware of this fact simply added to his overall charm.

'Well, it's official, I can't find my damnable hat,' Frankie declared as she clambered down the double oak staircase. It was a graceful centrepiece to the home, polished in deep honeyed hues with a rich velvet-red carpet runner and lit by a large leadlight window that caught the gold in Frankie's hair. The beauty of the setting was somewhat spoilt by her chaotic descent, however, and the colourful ranting as she continued. 'Flippin' flamin' blasted hell.'

'An interesting expression, dearest, but do take a break from swearing and stomping about like an old farmer and sit down for tea,' her mother said between pours. 'Old farmer' was actually about right. Frankie's penchant for country slang and swearing had long been laid at her great-uncle Frank's door. She'd adored him when they'd lived near him as a small child. Country Queensland had never quite left Frankie's blood.

'No time for it today,' Frankie informed them as she searched the room, messing up cushions and peering under furniture. 'I've got a deadline to meet down at the paper. Where's the stupid bugger of a thing?'

'Language again, Frankie,' her mother warned offhandedly.

'Just wear one of mine,' Ivy suggested.

'One of *yours*?' Frankie said, looking momentarily and comically incredulous.

'I do have quite a few,' Ivy said, with a shrug and a nod at the hatstand, 'amazingly hanging on hooks over there and not lost on the floor of your bedroom.'

Both their parents glanced over at Ivy's outlandish array of headwear with amusement then back at Frankie. 'I doubt you've something less colourful than Pretty Boy, which won't exactly impress that pelican of a man.' The 'pelican' in question was Mr Forsyth, head editor of the district paper, an individual fast becoming Frankie's nemesis.

'Beggars can't be choosers,' Ivy sang, feeling rather entertained as Frankie glared, her exasperation evident, before hurrying over to peruse the hats.

'Blimey, don't tell me you wear this in public?' she said, screwing up her nose at a brilliant red hat decorated with holly.

'Wore it this morning, actually,' Ivy enjoyed telling her, 'when I delivered my invitations.' Patrick had complimented her on it, saying red was his favourite colour, but her family didn't need to know that much.

'You must have sent half the neighbourhood blind,' Frankie remarked, squinting at it.

'God coloured me brightly so I may as well …'

'Yes, yes, join the ruddy party,' Frankie muttered, tossing the red one aside and choosing a bright purple bonnet instead. 'I suppose this is less ghastly but I'm still going to look like a god-awful peacock,' she bemoaned as she tied it over her tightly bound blonde hair.

'I think it looks stylish,' Ivy said, partly in defence of her bonnet and partly because Frankie truly did appear rather fetching in it.

'Oh well, perhaps he'll actually look at me today. Usually all I get is grunts.'

'Must be something wrong with the man,' Albert observed and Frankie's purple-framed face broke into a smile.

'You're just biased, Daddy,' she said, blowing him a kiss then waving at the others. 'See you a bit later on.'

'Why don't you take Shadow?' Harriet called. Shadow was their horse and was usually fought over for transport but Frankie was in too much of a rush.

'No time to saddle him. See you tonight!'

'Don't be late for carols,' her father reminded her as she left. Frankie always heartily enjoyed the traditional neighbourhood carol singing on Christmas Eve.

'I won't.'

'Good luck,' Harriet called after her as the door slammed shut. 'She shouldn't need it but still.' *The Sydney Morning Herald* had published several of Frankie's articles by now but the local paper was less enthused by her feminist themes, severely censoring her writing if publishing it at all. With the *Herald* and the women's bulletins openly accepting of her work Ivy didn't really understand why she persisted with 'the local rag', as Albert termed it.

'She should focus on the *Herald*,' he said, voicing Ivy's thoughts.

'She wants local awareness raised and I quite agree,' Harriet said as she settled down with her tea. 'I just wish they'd do something about that Father Brown. Aggie told me he turned away another girl – not yet fifteen years old. That's a *child* and with no parents or kin. Where's the Christian charity?' she added angrily.

'Hypocrite. And at Christmas time too, as Aggie pointed out. How can he possibly call himself a man of God?'

'In the family way, I take it?' Albert said.

'Yes, but hardly her fault. Some low-life attacked her.'

Ivy shifted, uncomfortable now, and Albert cleared his throat. 'Perhaps not a topic for young ears.'

But Harriet stirred her tea angrily. 'What of that child's young ears? What will she be hearing out on the streets while she and the baby starve? I'm telling you, Albert, they need to hurry up and give we women the vote so we can make laws to protect each other. It's about time.'

'The vote for women will pass soon, I'm sure,' Albert tried to placate her. 'With all the work you've done the new parliament is already moving on it and South Australia and the west have passed the state vote so it surely can't be far off,' he reminded her. '1902 will be your year – and a world first, let's not forget, if they let you ladies actually stand for election.'

'Humph. If the men can stop patting each other on the back long enough over Federation. Nine months later and we're still hearing them carry on.'

'We're not entirely a nation though, are we?' Ivy said tentatively. 'I mean, we are still bound to England.'

'True, Ivy girl, true,' Albert said, obviously pleased to see her joining in, 'but we are a nation and that's a start, although I agree with your mother about all the backslapping. This should amuse you, my dears,' he added, reaching for the paper to read aloud. 'Saw this one this morning:

> *Ah! See, now the sun uprises with a glow like firelit gold,*
> *With glory flooding a country where never a slave was sold.*
> *With her new-born flag saluting, Australia greets the sun—*
> *The bright sun of Federation, whose day at last hath begun.'*

'"Never a slave was sold"? We're a nation based on convicts whose very flesh was sold as they built the place! Never a slave ...' Harriet tutted, tapping her spoon furiously. 'Besides, every woman is a slave when she has no right to vote nor protect herself from injustice and tyranny! I mean, here we are, living in an age where a man can take a woman to court to enforce her *bedroom duties* and yet ...'

Albert cleared his throat once more as Ivy looked uneasily down at the floor.

'Yes, well,' Harriet said, slowing a bit now, 'I suppose enough said for today, but you have to know these facts, Ivy. The truth may be unpleasant sometimes but it's still the truth,' she continued. 'I didn't spend all those years fighting for my right to an education only to raise you a ... a protected *ignoramus*.'

Ivy flinched at the word, ashamed to not want what her mother had so desired and was still denied. Raised in London, Harriet had completed her studies in natural science at Cambridge University with second-class honours, no less, but the university wouldn't grant a degree to a woman. She was still campaigning to have her work recognised via correspondence and the ramifications of that ongoing injustice these past twenty years echoed in her parenting. A woman's worth was measured largely in intellect and passion, in Harriet's books, and Ivy felt well below par in both. Especially when compared to her sisters.

Her father looked over, eyebrows half raised at Ivy, and she knew he was encouraging her to raise the idea of pursuing her art but she didn't have the nerve. It seemed a rather trivial purpose once more.

'You need to broaden your horizons. Come along to the rallies and listen, and read like Frankie and Aggie,' Harriet continued, ramming Ivy's sense of inferiority home. 'Like what you find or not. The laws are against womankind and that includes you.'

Ivy nodded, torn between relief that the conversation seemed to be ending as her mother stood up, and guilt that she wanted it to. The strain of the moment was interrupted by Pretty Boy.

'Ignoramus. Ignoramus.'

He said it with a quizzical cock of his head and looked so cheeky it broke the tension. 'He'll never let us forget that word now,' Ivy said, unable to hold back a giggle.

'Oh dear. That could get us in trouble, especially if Father Brown ever drops in,' Albert said, chuckling too.

'I might have to take Pretty Boy with me next time I go by the presbytery,' Harriet suggested as Albert rose to make his way outside to smoke his pipe. Ivy couldn't help being further amused at the idea of her mother striding past the conservative priest with Pretty Boy crying 'ignoramus!' from her shoulder. Her father was still smiling too but he also looked a little worried. Knowing Harriet, she wasn't joking.

Three

Sydney University, 24 December 1901

Patrick Earle figured he must be the only student stupid enough to be studying on Christmas Eve but he wasn't really there to improve his marks come next year. He was there for the cricket. Professor Jacobsen was announcing the Sydney University first-grade team to go on interstate tour. Patrick figured he may as well study as he waited for the list to be posted outside the library. Not that he was getting much done. The historical significance of court structure and writs hardly had his attention, especially since he'd seen Ivy Merriweather that morning in a Christmassy red hat, standing on his doorstep with an invitation to her birthday 'box' party, her gorgeous smile in place. That the girl was a knockout was an understatement and the image of her as he'd opened the door, coupled with the cricket team announcement, left scant room for boring facts.

The party promised to be a good one, set down at Apple Tree Bay on New Year's Day, which seemed a fitting birthdate for so unique a person. They'd have to lumber down the forest track in carriages to get there but it was a pretty spot and well worth the journey to bask in Ivy's presence all day. She was bound to look ravishing in one of her colourful outfits as they played croquet and drank champagne and did whatever else you did at a box party. There was one thing he was definitely keen to do, but would she allow him to give her a birthday kiss? He suspected she liked him but he wasn't sure she liked him *that* much.

Plus he'd have to get past that mad sister of hers first. Frankie would be a looker too if she bothered with herself, but she was always too busy trying to whip the men at sport to show any inclination towards femininity. Feminism, on the other hand, the woman had down pat. Patrick supposed women deserved the vote, he just didn't want to hear about it from a fired-up blonde all day. The third sister Aggie was just as political, and just as attractive, but she'd been snapped up by his mate Robert years ago and she was also a bit understated for his tastes. No, it was uncomplicated, rainbow-coloured Ivy who had his attention. Ivy and that cricket list.

Thinking about either made him nervous though, and he stared out the window at the gothic turrets rising against the blue sky, forcing his thoughts towards law after all. How far they'd come in so short a time, especially this momentous year. Not only had Australia gained independence with Federation, influential men and politicians had also formed an entirely new government *and* agreed upon a constitution. As a budding lawyer, he understood that to be nothing short of monumental. Such things usually occurred when countries were defeated in wars or overrun but all had proceeded rather smoothly in the end, and in peaceful fashion. It was literally history in the making and especially personal to Patrick with his own father involved.

Maybe that was part of the reason he was so keen to get into the prestigious cricket team. He had a lot to live up to, being Douglas Earle's son, a man who presided as a judge as well as being a member of the new parliament. A cap in the Firsts would earn recognition and respect, two things very important to him at this point. Hopefully he'd done enough at grade level, earning a batting average of thirty-eight and being a handy spin bowler, taking a wicket in most games. It sounded impressive … didn't it?

He was staring up at the clock, wondering how many others would show up to see the list in person, when he heard a familiar voice call out from the corridor.

'It's up!' It was his friend Nick Johnson and the announcement caused Patrick's heart to leap hard. He ran out, shoving books in his bag as he went, spinning with a skid to rush over and see the verdict.

'Barnett, Craig, Earle, Johnson – we made it!' Nick cried as Patrick landed and they clapped each other on the back as a few others crowded in to read.

'Thank God,' Patrick said, the relief stronger than he'd expected. His hands shook and he shoved them in his pockets. His father would be proud now, no doubting that.

'Come on, let's have a drink and celebrate,' Nick said and Patrick gladly went along. News such as this deserved a beer and, besides, it was Christmas.

'Bloody ripper,' Nick toasted as soon as the ales arrived at the Royal Hotel and they clinked glasses with a few other mates who'd been selected. 'Think it's time for us to sing the club song, lads,' and so they did, in resounding fashion.

We are the good ol' Sydney Uni;
We are the good ol' gold and blue;

Did we win? We shit it in!
How'd we do it? Eaaaasssyy!!!

Patrick relished every word, euphoric to consider he'd be singing it all season now, assuming they won their games. Yet surely they were bound to do well, he thought, looking around at the talented bunch who'd made the cut. Nick could really swing a ball and left-hander Greg King was a gun batsman when he was fired up. Predictably most of the talk and banter centred around cricket and their upcoming tour but the topic of women eventually came up. It always did with this lot.

'Did you score an invite to the Merriweather do?' Nick asked Patrick.

'Certainly did, my friend,' Patrick said, patting his top pocket where the invitation lay.

'Think I might make a play for Frankie this time around,' Nick said with a grin. 'She's bound to succumb to my charms now I've made the Firsts.'

'Ha! I suspect envy would override admiration there, I'm afraid.'

'Well, she can hardly join the team,' Nick pointed out. 'Women simply can't play like men.'

'I wouldn't say anything along those lines either,' Patrick told him. 'You know how riled up she gets over women's rights.'

'A feminist, eh?' Greg piped in. 'Not sure I'd be too interested in a bluestocking.'

'You might be if you saw her,' Nick said. 'Anyway, I can hardly try for Ivy. You seem to have cornered that little filly nicely.'

Patrick was pleased with that but he tried to shrug it off. 'Maybe.'

'Maybe? She was hanging on your every word at Mariel's party, half your luck,' Nick added. 'Bloody good sort. All that red curly hair and alabaster skin.'

'Alabaster skin,' Greg said with a sigh.

'Wouldn't mind seeing more of it,' Nick said, with a cheeky glance over at Patrick, 'especially past the neckline.'

'Watch your tongue there, Johnson,' Patrick warned.

'Woah, what colour's green then?' Greg teased.

'Someone under your royal skin, highness?' Nick said, laughing.

Having the last name Earle and a parliamentarian as a father often prompted such jokes.

'Just, you know … she's a lady.'

'She certainly is, a bloody gorgeous one and sexy as hell with those cherry-red lips,' Nick said, trying to goad further, Patrick knew, but this time he didn't bite. He threw back the gauntlet instead.

'So's her sister.'

'How many of these merry girls are there, then? Any left over for me?' Gerard Fawkner, the team's wicketkeeper, asked hopefully as he delivered another round of beers.

'Not if I score Frankie and he gets Ivy. The third one is already taken by Pat's old school chum.'

'Bugger. A good looker too?'

'They all are,' Nick confirmed. 'Like Neapolitan ice cream, or close enough: cherry, vanilla and chocolate. A redhead, a blonde and a brunette. Imagine getting the hat-trick,' he said with another grin at Patrick over his glass.

'Ladies,' Patrick reminded him again firmly.

'They certainly, certainly are.'

The banter and talk of cricket and girls continued until, a good half-dozen ales later, they were on the train home, singing the club song, laughing at how nervous they'd been and their new good fortune. Then they sang carols. 'Deck the Halls' and 'Good King Wenceslas' rang out above the clatter of wheels, but none of the other passengers seemed to mind, and so Patrick disembarked at Hornsby Station that afternoon in good cheer. A cap for the Firsts, an invitation from a much sought-after merry girl and now dinner tonight with his hopefully proud father. Life felt good for Patrick Earle this Christmas. Very good indeed.

Frankie was fed up with waiting but she forced herself not to fidget as she watched the editor, Gerald Forsyth, read her latest article. At least he had noticed her today, as predicted, but staring open mouthed and slightly horrified at her bright purple hat didn't necessarily bode well. He seemed to be finished at last and Frankie held her breath.

She'd taken her time with this one, outlining everything she could find on the plight of unwed mothers in northern Sydney, which was topical with the release of Maggie Heffernan from prison that week. Vida Goldstein, the woman behind it, was a powerful figure in Australian feminism, and Frankie's heroine. She'd successfully saved poor Maggie from a death sentence – a girl from country Victoria who'd been left penniless on the streets with a starving newborn baby, and had chosen to quietly drown it in the Yarra rather than watch it slowly die in her arms.

Vida had managed to rally the public and gather twelve thousand signatures asking the Crown for mercy, and so it had been granted. Frankie considered Maggie's timely release a Christmas present to all Australian women – sympathy for the tragic girl was high, despite her crime, and Frankie suspected the article she'd written would be widely read if published. However, as the editor raised his eyes and pinned her over his glasses, she knew immediately that the conservative man before her wouldn't print the piece.

'I'm afraid it's a bit much, Miss Merriweather. Perhaps if you'd chosen to focus on what services are provided for such young women ...'

'I can't write fiction, Mr Forsyth. There are no services.'

'Surely you're exaggerating.'

'Unless a hospital or charity takes them in, they're completely at the mercy of the streets, and believe me, few are so fortunate. It's one of the main reasons the prisons are so crowded.'

He gave her a derisive look at that assertion. 'The government isn't turning its prisons into nurseries for the illegitimate children of unwed mothers, Miss Merriweather. I suggest you choose a less controversial theme if you want to be taken seriously by the newspapers.'

Frankie swallowed the angry words that threatened to spill out, opting for persuasion instead. 'Controversy sells papers, as I understand it.'

'It also exposes them to ridicule and possible litigation, neither of which I am willing to risk,' he said with finality, glancing at his fob watch. 'At any rate, I must wish you good day now, Miss Merriweather. The office closes early for Christmas and the staff need to lock up.'

He stood, dismissing her, and Frankie glared at him. She stood too, ramming the purple hat on her thick hair.

'Well, I'll just have to see what the *Herald* has to say then.'

He merely smiled in condescension, as if to say that her chances were non-existent. 'Goodbye, Miss Merriweather.'

'Goodbye,' she gritted out before turning and leaving. Stupid, dratted man.

Frankie stomped her way outside, holding on to her hat lest it fly off in the strong hot breeze and cursing under her breath as she strode down the dusty main street of Hornsby, past the post office, the dentist, the menswear store and the grocer.

'Of all the insufferable, prawn-faced ...' she fumed as she avoided a stack of crates filled with fruit from the local orchards and rounded the corner near the Railway Hotel.

'Woah there,' said a familiar voice as she collided with a young man. Papers went flying, adding to the confusion, and she yelped and ran about catching them, still cursing.

'Tarnation, oh lord … not the trough.'

By the time she'd retrieved the final dripping page of her story from the water trough outside the hotel quite a few of the locals were watching on, and Patrick Earle was handing over what he'd managed to chase down after knocking into her.

'One way to meet 'em, mate,' drawled a flannel-shirted man as he leant against the post, his grin wide. It was Billy Higgins, one of the timber cutters from Old Man's Valley. His wife Emma volunteered at the orphanage where Aggie worked so Frankie felt obliged to give him an awkward nod. She arranged the sodden papers in her arms as she did so, prompting amused chuckles from the small audience of beer-swilling men surrounding him.

'My heartfelt apologies, Frankie …' Patrick spluttered.

'No, no, it was my fault, I'm sure,' she said, but her annoyance was plain, even to her own ears.

'I'm afraid I was in a bit of a hurry to get home …'

'It's fine, really,' Frankie replied, still flustered but looking at him properly for the first time as she pushed back her escaping hair. He was slightly dishevelled himself and the patrons she was trying to ignore nearby weren't the only ones smelling of beer. 'Been … out, have you?'

'Oh. Well, yes, as a matter of fact. I had to go into the university.' He spoke coherently but there was certainly a detectable slur, now that she noticed it.

'University, was it? On Christmas Eve?' she said, stashing the paper in her bag now and throwing it over her shoulder. He had enough manners to appear abashed and she raised her eyebrows, waiting. If Patrick Earle wanted to court her sister he'd have to show a little more propriety than this.

'On the first day of Christmas my true love gave to me,' sang Joe Collins, the man who drove the grocers' dray through the gorge and another familiar face.

'A partridge who's rather merry,' finished Billy.

Frankie glared at the two of them and the line was quickly amended. 'Not very merry today, it seems,' Billy said as the other men chuckled. 'A few ruffled feathers, in fact, I'd say.'

'The peacock seems a bit ruffled too …' Joe observed to general laughter and Patrick stumbled slightly to face them.

'Gentlemen, if you don't mind,' Patrick said with some semblance of dignity as he led Frankie away, his hand at her elbow. 'I do apologise for that.'

Frankie merely raised her eyebrows again and put a little distance between them so he could no longer touch her. 'They're harmless enough, although you do seem rather … merry yourself this afternoon, I must say,' she ventured.

Patrick paused and she knew he was choosing his words carefully. It was quite enjoyable, watching him be brought down a peg or two. He was always so annoyingly confident, and more than a little pompous, in her opinion. The working lads at the hotel may be rough around the edges, and not men she and her sisters would be likely to associate with, but at least they weren't snobs, as she was beginning to suspect Patrick might be.

'The fellas and I had a few ales in town,' he admitted, looking a bit sheepish, but then his usual cockiness resurfaced. 'I've had some rather good news today, actually.'

'Oh?'

'I've been selected for the First Eleven interstate tour for Sydney University.' He was obviously very chuffed about the news and with good reason. It was quite an achievement and Frankie tried not to feel jealous.

'Congratulations,' she said. What she wouldn't give to play in a real team and be celebrated for her achievements, let alone study law there herself. The dean of the law school wouldn't allow female students to enrol, although one woman was fighting her way through. Ada Evans had somehow slipped in and was looking at becoming the first woman to earn a law degree in Australia, perhaps as soon as that year, yet so far Frankie hadn't been able to copy her successes. Frankie was eligible to sit for an arts degree, however that seemed like a consolation prize in comparison. How unjust, the opportunities denied the fairer sex. It made her blood boil even further as she shifted her bag filled with soggy, rejected words to the other shoulder and endured Patrick's gloating.

'Can't wait to tell Father. I was more than a bit nervous about it, let me tell you; felt like they'd never post that list today but they did, finally, and my name's on it so it's all official.'

'What a feeling that must be,' she managed, striding forwards even more forcefully than usual.

'Yes, it is rather,' he said, tripping slightly as he matched her pace. 'Good grief, do you always walk this fast?'

'Time and tide wait for no man … or woman,' she replied brusquely.

'A pity they don't let women play,' he said, seeming to pick up on her envy. 'You could outpace the best of them and I've seen what you can do with a bat.'

'Yes, well, give us enough time and we'll change that too,' she told him. He didn't respond but failed to hide a smirk and she recognised what it signified. Feminism obviously bored the man. Another mark against him. 'Anyway, until then you can pave the way for Sydney with the men. Who knows? You may even end up playing for New South Wales or Australia.' She'd hoped that comment might humble him but he only seemed encouraged.

'Yes, you never know what the new year has in store,' he said cheerfully, grinning at her now. He still appeared a bit drunk but, annoyingly, the grin made him appear more handsome too. That was pretty much the last thing she wanted to be thinking so she changed the subject.

'There will be a wonderful party to start it off, at any rate.'

Patrick's grin remained as he kicked at a pebble and it scuttered across the wide dirt road. The corner where she would turn for home was coming up and Frankie braced herself for a good two minutes of hearing how lovely her younger sister was. How colourful. How pretty. Ho hum.

'Yes, I'm very much looking forward to it. Ivy dropped the invitation around herself in what I must say was a very fetching hat.'

'She has a few of those. I was forced to wear one myself today.'

'I was going to say … I mean, it is rather bright, for you,' he observed. 'The one Ivy wore was red. It even had some holly on it,' he added, rather dreamily.

'I'm surprised she didn't stick an entire Christmas tree on her head,' Frankie muttered and he paused to look at her in surprise before bursting into laughter.

'You know, I think she could actually pull that off.'

Frankie giggled too then, the image too comical not to.

'I'm sure she'll wear something marvellous to her box party. Perhaps a gigantic present?' she suggested and he laughed again.

'She's a gift enough in herself,' he said, all charm once more.

'Yes, she is that.' Frankie had to agree.

'I've been wondering,' Patrick said, 'what exactly *is* a box party?'

Mary-Anne O'Connor

Frankie shrugged. 'Oh, she read about something similar somewhere and dreamed up the plan. She loves the theatrical notion of bringing lots of mysterious boxes down to the bay filled with goodness knows what.'

'A change of hats, perhaps?' Patrick suggested.

'Hats, gowns, shoes. Anyway, I'm sure she'll be the centre of attention no matter what she wears.' She hadn't meant to sound so suddenly petulant and tried to soften it with a smile.

Patrick looked at her with a side glance. 'You know, there's one fellow coming who's rather interested in paying attention to you.'

Frankie momentarily slowed down, face flaming before she marched back on. 'I seriously doubt that.'

'It's true. Heard it from the horse's mouth this morning.'

'Does he look like a horse?' she joked, but the blush burnt. She was used to being considered a chum, not a woman who attracted suitors. And hardly one who wanted to.

'Not really,' he said, appearing to consider the comparison. 'He runs rather like one though, which hampers his scoring ability terribly, but he's good with the ball. Excellent in fact. Made the team too.'

'Not Nick Johnson?' Frankie said, slightly incredulous and stopping altogether as they arrived at her street.

'One and the same,' Patrick confirmed.

'But … but he always tries to run me out or smash my bowling around …'

'Yes, funny that.'

Frankie gaped. 'I thought he just saw me as a … a friend. You know, one of the boys.'

Patrick tipped his hat, facing her as he backed away. 'It's hardly my place to say, Frankie, but I don't think any man sees you as that.'

He turned and left then and she stared at his retreating back in astonishment, not just at the news that a young man was interested in her romantically, but because Patrick Earle had just done something she'd never thought she'd hear him do: he'd paid her a compliment.

Four

Sisters of Mercy Orphanage, Waitara

The curtain was flapping in the hot breeze and Aggie tiptoed towards it, breath held as she carefully lowered the window pane to ease the sound of Eddie and the other older children outside. The infants were almost all asleep although six-month-old Annabel, their newest charge, had fought against it, her big brown eyes watching Aggie intently as if asking her to promise to still be there when she awoke. It had prompted Aggie to stroke her soft cheek and smile until the baby's lids lowered trustingly, leaving Aggie teary, a familiar chasm forming inside.

'Tea,' she whispered to herself, casting Annabel one last look before squaring her shoulders and walking quietly away. The nursery was becoming a trap of late and she had no time to become ensnared. Least of all today, of all days.

Aggie headed down the open-air brick hallway that linked to the kitchen where the rare wafting scent of stewing fruit in sugary syrup tantalised her. The children would have it with custard tonight and Aggie wished she could see their rapturous expressions as they tasted it; a wondrous Christmas Eve treat for tastebuds usually deprived of sweet fare. Even the fresh, juicy apples of Father Brown's orchard were denied them, although Eddie didn't seem to mind risking the odd covert mission to pinch a few. His voice reached her and Aggie paused to look out at the grassy apron where Eddie was standing on a pile of rocks and swinging a stick about as he sang loudly. The others watched on.

> *We three kings of Orient are*
> *Drinking beer and smoking cigars*
> *Fully loaded we exploded*
> *Drunken and full of farts …*

'Blessed saints – Eddie!' exclaimed Sister Judith, rushing over. 'Get down from there at once, you naughty boy. Such language!' she scolded as she went, waggling an angry finger, her black habit flapping. Aggie moved on, smiling at how much Eddie was like a young Frankie. Some people were just born to a life of mischief-making.

The kitchen was busy today with two local women in attendance. They'd ostensibly volunteered to cook and prepare but Aggie knew they really worked in lieu of paying school fees, which few in the parish could afford. The nuns ran the local school next door as well, which doubled as the church, and they also had the convent to maintain along with the nearby presbytery. Father Brown seemingly had no qualms in extending their duties to cleaning, washing and cooking for him as well.

It wasn't an easy life for the Sisters of Mercy, by any means, Aggie reflected as she put on a fresh apron and joined the women in the kitchen, and without the help of volunteers it would certainly be a lot harder. However wondering how the nuns would ever cope without her if she did leave wasn't an advisable train of thought either so she forced herself to focus on the job at hand instead.

Ham and duck were both baking in the oven, a donation from Aggie's parents, and the large wooden table was covered in vegetables as the women peeled and diced and shelled, chatting endlessly as they worked. Unlike the Merriweather girls, who had attended the prestigious Anglican Abbotsleigh Ladies College down the road, these two women had been raised Catholic, local and poor. They knew each other well and the conversation was usually just gossip and chit-chat, topics that came as welcome relief to Aggie. Unlike in her family, no complex debating occurred here, just easy friendship as they discussed their husbands and children, but there were undercurrents when it came to chatting about their vegetable gardens. These precious plots were essential to their families' survival but they also inspired quite a bit of rivalry. As such the produce before them was being prepared with a mixture of envy and pride.

'Goodness, that's big enough to feed the lot of them,' Aggie observed, eyeing the massive pumpkin they were cutting up.

'Only won second prize though,' Tessa Collins lamented, pushing down hard on a wedge and grimacing. 'Coulda sworn I had you this time, Emma, but it wasn't to be.'

Emma Higgins looked smug at the admission but she replied politely enough. 'It was awful close, I'm sure.' Aggie picked up a knife of her own as the woman continued. 'It's a pity those sons of mine don't work as hard at getting ribbons for fare but there y'go. It's all about the woodchopping, ain't it?' she said with a grunt, pumpkin skin splitting. 'I swear, if I have to hear one more word about that bloody Royal Easter Show … 'scuse the French.' Someone else cleared their throat as they walked behind her and Emma turned and blanched. 'And yourself, sister.'

The mother superior, Sister Ursula, merely raised an eyebrow as she passed through but it was enough to leave Emma pink-cheeked. No-one liked to be in the bad books with the sternest of the convent's nuns. Aggie was a bit scared of the woman herself, but Sister Ursula's discipline was needed sometimes, especially when it came to keeping young Eddie in line. He was no doubt about to get a serving for his Christmas carol antics. The sound of a man's raised voice outside indicated she'd been beaten to it, however, and the three women exchanged glances before going over to the window to see what was going on.

'Disgusting boy!' Father Brown roared. 'Hold out your hand.' He held a leather strap high as Eddie looked up at it fearfully. The other children stood watching, each little face terrified, and Aggie's heart went out to them. Aggie had the run of the nursery most of the time but the school-aged children were firmly under the jurisdiction of the nuns and sometimes, unfortunately, the priest. There was nothing she could do but watch.

'What are you waiting for?' the priest demanded, his black-clad form menacing as he towered over Eddie. The child slowly raised his arm, his fingers visibly shaking even from a distance.

Aggie held her breath and Emma made a sign of the cross as Tessa muttered alongside.

'Bloody brute.'

Eddie squeezed his eyes shut, waiting for the cruel strap to slice the air and land upon his bare palm, but then a voice carried across the grounds.

'Father Brown, a word if you please.'

It was Sister Ursula, her black robes fanning around her as the hot summer breeze whipped them about. All eyes turned towards her as the priest lowered the strap.

'I am doling out punishment at the moment, sister, so it will have to wait.'

'I'm afraid I cannot let that happen,' she said, immoveable and undeterred. 'The bishop has clearly stated that he doesn't want the reputation of our priests sullied by menial tasks such as school discipline.' She held her chin high. 'Eddie, go to my office at once. I will deal with you myself.'

Eddie ran off before anyone could stop him and Father Brown glared at Sister Ursula.

'In this parish my authority is final,' he said angrily.

'Of course, Father. Pardon me for not acting sooner myself on this matter and saving you from feeling you had to do such a distasteful act.'

The priest straightened, red-faced above his white collar, but he could hardly argue the logic of her words when they were based on the bishop's orders.

'Very well, sister, I will leave you to it. Just make sure you keep these orphans in line during mass tomorrow. I'll not have the congregation scandalised by their unholy behaviour on Christmas Day,' he stormed before walking away, leaving the stunned children to gape at his retreating back.

The women quickly returned to their stations as Eddie ducked through the kitchen. Sister Ursula soon followed and not a word was spoken until she closed the door behind her.

'Well, good on her, I say,' Emma whispered.

'She needs to watch those children like a hawk around him,' Tessa whispered back. 'I remember what he did to Charlie Beatson a few years back, poor lad.' Aggie had heard about it too. Father Brown's strap had given the boy two broken fingers, and he'd ended up being billeted into trade not long after, despite being only eleven years old. Sister Ursula had arranged it, making sure he was well out of the priest's way.

'Eddie almost copped the same,' Emma said with a shudder. 'Why that boy doesn't keep his nose clean.'

'He's just trying to entertain the others half the time, I think,' Aggie said, 'even though I've tried to warn him to behave. He's a smart boy and he acts up because there's not much else to do, outside lessons.'

'Idle hands and all, it's true enough if you ask me,' Tessa agreed, picking up her knife again and continuing with her work. 'Some men never grow out if it, neither. Take our husbands. Once the crates are delivered, my Joe seems to find nothing better to do with himself but drink at the pub with Tessa's Billy. Tsk, can't see no rhyme or reason for such a sinful waste of time.'

'True, true, it starts young and it keeps on going. Not everything makes sense to we women,' Emma observed, 'although Billy doesn't usually start work until after breakfast. Your Joe is up before the birds. You'd think he'd be too tuckered out, starting so early, although Barney's the same.' Both Tessa's husband Joe and Emma's brother Barney worked for Fagan Orchards out at Galston, with Joe picking up Barney at the creek most mornings as he drove his dray through the perilous Galston Gorge from Hornsby. The track was carved straight through thick rainforest and filled with 'more hairpins than a debutante' as Tessa liked to say, which meant setting off at four to deliver the produce to the trains by nine. 'At least Barney is well up the river before he has his grog. How does Joe make that long drive back without nodding off to sleep if he's stopping to drink beer at the pub along the way?'

The valley where the Collins family lived was difficult terrain to traverse, and the question prompted a wry smile from Tessa. 'To tell you the truth, Chompers knows his own way home. Last week that horse pulled up with Joe fast asleep and snoring away in the back. God knows how long he'd been there.'

Aggie chuckled and Emma noted with amusement, 'So long as he gets the job done, I 'spose, awake or no.'

'I always thought that man could sleep through anything, although I never figured it'd be his job,' Tessa said wryly as she slid the chopped pumpkin into the pot. 'At least he comes home in one piece and gives me the coin.'

'True enough. How's that fruit coming along?' Aggie asked her and Tessa brushed her hands and went over to check.

'Looks good to me,' she said, stirring the contents and breathing in the sweet aroma.

'Might be an idea to get those potatoes washed now, I'd say. I'll put this pumpkin on too, although I'll need to get you to watch it,' she said as she hefted the pot to the stove and stoked the fire below. 'I have to head out soon, I'm afraid,' Aggie told them, trying to sound nonchalant. In the three years she'd volunteered her she'd never missed a day's work and sure enough curious eyes were raised her way.

'Where you off to then? Christmas shopping, is it?' Tessa asked.

Aggie hesitated before nodding but it was probably the best excuse, if one that would cause possible resentment. Being affluent wasn't something she liked to highlight around these women, especially at Christmas time. Their children would be given simple, handmade gifts at best, and wouldn't be attending the carols and the following party on Rosemead Road tonight, as enjoyed by their wealthier neighbours.

Sure enough, the topic of gift-giving inspired the next topic of conversation and Aggie's guilt increased with each rag doll and second-hand pair of shoes discussed. It was hard not to feel guilty, working here, at this time of year especially. Hard not to feel resentful on these women's behalf, too. They worked tirelessly as mothers and wives, with no pay for any of their backbreaking efforts, and little appreciation from their husbands who expected no less. They took whatever other work they could get as well and

Tessa confided that she'd somehow managed to afford a longed-for pink satin ribbon for her daughter Molly.

Something in her tone tugged at Aggie's heart, causing the chasm inside to return. For they had love in abundance, these women, despite the hardships they endured – the adoring smiles their children bestowed upon them were treasures only a mother could ever receive.

Aggie heard a horse and cart approaching and looked out to see her husband arriving with a cheerful wave. A small crowd of children ran to greet him and climbed up for a short ride down the drive. He was a favourite when he dropped by occasionally to pick her up, especially with the boys whose only adult male influence was Father Brown.

Robert always took the time to throw a ball or listen to their stories and jokes, unfailingly kind and patient while they clamoured for his attention. Just like now, Aggie observed, watching him allow Shirley Bennett to put tinsel on his hat as he picked up Johnny Hayes for a piggyback across the yard. Eddie came through the kitchen then, his expression woebegone, and Emma nodded outside at Robert. He followed her gaze and his face split into a grin as he took off through the building to greet him.

'Robert!' he called and Aggie saw her husband laugh as Eddie ran across the grounds and launched himself against him.

'Hey Eddie, how's it going, little mate?'

Robert made slow progress with so many children upon him and the sight of him approaching like St Nicholas himself deepened the chasm inside Aggie to almost physical pain. She tried to ignore the feeling as Tessa came over and stood beside her, knife still in hand as she peered outside.

'He's a natural with 'em, and that's a fact,' Tessa observed quietly as the sound of Emma's chopping echoed behind her. Aggie merely nodded, swallowing hard before untying her apron and turning around.

'Back soon,' she announced before briskly walking out, bracing herself for the verdict she and Robert would soon hear; knowing that only time would reveal if Christmas would bring them the most precious of gifts or leave them forever empty-handed.

Five

Cicadas rang and small feet pounded the street but for once Frankie didn't envy the neighbourhood children the fun of being young enough to still race to each letterbox for the next carol. She felt rather strangely grown up this Christmas Eve as she followed along, keeping pace with her family for once, and she wasn't entirely comfortable with the concept. Not at all, in fact. 'Grown up' had connotations for women, paralysing ones Frankie was unwilling to face.

'I swear, it comes around faster each year,' John Hunter from number eight was saying, his wife, Dossie, nearby. 'No sooner had I put the old girl away than I was hauling her back out.' The 'old girl' was his Christmas milk crate – an ordinary wooden box that had been transformed by a coat of green paint and a some glitter and glue from their daughter Constance years ago. Constance was now a married woman with children of her own – nine-year-old Lydia and baby Josie, both the pride of their grandparent's lives, although Dossie fussed over them something fierce. She fretted about any medical calamity, real or imagined, and shook her head at her husband now.

'I tell him every year not to climb on that old thing,' she remarked with a tsk. 'It's an accident just waiting to happen.'

'I certainly wouldn't trust myself not to fall off,' Harriet remarked as Pretty Boy flapped about on her shoulder, excited to be outside.

'Yes, I'm probably getting too old for it …' John said, but they all knew he wouldn't relinquish the role of choirmaster lightly when the time came.

The conversation continued but Frankie had lost interest. Patrick Earle's words were too much in mind.

She knew men sometimes noticed her but she'd long thought she'd mastered the art of ensuring any potential interest was quickly shut down. It wasn't difficult to squelch their attraction: men usually disliked being shown up by a woman, and smashing them for four or acing a serve usually did the trick. In fact, spoiling any illusions they may have about courting her by besting them at sport was actually rather enjoyable.

Certainly there had been one or two times she'd felt a bit flattered or even attracted to a man herself – including Nick Johnson, if she was honest – but Frankie's ambitions in life centred on using her wits and skills to bring about suffrage and fight for women's rights. There was zero room for romance. A husband and children would tie her to the home and she could hardly go to rallies and exercise what freedom she had to support the Cause with someone else in charge of her life. Besides which, the law forbade married women from working in most professions, and she fully intended to have her writing lead her into a political career of some sort. Marriage would curtail any such aspirations and render her a man's possession, his legal chattel, she thought grimly, grinding her teeth at such inconceivable injustice.

Well, Frances Merriweather would be no man's property and she would answer to no-one but herself. Just see Nick or anyone else try to change that state of affairs. The thought made her square her shoulders and march forwards resolutely. So what if he had plans to pursue her, or that Patrick Earle had said something complimentary? That didn't change a thing as far as she was concerned, and it certainly didn't give them any new power over what she felt or thought or did. She was passionate about politics, not men; that was what being 'grown up' really meant. Taking social responsibility. Leaving the world of courtship to the romantics like Ivy – Frankie was forging an independent path.

'Blast and tarnation,' Pretty Boy crowed from Harriet's shoulder, prompting a few chuckles as Frankie drew ahead.

'Looks like she's suddenly remembered her marching,' Frankie heard her father say behind her.

'Well, the truth does march on, remember,' Harriet reminded him. 'It doesn't dawdle, as far as I know.'

'Save us a seat,' Ivy called. The fallen log outside the Jespersens' home was a sought-after resting spot after one of the longer walks between houses, and a decent enough excuse for her increased pace, Frankie supposed.

It was a scenic road to walk and Frankie took deep, calming breaths as she strode. Rosemead was the newest and wealthiest street in town and the elegant homes and gardens dotted along it were like Christmas decorations on an extensive forest of trees. The tallest and grandest house, Mount Errington, had recently been built by Oscar Roberts, president of the shire and a successful jeweller. He and his wife were making their way to the Jespersens' too, her adornments glinting in the sun even from a distance. Their home had featured in architectural journals, as had Kuranda, but the Merriweathers' home was more of an artistic retreat and seemed welcoming and homely to Frankie compared to the stately and rather imposing Mount Errington.

It wasn't just the chance to build an impressive house on a fashionable street that attracted some of Sydney's wealthy to Rosemead Road, however, it was the natural surrounds. Real estate salesmen sold it as 'the mountains by the city'. Mountains was an exaggeration for the thickly vegetated hills that stretched back in hazy blue and green vistas towards the horizon but they were ruggedly beautiful in their own unique way. The untamed wilderness certainly stirred something within Frankie and she resonated with the restlessness that danced in the hot breeze and roused the native birds as she went along.

Rosellas and lorikeets fluttered across the sky in flashes of brilliant colour, calling to each other to follow, oblivious to the festive occasion. Her eyes followed them as they sought roost for the night in the calm, deeper folds of the valleys, mysterious and dark places where the dense forest hid the creek and duck ponds. It was secret home to a plethora of local wildlife, from rock wallabies to her father's cherished dragonflies, all seeking to follow water, as he liked to say. The lifeblood of the Australian bush.

How simple life was for other creatures, Frankie reflected with a sigh, and how complicated it was for human beings. Animals and insects weren't beset by the longings and ambitions that plagued humankind, yet nor could they advocate for the betterment of their species. Humans, however, had choices to make for their own kind; values to apply and emotions to sort through. Responsibilities to adopt and roles to assume.

Frankie had always known that her role would centre on the Cause. Feminism consumed her. She'd been influenced first by her mother then the inspirational writings and actions of key suffragettes. Her every day was driven by the desire to realign that age-old imbalance between the sexes and give the female of the species the right to have an education and to vote. To protect one another from the laws that deemed women the property of men, to make an impact on the plight of the poorer classes, especially, and to herald in change – something on a grand scale. Something that embraced the passion and enlightened views of her parents, a calling she truly believed she was born to.

Like Vida Goldstein had said at a recent rally down in Melbourne: 'Surely those with a brain to think, eyes to see and a mind to reason must realise that a capitalist system must cease and a co-operative system prevail in its place.' Yes, the age of equality was dawning; history was being made and Frankie was determined to be a part of it all; to wield the power of words and protest for the advancement and protection of her species, just like the indomitable Vida.

Frankie considered her heroine's enviable achievements. Not only had she famously secured Maggie Heffernan's release, she'd also excelled at her studies, opened a school of her own, worked firsthand in helping the underclass in some of Melbourne's worst slums as well as establishing Frankie's favourite bulletin, *The Women's Sphere*. There were no recipes and home hints in this esteemed publication, Frankie reflected with a satisfied smile, it was all politics and reports and real news, without a corset advertisement in sight. Frankie's greatest contribution to feminism so far was having her articles included in a few publications. It didn't seem much of an achievement in comparison, but then again she was ten years younger than Vida.

Yes, Vida had been born into a life of privilege too but she'd turned it into a life of purpose. Frankie craved that. A life that mattered. And Vida had reportedly turned down several offers of marriage, demonstrating her great commitment to the Cause. Frankie vowed to do the same, should such proposals come her way. How could any romantic sentiment possibly compare to the lure of revolution and empowerment? To choose the former instead was well beyond Frankie's comprehension.

She was roused from her musings by the children, who'd been running about catching cicadas and were now climbing the big gum nearby, crying out when they managed to find one. Frankie found herself smiling in fond memory of doing the same not so long ago.

'Greengrocer!' young Lydia called triumphantly, jumping down from a wide branch and holding the cicada aloft to show Frankie, who gave her a nod of approval. *A strong-willed, capable child, that Lydia. She'll never let a man rule her life either*, Frankie wagered to herself.

Lydia ran to show her mother as the other adults arrived and Frankie watched Constance's face light up with obvious pride at her gregarious child. *Perhaps I'll have a daughter like that one day*, Frankie supposed before blanching. Wherever had that come from? Her resolution felt rocked but fortunately her own family were now here to save her from further examining it.

Flapping hats at flushed faces from the heat and exertion, Ivy and their parents sat on the log next to her, with Robert and Aggie arriving behind them. Her brother-in-law chose to stand quietly behind Aggie as he often did, and Frankie turned to tease him, determined to squelch any more deep, reflective thoughts and to enjoy herself.

'Decided to join us did you? Well, I hope you're ready to take the lead on this one, Rob,' she began, relishing the idea of her crowd-shy accountant brother-in-law stumbling along centre stage. 'I dare say John would give you a turn on the old girl.'

'What's that then?' John said, pausing while lifting the crate. 'Oh, well, yes of course, son, if you feel the, er … need.'

Frankie looked up at Robert, feeling wickedly hopeful at the thought of him trying to sing up the front, red-faced and awkward, but it seemed he wasn't rising to the bait today.

'I don't think anyone would even hear me over you, Frankie,' he replied, disappointingly serious. 'Why don't take the crate yourself?'

She would have been tempted to do so, having long coveted the idea of standing on the marvellous contraption, but John was looking decidedly put out by now so she resisted.

'Oh, I don't think I could do this one the justice it deserves, especially when you do such a wonderful job, John.'

John sent her a pleased toothy grin as he lowered his crate and took out his songbook.

'Very charming, Frankie,' her father muttered.

'I told you it wasn't an impossibility,' Harriet returned in an undertone and Ivy giggled.

'Who remembers what song we sing here?' John asked jovially in his deep baritone and Frankie exchanged amused glances with her family at the familiar routine.

'"Jingle Bells"!' one of the boys called out hopefully, swinging from the branch above with excitement.

'Watcha doing?' Pretty Boy enquired, twisting upside down to watch him.

'"Jingle Bells" is the very last song of the night, as you well know, young man. Now, what's the carol we always do, here, at number four?' John Hunter said, his arms extended to invite further response.

'"O Christmas Tree",' Lydia said before scrunching up her nose, 'although it seems a bit rude to sing that in front of a dead old log, doesn't it?'

Frankie couldn't quite swallow a chortle as Lydia looked guiltily at the log the Merriweathers sat on.

'At least there's a real Christmas tree there,' Ivy said, pointing at the big Christmas bush across the road, and the children looked over with smiles, seemingly appeased.

'Yes, well, let's sing to that then, all right? Best voices now,' said John, lifting up his book.

The song rang out, led by the man's impressive voice, and Frankie soon found herself joining in, buoyed by his enthusiasm. It really was a lovely, sweeping melody and she couldn't help but feel Chrismassy all of a sudden as the treetops above let through the last of the burnishing sun. Even the Christmas bush seemed to be getting into the spirit of things as it nodded and bowed in pretty shades of green and scarlet, like a benevolent guest of honour.

O Christmas tree, O Christmas tree
Your branches green delight us

Each child's face was filled with earnest worship and it was touching to see baby Josie blink in wonder at her entertaining grandfather from her mother's arms, entranced. Aggie was watching her too, tears in her eyes. If she hadn't been feeling so suddenly emotional herself Frankie might have been more mindful of the fact that her sister's knuckles were white as she gripped her husband's hand at her shoulder, but Frankie was really, uncommonly choked up. So much so she paused mid-song, swallowing against such sentimentality in surprise.

'What's wrong?' whispered Ivy looking from Aggie to Frankie in confusion but Frankie could only shrug, because as much as she did consider herself one of the boys, Patrick Earle's words had reminded her that not everyone saw her that way. And ever since he'd uttered them she couldn't seem to stop feeling the raw truth of the fact that she was, indeed, very much a woman.

Six

Ten houses, ten carols and cake and refreshments at the conclusion had made for great excitement for the dozen or so youngsters among the neighbourhood crowd but Ivy was wondering if her mother regretted hosting the end party this year. Albert had made a very convincing St Nicholas but promising Lydia a bicycle when her mother had bought her a doll had left Harriet mortified, Dossie in a flap and Constance in a pickle. Adding to that, the wisdom of allowing a dozen children to splash about in the main pond may have been misguided, judging by the state of the carpets.

Fortunately there was an old bicycle of Ivy's in the shed and John and Albert were out hastily fixing it up with a coat of paint and a few repairs. Meanwhile the children were redirected to play on the tennis court and dry out as the party rolled on.

Ivy had enjoyed it all, despite the minor dramas. So far Christmas was passing by swimmingly, what with Patrick's obvious excitement over her personal invitation to her party and an early Christmas present from her parents. (Red boots – was there ever a more wondrous thing?) If it wasn't for Aggie's sad expression earlier and Frankie's strange mood she would have described herself as perfectly happy this evening but something was definitely amiss and neither sister looked keen to discuss things. But Harriet did, despite being harried. There was always time for prying.

'What on earth's the matter tonight, Frankie?' their mother asked again as she sorted out napkins and plates in the kitchen.

'Cat's got her tongue – don't think I've ever seen that before,' Dossie observed over her spectacles as she helped. 'Are you ill, girl?'

'No, no, I'm fine,' Frankie assured her quickly. 'Just a bit tired.' It wasn't just that Dossie was a well-known hypochondriac, she was also a notorious gossip and the last person Frankie would be confiding in, Ivy knew.

'Bit disappointed too, I'd say,' Dossie said, nodding. 'That horrible Mr Forsyth never publishes the truth of things, dearie, pay no mind. He wouldn't even report that bout of tuberculosis I caught two years back and that was a matter of serious public concern!' She pushed her spectacles up and sniffed her outrage.

'Saying you had tuberculosis is as ridiculous as assuming that man was born with an ounce of good sense,' Harriet said in her usual blunt way, ignoring Dossie's offended look.

'I most certainly did have it but I hardly expect *you* to believe me. You're always saying I'm in fine health when I'm obviously not. My poor back has been troubling me something terrible actually … I think I may have to see Dr Pratt again,' she confided to Aggie, who looked immediately flustered and dropped the teaspoon she was polishing. 'Whoops-a-daisy,' Dossie said, continuing on unperturbed. 'He'll know what to do, bless him.'

'Pratt by name …' Harriet muttered. It was a great joke between her parents that the local doctor was, indeed, an egotistical prat, yet Dossie was his favourite patient. She fed that ego to perfection by raving on ad nauseam about his miraculous cures for her many claimed ailments.

'What was that?' Dossie said. 'I haven't got my ear horn, I'm afraid, and the doctor is due to clear them out. Bit of a wax problem,' she whispered loudly, this time seemingly to no-one in particular.

'Go and fetch it for her, Aggie,' Harriet instructed. Her sister looked glad to get away for a minute. 'Anyway, why don't you just try the *Herald* with this one, Frankie? Show that Forsyth a thing or too.'

'Once you dry all those papers off, of course,' Dossie added. 'I heard quite a few ended up in the water trough this afternoon.'

'Why did your papers end up in the trough?' Ivy said, surprised it was the first she'd heard of it. Normally Frankie would have been screaming blue murder about anything happening to one of her precious stories.

'The water trough!' Harriet exclaimed, but with amusement. 'What were you up to this time? Marching along and not looking where you were going again, I suppose?'

'A little bird told me she walked straight into young Patrick Earle,' Dossie told her. 'In front of the entire Railway Hotel, unfortunately.'

'It was an accident …' Frankie began.

'Patrick?' Ivy interrupted, suddenly on alert at the mention of his name. 'What happened with him?'

'Nothing, nothing,' Frankie said. 'I just ran into him this afternoon – quite literally, I'm afraid.'

'You ran into Patrick? Why didn't you tell me?' Ivy knew she sounded put out, and flushed at the knowledge but Frankie looked cagey, which was disconcerting, to say the least.

'Why should I tell you?'

'Be … *because* …' Ivy spluttered, searching for words. 'Because I just thought you would have done.'

'Is he your beau nowadays?' Dossie asked with keen interest and Ivy blushed.

'No, no, he's not my beau. He's just a … a good friend, is all.'

'She asked him to her birthday party in person this morning. Wore her very best Christmas bonnet with the holly on it,' Frankie told the neighbour, obviously glad to get the focus off herself.

'Did you now?' Dossie asked with a glance at the green one she was wearing. It boasted actual ivy and Ivy touched it self-consciously, at a loss.

'As long as it wasn't mistletoe,' Harriet said. 'Still a bit young for romance, Ivy girl,' she added, much to Ivy's further humiliation and annoyance. Aggie had married at eighteen and Ivy would turn that age next week, which in her opinion rendered the comment most unfair. 'Anyway,' Harriet continued, her attention back on Frankie, 'is that what's been bothering you tonight? That silly editor and a mishap in town? I wouldn't have thought you'd let things like that concern you by now.'

'Goodness, it's a miracle to me you don't end up in the good doctor's office every day of the week the way you march along every which way,' Dossie added. 'It's not very feminine, Frankie, if you don't mind me saying so.'

'The only "fem" she's interested in is femin*ism*,' Ivy pointed out, still annoyed.

'Feminists can be feminine as well as political,' Dossie asserted. 'A little powder and a pretty bonnet may not get you the vote, Frankie, but it could go a long way towards getting you a husband.'

'Ha! She's definitely not looking for one of those,' Ivy said, thinking Frankie would roll her eyes or smirk too but she didn't. She just looked … odd. Very peculiar, Ivy decided with a frown.

'Perhaps not quite ready for romance either,' Harriet said, gently now as she lifted Frankie's long braid back off her shoulder and met her gaze.

What on earth was going on? Ivy wondered, uncomfortable that Patrick was somehow involved in this. Surely Frankie wasn't interested in him at all. Ivy wasn't certain her sister even liked him.

'Aggie was married at eighteen,' Dossie pointed out, a fact Ivy would have liked articulated only a few moments ago but not so now. 'Frankie's twenty come Valentine's Day. I'd start shopping for a new bonnet or two, dearie, if I were you,' Dossie warned.

'I don't want a new bonnet, I just want to find my old one,' Frankie said, setting biscuits out on a tray, her more usual resoluteness returning, 'and Ivy's right, I'm not looking for a husband. I'm looking for the right to vote, parliamentary representation and equality for Australian women.'

Ivy felt comforted as the world set itself back to rights at those words but Dossie wasn't done.

'You can have women's rights and the vote until the cows come home but it won't give you a husband and babies any sooner,' she warned.

'Husband and babies,' Frankie said, taking out the cream and whipping it hard. 'It's not the only thing we're made for.'

'True, true,' Dossie said as Aggie returned. She took the ear horn gladly and Ivy hoped it didn't improve her hearing too much. Frankie was beginning to sound rude. 'Still, all the speech-making and fancy newspaper articles in the world won't give you the contentment that comes from having a family of your own, mark my words. Caring for Constance and my John has been the greatest privilege of my life, and now that we've got grandchildren to bless us in our old age, well … all I can say is that it's a joy only a woman knows and one you shouldn't be so quick to throw away.'

Just leave it at that, Ivy pleaded silently to Frankie as Aggie quietly turned her back and began to fill the kettle. There's no winning an argument with Dossie. But of course her stubborn sister didn't.

'I'm sure you're very happy with the choices you've made but that doesn't mean that's what every woman should do. Where's the law saying that's the only future we can choose? In the heads of men, I suppose?'

'Healthy debate is one thing, Frankie, but mind your tone,' Harriet warned her.

'Choose what you like,' Dossie said, ignoring Harriet and straightening out a napkin with a sniff, 'but having a family will make you happiest.'

'Depends who you ask, I'd say,' Frankie returned.

'Yes, well,' Harriet concluded, 'no use fighting over things, in any case.'

'Who's fighting?' Dossie replied, grey eyebrows raised. 'I'm just trying to point out that you don't want to make a mistake and miss the boat on marriage and having children, Frankie, that's all. You're not getting any younger, are you?'

'Who gets to say when or if I have children – or not?' Frankie said, setting the bowl down with a sudden loud clatter. 'I say it's *my damn choice* and no-one else's.'

Dossie let out a gasp and Harriet looked set to admonish Frankie for such profanity and anger but surprisingly it was Aggie who spoke.

'Actually it's Mother Nature's,' her sister said softly, turning around to face her sister. 'Just pray that you never have to take up this fight with her.'

And with that the strong, ever-practical Aggie dissolved into sudden, broken tears.

Seven

Silent night, holy night
All is calm, all is bright
Round yon virgin mother and child
Holy infant, so tender and mild,
Sleep in heavenly peace
Sleep in heavenly peace

Lydia's slightly offkey yet wistful singing floated up towards them with bittersweet irony as the three sisters sat in the bay window of their parents' room, quiet for a change. Words were hard to find for Ivy and Frankie, Aggie supposed, and as for herself, well, Lydia was doing an exemplary job of articulating the ache she'd never shared until tonight. The voice of the child seemed to say at all.

Aggie hadn't elaborated further after her outburst downstairs. The admission and what it could mean was simply too huge a subject for a Christmas kitchen debate and the mind-numbing realisation that she'd blurted out her darkest secret in front of the town's biggest gossip was enough to make her run and hide without hesitation. She'd left the dumbfounded group in the kitchen immediately, seeking refuge here.

The seat was a favourite retreat of the sisters, with its expansive view of the gardens, tennis court and bushland beyond, and it was a comfortable nook in which to read or ponder. Harriet had many cushions stacked along it, souvenirs of their parents' long-ago honeymoon in India, and the velvet drapes were soft and thick, perfect to lean against and gaze out.

Ivy and Frankie had given Aggie a little time before joining her and she wondered how to explain, and how much to reveal to her two unmarried sisters. Her mother would have greater insight and understanding but Harriet had to get every man, woman and child in the neighbourhood out of the home first – which Aggie didn't consider too terrible a delay. How much comfort could even Harriet bring when God had never denied her this, granting her three children, all in a row. So natural, so easy, so perfect.

So why were she and Robert, one of three siblings himself, being punished so?

The thought of the dear, kind man she'd married brought fresh tears, the damnable things seemingly unstoppable now, and Aggie brushed at them and hugged a tasselled velvet bolster tight. Her knees curled up like a child's. The action seemed to move Frankie to speak at last.

'I'm so … oh Aggie, I'm so, so sorry,' Frankie said, her expression pained. 'Me and my big, stupid mouth.'

'You weren't to know, although I suppose you've wondered …' Aggie said, trying to smile to reassure her.

'I wasn't sure you were, er … wanting to … I mean, trying to …'

Aggie just nodded, sparing her sister further awkwardness as Ivy watched on, wide-eyed.

'Have you … have you seen the doctor?' Ivy ventured.

'Yes,' Aggie said, sitting straighter to clear her throat. 'Had the last appointment today, actually. I've never been, you know, in a normal pattern of things like the two of you but I thought that was just … just my body's way.' She was blushing at the subject matter now but it seemed ridiculous to be overly polite to her own sisters at a time like this. 'The doctor said I could consider myself much like a faulty clock, although that seems a rather ludicrous comparison. Then again, who can explain such a thing?'

'Well, he is a prat so certainly not him,' Frankie noted. That prompted a sniffly giggle and Aggie reached out to squeeze her fingers gratefully.

'Oh Aggie,' Frankie said as she gripped them, the sorrow returning to her countenance. 'I wish I … I wish …'

'Yes … yes, so do I,' Aggie whispered brokenly, her bravery slipping once more. 'You know, as … as I sat there in his office today all I kept thinking about was that poor girl Julia, out there alone on the streets at Christmas, an unwanted child in her womb,' she said, wiping at tears with her handkerchief, trembling fingers clenched. 'How can … how can one woman be cursed with a child and another cursed without one?'

'You're not cursed—' Ivy began but Frankie interrupted her.

'Julia's only cursed because the world thinks the *weaker sex* need men to support them, and our children,' she said, bitterness in her tone. 'Heaven forbid we be allowed to raise babies without a ring on our finger or a man by our side, but no, our only choice is to give them up or struggle and starve.'

'They allow other women to raise them, but not the mothers themselves,' Aggie reflected with a small helpless shrug. 'Widows and such. Nuns and people like me who work in orphanages and … and love the babies no-one wanted.'

'It's the government who doesn't want them,' said Frankie with disgust, 'and some men of the cloth like that Father Brown.

He'd rather see that baby a respectable orphan than some woman's bastard child.'

Both Aggie and Ivy flinched at the term and Frankie shifted angrily against the cushions.

'Sorry, but it's true, and why is that such a dirty word anyway? Who wears the stigma? The authorities? Ha – the innocent, that's who,' she declared, but her tirade came to an abrupt pause as Ivy cleared her throat and Frankie looked at Aggie's stricken face. 'Anyway, it's just … just so bloody unfair …' she finished, more quietly now.

'Yes, that it is,' Ivy said gently, reaching over to brush a tear from Aggie's cheek. 'Terribly, terribly unfair.'

Then Lydia's voice rang out as if God Himself had had the final word on the matter.

Jesus, Lord, at thy birth
Jesus, Lord, at thy birth

Frankie leant her head on Aggie's shoulder then, and Ivy did the same, as they gazed out together beyond the dispersing crowd below towards the clear, deeply burnished horizon; gold, brown and red hair catching the last of the warm light.

'Mother Nature won't deny you this, dearest,' Ivy told her, her conviction so strong it seemed to glow too. 'You've too much love to give. You've always been such a wonderful big sister, caring for we two, and look at the way you are at the orphanage with all those little ones. It's meant to be, you'll see.'

But, as Lydia's voice faded, Aggie's arms felt as empty as the now silent, cloudless twilight. And the fear of being forever barren burnt within her like an endlessly setting sun.

Eight

Crack.

The sound reverberated off the valley walls with a pleasing thwack and Patrick took off down the makeshift pitch as the ball bounced merrily along, disturbing a flock of rosellas who'd been grazing in the dry grass. It was as picturesque a setting as could be as the first day of 1902 sailed on, with the haze of the blue and green hills mirrored in the still, wide bay that lay there. The flat grassy area they played upon was just around the corner from Bobbin Head, the area's main port, and it was usually a peaceful and quiet sanctuary. Not so today.

A goanna had ambled by earlier, eyeing the cricket game with a wary disdain, blue tongue flicking as he found a wide trunk to climb and bake upon, the intricate patterns on his skin like pale mint lace on a textured slate background. A nearby wallaby watched occasionally too, eventually flicking an ear before loping away, but the wildlife mostly seemed to tolerate the disturbance of the human activity on display.

It was surprising really, considering the racket they were making. Ivy and the other young ladies sitting in the shade were loudly cheering Patrick on, and Frankie's displeasure at being dispatched earlier was still evident as she paced and fumed, yelling at Greg King to fetch the ball with more alacrity.

'I've known chickens that can run faster than that!' she called after him, causing Patrick to chuckle as he ran. God help the man who ended up with that particular sister. Ivy, on the other hand, well, if the cheering and dimpled smiles she was sending his way weren't enough to encourage him, her elaborate birthday outfit surely was.

She seemed to glow in her all-white blouse and skirt, as was the choice of many of the girls, but the commonalities ended there. It seemed no conservativism prevailed when it came to Ivy's choice of embellishments for her day in the sun. The neckline and sleeves were embroidered in bright green ivy and her new red Christmas boots poked out cheekily at the hem. The whole effect was topped with an enormous sun hat that boasted a centrepiece of real flowers from her garden. They were mostly daisies but it was the perfect red rose at the centre that had him encouraged.

'You said you loved my boots so I thought a red flower too …' she'd told him with a blush when he'd complimented her on it. That she'd remembered he'd said so when he'd seen her briefly in town and gone to the trouble of showcasing the rose just for him had Patrick in especially good spirits. So much so, he didn't even mind that his parents were here too. They were long-time acquaintances of the Merriweathers, after all, and had every right to join the other cricketers' parents with the rest of the older crowd beneath the marquee. If only his mother's voice wasn't quite so loud. He grimaced, trying not to take any notice as her comments carried clearly across the grass.

'Really, with a stroke like that it's no wonder he's made the team for Sydney University,' she was saying, 'and still not yet twenty-one. Of course his coaches have always said he was a natural talent, all the way through school, but one doesn't like to brag.'

'You seem to be doing a good enough job of it now, Sybil,' Douglas Earle said dryly and Patrick could hear the general sniggering that followed as he faced another ball from a determined-looking Frankie.

Crack.

Straight for the edge of the bush, which meant four this time. Frankie tossed her hands in the air in frustration as the crowd applauded loudly and poor Greg took off after it in the blistering hot sun.

'Your Patrick will be playing for New South Wales at this rate,' Harriet Merriweather said as she clapped. Her parrot Pretty Boy let out a squawk of excitement.

'Well, his coaches at university have said as much, but one doesn't like to talk *out of school*,' Sybil said, ignoring her husband's previous censure and with a giggle at her own witticism.

'Beating girls and a few friends for a lark is one thing,' Douglas said dismissively, 'a first-grade team is quite another.'

That remark deflated Patrick a little and earned a scathing glare across the field from Frankie, not to mention a thinly veiled reproach from Greg's father, Tristan, standing nearby.

'I'm sure *they* will all hold their own when the time comes.'

'Indeed,' Alistair Johnson agreed. 'Up next are you, Nick?' he asked his son and Patrick felt a bit embarrassed as Frankie marked her run-up once more, flushed in the face and swatting at her hair.

Perhaps it was time to just get out and give everyone else more of a go. But then Ivy called out, 'Go, Patrick!' and he looked over to see her holding her hat brim and smiling so sweetly at him he let out a low whistle and took a determined stance once more. Maybe just one more four.

'Better watch out, your highness,' Greg heckled in support of Frankie and down the grass she ran, impressively fast for someone wearing a long skirt. The ball flew at a pace, surprising him around the legs and whacking the empty box wicket. Clean-bowled.

'Yes!' crowed Frankie ecstatically. Aggie's umpiring husband Robert lifted a single finger in the air and the verdict was sealed.

Patrick was disappointed, of course, but he had to hand it Frankie.

'Great ball,' he told her as he walked off and she looked at him with surprise, then with a hugely satisfied grin as her teammates landed upon her, full of cheers and congratulations. *Great smile*, he added to himself. She was pretty gorgeous when she wasn't trying to annihilate him at sport or shove politics down his throat. Patrick could read the similar thoughts in Nick's expression as his mate stared straight at Frankie and tapped his bat as he passed him.

'Bring it on, Miss Merriweather,' his friend called.

'With pleasure,' she called back, and Patrick didn't need to turn around to know that she'd be wearing the same mask of determination in her quest to get Nick out too, although Patrick wondered if the news he'd imparted on Christmas Eve would negatively impact her game. Or enhance it. The laws of attraction were funny things, he mused, looking at Ivy and taking a deep breath as he approached her, Aggie and the other girls gathered under the big gum tree. It was hard to think straight when the body started thinking for you.

'Thirty-eight runs,' Ivy exclaimed, her big blue eyes shining beneath the wide hat brim. 'My hero.'

'Would have liked to have made fifty but that sister of yours had other plans,' he said ruefully, flopping down on the grass and taking out his handkerchief to mop his face. 'Phew, certainly is hot out there.'

'Here,' Ivy's school chum Mariel Chambers said as she poured him a glass of lemonade and passed him an orange from one of the many crates the family had strapped onto the convoy of carriages for the box party today. 'Refreshments, kind sir.'

'Thanks,' he said, taking them gratefully and trying not to appear too pleased that Ivy looked jealous. He drank thirstily as Ivy and her friends were distracted by the banter both on and off the field.

'Hope they've put the champagne on ice,' Nick called over to Greg in the outfield. 'You're going to need gallons of the stuff by the time I've run you around.'

'I'll be toasting our victory,' Greg called back, 'and our woman of the match for getting you out.'

Nick just laughed and Patrick wanted to tell him not to get too cocky. As surprising as it was, that girl could really bowl.

'Yes, let's see if your girl can get Nick out too,' Tristan King said to Albert Merriweather. 'She certainly cleaned Patrick up.'

'I doubt our Nick will be so easily bested,' Alistair said with a sniff.

'... and I doubt that wicket was anything more than Patrick being a gentleman and letting it through,' Sybil said in a too-loud whisper and Frankie paused in her run-up, staring across with one hand on her hip. Ivy looked nervously from one woman to the other.

'She got me fair and square, Mother,' Patrick called over, peeling his orange. 'No shame in it when she's as good as she is.' That earned a look of relief from Ivy, however Nick's father was scornful.

'Humph. I wouldn't go that far.'

Albert took off his spectacles, looking set to defend his daughter lest a miffed-looking Harriet beat him to it, when Pretty Boy commented for them both.

'Ignoramous, ignoramous.'

Patrick looked at Ivy in surprise before joining most of the party in laughter and shaking his head. She really did have the most eccentric family.

The afternoon wore on and Frankie was on a roll, cleaning up Nick for a mere twelve runs and taking to the field to make the final catch as Greg finished off the rest. She was happily glowing as she walked off, red-faced from all the exertion and excitement, but Ivy looked embarrassed as Frankie shoved at her escaping hair and wiped dirt from her palms onto her already grubby skirt. Such unladylike dishevelment hadn't escaped Sybil's notice either – her eyebrows were certainly raised as Frankie tossed the ball in the air and gave his mother a smug stare.

Frankie's team were declared the winners by a mere three runs and a magnanimous Greg suggested they say it was a draw, being 'among friends'.

'Blow that,' Frankie exclaimed before gulping down a glass of celebratory champagne, and although Ivy looked over at Sybil worriedly, Patrick had to shake his head in amusement once more. Eccentric was the word, all right, but to his surprise he decidedly liked it.

The cicada song had risen to a loud, echoing cacophony as Ivy fixed her curls and powdered her nose in the tent-come-makeshift-parlour the men had erected for the day but, despite all the noise, heat and discomfort, she was excited. Although, if the mirror on the box was anything to go by, she was also a bit drunk. The tell-tale flush in her cheeks and her giggly state betrayed the fact that she'd had three glasses of champagne – the very first time she'd ever had more than one. Coupled with the fact that Patrick was here at her eighteenth birthday party and would be accompanying her on the bushwalk about to take place, it was little wonder she could barely put her hairpins in and her hat on without needing to take deep, calming breaths.

Despite Frankie's embarrassing behaviour and the peculiarities of her family, Patrick had made it very obvious today that he liked her regardless. The tantalising prospect of an impending court-ship beckoned and Ivy closed her eyes, savouring this longed-for moment.

Maybe she would let him hold her hand today. Maybe she would even let him kiss her, and the thought made her eyes flick open and go round in the mirror as she touched her fingers to her mouth. Perhaps, perhaps, she'd even …

'What's taking you so long?' Frankie demanded, knocking on the tent flap before peeking in.

'Hurry up, everyone's ready to go and waiting for you.' Aggie looked in too before sighing and leading the way through. 'What are you doing in here? Primping?'

'Well, it *is* my birthday,' Ivy reminded her sisters as she re-adjusted her marvellous hat.

'Lest anyone forget *that*,' Frankie muttered, eying it with derision.

'What's that supposed to mean?' Ivy said, feeling bolder than usual. Perhaps it was the champagne. Frankie didn't answer under a warning look from Aggie but she did roll her eyes, which Ivy found annoying.

'Anyway, are you ready now?' Aggie asked her, tidying a few strands herself and looking at Frankie's completely messed-up hair with a slight frown. 'You may want to fix yourself up a bit, while we're at it.'

'I don't care,' Frankie said with a shrug. 'I'm here for fun and adventures, not to impress the men.'

'Just as well.' Ivy pinned a stray curl.

'And what's *that* supposed to mean?' Frankie demanded.

'Just that you couldn't make less of an effort to act like a girl if you tried,' Ivy said, her annoyance at Frankie rising, 'and besides, I would have thought you were also here for my birthday?'

'We're all here for your birthday,' Aggie said, in a reassuring tone. 'Although people may be getting impatient waiting—'

'Not everyone thinks the pinnacle of a woman's worth is to marry some snooty man and become his doormat, you know.' Frankie faced Ivy.

'Patrick isn't snooty!' Ivy was offended. 'And who says I'd ever be someone's doormat?'

'Who said I was talking about you and Patrick, let alone *your* marriage?' Frankie said. 'I'm just talking about all this ridiculous ... bait women like you throw out to land the stupid ruddy fish.' She flicked her hand at Ivy's hat.

'Well, it's better than stomping about like a man and ... and making a spectacle of yourself.'

Frankie frowned and Ivy wondered momentarily if she'd offended her sister but then Frankie kept going. 'I'd rather be an authentic spectacle than a fake one on display all the time. That just sickens me, the way women do that, like we have to advertise our prettiness to be worthy as a potential mate.'

Ivy gasped. 'Don't be crass!'

'Don't be so pathetic then! Honestly, if you gave half the thought towards bettering the world as you do to the state of your bonnet rack—'

'Frankie, that's enough,' Aggie warned but Frankie continued.

'—you could offer something of substance to society, something that counts in the bigger scheme of things. That's what you should be thinking about turning eighteen. Not all this ... this ... self-decorating.'

'There's nothing wrong with trying to look attractive,' Ivy defended herself, despite reeling from Frankie's attack. 'It's one the nicest things about being a woman, not that you'd know anything about that.'

'It's a shackle,' Frankie stated flatly, 'and a way to make us focus on the very least thing that matters. What possible use does it offer womankind to bat your eyelashes when you could be changing the very law and having *true power*, Ivy? Think about that, why don't you? Maybe beyond just your own little world for once,' she added, circling the air above her.

'That's too far,' Aggie pleaded.

'I'm afraid it isn't far enough. You've been too spoilt by flattery for too long,' Frankie declared. 'When are you going to wake up and see that far more important things are happening? Things you could be a part of, and live a life that matters?'

'I don't care about your ... your revolution and your arguing and awful stories about poor women cast onto the street and in gaol. I just want to settle down and be happily married and away from all that ... that ...'

'Reality?'

'*Horribleness.*'

'But what about *purpose* and *meaning*?' Frankie said, spreading her arms wide. 'What will your life be worth just as somebody's wife?'

'It's worth something to have a husband and children and raise a family! How could *anything* matter more than being a ...' Ivy pulled herself up abruptly and looking guiltily at Aggie.

'... than being a mother.' Aggie finished for her as both sisters finally went silent. 'How, indeed.' The look she cast them both was one of the deepest hurt and Ivy dipped her head, ashamed to have affected her so.

'I'm …'

'Aggie, I …'

'Yes, you're both sorry, I know,' Aggie said, squaring her shoulders. 'Let's just go on that walk then, shall we?'

Aggie left the tent and Frankie followed her, not meeting Ivy's eyes. Hurt and ashamed too, Ivy supposed. She wondered how this latest 'healthy debate' had got so unhealthy, so quickly, supposing the champagne must be somewhat to blame. Her mother had often warned her that it loosened the tongue. Certainly that was a lot more arguing than Ivy would usually engage in yet the emotions of the day were high, and now they wrestled for dominance as she stared back at the mirror. There was guilt and pain in her expression, but excitement remained there too, as selfish as that made her feel.

For it was still her birthday. Surely that made selfishness somewhat less of a sin.

The thought made her feel rebellious and a budding recklessness began to grow as the best effects of that golden champagne returned. Suddenly she wanted to drink more of it with Patrick, leaving the deeper ponderings about life until tomorrow. For turning eighteen wasn't only a time to consider her adult responsibilities, it was time for some adult fun too. However much of it she dared to try.

Nine

Something was up with the three sisters. As little as he really understood women, Patrick could see that much, as Frankie marched along silently up front and Aggie walked quietly beside Robert behind her, both seeming preoccupied since fetching Ivy. As for the birthday girl, she'd barely said a word, so he'd prattled on about the scenery and cricket and really anything to keep her engaged and by his side. Somehow they'd fallen further and further back until they were the last ones visible on this stretch of the path that rose above the river.

Turning to remark on that fact, she surprised him instead.

'This way,' she whispered, taking off into the bush in a sudden dart, and Patrick's heart leapt as he hesitated, knowing he should dissuade her. But, oh, the temptation of following her as she dipped below a branch and threw him a daring look such an innocent girl shouldn't know how to send.

And so he followed, against good sense, his blood pumping as they broke off from the party, voices fading behind them as they dove deep into a shadowed pocket of ancient rainforest that ran along the gully. It was soon cooler and the air was dank with moss and earth, a primeval, welcoming scent that enticed him to breathe it in deeply and squint up at the dappled light of the canopy above.

'Look,' Ivy said, pointing at a dragonfly and he watched, entranced, as she followed it. 'It will lead us to water, they always do.'

She seemed ethereal and fairylike here, much like a dragonfly herself as she moved down through the bracken, no longer a girl but a wood nymph in a mysterious, abundant paradise. Then they came to a tinkling waterfall and she turned to him, pausing as the dragonfly hovered nearby.

'We could drink from it, I suppose, but I thought it might be more fun to have another champagne.'

'Did you bring some?' he asked, drawing closer, mesmerised by her skin, which looked impossibly smooth and soft in the shadowed light.

'No,' she said, her eyes on his mouth as he dared to draw even closer. 'But I hid a bottle behind the parlour tent, which isn't very far … as the crow flies …' Her voice was trailing off as he stared at her mouth too.

'Then I'd have to drag myself away from you,' he said, eyes moving to her neck as he raised one hand to brush a red curl away and she sucked in her breath.

'I'll be here, waiting to give you your reward.' It was a bold thing for Ivy to say but she seemed suddenly daring. Transformed, and so close now he was breathing her in. The pull of her was like a drug but he managed a reply.

'Can I claim a little of it now?'

She didn't answer. Instead her soft lips were suddenly on his in the lightest brush, like the silvered wings of the dragonfly. It was as if she'd cast a spell and he fell deeply under it as she pulled away and their eyes met. Something snapped inside him then and he pulled her against him in a rush and kissed her back, a passionate, unrestrained kiss that seared through his body as skin met skin and she clung to him, soft, yielding. Woman. Yet Ivy, still Ivy, he forced himself to recall. He knew he had to end it before it led to more so he pulled away. Their breathing was laboured as they broke apart.

'I … I'd better get that champagne,' he said, backing away.

'Hurry back,' she said, her beautiful face filled with promise and longing. He nearly changed his mind, but then he turned and took off through the forest at a run, every precious second counting before someone noticed they were gone. Still, it was only ten minutes there, ten minutes back, he reckoned. Not too concerning an amount and surely enough time to cool his blood and regain control. However the thought of returning and drinking champagne then kissing her again both tantalised and tortured and Patrick knew he'd have to be strong enough for both of them today. Because as ladylike and angelic as Ivy Merriweather may be, she was flesh and blood too, and deep in this age-old rainforest she became more than a beautiful girl. She became a powerful, primal seductress.

It was one of those moments Ivy knew she'd remember always: the time she shared her first-ever kiss with the man she loved deep in the cradle of paradise. For she did love Patrick Earle – the feeling in the kiss they'd shared was too powerful to be anything less. It was like nothing she'd ever felt before, this sensation of being emotionally blended with another being and physically consumed by them at the same time. Every part of her had felt suddenly more alive and driven by a strange, aching need, almost like hunger but far more wondrous.

'Adult fun' was surpassing all her daydreaming and expectations, but, as the minutes ticked by and she waited for him to return, those other emotions began to resurface and take over.

Adult responsibility began to gnaw. For this was also the day she'd hurt her sister Aggie and that pulled at her conscience as she paced the forest floor. It was all Frankie's fault, attacking her like that, she fumed, but Ivy was a fair-minded girl and she soon had to concede that she couldn't really lay all the blame at her elder sister's door. She couldn't really blame the champagne either.

Truth was, she was just plain angry at them both, and her mother too. That admission made her stop now and stare at the trickling waterfall and creek, trying to sort through such an enormous thought. There was no other word for it, she realised with sudden clarity as the water seemed to wash the truth clean.

She was angry, even at poor Aggie.

Her sisters and mother infuriated her with all their passion and fire over feminism and women's rights, because it made the world seem an ugly place and Ivy's world was all about beauty. Why should she be made to feel guilty about that? Loving beautiful things, wanting to be beautiful and attract a handsome man, appreciating the beauty of all that surrounded her with an artistic eye … wasn't that simply part of being a woman? The best part, perhaps? Her father even claimed it to be a form of intelligence and he was a professor, after all.

Yes, Ivy was angry, and sick to death of being made to feel inferior within her family, and adding that to the incredible feelings Patrick had awakened in her was a dangerous game. Passion and fury were combining with that budding recklessness of before and she was alone. In the middle of the forest at the heart of this wilderness.

An inner wildness came over her then, a need to immerse herself in it further and become part of its very veins, and so she began to follow the water, down further into the gully, where only the dragonflies would usually go. Creeping through thick undergrowth and guided by the building flow, she emerged at its place of release: a small cove alongside the river. It was lined with rocks that gleamed in the sun and Ivy blinked against the glare and heat, her dress feeling heavy all of a sudden, her hat ludicrous now. Off they came, and, clad only in her underthings, she picked her way over the rocks to the water and waded in, the coolness like silk against her skin. Patrick would be back soon, and his fingers might trail against some of the places the water caressed. She allowed the sensual pleasure of that scandalous thought consume her as the river washed the anger and recklessness away, leaving her with passion alone.

She felt calmer now as she made her way out and climbed across the rocks towards her clothes, every inch of her skin refreshed, alert. Alive to the sensation of touch. Water, sunshine, moss.

Perhaps if she hadn't been thinking about the feel of the soft, slimy stuff beneath her feet she would have relied more on her sense of sight and noticed a batch of oyster shells clinging to the rock. And perhaps she would have avoided the soles of her feet being cruelly sliced as she stepped on them and cried out in pain, slipped hard and fell. And perhaps her world would have stayed lit by the sunlight on her eighteenth birthday on this, the first day of 1902.

But instead it all turned black as her red curls hit the rock. The warmth of her very essence began to trickle into the water; a dark crimson stain soon to clear when the tide washed it away and Ivy became one with it. Flowing with the lifeblood of the Australian bush.

Ten

'*Ivy!*'

Frankie's voice was growing hoarse and Aggie was growing more and more agitated as they scoured the bushland along the path.

'She'll be with Patrick, exploring,' Robert reassured them yet again but both sisters looked at him askance.

'That doesn't help much if we can't find him either.' Aggie's tone was clipped. That she spoke to him in such a manner revealed just how worried she truly was and Frankie felt her gut tighten. What a drama to cause so late in the day, she fumed internally at Ivy, supposing this was her sister's idea of revenge after their fight. Yet fear was overriding anger as the shadows lengthened and the light began to grow golden. The danger of her sister being lost in the bush overnight was becoming less nonsensical with every passing minute and she doubted Patrick Earle would risk her sister's reputation by disappearing with her as long as this. No, something was wrong, and Frankie knew Aggie sensed it too.

'Look,' Aggie said. Frankie came over to see her pointing at a single bright red rose in the undergrowth. 'There seems to be a path here. Come on.'

The trio followed it and Frankie knew instinctively that this was the way she would have come. Ivy loved rainforest and water and the dampness in the air indicated that there would be both soon enough. Sure enough, within a mere few minutes they were deep in the cool, thick greenery and alongside a trickling waterfall. Dragonflies danced about and the sunlight found droplets among the sweeping bracken beside it, some of it appearing recently broken.

'Perhaps she followed it down,' Aggie guessed and Frankie knew she was right about that too. Ivy heavily romanticised the idea of dragonflies following water, spending as much time with their father as she did. The thought of her parents and how worried they'd be once they realised Ivy was missing spurred her on and she began to pick her way downstream. There was only one way to prevent this turning into a scandal or, worse still, an emergency, and that was to find the silly girl before the day fell into night. Everyone raised near this local bush knew that the exotic creatures within it were also sometimes deadly. As beautiful as this paradise could be, you'd never want to find yourself lost and alone in it after dark.

Patrick was sweating, despite the coolness of the water as he picked his way downstream, champagne and glasses discarded in the bushes further up. Navigating the creek had seemed a better idea than fighting through the vegetation beside it but it was slower than he would have liked as his panic began to grow. Why would she go off without him? Why not just wait for his return? Didn't she share the same desire he felt to explore the explosive passion they'd unlocked together? He'd run all the way back in his eagerness to hold her again but now his lust was replaced by fear as time ticked on and the day began to fade.

You're being ridiculous, he told himself over and again but deep down he knew Ivy wouldn't leave him to worry so long. Going off on a small adventure by herself? Certainly. Going missing for what must be nearly half an hour? Highly unlikely. He cursed himself for waiting by the waterfall and not going looking for her sooner but it couldn't be helped. Besides, the light up ahead signified that the creek was reaching its apex and that the river was nearby. Surely that's where she'd be, perhaps having a swim.

The thought spurred him on, half hopeful of seeing her in a state of undress, half fearful she wouldn't be there, but what he did see when he emerged from the shadowed forest into the bright, orange light made his heart leap from his chest. Making his way across the slippery rocks, Patrick picked up Ivy Merriweather's extraordinary hat to see her white dress and red boots discarded beneath.

'Ivy? Ivy!' he called but the deep water was mirror-like and still, eerie and without any trace of the girl who'd seemed a part of this landscape a short while before. A wood nymph in paradise. Casting her spell.

The magic had disappeared and only the landscape itself knew the truth of where Ivy had gone and what fate had befallen her as Patrick searched along the shoreline, desperate for answers. Then he found one, the most unwanted, dreaded clue of all and he fell to his knees in horror, reaching out to touch a pool of blood that the tide had yet to wash away.

Ivy, his mind screamed as the sound of footsteps could be heard and he turned to see Frankie and Aggie emerge, taking in the scene in horror as Robert followed behind.

'What …' Aggie said, picking up Ivy's hat in confusion and fear.

'Where …' Frankie began but then she looked over and saw Patrick and glanced down at his fingers before her eyes clashed back with his. And in that frozen moment Patrick Earle knew what it meant to literally be caught with blood on your hands.

Part Two

The life of Riley

Eleven

Numerous crates vied for space on the cabin floor below deck but it was the last addition to *Hawkesbury Queen* that had Riley Logan's pulse beating hard. He drew deeply on his cigarette as Donovan's boat neared his. The man was already studying him intently, the way Donovan often did, so crooked himself he rarely missed any hint of foul play. Nor an especial load being conveyed along this smugglers' route. Riley ashed his cigarette and forced himself to look calm, knowing he would need to steel his nerves despite his rapid heart rate. There was far too much at stake this time.

'Whatcha doin' heading back so late for?' Donovan asked, not wasting words on pleasantries. He didn't even waste words when it came to his own name. Riley had no idea if Donovan was his Christian or surname, let alone whatever other names he answered to. Perhaps none. Children like him grew up wild along the river and many learnt to fend for themselves from a young age. Who knew where Donovan had come from or if he'd even known his parents at all?

'Taking my time,' Riley said with a flick of his eyes towards the half-covered wooden crates on the deck of Donovan's boat. 'Bananas?'

Donovan shrugged. 'People gotta eat somethin' healthy now and then. Don't want to end up a bunch of scurvy ol' pirates. What are you running?'

Riley drew on his smoke. 'A bit of this an' that.' Donovan would hardly be surprised at Riley's noncommittal answer. Most knew better than to ask a man his business around here but Donovan was always a nosy bugger. Far too much so for Riley's liking right now, as the sweat trickled down his back.

'Saw Petey and Deano 'round the bend. Might settle in for a drink at Mozzie Point.'

It wasn't an invitation. Donovan was no friend of Riley's; if anything he was a nemesis, even to the point of naming his boat *River King* just for a bit of one-upmanship. It was really more of a territorial brag, mentioning he had cronies along the river and therefore jurisdiction tonight. However it was good news for Riley that the three men would make camp and be well out of his way. He was careful to hide that as he responded.

'Hot enough night for it,' he said, throwing the stub of his cigarette overboard and reaching down to start hauling up the anchor. He'd dropped it in a rush before. Riley blocked the recollection of the panic he'd felt.

'Guess I'm off then,' Donovan said.

'Right you are,' Riley said, not looking at him as he made ready to go. The time between Donovan's engine rumbling to life and his departure seemed torturously long but Riley continued his preparations as normally as he could until a glance at the bend in the river confirmed Donovan's boat had disappeared from sight.

Riley dashed below deck, his boots skidding on the rungs, but nothing had altered. The crates remained stacked, the equipment, ropes and supplies lay in semi-ordered array and the clock he kept on the wall still ticked away.

In fact, nothing was terribly different on Riley Logan's boat this late summer afternoon, save the last addition in the corner. He rushed over to check if there'd been any change these last few minutes but as he pulled back the thin blanket he saw that his latest impossible cargo remained the same. Staring down, he wondered what on earth he was supposed to do as fate delivered yet another sharp twist in the convoluted journey that had so far been his life's path.

For it wasn't every day you found a beautiful, half-naked and unconscious woman glistening in the sun on the edge of a secluded cove. His reasons for hauling her on board and getting her out on the river had seemed inarguably logical at the time but looking at the blood-soaked bandages at her temple and around her foot, and her alarmingly pale complexion, he was starting to question himself now. How to explain his actions when they came looking for her, as someone undoubtedly would? How to explain it to the girl herself when she eventually came to?

The time for solving that particular dilemma suddenly arrived as the girl groaned softly and a frown puckered her features. Riley held his breath as her lids fluttered open and blue eyes focused on his, filled with confusion then dawning fear.

'Where … where am I?'

'You're on a boat, my boat actually, the *Hawkesbury Queen*.' Riley figured saying its name might reassure her, like it was a known, respected vessel, which it was. Well, in its own way.

The girl stared at him, her eyes darting around. 'Why?'

'You had an accident and I brought you aboard to tend to your injury. You've a nasty gash on your foot and your head,' he added with a nod at the wound. 'A pretty massive lump too. You've been passed out cold.'

'Passed ... passed out?' She started to rise, wincing, and he gently pushed her shoulder back down.

'I think you'd better stay lying down.'

'I can't ... I can't be here ... on a boat. They'll all be worried ... looking for me.'

'I'll take you back as soon as you've recovered.'

'Back? How far away are we?'

'A few miles,' he hedged.

The girl looked at him, her pain evident as she tried to process that. 'Why didn't you just find someone ... nearby ... rather than bring me here? My family and ... my friends ...'

'I thought you were there alone,' he improvised, looking away as he filled a cup with water and handed it to her.

'Why would I be alone?' she said, in a way that suggested the very idea was unimaginable, and Riley knew he was definitely in deep trouble now. She was obviously a well-protected girl and would likely have half the district looking for her by nightfall.

'I couldn't see anyone else about and I could hardly leave you there. There's rough types along this river,' he said, his earlier logic returning as Donovan came back to mind, 'and you were ... er ...' Riley cleared his throat, unsure how to refer to her state of undress. She seemed to understand and drew the blanket higher towards her chin, despite the warmth in the cabin.

'Did you ... Have you got my ... things?'

'I'm afraid I was too worried about your welfare to look,' he told her. Too worried about being caught by authorities with his other cargo on board too, but that was a hell of lot harder to explain.

The girl touched her fingers to the bandage and watched him nervously. 'How long has it been ... since you found me?'

Riley looked at the clock. 'About half an hour or so, I'd say.'

'Half an hour?' she said, looking at the clock too, aghast. 'Oh, oh lord. Please,' she implored, 'you have to take me back. It'll … it'll be dark soon.'

'I don't think you should stand or be moved about yet,' he told her. 'I think we should get you to my sister who can tend you then I'll take you home.'

'You don't understand, my family—'

'I'll send word as soon as we arrive. It's only up the river a way.' Actually it was another hour and a half if they had a good run but she didn't need to know that.

'No, really, I'm fine. I think you should take me back now,' she said quite firmly as she sat up, but immediately she looked set to faint, clutching at her temple with a grunt of pain and Riley steadied her then lowered her back down.

'You're not fine,' he said, gently, 'and you need attention. My sister has some good nursing skills passed on from our mother.'

'No, no, please … just take me …' She tried again, but the exertion of attempting to rise had cost her and she was beginning to fade. She really did need medical attention, that part of the reason for heading up river was true enough.

'Rest,' Riley told her, drawing the blanket back up. 'I'll have you looked after and send a message to your family in no time. Trust me.'

Those two words hung between them and he knew she didn't at all – why would she? Yet what choice did she have.

'I don't even know … your name …' she muttered as her eyes began to close.

'Riley,' he said. 'Riley Logan. And you are?'

'Ivy … Merriweather.'

Riley almost smiled at the prettiness of her name, it suited her so well, but he had no room for anything but concern right now because she was also in pretty bad shape. And not only was she losing consciousness once more, she was doing so alongside a full load of illegal booze and stolen supplies on his smuggler's boat, which meant one thing was for sure right now: Riley Logan couldn't possibly take Ivy Merriweather back.

She was holding a lantern with one hand, using the other to stroke her belly absently, but Riley knew his sister Fiona would already have surmised that something was amiss. She was too astute and too logical for things to be otherwise.

The comforting green hills that lined these twisting waterways by day were dark and shadowed, and they loomed behind her home, rendering it a half-lit speck on the riverbank, a glint on the shoreline until you drew close as Riley was. The shack was a sorry sight, appearing worse for wear after the summer storms over the past few weeks, even in this pale light, and Riley wondered what her good-for-nothing husband George was planning to do about it. Nothing, most likely. The man spent most of his time drinking and fishing, which at least put some fare on the table, otherwise Fiona and their young twin girls Tricia and Annie wouldn't eat much. The produce from their meagre vegetable patch and the eggs from the chicken coop out back weren't really enough to survive on. Riley knew they relied on the stores he delivered each week more than his proud sister would ever let on.

Little Annie ran down towards the boat as he approached, calling out to her sister, who stumbled in her haste to join her, each carrying their own small lanterns, a recent gift from their Uncle Riley, along with their own small and precious stores of fuel. It was an indulgence, to be sure, but certainly they deserved some in their otherwise bleak lives. At four years old they were curious souls and cherished the explorative opportunities the gifts provided, Riley's boat in particular was a source of great fascination, with its eclectic assortment of equipment and variable cargo. He wondered what their reaction to his latest addition might be and what Ivy might make of his sister's world too, but there was little point pondering that until the girl was well enough to take anything in.

She'd been drifting in and out of sleep and he went down to ready her as the *Hawkesbury Queen* peppered its own way towards shore. Those blue eyes met his in the lamplight and he tried to reassure her once more.

'My sister Fiona lives here. Let's get you up then, if you can stand?'

'All right,' she said, but she clutched at the blanket as she sat up gingerly, and winced as she moved her foot. Riley saw he would need to carry her.

'Here now,' he said, 'let me help you.'

She appeared too weak to really protest and he wrapped her in the blanket and lifted her awkwardly in the confines of the cabin before taking the steps carefully, one at a time.

'There,' he said, lowering her down gently once on deck to sit on a crate and lean against the wall. Riley moved over to cut the engine and drop anchor as quickly as he could.

'Who's that?' Annie called out.

'He's found a dead person,' Tricia said. 'Did ya kill someone then, Uncle Riley?'

'Nah, he's not a mudderer, are ya, uncle?'

Riley ignored them but he could feel Fiona's stare as he worked then made his way back to Ivy, who had slumped and was groaning. It was no easy feat carrying her over the boat's side and through the shallows to reach the shore and by then the twins' eyes were round in the lamplight. Fiona had rushed inside to make preparations in her usual brusque way, no questions asked. Yet.

'Told you she wasn't dead,' Annie said in a loud whisper.

'Yeah,' Tricia said, sounding a bit disappointed. 'Maybe she's a mermaid,' she added hopefully. 'She's got mermaidy hair.'

''Scuse me, but are you a mermaid?' Annie asked hopefully as Riley carried her inside.

'Hush, girls. Put her on the bed, Riley,' Fiona instructed, pulling back the sheets as he lay her down. Ivy let out a groan. 'There now, I'm Fiona. Everything's going to be just fine,' she soothed as she unwound the bandage while the others looked on. 'Fetch a bowl of water and some cloths, Annie, and my kit,' she added with a quick nod at Tricia. The girls did as they were told and Riley watched as Fiona examined the wound on Ivy's head. 'Nasty,' she muttered.

'There's more on her foot,' Riley told her.

'Looks like oyster cuts. Slipped, did she?'

'I've no idea,' Riley replied. 'Just found her like this, unconscious though.'

'How long was she unconscious for?'

'About half an hour, I'd say.'

Fiona frowned at that. 'Where was she?'

'Apple Tree Bay.'

Fiona glanced up. 'Long way to bring her for attention.'

Riley didn't comment. He didn't need to. Fiona would know the reason why he couldn't very well drop anchor and have a bunch of strangers ask a lot of questions.

'I couldn't just leave her there,' he said instead.

'Might have been a better idea,' she muttered as Annie returned with the bowl, holding it carefully with her little hands, the cloth over her arm. Efficient young girls, his nieces, Riley observed as Tricia dragged the kit bag behind her. Just like their mother.

Fiona cleaned the wound carefully and Riley sucked in his breath when Ivy flinched.

'I know, love, just let me see what we're dealing with and clean this all up, eh? Don't want an infection setting in, now do we?' Fiona told her as she worked. 'What's your name, then?'

'Ivy ... Ivy Merriweather.'

'Pretty,' Fiona said, eyes flicking momentarily to Riley. 'I'm Fiona Ryan and these are my girls, Annie and Tricia. What do you say, girls?'

'Nice to meet you,' they both said, their voices singsong.

'Do you have a fish's tail?' Annie added, still hopeful as Fiona unwrapped the blanket from her lower body.

Ivy managed a small smile between frowns of pain. 'No, just boring old legs.'

Nothing boring about them, from what Riley could observe, but he tried not to focus on that, nor on the fact that Ivy's arms were still bare and a good deal of creamy skin was on display.

'You may have a few fish-like scales on your head for a while,' Fiona noted with a small smile herself, 'but I think you'll heal up just fine. Let's get you rested up but no food for now, I'd say, although a cup of tea and a fresh night rail would be in order. I take it you'd been swimming before you fell?'

'Yes,' Ivy said, blushing as she glanced down at herself. 'I'm sorry, I quite forgot ... I ...'

'No mind, no mind,' Fiona said. 'I'll help you change. Out with you then,' she said with a nod at Riley and he made his way out to light his pipe and wait for her interrogation, which he knew would shortly follow. At least George wasn't at home, giving him one less problem to deal with today.

The twins' chatter could be heard as Fiona tended to Ivy but soon enough his sister was outside, handing him a cup of tea too, eyebrows raised in the lamplight.

'Quite a cargo today then?'

'Yeah, bloody risky though. I finally got the medicines and herbs Eileen's been waiting for,' Riley said, avoiding her gaze. 'Not to mention enough booze to put me in gaol for …'

'I meant the girl.'

Riley sipped his tea, pausing before explaining further. 'Donovan's been skirting around the bay with Deano and Petey. I couldn't very well leave her there for them to find.'

'No,' Fiona agreed, 'but you could have sought out her family or friends.'

'I told you what's on board. It wasn't worth the risk.'

'And this is?' Fiona said, shaking her head. 'Of all the foolishness, Riley. That girl is wearing underwear I couldn't afford in a month of Sundays and I've heard that name, Merriweather. Pretty sure her father is a famous scientist or something; the family built some incredible house in town a while back. I remember reading about it in the papers.' Fiona was always reading something 'in the papers'. She had an amazing memory so Riley didn't doubt her word. 'What will you say when they come looking for her? You may well be up for kidnapping.'

'Didn't really give it much thought at the time,' he admitted, slapping at a mosquito. 'There was so much blood. I just wanted to help her and get her out of sight.'

'You and your heroics,' she scoffed. 'She may well have been a damsel in distress but now she's a wealthy man's daughter gone missing, and you're hardly a knight in shining armour in the eyes of the law, are you?'

Fiona was making far too much sense now and it was beginning to irk him. 'I'll take her back downriver tomorrow and no harm done, Fi. It's not as if I've actually kidnapped her in reality, for God's sake.'

'Her family won't see it that way.'

'So I won't see her family,' he reasoned.

'What, you're just going to dump her back on the riverbank at Apple Tree Bay, are you? And how's she supposed to walk anywhere, the way she is?'

'I'll figure something out,' he said, annoyed at her logic. 'Meanwhile I'll get Barney to send word.' Their neighbour Barney worked at the orchards near Galston and made the trip downriver in the wee hours. He could well leave an hour early and make the diversion into town.

'Better get over to him now before he passes out. He and George have been fishing all day and are sleeping on the boat.' Riley went to ask why he wasn't at work then realised it was New Year's Day and most people had taken a holiday. Days off for river men meant time to go fishing, but with the focus more on heavy drinking than the usual job of ensuring dinner was on the table. Barney would be going at it hard with George on board for company, which meant they were both probably pretty drunk. 'Be best to write a note for the family, I'd say. Goodness knows how Barney might explain things, especially if his memory is scattered from the drink.'

'True,' Riley said with a sigh. Barney wasn't too bright at the best of times, let alone hungover. What a bloody mess he'd got himself into, saving that girl today.

'Let's just hope she's better come morning,' Fiona said, with a glance down the river to where the faint light of Barney's boat shone. 'She can't stay here once George comes home.'

There was a finality in her words, and a trace of the fear that Fiona never quite managed to hide when it came to her husband. It made Riley's teeth grate but she'd sworn George didn't hit her whenever Riley pursued the matter and there wasn't much he could do about the man's boorish personality.

'Guess I'd better be off then, see Barney and unload this cargo. Any messages for George?'

She avoided his gaze, responding over her shoulder as she made her way back in. 'Just make sure the fish are cleaned before he brings them home.' If he'd bothered actually fishing, the thought hung between them.

Riley waved away another mosquito, not relishing the idea that he would have to contend with his drunk, obnoxious brother-in-law while ensuring the likely equally inebriated, dim-witted Barney would carry the message in the morning. On top of that, he would need to deliver Margie's load in the wee hours and unload the rest into his hidden cave upstream before heading back early tomorrow, but there was nothing else for it. He'd have to appear clean as a whistle if the need arose to explain to the authorities how an injured Ivy Merriweather was being returned a day after being found. And she'd have to appear well-tended and fully dressed, perched upon the deck, with no mention of the hours she'd spent half-naked in a bachelor's boat cabin. Everything completely above board.

Twelve

It was hot. Ivy tried not to think about that, as she was in no position to complain. Fiona Ryan had literally given her the clothes off her back and tended her with care, and Ivy was pretty sure the salted bacon she'd been given with the fresh eggs for breakfast was a precious commodity, judging by the impressed looks the twins had directed at her plate. They hadn't complained, though, satisfied with just having eggs, which they claimed were their 'favvit food'. Fiona said they practically lived on them and, looking at the poverty around her, Ivy could believe that was true.

The food had tasted wonderful at the time but now it was beginning to churn and her head was pounding. She didn't welcome the time ahead spent rocking on a boat, especially while the sun beat down so mercilessly on the coarse material of the dress. Yet the woman and her children had been so kind. Any churlishness would be unforgivably rude.

Riley Logan had been kind too, although she didn't trust him the way she trusted his sister. It wasn't his fault. He'd done everything he could to help her, but something didn't sit right with his reasons for not looking for her family and friends and instead taking her onboard and then upriver. It felt like he didn't want anyone to know he'd saved her. Yet, here he was to take her home, chugging around the bend in the river in his boat with another man sitting on the prow. Fiona's husband George, she'd been told, although it had sounded more like a warning when Fiona had uttered his name.

The crate she sat upon on the shore was uncomfortable and perspiration seeped into the bandage at her head. She touched her fingers to it, gingerly, wondering what the wound beneath looked like. She supposed she was a rather hideous sight. Then all vanity receded as she swooned from the effort of moving, almost falling off her seat. *Why is the sun so cruel today?* she lamented, forcing herself to keep her eyes open and to stay alert, focusing on the two men as she watched the boat slowly approach.

It was the first proper look she'd had at it, having spent most of her time below deck, and it was larger than she'd thought. By day it looked long and sturdy, and impressively well-equipped with fishing rods and nets and multiple lines of well-fastened rope. The rear and front mast stood tall, their sails tightly bound in readiness for a more windswept day, meanwhile steam billowed from the funnel like fanfare, as if to announce the boat's arrival. The name *Hawkesbury Queen* was proudly on display near the prow.

The vessel spoke volumes about her captain. Ivy observed him as he spun the wheel and moved about deck, confident and strong. That he'd been boating all his life was easy to see. He had that sea-worn look about him with his sun-bleached hair and tanned forearms. Ivy vaguely wondered at the colour of his skin above the shirtsleeves, thinking of Patrick's claim that he had 'cricket tan' in summer: brown hands and wrists but then pale elsewhere. Thinking about Patrick's 'elsewhere' was far too distracting a thought, however, and made her feel unbearably guilty. He and her family must be so worried. At least word had been sent on ahead in the early hours of this morning, Fiona had assured her, so they'd know by now that she was all right. Even so, she wasn't sure she could stomach feeling this ill coupled with remorse, so she studied the boat's passenger, George Ryan, instead of dwelling on everyone at home.

If ever a man looked hungover it was he. In fairness, Ivy supposed her current poorly state could be partially attributed to her own forays with drinking yesterday, however there was obviously no comparison when it came to George. The man was hunched over, with his head in his hands as if to push the pain away, and Ivy could see already make out the greyness of his pallor beneath his unshaven skin.

'How are you feeling?' Fiona asked Ivy, coming to stand nearby as the twins raced about along the shore.

Not very well but better than your husband, I'm guessing, Ivy was tempted to say, but didn't, of course. 'I'm fine,' she said instead, trying to smile, but it was an effort and Fiona watched her dubiously.

'Hmm. Well, I'm sure you'll be glad enough to get home. Your poor family must have been beside themselves.'

'Yes,' Ivy said, feeling horribly guilty again. She changed the subject. 'At least it's a nice day for the trip. Riley looks so at home on that boat.'

'He loves it,' Fiona said simply. 'Never happier than when he chugs along this river and drifts off in his way. Bit of a dreamer, our Riley, but he gets the job done too.'

'What job is that, exactly?'

Fiona paused, pushing a strand of brown hair behind her ear before responding. 'He brings supplies in and out between Pittwater and Wisemans Ferry. Sometimes even as far up as Windsor.'

'What kind of supplies?' Ivy asked, curious now and a bit suspicious as she studied the *Hawkesbury Queen* and considered what lay in the crates she'd seen below deck.

'Food, medicine, items for the home, all sorts of things, really. Not that he makes as much money from it as he should, always giving things away with that big heart of his, including to us, bless him. There's not a lot of industry besides timber cutting and fishing up here, except the main mills but they're much further up. People need more than this river country can provide,' Fiona told her. 'Much more.'

There was something in the way she said it that made Ivy look up and she caught a wistfulness in Fiona's expression. A sadness too.

'I suppose … well, I guess it isn't easy for you, living here,' she said, hoping she didn't sound rude.

Fiona seemed to collect herself then and pulled her shoulders back, her hand resting on her belly as it often did, Ivy noticed. 'We get by,' she said with a forced smile. 'It's always a woman's lot, having to work hard to care for her family. I can't complain.'

I would, Ivy couldn't help thinking, especially as she watched George returning from doing as he pleased and Riley moving happily about the boat, the sound of his whistling carrying to shore.

'The men seem to have a better time of it,' Ivy observed.

'Yes,' Fiona said with a sigh but then a fond smile as she watched her brother. 'Our mother always said "he lives the life of Riley". Born to the name, born to river life.'

Riley was dropping anchor now and Ivy couldn't help but think of her sisters and mother and what they would have to say about such disparity. Why should the women be left to eke out an existence while the men galivanted about on boats all day? Men like George didn't even show up half the time, by the looks of things.

'Take me boots,' he was bellowing now, standing up unsteadily before tossing them over, and the twins ran to fetch them immediately.

Ivy glanced at Fiona, who looked agitated, the organised, competent woman Ivy had witnessed so far now a nervous one, her hand at her belly once more, mouth drawn in a tight thin line. This was not a husband welcome home, Ivy observed as she watched George jump heavily from the boat and wade over.

'What are them chickens doin' out?' he said, nodding at the pair of white hens pecking at the spindly grass near the pen.

'Twins have been getting eaten alive playing over there,' Fiona told him. 'I read in the paper that letting the chickens have free run near the home helps reduce the larger insect population, march flies in particular.'

'Ha. There's probably thousands of bloody things biting 'em. Fat lot of good that'll do,' he said, reaching shore and squinting at Ivy. 'You the patient, then?' he said, raking his eyes down her body before landing back on her bandaged face. It was an undisguised leer and Ivy tried not to recoil as she answered.

'Yes, Ivy Merriweather. I must thank you for your hospitality, Mr Ryan.'

'Oh, la-di-da,' he said, leaning in closer and grinning now. 'Call me George.'

Ivy didn't reply, thinking if the heat didn't do her in soon his rancid breath would.

'She won't have time to be calling you anything,' Riley said, overhearing. 'Ready to go, are you then?'

'What's your hurry?' George protested, still eyeing her, and Ivy glanced at Fiona. Her expression remained stiff as she placed one arm around each of the girls.

'Have to make use of the tide,' Riley replied. 'Best say your goodbyes and we'll be off.'

'Seems a shame to hurry away. We don't get many new females up here,' George said as Ivy struggled to rise. 'Nice to have a change of scenery.'

'Look at the river if you want scenery,' Riley said firmly. 'We're going. See you tomorrow, Fi.' He kissed his sister on the cheek before reaching down to pick Ivy up in his arms.

'I … I'm sure I can manage on my own,' Ivy protested but it was half-hearted. Truth was she could barely stand.

'Looks like the man's got his fish and he's away home,' George observed, eyes narrowing.

'She's not a fish, she's got legs,' Annie said, but then she clamped her mouth shut and Ivy noticed her nervous glance at her father. He didn't comment, however, merely watching Riley as he carried Ivy to the boat, the girls following.

'Bye, bye.' They waved and Ivy felt sorry to leave them. Sorry to leave Fiona too as she stood in front of her home. The house looked no more than a broken-down shack when viewed from offshore and Ivy noted it was really just a collection of mismatched materials, roughly constructed into a two-room dwelling. It clung precariously to the rock-strewn hillside and the sandy soils made for a very sorry-looking vegetable patch beside it. Kuranda seemed like a palace in comparison and Ivy longed to get home to the comforts it offered and her loved ones, leaving this unfair river world far behind.

They'd reached the boat and Riley lifted her on deck. Ivy managed to stand on one foot and grip the rail to look down and say goodbye to the twins, who had waded out waist deep to farewell her, their little faces woebegone as they wiped at tears.

'Bye,' Annie said again, her bottom lip trembling.

'Hope your scales turn out okay,' Tricia added with a sniff.

Ivy smiled at that and blew them both a kiss. She waved to Fiona then, her heart breaking for her as she bravely smiled and waved back. How she wished for a better existence for this strong, kind woman. How she wished for a better existence for her young daughters too, feeling wretched for them all as George stared across at her. What an isolated, depressing place to spend such a life, and what a man spend it with.

The engine began to rumble as the boat began its journey and Ivy slumped on the only cleared bench where Riley had laid down some blankets, too unwell to consider Fiona's fate any longer. He'd strung a blanket above the bench as well and she closed her eyes, grateful for the shade.

'You all right there?' Riley said, pausing in his work to look down at her.

'Just hot,' she mumbled.

'I'll get you some water.'

He took off below deck and Ivy tossed about, unable to get comfortable, and longing for that drink as the land passed by in a eucalypt haze. The trees looked thirsty too. Everything did. *How can a landscape surrounded by water appear so dry?* she wondered vaguely as Riley returned.

'Here you go.'

She drank thirstily before collapsing back against the bench.

'I'll have you home soon, don't worry,' he told her with a quick smile before cheerfully getting back to the wheel, and Ivy observed that it wasn't his fault he lived the life of Riley while his sister toiled away. He'd been nothing but good to Ivy. His smile was a nice one too, filled with reassurance and surprising gentleness for a man from such a rough place. She'd been lucky he was the one who'd found her, that was for sure. The idea of someone like George stumbling upon her half-naked and unconscious made her shudder.

Riley began to sing as he worked. 'Many years have passed since I strolled by the river ...' and Ivy smiled at the sound, drowsily watching the blue sky drift beyond the blanket. She was still terribly hot and her head was throbbing, but she felt grateful now, too. Fortune had smiled on her and her lifeblood remained intact as this decent man followed the water to take her home, she mused, thinking she must phrase it that way when she told her father of her escapades.

Now this drama was simply a story to tell in the years to come: the grand adventure of her eighteenth birthday when she dared to go for a swim and ended up being kidnapped, mistaken by a mermaid by twin little girls and returned dressed in homespun on a riverboat that carried dubious cargo. No harm done other than causing worry to her family and a probable scar on her temple that her hair would mostly hide. A permanent reminder of the cost of recklessness, certainly, but also of how very lucky she was, not only because she lived a life of comfort and plenty but because of the people she lived it with. 'The life of Ivy' now seemed a very fortunate existence, indeed.

I won't take things for granted any more, she vowed as she closed her eyes. *And I'll never get angry enough at my family to rush off and do something foolish ever again*, she added as each dear face came to mind, her father's lingering. *Less of an ignoramus, Dad, I promise.*

Thirteen

It was nothing short of a squall and no man alive could have seen it coming but Riley cursed himself, just the same. The clear mid-morning had turned suddenly windy and grey with menacing clouds rapidly approaching and there was no way to avoid the summer storm as they neared the sharp bend in the Hawkesbury River. It was too late to head back to Fiona's and too dangerous to keep going. The best he could hope for was to turn left into Mangrove Creek and seek safety in a small bay he knew of until it passed.

Ivy had remained asleep for the half-hour since they'd left but a huge gust of wind whipped at the blanket above her and Riley saw her wake, startled, as one corner broke away and slapped against the wall. She tried to sit up, nursing her head, and looking around in confusion.

'What's happening?' she called over to him.

'Need to avoid getting caught in that,' he said, nodding over to the ominous cloud mass. It was almost green at the centre and Riley knew hail was on the agenda. Leaves flew in darting flurries as the *Hawkesbury Queen* drew closer to land, haphazard and frenzied, as if to escape the impending onslaught. Lightning split the sky as thunder rumbled in dark warning and Riley realised they'd need better shelter than the boat.

'There's a cave we can stop in,' he called over to her, pointing towards the approaching cove. 'Should be safe and dry enough.'

He had to work fast to get the boat to the beach and the wind was against him, tossing the vessel about like a cork. Dropping anchor in a hurry, he made his way to Ivy, gripping the rail lest he fall from the force of the gale and somehow managing to lift her over the edge of the boat once more. It had been difficult enough the other times he'd got her to and from shore but it was quite a strenuous challenge in this wind. She was gripping on to him hard too, burying her face against his chest, and Riley realised she was frightened. And still damnably hot. For the first time it occurred to him the wound may be festering and she might have taken a fever, meaning getting drenched in a storm was the last thing she needed right now. He broke into a jog, desperate to get her into the cave as she-oaks flung needled branches against them and the rocks threatened to trip him every few feet.

Somehow he made it, checking for snakes in the dim light then placing her well inside on the sandy floor. There were tracks but no reptiles that he could discern and he reassured her before setting back out into the wind.

'You'll be safe here. Hold on while I get a few supplies.'

The gale force of the wind was almost toppling him over but soon enough he was able to throw a few things in a sack and battle his way back as heavy drops began to fall.

Ivy was slumped once more, her face pasty as she blinked his way. 'Do you have any more of that water?'

Riley set the sack down and pulled out a jug, uncorking it and offering it to her. 'No mugs this time, sorry.'

She drank and watched him as he unpacked a few more things: a candle, matches, a few peaches and plums and the blanket he'd used as shelter before. He wrapped it around her and drew her away from the cave's entrance as the wind carried in the pelting rain, but it was a battle trying to keep her completely dry. He clamped his hand to her forehead, his concern rising.

'What are you doing?' she murmured.

'Feeling your temperature.'

'… how is it?'

'Not good,' he replied grimly. She was burning to the touch. 'Here, lie down on this.' Riley spread the blanket on the sand, figuring it'd be better beneath her rather than over her heated skin and she lay down like it was an enormous effort to do so.

Shit, shit, shit. What to do? he wondered, looking out at the storm. It was raging now, the din of it rising as trees thrashed about and the thunder boomed ever closer. Flashes of lighting illuminated the cave and Riley looked back at Ivy. She was groaning, her head moving from side to side, and he knew she was actually in worse shape than when he'd found her.

What would her family have to say about that if he took her back now? He'd protected their injured girl, to be sure, but to return her this ill would cast him less in the light of saviour and far more in the role of irresponsible stranger. Questions would be raised, and it was one thing to hide his illegal cargo in a cave, quite another to hide his entire profession from the authorities. What if he ended up in gaol? Who would look after Fiona and the twins and all the other people who relied on him then?

Yet this girl needed help, his heart reasoned, as he gazed down at her young, pallid countenance, her breathing laboured, brow furrowed in agitation. Compassion for her took over and he knew that her dwindling health was the priority, above any of his own concerns, but which help to choose: to turn back for it or continue on?

Her wealthy family were bound to have a decent doctor at their disposal, yet the journey back to Hornsby was an arduous one. It would mean a good hour and a half on the choppy river followed by a steep climb by omnibus up the coach track from the main port at Bobbin Head to town. How was he supposed to manage such an ill patient under those extreme circumstances? What if ... what if she got far, far worse?

Riley took a deep breath, forcing his racing mind to slow down and focus on the other alternative. *You can take her back to Fiona's,* he told himself. *She isn't far away and she'll know what to do. You just need to nurse Ivy through this storm.* Such practicality calmed him, almost as if his sister stood by his side, and he knew she was Ivy's closest, safest option for help right now.

That decided, he focused on doing what he could for her now until the storm passed. Fortunately he'd picked up a few nursing tips from his mother too, starting with the fact that he needed to cool her down, but not too fast.

Riley rummaged around and grabbed a cloth from the sack, pouring some water over it, then he used it to dab her face as best he could as she twisted about.

'Try not to fidget,' he advised. 'You'll overheat even more if you move around too much.'

She lay stiller then and he was able to cool her neck as well, knowing he needed access to more of her.

'I'm really sorry, Ivy, but that dress has to come off.'

Her eyes opened drowsily but it was a mark of how unwell she was that she didn't protest as he undid the buttons and lifted it over her head. He cooled her arms and legs then, trying not to register the beauty of the young body before him. Riley decided to distract them both by chatting, looking for anything to talk about as she watched his administrations blearily.

'So do you have many siblings?' he said, having to raise his voice above the din of the storm. 'You mentioned you had family but not who they are or what they do.'

'Yes ... two sisters: Frankie and Aggie.'

'And are they much like you?' he said, liking the idea of three women who looked like Ivy.

'No,' she said, weakly moving her head, damp curls clinging to her skin. 'Frankie is blonde and tall and Aggie is dark and smaller. They are both very passionate though ...' she trailed off thoughtfully, a bit misty-eyed.

'About what?'

Ivy considered that. 'Womankind.'

Riley was intrigued but also wary. In his limited experience, feminism was a dangerous subject, so he changed it.

'What about your parents? Fiona said she read in the papers that your father is a scientist?'

'Yes,' she said smiling a little, her fondness for him evident. 'He studies dragonflies.'

'Really?' Riley said, surprised and amused. 'Imagine earning a living from that.'

'My mother is a scientist too but the university ... wouldn't ...' she paused, her eyelids dropping momentarily but then she opened them again at the coolness of the cloth as he wiped her arms. 'Wouldn't give her a degree. She's still ... fighting that.'

'I don't know any women who've been to university,' he told her. 'Seems a waste of time to me, I mean, all that study if you can't use it.'

Ivy frowned. 'Why shouldn't they use it?'

'I'm not saying they shouldn't, more that they can't if they're raising a family. They already have a job doing that.'

'Doesn't mean they can't work too,' she protested, and Riley wondered how he'd landed in a feminist debate after all, but the subject seemed to give Ivy strength so he continued it.

'They do work. Harder than men, I'd say.'

'My mother is always working in other ways too, writing to the universities and helping Dad—' She paused, wincing as his hand grazed the bandage on her forehead, ignoring his muttered apology to continue, '—with his research. Why waste intelligence?'

'Maybe for women who can afford the time and where it can be used in such ways, I suppose,' Riley conceded, 'but it isn't of much use to women up here. They've got their work cut out for them raising a family and they need all their wits focused on that, let me tell you. What's the point in them learning about insect behaviour, beyond treating their bites?'

'Fiona is intelligent, applying what she reads in the papers from what I saw,' Ivy pointed out. 'Maybe if she could study the insects properly she could find other ways to … to prevent such things, who knows?'

It was an interesting point, if a little far-fetched, but still. 'She is a smart one,' he agreed. 'Got educated by our parents. They were both schooled, and quite well-off but … well, that's another story,' he said.

'Tell it,' she implored and she was hard to refuse, lying there so ill, and so he did.

'My dad was the son of a convict,' he began, chuckling a bit as her mouth formed an 'o' of surprise. 'It isn't any great shame to us. Old Da should never have been sent here just for stealing a horse on a drunken lark back in Killarney … anyway,' he continued, wondering how much he should really be telling her about his colourful family past, 'he only got few years and when he got out he decided to make the most of things and began building oyster farms. All along the river up here, they were, did pretty well for himself and gave Dad a decent education while he was at it. He was an only child so when Da died Dad took over and married Mum.' Riley smiled fondly, remembering his very much in love parents. 'She was probably a bit out of his league, being the daughter of a lawyer and all, but they were always smitten, those two.'

Ivy was hanging on his every word, smiling too. 'My parents are like that.'

'Are they? Well, it's rare in my experience but it gives a man hope,' he said, and immediately wished he hadn't, considering he was currently stroking her leg with the cloth. Riley cleared his throat and stopped to pour more water before continuing.

'Anyway, I was luckier than most until the day they took sick. Everything changed after that.'

'What happened?' she asked, her eyes filling with concern.

Riley paused, forcing the most hated word he knew out. 'Diphtheria,' he told her. 'Fiona tried so hard to save them … took weeks but, anyway, they didn't make it.' His throat was tight now, the image of the two graves weathering this storm downriver on Bar Island a painful one. 'Died the same day. That was ten years ago.'

'Oh. Oh Riley, I'm so, so sorry.' Tears slid down her face, mingling with the rain and the perspiration in her wet red hair. Most women would probably look a sight in such a state but, looking at that heartfelt expression as he revealed his deepest sorrow, Riley had never seen anyone more beautiful.

'Thanks,' he said, no other words coming to mind as he gazed at her and choked back tears himself. He'd never told anyone that story before. He never cried, either, hadn't since that terrible day.

'What happened to the oyster farms?'

'Algae came that summer. Choked the whole river and killed off the stock. There were debts to be paid and ... I don't know. Maybe if we'd been older ...' He shrugged. 'We lost everything.'

'Not everything,' she said softly, lifting her hand weakly to place it over his where it held the cloth. 'You have each other.'

He gazed at the spot, transfixed. 'Yes. Yes, that we do.'

'And their intelligence, I take it,' she said, letting her hand fall. It dropped listlessly and he couldn't help but stare at it, wishing it back.

'They were very bright,' he said, rousing himself back to tending her, 'both of them. And educated, as I said. That's why we can both read and write, unlike most around here.'

'Why didn't ... why didn't you go to school?' she asked and Riley sensed she was fading again.

'Better off being taught by them. Besides, we were living right up the river at the time and the closest school was at Wisemans Ferry, an hour by rowboat in all weathers, which seemed too far. Still is for a lot of children living in remote spots so they don't bother going,' he said.

'But ... but that's against the law ...' she said, a confused frown appearing.

Riley shrugged, stroking her shoulder with the cloth. 'So are a lot of things.'

'They should ... every child has the right ...' she muttered before looking at him, aghast. 'What about the twins?'

'Fiona will do what she can,' Riley said by way of an answer, not wanting to upset her further. George would be against the idea of the girls being schooled, Riley knew. 'Anyway, enough of all that. How are you feeling? Any better?'

Ivy closed her eyes, the frown still there but she appeared too exhausted to deal with more. 'A bit, I think.'

She seemed slightly cooler but she was still very pale and feverish and would soon start to burn up again, he knew, the memory of his parents' deadly fevers haunting him now.

Riley stood, letting her rest, and wondered how long it would be until he could get her out of here, his concern for her mounting as he stared out at the storm. The squall didn't seemed to be waning. If anything it had gained momentum, with churning waves thrashing against the beach and whole mountainsides of trees bowing and whipping in unison. His boat dipped and rocked precariously and Riley wondered if the situation could get any worse. Then he heard the shouts of men's voices, and it did.

'Riley!'

Deano was standing on the rocky edges of the cove, calling his name. Riley could see him clearly despite the lashing storm – clad in the same blue sailor's jacket he always wore when it rained, a remnant of his days in the navy.

His mate Petey was visible too, his long beard trailing in the wind as he rowed to shore and tied their rowboat to a large log. In such conditions and in their exposed two-man vessel it was no wonder they'd sought shelter. Unfortunately Donovan was seeking refuge too, his larger boat chugging to shore. Of all the people in the world they were the last ones Riley wished upon Ivy right now. A beautiful, vulnerable woman was worth more than gold up in these parts.

Women were vastly outnumbered and the ones who grew up here were married off young, often after heated negotiation. Others were simply stolen, especially Aboriginal women unlucky enough to be caught alone. Once they were married they were at the mercy of their husbands and some were shown very little of it, often beaten and raped as the men pleased. It sickened Riley to the core, and the other decent men he knew along this river, but there were too many of them who adhered to the violent way of things. Donovan being the worst.

Riley watched him as the engine cut beneath the storm's roar, the waves whipping to a frenzy against the sides as he jumped out and waded hurriedly in. Just one man, small against the elements, but enormously dangerous to all who crossed his path. Riley had managed to hide Ivy from him before but he didn't like his chances of doing so again. There weren't many caves to take shelter in within this cove. The realisation made him snap to a decision and he turned back to Ivy.

'I have to go out and see a few fellows for a minute but I'll be right back. Don't move, all right? And whatever you do, don't call out or come looking for me.'

'Why … who …?' she mumbled.

'Men I don't want you to meet under any circumstances,' he told her firmly before softening his tone. 'Back in a moment.'

Better he find them than they find him, he reasoned, dashing out into the storm. As menacing as it looked from the cave it was brutal firsthand and Riley battled unsteadily to the shoreline, wet rocks threatening each step, and the wind causing the rain to angle and pierce like needles. It looked to be a long one too, the dark clouds roiling towards them from the south like a sinister army on the march, the green he'd noted before nearly upon them.

'Hey!' Riley called and Deano looked over, raising his hand in a wave. Petey had found shelter under a large rock overhanging a hollow not thirty feet from the cave and Donovan was dragging an oilskin cloth towards it. At least they had found their own spot. But how to keep them away from his?

The answer presented itself as he witnessed Deano trying to lift a keg from the rowboat. Sober and with their adrenaline up they were a threat, drunk and mean even more so, but passed out cold Riley could give them the slip. It seemed his best option but it would take some doing, including offering some of his own good rum and being friendly after all these years. Deano was calling his name purely because treacherous situations called for such rudimentary courtesy, Riley knew, not because he suddenly cared much about Riley's welfare. Riley had been in enough danger with other men over the years to recognise that.

Still, he went over and helped Deano with the keg, earning a surprised glance from the man, but no comment. Together they carried it across the wet sand and plonked it inside the shelter, which was proving quite a good spot. Donovan looked over at him, wary yet nosy.

'Where'd you spring from?' he called over the storm's noise.

'Found somewhere over there,' Riley called back with a nod towards the cave.

Donovan looked over at it. 'Bit small.'

'Yep, this spot's definitely better,' Riley assured him, feeling fairly certain Donovan wouldn't explore the cave if he felt he'd found superior shelter. Banking on that, Riley added, 'Just getting some more supplies.'

'Got anything better than this?' Petey asked him, tapping the keg, the elements and his long beard muffling his words to the point that he actually had to shout. It was as good an invitation to join them as he was going to get.

'I'll see what I can find.' Riley headed over to his boat. Maybe ingratiating his way in for a change wouldn't prove too difficult under such extreme conditions. Men were more accommodating in life-and-death situations, even men like these, and Riley could surely pretend he thought any company looked good in a storm.

❖

'King of the river, that's me,' Donovan slurred, twirling his bottle about as he looked out at his boat bobbing in the rain. 'The *River King!*'

They were good and drunk, well, drunk, anyway. Except Riley, who'd tossed a lot of the stuff away when the others weren't looking. He'd even managed to sneak over and check on Ivy a few times under the guise of relieving himself or grabbing more supplies. Her temperature was up again but he'd expected that, and there was nothing he could do about it save bathe her face quickly before rejoining the others. The storm had raged for quite a while, the hail arriving as predicted, which kept the men entertained. Deano had collected some pieces that were the size of a plum before hurling them against the rocks for sport and altogether he was a rather merry drunk, telling some ribald jokes and breaking into the odd song with Petey. But Donovan had turned mean in the past half-hour and the three had nearly come to blows several times.

Riley had managed to keep in the background and just observe, mostly – not a friend by any means but tolerated due to the circumstances. The brief armistice seemed to be wearing thin, however, as the storm calmed to a steady rain, the grey curtains of water rendering their world eerie as Donovan's focus turned Riley's way.

'So why aren't you hiding in your cave?'

'Bit boring on my own,' Riley said with a shrug, wondering if he'd just heard Ivy moan or merely imagined it. He took a swig of his drink, hiding his nerves.

'Cosy places if you have a woman with ya.' The comment made Riley's stomach coil, hoping to God Donovan hadn't heard Ivy or suspected anything.

'Haven't had one of those in a while,' Riley said. It was a comment designed to deflect and it worked. Donovan loved nothing better than to brag about his conquests, as sickening as it would be to hear it.

'Problem with you is y'too fussy. I've had three wives in three years, two at once last winter,' he bragged, 'a brown girl and a white girl. Had me way with both of them at the same time after I beat them into agreeing to it,' he said, chuckling to himself as he stumbled forwards to fill his glass.

'Is that what did her in? That brown one, I mean?' Deano commented. The girl had been found dead by her tribe one cold August morning, her body left in the rain onshore, bruised and lifeless. Donovan had denied it was by his hands at the time. 'Thought you said she fell.'

'No law against it,' Donovan said with a shrug, sculling his rum. It made Riley want to punch him, his fist curling by his side. Donovan noticed it, despite his inebriated state.

'Got a problem with that, have ya?'

'Well, it is against the law to commit murder,' Riley said, fury and alcohol driving his words, despite his efforts to not get drunk.

'Ah, she was just a stupid native. Besides, my wife, my property,' Donovan slurred. 'You should try getting y'self one.' He moved closer to Riley, talking straight into his face, one hand on the knife at his belt. 'Might improve that carrot-up-your-arse attitude of yours.'

Riley itched to fight him, would have done, in fact, if not for Ivy lying sick and needing his help nearby.

'Think I might see a man about a dog,' he said instead, sending Donovan a warning glance before moving off.

'Yeah, yeah, piss off then,' Donovan called after him. 'Pass me his rum, Deano.'

Riley made his way over to the cave to check on Ivy and to his dismay she was sitting up trying to put her dress on.

'C-cold,' she stuttered.

'Hush now,' he said as quietly as he could. 'The storm's died down and we can't let those men out there hear you, all right?'

'I c-can hear them …' she told him and there was fear in her eyes, making Riley wonder just what she'd heard, and how much. God knows it would shock a girl like her to the core.

'You're still very warm, Ivy,' he told her softly, focusing on that instead and stroking her face with the cloth. 'I know you feel like you're cold but you're actually not. Lie down now. I'll get you out of here as soon as I can.'

'When …?' she moaned, collapsing back and clutching the dress.

'As soon as the coast is clear,' he whispered, grabbing a few pieces of fruit to justify his visit and climbing back out.

Fortunately the rain had eased to a drizzle and blue sky could be glimpsed between cloud masses, meaning there was enough daylight to make his way back to Fiona's if that was truly what he needed to do. Thinking of Ivy's weak and shivering form he knew it was, as further complicated as that made things, but he'd have to leave soon. *Just pass out already*, he silently begged as he made his way back but Donovan had started an argument with Petey now.

'Go near her and I'll kill ya,' Petey yelled.

'I wouldn't go near your sister in for all the tea in bloody China.'

'What? Not good enough for y'then?'

'Not if she's as hairy as you. Reckon she could have a beard downstairs!'

Deano guffawed at that but Petey had grabbed Donovan by the shirt and Deano scrambled to pull them apart.

'Hey … hey!' Deano called.

'Have a go then, ya grizzly mongrel,' Donovan yelled at Petey, reeling about and nearly falling over his feet.

'Just settle down already,' Deano said, rocking as he stood with his arms out between them.

'My bloody sister ...' Petey was muttering as he sat heavily down. 'No respect.'

Donovan noticed Riley's return then and a lecherous grin split his face. 'Riley's sister's the one I would have loved to get me hands on, that Fiona,' he drawled. 'I woulda beat the snootiness out of her in no time.' If Riley had wanted to hit Donovan before it was nothing compared to now.

'Hasn't worked for old George so far,' Deano replied, not noticing Riley as yet. 'He said a good beating only makes her angrier.'

'He said what?' Riley said, heated fury flooding through him in a rush.

Deano swung around at his voice and blanched. 'I'm sure he ... I mean, I'm pretty certain George was lying 'bout it.'

Riley glared at him, trying to discern the truth through his anger. 'He'd better pray to God he was,' he said switching his focus back to Donovan, the menace in his tone clear. 'Any man lays a finger on her and he's dead.'

For all his bravado it seemed Donovan had finally been shut down, showing his cowardice in the end, and a tense silence followed. Then Donovan stumbled off to relieve himself, muttering, and fell over in the process. Snores soon followed and after a few minutes it seemed the others had begun to doze off at last too. Riley could finally make his exit and smuggle Ivy on board and back to Fiona's but he waited a bit longer, just in case, before going to her.

He'd expected to find her still feverish but he hadn't expected to find her crying.

'What is it? Do you feel that poorly?' She shook her head, her expression filled with despair. 'I'll get you home as soon as I can, don't worry,' he said, soothing her face with the cloth, figuring she was probably scared or perhaps homesick. 'In fact we can get out of here now.'

But tears continued to fall and her face crumpled as she whispered, 'Fiona.'

Riley's heart shifted at that, her sweet compassion touching after so much belligerence and cruelty this afternoon.

'I'm sure there was no truth to it, Ivy. Take no notice of what drunken men like that say. All right?'

She nodded, her trust evident, but she remained emotionally shaken, and literally still shook from fever as he wrapped her in the blanket, grabbed the hessian bag and gathered her in his arms, holding her against him protectively. Then he set off to sneak quietly to his boat with the most precious cargo the *Hawkesbury Queen* had ever carried, a fact vehemently reinforced by these dangerous men. His need to guard her intense, his senses on painful alert, he lifted Ivy aboard for the third time in less than a day and headed back for urgent attention from Fiona, her safest option for recovery. To the one person who'd always been his home, his family, his rock. To seek healing and support once more, and, while he was at it, to find out how much truth there really was in the words drunken men say.

Fourteen

The moon was rising, cresting the hill across the river in a luminous half-orb, slightly golden as it slowly revealed its form that night and cast a glittering lane across the water that ended in rhythmic waves onshore. It rendered everything magical, a beautiful spell cast over the landscape as its soft light touched every tree, every rock, every tuft of grass. The ordinary now extraordinary. It was Riley's favourite part of living here: the moonlit river. It spoke to some primal part within him, soothing him and chasing shadows away, but tonight two shadows remained and Fiona had carried one of them with her when she'd waded out in her skirts to meet the boat.

'What's wrong? Was it the storm?' she'd said immediately, the shack behind her bearing fresh scars from the recent onslaught.

'Yes, we got caught and Ivy's not good. She's taken fever ...'

'But you can't stay here,' she'd interrupted, eyes darting to shore. 'George is drunk and in a mood.'

'What kind of mood?' Riley had demanded, glancing over at the shore too.

Fiona had paused before replying, her expression closed. 'Nothing for you to worry about.'

Riley had wasted no words then. 'I swear, Fiona, if he's been laying into you I'll kill him.'

She'd merely lifted her chin and scoffed, pride and haughtiness in her reply. 'Of course he hasn't! As if I'd let any man hit me in a million years.'

If she was lying she'd become damn good at it all of a sudden. Fiona had been a terrible liar when they were growing up. He hadn't pursued it, however. She would hardly start confessing in the middle of the river and in full view of George as he lumbered outside to sit in his fishing chair, even if it were true. Besides, Riley had needed Fiona's help with that other shadow over his day, his very ill and feverish passenger, and it wasn't the time to argue. That time would come though. This matter was far from over.

In the end Fiona had tended Ivy on the boat rather than move her or contend with George and the patient remained below deck as an exhausted Fiona came up for a breather.

'Any change?' Riley asked, pausing from filling his pipe.

'No,' Fiona said, stretching her back and sighing. 'You were right to bring her back to me, though. She would've struggled to make the long journey home and that's a fact.'

'Do the wounds look worse to you?'

'Not really,' Fiona said, frowning as she stared at the water.

'What then?' Riley said, studying her, his stomach knotting.

'Well, I was thinking,' she said, dropping her tone to a whisper, 'it could be the plague.'

'*The plague?!*'

'Hush! Keep your voice down,' she warned before continuing. 'It took nearly a hundred lives in Sydney last year, is all.' His horror at that fact must have showed for she'd quickly added, 'but most newspapers say that's as good as over.'

The plague. Could anything else happen in this calamity-filled new year? Only two days old and already 1902 had taken his quiet life of smuggling along the Hawkesbury River and thrown in an unavoidable kidnapping, a local hurricane and accusations of wife-beating along with admissions of murder at a violent rum party. No wonder he felt sick and exhausted.

There was no time to rest, however. Ivy was still very ill and Riley needed to get word to her family. Fortunately, Barney's boat was due to come by soon so he was keeping vigil to send another message. Barney always went fishing on Thursday afternoons but would be back home by nightfall and his boat would chug straight past when he did.

And so it was just Riley and the river, his closest companion, left to soothe his tumultuous emotions in the moonlight. The tide drifted slowly, as if to mark the painfully slow passing of time as Fiona tended Ivy down below, the occasion scrape of a bowl or groan from the patient the only human sounds. The river itself had its usual living language, lapping steadily against the boat's sides and the shore, while the fauna that depended on it added to that constant sound like an eclectic orchestra.

For a while it had been the diurnal animals keeping chorus but they had all disappeared when twilight fell; the cicada's drone fading as the last of the wood ducks flew off in drumming flutters and flocks of cockatoos called to their families to take roost in the hills. Riley wondered where they'd all got to while the violent squall had raged, but a perfect calm had settled in after the storm. Yet it wasn't a quiet calm, nor was it still, as the nocturnal animals took reign.

Frogs, crickets and all manner of insects started the nightly song and it was peppered by the leathery swish of fruit bats flapping overhead, making their nightly pilgrimage to the orchards. The swoop of tawny frogmouths could also be heard as they moved among the trees, and Riley knew that many more creatures would be visible beneath the moon tonight, but the twins hadn't sought to investigate the riverbank with their little lanterns, nor had they rushed out to greet him as they often did. They hadn't emerged at all.

Riley stared over at George, asleep in his chair, and seethed anew at the possibility of this man hitting his sister. He was a good-for-nothing type, and lazy as the day was long, but he'd managed to woo Fiona a few years ago, somehow, and at the time Riley had figured she could have done worse. He'd seemed rather harmless back then, especially compared to the likes of Donovan. George's drinking had got worse since the twins were born, however, and there were more notable and regular absences as he took off fishing. To say the honeymoon was over would be an under-statement but he'd never have expected the man would actually hit her, if for no other reason than the fear of Riley knocking his lights out.

But who really knew what went on behind closed doors, and Fiona was proud, as her reaction today had proven; potentially proud enough to hide this from him. There was something in the way she kept holding her hands across her belly too, and the purse of her lips as she drew the twins closer, and away. The image of George's fist colliding with Fiona's pregnant form flashed through his mind and he gritted his teeth as he looked out at the water. Maybe he wouldn't wait to have this out with Fiona properly. Maybe he wouldn't just hit the bastard, either. Perhaps he really would help him find a watery grave along these shores instead.

Such disturbing, murderous thoughts were interrupted by the rumble of Barney's motor and Riley picked up the lamp nearby and signalled for him to stop. At least that was one piece of action he could take right now, and it felt good to be able to help Ivy contact her family again, at least, especially after hearing how much she cared for them today.

Barney's boat approached, low in the water with all the equipment he had on board along with the crates he'd not yet delivered from the orchards. It was part of his job that he deliver up here each afternoon but the produce turned up on doorsteps in the wee hours on Friday mornings due to his Thursday fishing jaunts.

'Ahoy!' Barney called cheerily, trying to wave and tie down a crate at the same time.

'Ahoy!' Riley waved back, thinking it would be good to see a friend after such a day. He was actually a decent bloke, if rather dim and easily distracted.

Barney finished tying the ropes and drew the boat alongside. 'What's with George?' he said, nodding over at the man's slumped form.

'Out cold,' Riley told him, his earlier thoughts of punching the man and achieving the same end still fresh.

'Again?' Barney said, with a shake of his head. 'He's really not handling the grog too well lately, is he?' he said, swigging at a bottle himself, although not unsteadily. 'Anyway, what's your story then?'

'What do you mean?'

'I mean why'd you call me over? Need a hand with somethin'?'

'No, no, just another message delivered, if you don't mind.'

Barney looked at him blankly. 'What do you mean another one?'

Riley stared, dread in his tone as he replied. 'Don't tell me you forgot?'

'Forgot what?'

Riley took a deep breath, cursing himself for entrusting such a man with such an errand.

'I gave you a note to deliver last night. To the Merriweather family in Hornsby?'

'A note?' Barney was frowning in the lamplight and Riley rubbed his face as yet another huge problem arose.

'Good God, they must be beside themselves.'

'When did you give me a note?'

'When you were pulling the nets in, remember? I said whatever you do, don't forget to deliver this note …'

'… pinned on the door,' Barney said, memory dawning as his eyes grew wide. 'Shit.'

'Is it still there?' Riley asked, trying not to lose his temper, and Barney went over to the door to investigate. He lifted the oilskin coat that hung on the peg and found the note beneath it, turning to show it to Riley.

'Stuck me oilskin on there this morning. Felt too bloody humid not to storm. I was right about that much, anyways,' he finished lamely.

How a man could read the weather so well yet not notice a note on a door when you hooked and unhooked a coat over it, let alone forget something as important as telling a missing girl's family she was safe, was beyond Riley's ken. But there was no use berating Barney, as frustrating as he could be.

'Anyway, she's back now, ain't she? Didn't you say you were taking her home today?' Barney said, his memory of the previous night obviously beginning to return.

'No, she's taken sick with a fever. Fiona's tending to her down below,' Riley told him, closing his eyes momentarily.

'Bloody hell, that's bad luck,' Barney said, looking below deck guiltily. 'I can take another message if you like. The moon's up. I could make my way right now, I reckon, just need to drop off these fruit crates but then I'm good as gold.'

'How will you get up to town, though?'

There were no omnibuses running from Bobbin Head at night. Normally Barney got picked up by his mate Joe near where he moored his boat in the gorge, but this would mean leaving his boat at the wharf instead. Heading up to Hornsby in the middle of the night would be both treacherous and too far on foot.

'I'll borrow one of Jimbo's horses, I guess.' Jimbo managed Shaw's Boathouse near the pier and had a few mounts that he occasionally rented out. He probably wouldn't be too impressed at being woken in the wee hours but Barney had a way about him that saw people easily forgive his transgressions, right now a case in point.

Still, Riley hesitated. It was dangerous navigating the smaller creeks up near Hornsby, despite the aid of the partial moonlight, but ultimately Barney was a riverman, born and raised, and he made this journey most days of his life. What he lacked in everyday intelligence he made up for in his knowledge of these waters.

'All right,' Riley agreed. 'I'm giving you a second note to go with the first but head straight to the girl's family home this time, all right? And no more grog.'

'Yeah,' Barney agreed, still with an air of guilt about him but seeming relieved to make amends. 'I was done anyways.'

Riley went over to the boat's cabin and rewrote the second note to include a line about the first letter being waylaid. Let Barney explain it better in person. It was probably more believable that anyone could forget to deliver such an important message if they met the man himself.

That done, he made sure the family's address that Ivy had provided was clearly printed on the front. Barney could barely read but he knew numbers, at least, and Rosemead Road was an easy street name to memorise.

Barney set off and Riley watched his departure until he disappeared from sight, wondering what other twists and turns these startling few days of 1902 could possibly bring, guilt gnawing away within him too. He was the one who'd picked Ivy up and brought her here and he was the one who'd trusted Barney to deliver the news of her location and wellbeing. As a man of usually good common sense neither decision seemed very smart now.

The sound of his sister's muffled administrations prompted him to go to see the patient, debating with himself whether he'd tell her this new piece of bad news. One look at her ill white countenance made the decision for him, however – best she fight the fever without this additional worry. Fiona's eyes raised at the sound of his tread and she looked worn out. Riley hadn't considered how much physical strain this crisis was putting on his sister, especially in her current condition, and he placed a hand on her shoulder.

'Why don't you head over home to bed and I'll sit with her now.'

Fiona hesitated but it was a mark of how drained she really was that she nodded and agreed.

'Just a few hours' sleep and I'll come back.'

'It's too much effort for you, wading back and forth and getting on board again. I'll carry you.'

'Ha. Not while I'm the size of a house, you won't,' she replied, considering things. 'Perhaps I could just sleep on the bench upstairs awhile. Out in the fresh air.'

The porthole was open but it was still stuffy here below deck and Riley agreed. He'd move Ivy too only he didn't really want her exposed to any other nasties at this point.

'Come on then,' he said, helping her stand.

He settled her above deck on the same blanket that Ivy had used and took out his pouch to roll a cigarette, delivering the news about Barney and the failed message. Fiona's mouth dropped open.

'Bloody hopeless,' she muttered. 'Imagine her poor parents … not to mention what the authorities might make of this now.'

'Let's just focus on getting her well and back in one piece,' Riley said, nervous about that himself, and the added pressure of ensuring Ivy's wellbeing hung between them. Bad enough she was here unbeknown to her family, far worse she perish in Fiona and Riley's care.

Riley lit his cigarette and looked out to the moon that was sailing along through scattered clouds. They passed before it like shadows, obscuring its brilliance, as if they were secrets hiding the moon's clear truth. Riley's concern over Fiona returned at the sight and he tried again to question her, to reassure himself that this shadow, at least, was a false one. The mere folly of a drunken man's words.

'Speaking of staying well,' Riley said, looking pointedly at the beach where George snored in the night.

'Oh, for God's sakes,' Fiona protested, shifting uncomfortably on the bench, 'leave it alone, Riley. Where on earth did this idea spring from again?'

Riley studied her face in the moonlight, searching for any reaction as he told her. 'Donovan and the boys were caught in the storm with us today.'

She stared at him, her bleary eyes widening in concern. 'Don't tell me they saw Ivy.'

'No, I managed to keep her hidden away in a cave but she could hear them well enough, I'm afraid,' he said, telling her the rest of what had transpired, including Donovan's brags of violence. 'Hopefully she'll forget,' he finished, 'think it was all bad dream.'

'Must have felt like a nightmare for a girl like that,' she agreed. 'Poor thing. How frightening for her, being exposed to such talk, and near enough and weak enough for them to … God, Riley, how frightening for *you*. The very men you wanted to protect her from.'

'Yep, it's been quite a year so far,' he quipped, sharing his earlier reflection, and she sighed.

'Not the best start, no.'

There was silence then and Riley watched her again. 'Fi, you can tell me, you know. I won't kill him, I promise … well, maybe mess him up a bit to make sure he never lays a hand on you again, but that's about it.' He paused, earnest now. 'Tell me the truth.'

She was looking him in the eye and then she surprised him by actually smiling. 'Bless your heart, Riley. I am telling you the truth. I'm perfectly fine, I promise. I'd tell you if I wasn't, or hit him back myself. You know I can pack a mean punch – walloped you once, didn't I?'

'I was ten years old—'

'—and laid down by your eleven-year-old sister,' she said, giggling a little.

'Humph,' he said, but he was smiling now too.

'Now let this go, all right? It's just rum talk and a waste of our precious time,' she stopped to yawn, 'and energy. Speaking of which, I'm having a nap. You all right to watch over her?'

'Yeah,' he said, rising and stretching. 'You rest up, Fi. I'll see you after a while.'

'Night,' she said, eyes already closing.

Riley watched her, hoping she'd been telling the truth but unable to do more than that as he tossed his cigarette away. 'Goodnight.'

He made his way below deck and sat heavily beside Ivy, reaching over to gently stroke her face with the cloth. Even white and feverish in the lamplight it was a beautiful countenance, and a young one. Riley studied it with a sigh, wondering how much more protectiveness for women he could possibly feel. It was a natural instinct, a moral obligation that his parents had always encouraged and instilled, but it came at a cost.

Ivy was beginning to toss once more and he stroked her cheeks with a fresh cloth from Fiona's neat pile nearby; dipping it in the water, soothing her quietly with his words.

'Dad,' she moaned. 'I'm sorry …'

Delirium wasn't a good sign but perhaps it meant the fever was at its peak so Riley continued to bathe her, trying to keep her calm.

'It's okay,' Riley said gently.

'I'm so, so sorry … Mum … where's Mum?'

'You're all right, Ivy, you're safe.'

'Tell Frankie I'm sorry too … and Aggie …'

She was crying now, her hands clutching at the blanket.

'There's no need to be sorry, there's the girl.'

'I just want to go home,' she said on a sob.

'I know, love,' he said, the word coming out so naturally it gave him pause.

Her eyes fluttered open and she seemed to focus on him. His heart skipped at the trust there.

'I just want … I want …' But then she shut them tight and he couldn't resist a prompt.

'What is it that you want, Ivy? What is it, my love?' There was that word again but Riley didn't care.

'I want …' and he held his breath as she whispered, 'Patrick.'

The word was like a punch and Riley felt a wave of jealousy towards the owner of that name so intense it made him sit back in his chair. *Who's Patrick?* he desperately wanted to ask, equally desperate not to know.

He could be anyone, he reasoned to himself, he could even be a pet, for all Riley knew. *Why should you care if she cries out another man's name, anyway? It's not like you're in bed with the woman.* He shook that disturbing thought away but others rushed in. *It's not like you expected her to say your name. Or use a word like love.*

Riley stood then, needing air, and he climbed the stairs to the deck to lean against the rail and stare out to where the clouds drifted, edged in silver and hiding the moon once more. Shadows and truth, truth and shadows. He didn't want to understand what he felt for Ivy Merriweather as she fought for her young life aboard his boat on this mysterious night. Let the grey clouds shield that truth for now. Let them shield the underscoring worry that Fiona could still be lying too, and the fact that somewhere down the river Barney's boat chugged away, closer by the minute to delivering the one truth that couldn't be avoided. One that would inevitably draw Ivy's world his way and with it the people whose names she called.

Two feminist sisters and two scientist parents – smart people who would question his not-very-smart decisions. People whose protectiveness over women extended far beyond their own flesh and blood and to all womankind. How would they judge his efforts? What verdict would they make? And what state would Ivy be in when they came here, to her sickbed on an old boat far, far removed from a soft bed in a rich man's home? Who, indeed, would come for her? All of them? A few? The police? Or simply a man called Patrick – a single word breathed in her delirium, yet a name that deeply mattered to her, it couldn't be denied.

Whatever happened and whoever came, this moon would sail on until the dawn hid the night and the third day of this dramatic year arrived. And whatever truths were shielded or revealed, two very different worlds were set to collide and erupt, regardless, in the broad daylight of tomorrow.

Part Three

Rule of thumb

Fifteen

Patrick was alone and he'd never felt more so in his life. It was nearly one o'clock in the morning and sleep had eluded him for the second night in a row, his occasional fitful naps ending in fractured nightmares that left him shaking and in a sweat. It didn't help that a policeman slept outside his bedroom door, part of the bail arrangement negotiated by his father. He was lucky to be under house arrest and not in gaol, the lawyers had told him. Lucky to be the son of Douglas Earle.

Lucky. What a word to use in association with these cursed few days when everything that was promising and wondrous in Patrick's world had ceased to be in one singular, gruesome moment. It was all a blur, and it seemed impossible to believe such a thing had truly transpired; that there could have been so horrifying an end to such a perfect day. So horrifying an end to such a perfect woman.

Patrick's head fell into his hands. *No, no, no. She can't be dead. She can't.* Like Frankie had said, 'I'll believe it when I see it'. She actually believed in Patrick's innocence too, despite finding

137

him in such incriminating circumstances. Blessedly all of the Merriweather family believed him, but that's where the blessings ended. The police looked set to lay charges against him by the end of the week if Ivy couldn't be found and even the son of Douglas Earle wouldn't be spared a trial, if so. Being found with the victim's blood on his hands and the last one to be seen alone with her was pretty damning. Even Patrick could see that.

He stood and walked over to the window to gaze out at the half moon gliding behind random torn clouds, as if it were fighting for the right to sail free upon the black canvas of night. As he watched it, Patrick wondered what his own chances of ever being free again were. Even if they found her body and proved it wasn't murder after all, he would still forever be a prisoner, the scars of losing his first love so suddenly and so cruelly, then being accused of causing her death, were chains that would forever bind. All else that had seemed important only a day and a half ago mattered nil: cricket tours and degrees. What foolish human folly. Mere games. The only thing that had truly mattered was his beautiful Ivy, the woman he loved, and now his heart was broken, all the life gone from him if it had gone from her.

If. It was the only word giving him any hope but it was fading with each passing hour. If she was alive they would surely know by now, but if not, then how had she died?

Imagining all the possibilities was sending him mad, as it was surely doing to her poor family. Did she take a swim then slip and a rogue wave take her, pulling her down? But no, all day yesterday they'd had men dive down and scour the water near where her clothes and the blood lay. She had simply disappeared. So what then? Perhaps a shark? There were plenty of bull sharks in these waterways but not usually in the shallower waters near Apple Tree Bay. Still, it was plausible, although he felt sick even considering it. Then there was the last possibility, perhaps the worst of all: that this tragedy was caused by man. The river was notorious for unsavoury characters, smugglers and thieves. Was she set upon by a band of murderers? Rapist thugs?

Patrick leant against the window frame in despair, hot tears falling as he cried in the pale moonlight. *Where are you, Ivy? Where are you, my love? Please come back to us. Please.*

But there was only the moon and those guarding clouds, with no end to them in sight. No way to break free.

Frankie hadn't bothered putting on her night rail. She hadn't bothered eating either, all routine seeming an insult to her missing sister somehow. As if she were allowing life to go on normally. As if it ever could again.

She sat out on the grass by the main pond in the middle of the night because that was something she'd never usually do either, which made Frankie feel better, illogically. It was a peaceful place to sit, yet there was no true peace to be found in Frankie's world right now. Only this hellish and distorted version of reality. And fear.

All was quiet at Kuranda, save the hum of insects, and the occasional hacking cough coming from her parents' room window. Frankie listened to it worriedly. Albert had reacted to the news of Ivy's disappearance with physical shock, his body racked with severe chills by the morning. It probably hadn't helped that he'd searched along the shores of the bay until the wee hours, calling her name until his poor throat could produce no more than a rasp.

Harriet had taken things very badly too, and Dossie had sat up with her to hold her hand and fetch her cups of tea or brandy with surprising docility, not even offering to fetch Dr Pratt for Albert. Just being there. Letting Harriet cry. And cry she had, in a terrible aching wail as she rocked back and forth, holding Ivy's now-bedraggled birthday hat in her arms, hugging it to her like it was the most precious thing on earth.

Aggie hadn't left her family's side, sleeping in the spare room that would have been hers if she hadn't married before they'd moved in, and Robert had fallen asleep on the lounge, after spending the previous night and all day with the police, doing whatever he could. But there was nothing to be done now except wait while the authorities searched and tried to find a single girl missing somewhere within the vast waterways and wilderness in and around Apple Tree Bay.

It didn't come naturally for Frankie to sit and let others take action so she'd joined the police in their search as well but they'd called it off when darkness fell, saying it was no use looking for her in the dark. There was some moonlight, Frankie had argued, but the sergeant had been firm in his decision.

'There's little point continuing on now. We'll come back at dawn.'

Little point? The point was that her sister be found, alive and well. Frankie couldn't bear to envisage her otherwise. For her voice never to be heard, her laughter never to ring, to never see her sketch out there with her father or don one of her marvellous hats was unthinkable. And to consider that the last words ever spoken between them were hurtful and anger-fuelled was too much of an aberration for sisters who loved each other. So very, very much.

All day as they searched, old memories had kept coming to her as she'd tried not to fear the worst. It was like her mind was conjuring evidence of Ivy alive to thwart the possibility of them finding her otherwise. Ivy running down the road at Christmas time when she was little, dressed in green and red from head to toe; Ivy being piggy-backed by their father up the hill, her bright curls bobbing about as she hugged him tight, ever his cherished baby. Ivy drawing her a birthday card last year that had Frankie holding a cricket bat with words 'nineteen not out'. Not out. She couldn't be 'out' herself on her eighteenth birthday. She *wasn't*, Frankie affirmed, as she stood and began to pace, despite her exhaustion.

But where was she? And what happened to her? No-one had any answers and every theory was a sickening one, but Frankie was certain that Patrick Earle had had nothing to do with it. He may well be bit pompous and, yes, perhaps even a snob, but there was no cruelty in the man that Frankie had ever witnessed, and the expression on his face when they'd seen him crouched with his fingers touching blood was one of true shock and horror. That they'd have to deal with him facing trial seemed an unnecessary nightmare upon the one they were already living through. In truth, Frankie didn't know how much they could all bear as each wretched repercussion of Ivy's disappearance unfolded.

Disappearance. Frankie clutched onto the word, a precious reminder that there was still hope. There was no answer to Ivy's whereabouts and therefore no tragedy had yet come to pass. Her investigative journalism skills kicked in then. Let others deal with this as they must but Frankie needed to face this the only way she knew how: facts first and head on.

Her pacing had turned into a determined march and she went back through the house to gather her things, deciding she needed to have another talk to Patrick, the last one to see Ivy, to try to ascertain any further possible clues. She doubted he was getting any sleep either.

Frankie hastily scribbled a note for her parents before grabbing a hat from the stand and swinging open the front door. She screamed at what she saw.

Sixteen

Aggie woke with a start, leaping from the bed. Frankie was shrieking. She tried not to panic as she grabbed her dressing gown and ran down the hall. Pretty Boy was screeching as Robert's hurried footsteps pounded and Aggie braced herself for whatever terrible scene she might find.

'What is it?' Harriet asked from her bedroom door, her expression terrified.

'I don't know,' Aggie threw over her shoulder, rushing down the stairs. Harriet followed, along with a coughing Albert. Aggie landed at the bottom as Robert rushed to stand in front of Frankie, shielding her from the rough-looking man on the doorstep.

'I'm sorry, miss, I'm s-so sorry,' the man was stuttering.

'What's going on here?' Robert demanded. Aggie drew closer and put her arm around her sister.

The bushy-faced man gaped at them all, twisting his hat nervously.

'Who is this—' Albert said as he arrived with Harriet but he was interrupted by a terrible sneeze.

'Bless you,' Aggie muttered automatically, still staring at the man. Dishevelled and smelling strongly of fish, he looked around at them all, obviously overwhelmed.

'I was just about to knock when she … she opened … I'm sorry, miss,' he said again. 'Didn't mean to give you a fright.'

'Who are you and what are you doing here in the middle of the night?' Robert said. The man looked rather afraid now.

'I don't mean no harm … I'm Barney Johns. I work over at the orchards. At Galston.'

'I've heard the name,' Aggie confirmed, remembering. 'You're Emma Higgins's brother, aren't you? You work with Joe Collins.'

'Yes,' Barney said, glancing at her, seeming relieved. 'At Fagans' farm.'

The family looked at him expectantly but he didn't say more so Robert prompted him again.

'So what are you doing here then? It's a bit of a way from the orchards.'

'Oh,' Barney said, patting his pockets before drawing out some letters. 'I've got some messages for you. I was supposed to deliver the first one yesterday but I forgot.'

He held out the notes and Albert took them. His hands visibly shook as they all watched on with breath held. *Please God, let it be news of Ivy,* Aggie prayed silently. *Good news,* she added quickly.

Albert opened the first and read aloud. '*Dear Mr Merriweather, please be advised that I have your daughter Ivy safely in my care …*'

'Oh dear Lord,' Harriet said, collapsing against him. Frankie let out a sob and Aggie closed her eyes, almost fainting with relief. '*She …*'

But Albert couldn't read on as his expression crumpled and he began to weep too, which set off more coughing. Robert took it from him and continued as both her parents sank to the bench near the door.

She was found unconscious and with a wound to her temple near Apple Tree Bay. As she was alone I feared for her safety and wellbeing so I took her aboard my boat and brought her to my sister Fiona Ryan for nursing care. We live not far from Wisemans Ferry. I apologise for your concern at her disappearance but I acted as the urgency of the situation required and could not get word to you sooner. She is much recovered and I will bring her back to you tomorrow. Please meet me at the wharf at Bobbin Head at approximately one in the afternoon.

Sincerely,

Riley Logan.

'Thank God,' Aggie said, hugging Frankie close before moving over to her weeping parents. 'It's all right, she's found. There now,' she crooned, crouching before them as they clutched at her hands.

'He … he's got her, she's safe …?' Harriet said tearfully, her hands trembling in Aggie's own as she sought confirmation that they'd all heard right.

'Yes, Mum, she's just fine,' she soothed, but then confusion set in, despite her elation. Frankie asked the question forming in Aggie's mind.

'Why didn't he meet us today then?' Frankie said, and all eyes swung back Barney's way. 'We were all down that way, searching.'

'It was the storm,' Robert guessed. 'Were they delayed?'

Barney twisted his hat and nodded awkwardly at the second note still in Robert's hand. 'Yes, but she … er … she's …'

Frankie grabbed the other note from Robert in a rush and read it aloud. '*Dear Mr Merriweather, Please be advised that Barney Johns, the man delivering these notes to you, forgot to deliver the first yesterday.*'

She shook her head in disbelief but continued. '*As you now know, my sister and I have Ivy in our care. Unfortunately we struck a storm on our return and more unfortunately Ivy has taken ill with a fever.*'

'Oh, no,' Harriet moaned, clutching at her heart, and Aggie felt her fear rise for her little sister once more.

We are tending her around the clock but advise you come to us rather than we come to you now as she is too sick to travel. Otherwise I can return her when she is well. Barney can give you directions to where we are or you can send word via him.
Sincerely,
Riley Logan.

'I'll go to her,' Frankie said, eyes flicking straight to her parents.

'No, no, it should be me ...' Albert began but his coughing stopped him once more.

'Dad, you're too sick,' Aggie told him gently. 'Let Frankie and Robert and I go. Mum can stay and look after you.'

Harriet nodded, relief and concern etched on her face. 'Yes, yes, you don't want to make each other worse. If she gets your cold and you get her fever ...'

'We can go to her,' Robert told her parents. Aggie looked over at him gratefully. 'But I do think someone should send word to Patrick before we do anything,' he added, 'and we'd better tell the police while we're at it.'

'Yes, do that for me, will you, Robert?' Albert wheezed. 'And Frankie and Aggie, perhaps you two could ... get word ... to Patrick.'

'Um, excuse me,' Barney began, shuffling on the doorstep and glancing over at his tethered horse. Aggie realised she'd quite forgotten he was there. 'If you don't mind, I have to set off for work so if you don't need me no more ...'

'Of course we need you. How else will we know where to find her?' Frankie said, frowning.

'Oh, right.'

Aggie was beginning to see why the first note had been forgotten. The man was obviously a bit dim-witted but he knew where Ivy was so she forced herself to remain patient.

'What's the quickest possible way to get to there?' Aggie asked, her tone gentle compared to Frankie's.

'Well, with the tides bein' so low there ain't much point setting off before dawn, less dangerous in the daylight too. If you leave then you'd get there round eight or so, I'd say.'

'That's good to know but, again, what *way* can we get there?' Aggie asked. 'Are there ferries running?' She'd never thought to ask how people travelled all the way upriver before.

'What way?' Barney said, appearing confused. 'Well, by boat, miss.'

Robert sent her a look and Aggie tried not roll her eyes.

'Yes, but whose bloody boat can we use?' Frankie said, obviously tiring of Aggie's patient approach.

Barney's jaw dropped at Frankie's swearing but he recovered himself. 'Don't know anyone who'd give you their boat,' he began slowly, but then an idea seemed to occur to him. 'But I could take you, if you like,' he offered. 'I've room enough for one or two, anyway.'

'That would be much appreciated,' Aggie said, standing up and nodding her thanks.

'Right then,' Frankie said brusquely. 'I'll get packing after we return from Patrick's. We'll meet you down there, shall we? At the pier?'

Barney looked like he couldn't have argued if he tried, simply nodding now as Frankie marched out the door. 'Oh,' she said, turning back. 'You'd better take this,' she said, giving Robert the second letter she was still holding. 'The police will want proof. You coming, Aggie?'

'Not in my night things. Give me a minute, all right?'

Frankie looked at Aggie's dressing gown in surprise. 'Well …
I suppose we can't set off for another few hours anyway.'

'Yes, just slow down a minute or two, Frankie,' Albert said,
sneezing once more before continuing with difficulty. 'There's
other things … to consider, like whether or not Dr Pratt can go.'

'That old shonk …' Frankie began, but Aggie left her family
to argue that one out while she dashed upstairs to get dressed.
Robert called his goodbyes, rushing off to tell the authorities the
wondrous news that Ivy had been found alive. Sick or no, Aggie
vowed to get her well and safely home with or without the help
of a second-rate doctor. Ivy was her baby sister, a relationship that
had never seemed more precious than these last few days. Just let
some fever try to take her away from Aggie now.

Seventeen

He was trembling as he waited, the muffled drone of voices carrying from downstairs. That it was Frankie and Aggie talking to his parents and the policeman who kept watch over him was clear. What the conversation was about was not. Patrick thought he might be sick, so coiled was his gut, so frantic the race of his heart. Whether it bode ill or well that Ivy's sisters were delivering news to the household in person, and in the middle of the night, his fear-stricken mind couldn't ascertain. All he knew as the sound of footsteps approached was that his entire future depended on the next words he would hear. A life in prison, a life in mourning, perhaps no life at all.

The doorknob turned and Patrick raised his eyes.

His gaze swung from Frankie to Aggie as they stood in front of him. Then Frankie did the very last thing Patrick would have expected: she smiled.

'Ivy's alive.'

Patrick's knees gave way as he slumped onto his chair and stared at her in disbelief. Then he looked to Aggie, silently pleading those words be uttered again.

'She is, Patrick, she's alive,' she said, smiling through her tears.

'She's …?' But the shock was too great for any words and he found himself weeping into his hands, not for sorrow, fear or despair, but for the sweetest of emotions, relief. He never thought anything could surpass his love for Ivy but this feeling eclipsed it as Patrick registered the enormity of such a wondrous truth. She lived.

Aggie placed a hand on his shoulder and he clutched at it gratefully, looking up at Frankie. His parents had entered the room behind her.

'The guard has gone home. You're a free man, son,' his father said, his voice shaking.

'Ridiculous business, having him here,' his mother Sybil muttered, but Patrick ignored her to look back at Frankie.

'Where is she? Can I see her?'

'Not quite that simple, I'm afraid,' Frankie told him. 'She's alive but she's not well. She was found unconscious and picked up by a passing boatman who thought she was alone so he took her home to his sister upriver and now … well, she has a fever, I'm afraid.'

'A fever …?' Patrick repeated as his common sense slowly returned. 'I … I have to go to her …'

He stood, looking about him in confusion.

'There's no need for you to do that. Her family are already going to her aid, Patrick,' Sybil said, disapproval creeping in to her tone.

'Aggie and I are going,' Frankie told him, 'and Robert and perhaps Dr Pratt. We'll need extra transport, though, as the boat can only fit two of us so …'

'I'm going,' Patrick said firmly. 'She … she was under my care when this happened to her. My responsibility. I have to see her for myself. I have to go.'

'Patrick, I really think—' his mother began again.

'Son, this simply isn't necessary,' Douglas interrupted with finality. 'Let the Merriweathers deal with this situation as a family. You can see her when she returns, soon enough.'

His mother merely raised her eyebrows as if to suggest Patrick should have nothing to do with Ivy at all after this and it made his next decision a swift and clear one.

'I am going to Ivy Merriweather and I'm going to sit by her side until she is completely recovered,' her said, looking from Sybil to Douglas. 'You can't stop me. I'm a grown man.'

It was the first time he'd ever stood up to his father and Patrick lifted his chin, defiant and expecting a fight, but Douglas didn't respond. He merely levelled a thoughtful glance at his son then nodded, a flicker of admiration there.

'You can't possibly let him go,' Sybil spluttered, but Douglas merely raised his hand, denoting an end to any further discussion.

'You heard the man, Sybil,' he said.

'Well, come if you must but we're going to need another boat,' Frankie said in her outspoken way, drawing Patrick's focus back to Ivy.

'We'll figure something out. Just give me a moment to get my things.'

They left, Sybil still voicing objections all the way down the hall.

'But how long will he be gone for? What about his studies? His, oh dear Lord, his *cricket tour*! What if he misses it? They can't possibly go without him.'

Such issues as potentially deferring study and missing out on sport, even procuring an extra vessel in the middle of the night, seemed ridiculously minor details now that Ivy had been found alive. Patrick briefly wondered if he'd ever worry about life's smaller challenges again.

He packed hurriedly, only pausing to look out at the moon through his window one last time before he left. It shone brilliantly in the sky now, all traces of cloud cover gone, and Patrick turned and left the bedroom that had been a cell this past day and night to journey to Ivy and help her fight this fever. To bring her home, healthy and safe at last, and to reclaim his freedom, while she reclaimed her life.

Eighteen

'Of all the bloody buggery things,' Frankie spluttered. Barney's expression was scandalised as he did his best to move the coils of ropes she'd managed to get her feet tangled up in. How Patrick had ended paired up with her while Aggie and Robert would follow with the doctor in a hired vessel later in the day was something he was still trying to figure out, but getting to Ivy as soon as possible suited him fine. Frankie's company, however, could prove another matter.

She was fired up with determination and concern over her sister, and the combination was resulting in a string of calamities that were distracting and annoying but, Patrick had to admit, unexpectedly amusing too. That she had him smiling a few times was rather miraculous considering all he'd been through and the lack of sleep he'd endured, not to mention the worry about Ivy's fever that hung over them both.

Still, when she'd tried to pat a pelican as they waited for Barney to bring the boat around and ended up being defecated on by the less-than-impressed bird, it was all he could do not to burst out laughing at her horrified expression.

'Eww, it smells like rotten fish,' she'd complained, swatting at the stains ineffectually. It did too, which rendered the situation even funnier. Watching her entangled as she was after tripping over a bait bucket was pretty comical too, especially witnessing poor Barney trying to assist.

'You all right there?' Patrick enquired and she shoved a strand of blonde hair out of her face as she fumed.

'Stupid, rotten, flipping …' Barney managed to free her then, ending further colourful phrases, and he was able to get the steam up so they could set off.

The morning was already warm, despite the early hour, and the water looked pristine and calm as Barney's boat cut a clear arrow on the glassy surface, breaking the mirrored reflection of sky and shore.

Patrick's amusement faded as they glided along through the otherwise still, empty place, soon passing Apple Tree Bay. It felt strange being here again, at the scene of the crime, or so that very spot had been supposed until the early hours of this morning. The residual fear over Ivy's disappearance still seemed to cling to the sandstone and gum-strewn shoreline, even though the mystery was now solved. Patrick had to remind himself over and again that she was alive and he was on his way to see that miracle for himself. The boat's chug was a steady reassurance of that fact as it echoed down the bay's tunnelled walls.

It was a blessing that Riley Logan had picked her up but questions had begun to form and he asked one of Barney as they made their way out towards the greater waters of Broken Bay.

'Two hours upriver seems a long way to take an injured girl. Why didn't Mr Logan look for her family and friends instead?'

Barney kicked more ropes out of the way.

'Not sure. Guess he figured she was alone,' he said finally. 'Best lose that mister business by the way. We're not too formal up home.'

'Why on earth would he think she was alone?' Frankie said, still flicking bits of pelican faeces off her skirt with disgust.

Barney shrugged and appeared confused. 'Because she was …?'

'Yes, but young ladies don't tend to go off on picnics by themselves,' Patrick pointed out. 'Surely that would have occurred to him.'

'I s'pose he didn't know what she was doing down here. Not a good idea to leave her on her lonesome, but. There's some rough blokes shipping back and forth along these parts you wouldn't've wanted her to have run into, that's for sure.'

'Anyone you know?' Patrick asked, wondering what kind of people they would encounter on this foray.

Barney nodded as he scanned the water ahead. 'Yeah I know 'em all right.'

'Who are they?' Patrick wanted to learn everything he could about people he may have to deal with in their quest to get Ivy home safe and well.

'Donovan's the worst,' Barney told them. 'Mean right to the bone, that one. Wouldn't trust him as far as I could throw him, and that's a fact.'

'What does he do?' Patrick asked.

Barney took out a cigarette pouch, not looking his way. 'Best lose questions like that up there too.'

Patrick considered that. The world Ivy had landed herself in seemed less appealing with each passing mile.

'What's Mr Logan, I mean Riley, like?' Frankie asked, and Patrick noted she was listening very closely too.

'Riley? Oh, he's a real good bloke,' Barney said as he rolled his cigarette.

Frankie prompted him. 'How so?'

'Always doin' stuff for people, y'know. Helping them out. Don't know how he makes much money half the time, he gives so much away.'

'Gives what away?' Patrick asked.

'Food, tobacco, medicine … household stuff. He, er … runs deliveries up and down the river.'

Patrick glanced over at Frankie and she raised her eyebrows. Riley did indeed sound like 'a real good bloke' but perhaps not an entirely law-abiding one. Patrick had heard smuggling was rife in these parts. Just what kind of people had been caring for Ivy these past two days?

Barney went to sit on a crate at the back of the boat to smoke his cigarette then and Frankie lowered her voice so it was muffled by the sound of the engine.

'Sounds a bit dodgy to me.'

Patrick nodded. 'I think there'll be a lot of dodginess where we're going.'

She looked thoughtful and neither spoke for a good while, each just watching the thickly forested shoreline until Frankie eventually closed her eyes. Patrick was tired too, of course, but the thought of Ivy tossing with fever and with a gash on her head kept him awake. Getting to her side couldn't come quickly enough but there was no faster way than by boat with no roads that far up, and nothing more to do than study the scattered houses and shacks that began to appear as the boat made its way along.

He'd never been upriver before and Patrick found himself viewing it all with unexpected interest, wondering how many people actually lived here as he glimpsed homes in quiet coves and among thick stands of trees. They were reaching a wide junction and Patrick looked down the waterway to the left to where more dwellings were visible.

'Berowra,' Barney told him, back at the wheel now. 'Place of many winds, a native bloke once told me. That's one of their words.' He seemed a bit proud of himself for knowing such a fact but then he ruined it by adding, 'Sounds like a place of many farts, don't it?'

Patrick had to chuckle a bit and Frankie smiled, not fast asleep after all. She opened her eyes and watched too as the boat moved past Berowra.

There wasn't much to it, just a few ramshackle huts, although there were several boats moored at a larger house that jutted over the water further down. Children ran along the shore and waved so they waved back.

'The Windybank kids,' Barney told them. 'Family lived in a cave before Ed Windybank built that house and started making boats. Does it all by himself too,' Barney said, gesturing towards the vessels as they bobbed gently along the wharf. 'Maybe you should get y'self one. Live a little of the ol' river life.'

Patrick doubted he'd ever want to do that. The Windybank house wasn't too much of an eyesore but the rest of the small settlement seemed a poverty-stricken, depressing place. He couldn't see much attraction in coming up this way to observe more of the same.

'Not many people seem to be taking on this river life of yours,' he commented as they drew away, the children waving once more.

Barney simply shrugged. 'You'd be surprised. They're building a road down here from the railroad right now – straight over that mountain. Should open things up a bit, I'd say, mind you they've got their work cut out for 'em.'

Patrick could see why, looking up at the steep mountainside that Barney had indicated. It seemed an impenetrable wall of forest, a formidable fortress holding civilisation at bay. He pitied the men trying to force a way through such thick foliage and heavy rock under the hot summer sun.

Barney went over to add more coal to the furnace and Patrick noticed Frankie studying the river and its shores, her expression a thoughtful one.

'And what do you make of it?' he asked her, expecting a raised eyebrow, but she surprised him.

'It's beautiful,' she said and he followed her gaze, wondering what she found so entrancing. The sun had hit the waterway up ahead and it was rather picturesque, he supposed; light blue at the river's centre, a deeper green in the shadows where the edge found the towering bushland's reflection.

'I guess it is,' he replied.

'Imagine living in a cave, though,' she went on, looking up at the many sandstone rocks that interspersed the trees in brilliant shades of gold in the morning sunlight. 'However would you manage with all those children?'

'They've a decent enough home now,' Patrick reminded her.

'Plenty of folk camp out in caves,' Barney said, overhearing as he stoked the fire. 'I've got one meself upriver. Good for storage and the like, although the snakes tend to get in.'

They passed another shack now, then another, each sorely dilapidated. A woman stood in front of one, several small children at her skirts. The youngsters waved but the woman merely watched them, her expression wary even from there.

'Who is she?' Frankie asked Barney.

'Dave's missus. He's one of the timber cutters,' he replied, glancing up.

The shack barely looked held together for something lived in by a man who dealt with timber all day but Patrick didn't comment. Frankie looked set to do that for him.

'Doesn't look like he spends a lot of time working on his home. How on earth do they fit all those children inside?'

Barney squinted over as the sun hit the water in front. 'They get by,' he said.

Frankie studied the woman and raised her hand but she still didn't respond. 'She looks unhappy.'

Patrick looked over at her too. Frankie was right. She did.

'She's got a roof over their heads and they get fed,' Barney responded. 'That's more than some folk.'

The woman turned away and walked inside, and Patrick noticed that she was lame, limping heavily.

'What's wrong with her leg?' Frankie said, looking worried.

'Dunno,' Barney said but he didn't meet Frankie's eye. She wasn't letting it go, despite that.

'Does he … does her husband beat her?'

Barney took out his tobacco pouch. 'Could do,' he said, leaning back to roll his cigarette, still avoiding her gaze.

'But that's disgusting! The poor woman has been crippled,' Frankie exclaimed, turning around to stare back at the place. 'Why haven't the police intervened?'

'No law against it, is there?' Barney muttered.

'There must be … I mean surely …?' Frankie looked over to Patrick.

'Well, no, there isn't,' he admitted. 'Although if a woman is severely beaten she can take her husband to court, I suppose, but there wouldn't be much point.'

'Not much point?' Frankie blustered and Barney moved to the back of the boat again, obviously uncomfortable. Patrick didn't imagine he dealt with many feminists in his life.

'Only that they wouldn't be likely to win. A woman officially becomes a man's property when she marries. I would have thought you'd know that, being so involved with women's rights and so on,' he added.

Frankie stared at him. 'Yes, but to actually maim a person!' she said, outraged. 'Don't tell me they have no protection whatsoever?'

'Well, there is the rule of thumb …'

'Isn't … isn't that just a general expression?'

'Yes, but it's, er, also been used in law courts. Some judges have ruled that a man has a right to beat his wife, but only with an implement no wider than his thumb.'

'*What?*' she exclaimed and Patrick sorely wished he hadn't brought it up. 'How can that possibly be legal?

'She signs a contract when she marries …' he said, the reasoning sounding lame to his own ears.

'Contracts and *property*.' She practically spat the word. 'We're not bloody houses, for goodness' sake.'

Patrick shifted on the crate he sat on, wishing he could go and hide with Barney. 'Laws have been changing since the turn of the century. It's a new country now, remember? I'm sure it's only a matter of time until women are treated more fairly.'

'Not while men control the laws – this is exactly why we need the vote, to protect each other. No man is going to rally for women not to be controlled by their husbands. It suits you all to have us downtrodden and enslaved, forced to … to do your bidding in the marital bed and be beaten whenever you feel like it.'

Patrick was more than uncomfortable now and one glance at a squirming Barney was enough for him to try to end this conversation. 'I really don't think we should be discussing such things …'

'What, the marital bed?' Frankie said, chin high now. 'I may not have realised how little the law protects women from being savagely beaten by their husbands but I am very aware a man can … can rape his wife whenever he feels like it. It's horrendous!'

There was challenge in the air but Patrick could only agree. 'Yes, it is,' he said, unable to add anything to the raw truth of that fact.

Frankie fell silent for a moment then fumed again. 'You're studying all this and yet do you have any intention of doing anything about these injustices once you practice? I know I damn well would if they'd let me have a proper say.'

'I hadn't really ever thought about it,' Patrick admitted, holding up his hand before she pounced on that comment. 'Not that I condone it in any way. I just hadn't.'

'Why would you, when you've never had to live with such threats in your life?' she said, glaring at him.

'Neither have you,' he dared to point out.

Frankie's eyes fairly blazed as she responded. 'No. And I never will.'

'Never going to marry or never going to marry a man who would treat you that way?'

'I'm never going to marry,' Frankie said firmly. 'No man will ever have control over my body, let alone my heart. I'm dedicating myself to the plight of womankind. For all the "Dave's missus" types out there – women who haven't got a voice. Well, I've got one and it's going to roar for the rest of my days until something is done.' She said it with so much fire and passion Patrick well believed her.

'Good on you,' he felt moved to say. She may be far too feisty for his liking but he couldn't help but admire her. Maybe he had been too ambivalent about women's rights up until that point. It did seem pretty horrific when he saw a victim of abuse firsthand.

'I reckon women should have the vote,' Barney piped up, back at the wheel once more.

'Why is that?' Patrick asked him and Barney shrugged.

'They worry more about people getting fed, my mum always did anyway. Don't reckon no-one would go starving if women ran the place.'

'You want women to get the vote because of food?' Frankie clarified and Patrick couldn't help but smile.

'Yep. Reckon that's what's missing in Australia: it needs a mum.'

Frankie smiled too as Barney's simple logic shone through. 'I think that would make a very fine placard,' she told him and Barney grinned through his whiskers.

'Well, I dunno what that is but I'm glad you're smiling and not so upset no more.'

Patrick looked over at her, thinking she looked far prettier when she did. Then Ivy's smile came to mind and his eyes were drawn to the river ahead where she lay, sick and injured amid this rough river world. Let Frankie help womankind but for now there was only one woman who held Patrick's focus. He just hoped she hadn't been too traumatised by what she'd seen and experienced up there. And that it hadn't adversely affected any views she might have on the subject of marriage.

Nineteen

Riley woke with a start as Ivy groaned and he sat up in the cabin chair to check on her. The fever still hadn't broken but she was asleep, which was one positive thing, at least. His mother always said nothing heals better than a good night's sleep. He stood and stretched, glancing at the clock and noting it was past seven-thirty. The family should be well up by now but when he headed up on deck he found Fiona still asleep too. The twins were awake, fetching eggs from the coop, but George was nowhere to be seen. Probably in bed, Riley supposed, sleeping things off.

It was clear and calm and a lone eagle circled above the river, looking for breakfast, which made Riley think of it himself. He wondered if he could get Ivy to eat anything when she awoke.

'Morning,' Fiona said and he turned to see her, sitting up with difficulty.

'How did you sleep?' Riley asked her, helping her by offering his arm. She leant on it, managing to rise.

'Ugh, can't say it was comfortable but I'm better for the rest,' she said, holding her back. 'How's our patient?'

'Still feverish,' Riley said, rubbing his hand over his face worriedly.

'You need a shave,' Fiona observed, 'and a good feed, I'd say. I'll go over and fetch something for you.'

'I meant to tell you I've got a crate of tinned beans. Hold on and I'll grab you a few cans. Might make a nice change for the twins.'

'Hmm, good luck getting them to eat anything but eggs. They'd live on them if I let them,' she said, her voice carrying as he went down to fetch them.

'Tell them beans are tiny eggs,' he suggested, returning with a few tins.

'You'd be very hungry waiting for your breakfast if I did – that would invite about a hundred questions, I'd say,' she said, grunting as he helped her climb out of the boat. 'Back soon.'

Riley watched her wade away, making sure she was all right, before managing a quick shave in the morning sun. Then he heard Ivy's voice.

'Riley.'

At least it was his name she called this time. He went straight below deck.

'Here I am,' he said. 'How are you feeling?' He placed his palm to her forehead. She was still warm, although he thought she seemed a little cooler. Hoped, anyway. Her blue eyes were wide open and she looked at him, confusion there.

'What time is it?'

'Past seven-thirty in the morning,' he said. 'You've been feverish all night but I think you seem a bit better.'

'Where's Fiona?' she asked and he couldn't help but push back a red curl that had fallen over the bandage onto her forehead.

'Making you some breakfast.'

'That's nice of her,' she said, 'but I don't think … I can eat.'

'You need to keep your strength up. We can't have you all skin and bones when your family see you.'

'When will that be?' she asked, resting her hand on his arm. 'Am I going home today?'

He closed his fingers over hers gently. 'I think you're a bit too unwell to make the trip just yet. Let's get this fever broken first then you can go home.'

Ivy looked at him, disappointment in her expression but trust too. 'All right.'

'Anyway, they may come to visit before that,' he added, guilty that some selfish part of him wanted to keep her all to himself.

She looked hopeful and nodded at him, a small grateful smile there, and he had a sudden strong urge to gather her up in his arms and hold her. But of course he couldn't do something so intimate to a girl in his care, especially as weak as she was. Besides, she was still so hot it was probably the last thing in the world she needed. He settled for letting her fingers go and soaking a fresh towel instead to stroke her lovely face. She smiled.

'Thank you,' she muttered. 'You really are the kindest man.'

Riley's heart swelled at her words. 'You're welcome,' he said, tenderly continuing.

Her hand brushed a book he'd left lying on the bed and she glanced down at it.

'What's that?'

Riley picked it up, showing it to her self-consciously. 'It's, er, Hans Christian Andersen. The twins have been asking me to read them more fairy tales, they love the Brothers Grimm, especially "Sleeping Beauty" for some reason. Anyway, I have to read them myself first because they can be a bit gruesome. Fell asleep reading this one last night.'

Ivy looked at the tome with interest. 'I always loved fairy tales too, especially illustrated ones. Have you found any suitable?'

'"The Little Mermaid" is a good one. I read it to them last week and they loved it, as you can probably tell from their disappointment that I hadn't brought a real one home,' he said and she smiled at him again, holding his gaze. 'I can understand their mistake, I suppose,' he added softly, tracing her long red curls with his eyes. 'Thinking you were a sea princess.'

An indiscernible expression crossed her face then but the sound of a footstep switched his attention. It was Fiona and the girls bringing breakfast.

'Quietly now,' Fiona instructed as they brought in plates of beans on damper but her eyes were on Riley, far too much knowing in her stare.

'Beans all done?' Riley said, ignoring the look and standing instead.

'Yes, let's make the tea, shall we? How are you faring this morning, Ivy?' she asked, bustling about now, and Riley took his breakfast on deck to give her more room. The twins went with him and jumped around, investigating everything as they always did.

'Did you eat the beans too?' Riley asked them.

'Nuh, we had eggs. Pink ones,' Annie told him.

'I thought I told you those colouring bottles I gave you were meant for cake icing.'

'Ain't got no cake,' Tricia said. 'Can we go fishing today, Uncle Riley?' she asked, peering into the bait bucket hopefully.

'Nuh, he's gotta look after Ivy, don't you? She's gone and got sick from the scales on her head.'

'Yes, not today,' Riley said, eating his breakfast. 'We may get some visitors though.'

That made the twins very excited and they fired him with questions, leaning their little hands on his knees and bobbing about.

'Who's coming? Do they like playing games?'

'Will they bring us lollies?'

'I hope they bring me a puppy.'

That last comment from Tricia made Riley chuckle. 'Now why would they bring a puppy?'

'I would if I was visiting somebody. When I grow up I'm going to give everyone puppies everywhere I go,' she declared, twirling about.

'Who's coming?' Annie demanded again.

'I'm not sure,' Riley told her. 'I just think some of Ivy's family may come to see her and check if she's feeling better.'

'Ohh,' they both said.

'Are they boys or girls?' Tricia asked.

'She has sisters and parents,' Riley replied, wondering again about the name Patrick. 'I'm not sure who else might come.'

'We could make them a cake,' Annie said, latching on to his previous comment, hope lighting up her face. 'If we had some sugar ...'

'Why don't you ask your mother if I'm allowed to give you some?' he said, remembering he had some packed away downstairs.

'Mum!' they immediately cried out.

'Shh, quietly now. If she says yes it's in the green barrel near the wood crates at the back. Use a cup,' he advised.

The girls went below deck and Riley finished his breakfast in momentary peace before they dashed back up and over the side of the boat to get cooking. There was a table outside the shack that they used rather than disturb their sleeping father and Riley watched them get organised with amusement. So capable, those two, just like Fiona. He wondered if the next baby would be a girl too, hoping that, whatever gender it was, it was nothing like George.

The shadows from last night threatened to return but he decided not to dwell on his brother-in-law this morning. He tried not to think too much about Ivy either but found it impossible. He could hear her voice as she made the occasional comment to Fiona and the trust in her eyes wouldn't leave his mind. Perhaps just another check on her, he decided as he stood, but the sound of an approaching vessel halted him in his tracks.

It was Barney. Riley recognised his boat at once, although he couldn't make out who was on board. Whoever had come for Ivy, he just hoped they would understand his actions and not judge him too harshly for having brought her here to be nursed in such rudimentary accommodation.

It made him nervous to think who may arrive and what that meant for his role in Ivy Merriweather's life, a short part but with devastating impact all the same. Perhaps any further involvement with her would end, should they decide to take her straight home. Riley wasn't ready for that, especially if the man called Patrick was the one who took her. She'd been in Riley's life less than two days but somehow, somewhere along the line, Ivy had got under his skin. He felt almost desperate to halt their approach, his entire being rigid with resistance, yet he could only grip the side of the boat and watch as the people who would ultimately take her from him drew ever closer.

Riley could make them out now: a man and a woman with Barney at the wheel. The woman held her hat and her hair was blonde in the sun. One of her two sisters, he guessed. The man looked fairly young and wore expensive-looking clothes. This was no river man. And Ivy had no brothers.

'They're here!' the girls cried, running down to the shore to wave, and Fiona came up on deck to watch too, sending Riley a thoughtful glance but no comment.

The boat came alongside and Barney called out a greeting before helping the two arrivals onto Riley's boat.

'One sister and one friend,' Barney told Riley and Fiona. 'Delivered safe and sound. Right you are then, I'll see you all later on.' He chugged off, leaving them to introduce themselves.

'Riley Logan,' Riley said, 'and this is my sister Fiona.'

'Patrick Earle,' the man told Riley, shaking his hand, and Riley's heart sank a bit further.

'Frances Merriweather,' the woman said with a nod, 'but please call me Frankie.' She was taller than Ivy, and rather gorgeous too, but Riley would never have picked them for sisters.

'Nice to meet you,' Fiona said. 'I expect you want to see your sister as soon as possible.'

'Yes, should we wade or …?' Frankie said, looking over to the house.

'Well, no, we have her here on board,' Fiona said, looking to Riley to explain.

'We didn't want to move her about,' he improvised. 'She's just down here.' He gestured towards the steps and the woman went first, closely followed by the man. Riley went to follow but Fiona halted him.

'I think we best let them have their privacy,' she murmured, looking at him meaningfully, and he nodded, knowing she was right but hating the fact.

So Riley simply waited, staring at the river, his closest companion, trying not to hear the depths of emotion erupting below deck as Ivy's world arrived on his smugglers' boat in the broad light of day. Already stealing her away.

'*Ivy.*'

Frankie was there, like a sudden apparition but also very much flesh and blood as she launched herself upon Ivy to hug her. She could barely breathe, but Ivy didn't care. Frankie began to cry and Ivy did too, so overcome with the joy of seeing her she couldn't speak.

'I was so afraid,' Frankie wept and Ivy clutched at her.

'I'm sorry ...' Ivy choked out but Frankie shook her head against her.

'No, no, none of that,' she said, her voice muffled by tears. 'Oh, we were all so scared, Ivy. Everyone thought the worst but I wouldn't ... I couldn't ...'

'I was supposed to go home yesterday ... but now ...'

'Are you all right?' Frankie said, drawing back to look at her properly and feeling her forehead. 'Damn, you're very hot. How's the injury? Show me your head,' she added, trying to peer under the bandage.

'I'm fine,' Ivy reassured her, smiling through her tears. 'Just a bit sick, is all.'

'Oh, buggery and tarnation, what am I doing, lying all over you,' Frankie said, drawing away now.

'I don't care,' Ivy said, lifting one hand to clasp Frankie's.

'I just ... oh Ivy, I love you so much,' Frankie said, pushing back her escaping blonde hair and holding Ivy's hand tight. 'We all do.'

'I love you too,' Ivy told her, tears gathering anew, 'and I never, ever want to fight with you again. *Never again, Frankie.* I mean it,' she emphasised, even though the energy of speaking was costing her.

'A little healthy debate is good for the soul,' Frankie told her, smiling fondly. 'But no angry words, I agree. Never again.'

'Imagine if they'd been our last?' Ivy whispered brokenly.

'Yet they weren't. No more talk of it now. You need your strength.'

Ivy did feel exhausted but then she noticed someone else in the shadowed corner of the cabin and she gasped.

'Patrick.'

He came forwards, the light from the open hatch hitting his handsome features, yet he was drawn and pale, the worry and suffering he'd endured apparent.

'I'm so, so sorry,' she began all over again.

'No apologies.' he said, shaking his head, and kneeling close as Frankie moved aside. 'Frankie's right.'

'I went for a swim. I don't know why I did it, it was so foolish,' Ivy told him, crying once more.

'It was hot,' Patrick said, swiping at tears of his own. 'People swim when it's hot. It's not your fault this happened, all right? Just so long as you're safe and you get well now.'

'What you must have been through …' Ivy hadn't really considered what the repercussions might have been for him, aside from the worry, but his haunted expression hinted at far more. 'You were the last one who saw me.'

'Yes, but now I'm seeing you again and it's a sight I'm never going to tire of,' he told her, taking her hand and kissing her fingers.

She smiled at such sweet, beautiful words but she knew he was hiding the truth of what he'd endured.

'Did they … blame you?' she asked him, frowning as she considered that.

'They were just trying to work things out. No harm done,' he reassured her. 'All that matters is that you're alive and we're here, talking to you, seeing you …' He paused as the words caught in his throat and Ivy saw the true cost. He really had feared that she was dead and, what was worse, the police must have considered him responsible.

'They … they thought you …'

'It doesn't matter now,' he said, his voice hoarse as he stroked her cheek. 'Let's just get you well and get you home.'

'The doctor's on his way,' Frankie said from behind him, 'with Aggie and Robert. Until then we're here to care for you and give these people a break. I wonder if we can get you off this boat though? It's a bit cramped.'

'It's fine, truly,' Ivy muttered. Moving seemed a great effort as all the emotion began to take its toll and her head began to ache.

'I guess we'll have to see what the doctor has to say,' Frankie said, watching her thoughtfully. 'Pratt that he is.'

Ivy smiled but she was fading now. To have them both here all of a sudden was a shock and as much as she felt loved and cared for, she also felt overwhelmed. And weak. Weaker than she'd ever felt in her life.

She closed her eyes and Frankie murmured to Patrick, 'I think she needs to rest. What if I take first watch and get her cooled down a bit while you go up on deck?'

'Of course,' she heard him say but he sounded reluctant, which was touching. She didn't ponder on it too much though because Frankie was stroking a cool cloth on her forehead and the sensation consumed Ivy's senses. Her loved ones had come to heal her and get her home and Ivy needed to focus on helping them achieve that end. Any deeper reflections about the heart would just have to wait.

Twenty

Ivy slept but Aggie hadn't stood still since she'd arrived with Dr Pratt a few hours ago, pacing then nursing her in turn. Her initial fear at finding her sister worse than she expected clung, even though the doctor had said that the fever should soon break. She hung onto that hope like a lifeline. These hours of intense worry had made both above and below deck purgatory on Riley Logan's boat and Aggie didn't know which was worse: seeing the others pace and suffer too or watching Ivy. Probably that, she decided, as her sister moaned and tossed and turned, wet strands of red hair sticking to her pink skin. She was barely even aware that Aggie had come.

It was only early afternoon but it seemed like an eternity that she'd been caged in here, restless and powerless to do more. Perhaps it would be better to sit. She did so, watching the rise and fall of her sister's chest worriedly, praying it would continue to do so. That life would remain in her young body for many years yet to come. The rhythm seemed to match the small clock that ticked on the wall, like her breath was being meted out in exact measures: in, two, three, four; out, two, three, four. And with it the river lapped against the boat, not quite so rhythmical but steady still, cradling the tense little cabin in an unsteady rock. Lap, rock, tick, breath.

It was nearly unbearable yet it was also acting like a drug, and despite the discomfort of the wooden chair eventually Aggie was lulled to sleep. The cabin became a nursery then and there were babies, so many of them, all watching her with lonely blue eyes. All with soft red curls and lifting their chubby hands towards her, aching to be loved. But Aggie's hands were tied and she couldn't hold them and they cried.

'No, no,' she cried too. 'Ivy.'

There were notes in her tied hands but the words were blurred from her tears and there was no-one to read what they said. No-one to tell of their fates. Then Robert was there, outside in the water, but he couldn't get in through the small porthole, and the babies all cried in a rising wail as he called her name.

Aggie. Aggie.

'Aggie.'

She awoke with a start. Then terror. Where Ivy had been restless, she was now still. Pale where she'd been flushed.

'Dr Pratt!'

He came immediately with a clatter, Frankie, Robert and Patrick close behind him.

'I thought she said my name but now she … she's …'

Ivy looked like a ghost as the doctor took her arm, and it was thin and limp in his hand as he felt her pulse. As he raised his gaze, Aggie felt her entire existence pause as she begged for good news. Kind news. Dear God.

'It's broken.'

Aggie stared at him then the enormity of that short statement sank through. He meant the fever.

'Aggie?' Ivy said again, opening her eyes.

'It's … you're …' Aggie collapsed on the sheet, clinging to her as Frankie fell against her too. The doctor moved back to let the three sisters hold one another and weep. For the second time in a day, Aggie felt a relief so great it consumed her entire being, culminating in great sobs as Frankie clutched her other hand and they lay together, not parted after all. The Merriweather girls, together and safe. Three hearts united, as they'd always been.

Aggie lifted her face to look at Ivy, who smiled, and even though it was faint and weak Aggie thought it was the most wonderful sight she'd ever seen. She looked to Frankie, whose tear-streaked visage reflected the same thought.

'Thank the lord,' Frankie whispered and although none of them were particularly religious, Aggie did thank a God that seemed suddenly benevolent. She looked over to see Patrick, collapsed on the stairs and crying, and raised her eyes to her husband who stood squashed behind him. Always there. Always strong. Gratitude filled her and the ever-present longing she carried like a stone in her heart receded as Aggie recognised just how much love she already had in her life. Even though there was always room for more, right now, in this cabin, it was overflowing. And enough.

'She looks like a different person,' Frankie whispered as they took one last grateful glance at a peacefully sleeping Ivy before going above deck. In a clean night rail and with her hair brushed and tied back she truly did seem transformed and Aggie and Frankie were able to leave her and take in some fresh air at last. Reasonably fresh, at any rate. Large, tell-tale plumes of brown smoke spiralled in the distance and Aggie felt relieved anew at Ivy's recovery. Bushfire haze would certainly have further hampered her breathing. She hoped her poor father's lungs weren't too affected back home.

Their ascent was well timed. Riley's sister Fiona and her little daughters had waded over with the doctor and were passing up tea and cake at the side of the boat.

'Oh, let me help you,' Frankie said, rushing with Aggie to help. She sent the empty-handed Dr Pratt a look. 'You shouldn't have bothered in your condition.'

'Not at all,' Fiona replied, although she looked exhausted. There'd been no help forthcoming from her lazy-looking husband either as he sat staring over at them from onshore. The man hadn't even bothered introducing himself and Aggie pitied the woman her obviously difficult life. The girls were adorable though.

'We mixed it but Mum cooked it,' one said. 'It's pink,' she added, unnecessarily. It was the pinkest cake Aggie had ever seen.

'Tricia dropped shell in it,' the other one informed them. 'Mum said it's just a special extra 'gredient.'

'Well, I look forward to being the one to find it,' Aggie told them and they giggled.

With the refreshments delivered and handed around, Fiona and the girls made their way back. Aggie found a spot to lean as Frankie questioned Dr Pratt as to what they should do next.

'I can't see much point in moving her,' he told her between mouthfuls. 'She's still in a very weakened state and any exertion would be ill-advised, particularly with that smoke in the air,' he added with a nod at the distant fire.

'But we can't just leave her here,' Aggie said immediately. 'I mean, surely you need your boat for work.' Aggie looked to Riley Logan. The man and his sister had been beyond generous and to keep him from being able to make a livelihood any longer seemed most unfair. Besides which, the cabin was hardly an ideal makeshift hospital ward and there was scant room for them all to stay there much longer.

'I have another run-around I can use,' Riley told her. 'You don't have to worry on my account.'

'It's also that, well, to be honest, it's just too cramped,' Frankie said. 'Sorry, I mean we really appreciate your hospitality, Mr Logan, but … well, it is.'

'It's a bed and she's comfortable and away from the elements,' Dr Pratt said. 'Do what you like with yourselves but I advise you leave her here to give her a little time to regain her strength before travelling. That was quite a fever.'

'Do you know what caused it?' Aggie asked. He still hadn't offered any real explanation and she wondered if he actually knew.

'Could have been the cut to her head, although it doesn't appear to be infected. Otherwise I suspect she just got sick from being damp, then hot after being unconscious for so long … there's only so much the body will take until it starts to weaken, you understand.'

Aggie's suspicion was confirmed: he really didn't know. That Frankie was thinking the same thing was evident by her sceptical expression.

'So she had …?'

'I'd say a bad case of shaking fever.'

It sounded made up, and most likely was, but there wasn't much use in commenting, although Frankie managed a scoff. He may well be a poor excuse for a doctor but he was the only one they had right now.

'How long until we can take her home?' Aggie asked and the doctor pushed his spectacles up.

'I'd say a good day's rest before travelling would do the trick, assuming all things turn out for the best.'

Aggie didn't like the sound of that last comment but she decided not pursue it. Better they focus on remaining positive after so much turmoil.

'Well, we can't all camp out on this boat,' Robert pointed out, turning to look at Riley. 'I don't think we should further impose on your sister either.' He was merely being polite by suggesting they even could, of course. The creepy husband hardly looked the hospitable type and the house onshore really wasn't much more than a shed. Besides, it was unrealistic that the poor woman continue to feed the lot of them when she obviously had little to spare, especially as heavily pregnant as she was. 'Is there somewhere else we could stay?'

'There's the inn,' Riley told them. 'Up at Wisemans Ferry. The Packet, it's called. It's fairly popular and only half an hour away – I can run you up there in my spare boat. I think that would suit quite well.'

'Sounds like the best bet,' Robert agreed, 'although I think perhaps I'll head back home with the doctor and tell Albert and Harriet the good news in person. What say you three care for Ivy in shifts and we'll get you all home tomorrow afternoon?'

Patrick nodded. 'I'll look after them, Robert.'

'Excuse me,' Frankie said, eyebrows raising, 'but I can bloody well look after myself.' Aggie felt the need to intervene as Patrick gaped.

'Yes, but it will be nice to have an extra pair of hands, thank you, Patrick.'

No-one else commented although Riley Logan looked amused, and Aggie had to hide a smile herself at Frankie being so outspoken. It felt good to see life slowly return to normal.

'Well, I'm ready when you are,' Riley said, finishing his tea, and it was soon arranged that the doctor and Robert would return in the hire boat they'd engaged and Aggie would stay with Ivy, which left Frankie and Patrick to make their way to the inn. Watching them depart with Riley not long after, Aggie couldn't help but chuckle before returning to Ivy's side, Frankie's voice carrying in the air.

'You know, I really quite enjoy boating. How does one go about learning how to drive?'

As much as he hated to break his vow that he wouldn't leave Ivy's side, Patrick could see the practicality of taking shifts with Ivy's sisters and staying at the inn.

Still, he wasn't sure if the sight of Frankie trying to feed the steam engine and drive this boat was an amusing one or a worrying one, or just too much to deal with after these past few harrowing days. Perhaps all three. Everyone reacted in their own way, he supposed. That Frankie had bounced from weeping relief to a sudden unbridled enthusiasm for boating was simply part of who she was, or so he was learning. That girl could feel every emotion under the sun and still want to take on the world in her next breath. Admirable as that was, give him a sweet, ladylike girl such as Ivy any day.

Well, perhaps minus her one act of recklessness that had nearly cost her life. Patrick doubted she'd ever do such a thing again, however. It was a lesson hard won and he looked forward to spending the rest of their days together with such rashness well behind them. If he survived this current adventure with her sister.

The Packet was coming into sight and Patrick followed Frankie's excited pointing as she manned the wheel, spinning it a bit too wildly. Riley took over.

'Think I'd better take her in.'

Frankie reluctantly moved over to sit beside Patrick and watch the town of Wisemans Ferry draw closer. It was an unexpectedly impressive sight and her face soon lit up again. The inn was a large one and Patrick was surprised at its graceful architecture, especially after what he'd so far witnessed of Hawkesbury River life. Double storey and perched on the rise, it had matching wrap-around verandahs above and below, the cream and green paint bright in the sunshine, with people leaning upon the rails with drinks in hand, watching the river view. It was surrounded by a few other decent houses near where the ferry went to and fro and in all there was a pleasantness about the place that had so far been sorely missing up here.

Riley drew the boat up to the wharf and they alighted and waited for him to moor it, looking about with interest as they did so. The dusty road was lined with horses and carts and the general store was so busy a line had formed outside, yet the hub of the town was certainly the marvellous inn.

'Is it always this crowded?' Frankie asked Riley as they walked over towards it.

'Not usually,' he said, scanning the faces of the men lining the railings near the bar.

A notice was nailed to the wall, flapping in the light breeze, and the reason for the large number of people was soon apparent. A woodchopping festival was on the next day and a dance was being held that night as part of the celebrations. The atmosphere was already a merry one as men drank their beer, and they watched Frankie pass by with interest, one letting out a slow whistle. She lifted her chin, ignoring him, as Riley sent them a warning glance.

'Nice day for it, Riley,' the long-bearded man called but Riley merely nodded.

'Friends of yours?' Patrick queried, glancing over.

'Not friends, no,' Riley replied.

He was an interesting character, Ivy's protector; quiet for the most part but obviously generous and kind-hearted, as his actions proved. Patrick had much to thank him for but part of him was jealous too. Any man spending that much time alone with Ivy and tending her in so intimate a situation would be bound to make him feel so. He was a rugged, good-looking type, just the kind of man women tended to admire, from what Patrick had observed over the years. Yet he was far removed from proper society and probably a bit too rough around the edges for a girl like Ivy. Probably not quite on the straight and narrow either, Patrick suspected. Still, he'd behaved as a true gentleman, as far as Patrick could see, and it seemed most ungracious not to express his own gratitude and to thank him on behalf of Ivy's father. Patrick paused as they reached the inn's door.

'Why don't you stay a while and I'll buy you a drink?' Riley hesitated and Patrick added, 'It's the least we can do, please. It would be my pleasure.'

'All right then, why not?' Riley acquiesced. 'Just let me get cleaned up a bit first.'

It was cool inside after the glare of the sun. Patrick's eyes took a moment to adjust as the woman behind the counter broke into a smile.

'Riley Logan! I've been wondering when you were going to turn up.' Riley took off his hat and raked his hair as she added in a whisper, 'I got your delivery. Didn't expect you to flit past in the middle of the night like that, though. We hardly get to see you as it is.'

'Sorry about that, Margie. I've had a few extra things on my plate,' Riley told her. 'Did you share the medicine and herbs around?'

'Yes, and not a moment too soon. Some god-awful fever has been going around and that thieving merchant at the store was all out anyway. Place has been like Pitt Street with people coming to pick them up, just to top off how damn busy we are.'

Patrick ears pricked up at that. That could explain how Ivy got so ill. More likely than 'shaking fever', anyway.

'Found enough time to put the decorations up, though?' Riley said and Margie beamed at him.

'Certainly did – and what a nice extra surprise they were, bless your heart! Looks right festive, don't it?' Margie said proudly of the streamers and rosettes festooning the foyer and beyond. 'And how's that sister of yours? Haven't seen her in an age although I suppose she's housebound with baby coming along.'

'Yes, she has her hands full. We've a few guests at the moment, actually. Thought we might trouble you for a couple of rooms.'

'Well, you've picked a hell of a day,' Margie told him. 'Half the district's come to town for the woodchoppin' and to see this band, although I can't say I've heard of ragtime myself. Sounds like cleaning the floor to me.'

Riley chuckled. 'Something different, I suppose. These are my friends, Frankie and Patrick.'

'Nice to meet you,' Frankie said as Riley stepped back. The woman looked her up and down.

'We're so sorry to arrive on such a busy day,' Patrick said, and she flicked her eyes at his expensive clothes curiously too. 'I don't suppose you've any rooms still available?'

The woman drew her glance back towards Riley and tapped her pencil on the register thoughtfully. 'Well, I don't really but I'll pull a few strings. You can take eleven and thirteen but if anyone asks you made a reservation a week ago.'

'You're too good to me, Margie girl,' Riley said.

'Now, now, go on with you,' Margie said, pleased, then she lowered her voice again. 'I just hope you've remembered about that other special request I made.'

'Next week, I promise,' he told her and Patrick wondered yet again exactly what Riley delivered up and down this river. Obviously more than medicines and party supplies.

They registered while Riley went to wash up and by the time they were settled in their rooms, Frankie seemed to have finally run out of puff. She stayed upstairs to rest, which sounded like a wonderful idea to Patrick, but he went down to the main bar to meet Riley instead to buy him that drink.

It was very busy inside and he had to shoulder through, muttering apologies as men made room, standing aside to stare at his clear-shaven and upmarket appearance.

'Pardon me, y'majesty,' said one.

'Crikey, didn't realise it were fancy dress,' said another. 'Shoulda worn me wig and frockcoat.'

It was unnerving but Patrick took it in his stride and soon enough he had two cold ales in hand. He sat down on a chair outside on the porch, relieved to be away from the throng and free to watch the river glide by in peace as he waited for Riley.

The water was clear at the edges but a murky olive colour further out, mysterious in its flow as it hid whatever creatures lived below the surface. It seemed appropriate that a deeply flowing, concealing river should be the main artery that pumped through this place. Everything he'd witnessed so far seemed covert: what went on behind closed doors that caused Dave's missus to limp; what Riley actually carried along these waters and where he acquired it; the reason why Fiona's husband simply sat and stared, ignoring their visitors. It held secrets, this river, and so did the people who lived along it.

Riley approached and sat beside him. Patrick slid over his beer, holding his own aloft.

'Bottoms up.'

'Thanks,' Riley replied, sipping it gratefully. 'Bit of a crowd they've got going. Should be quite a shindig tonight.'

'I doubt I'll be doing anything other than sleeping,' Patrick said, supposing he'd go to bed very early tonight no matter how much noise rose from below. This stay at the inn was simply time to be endured until he could relieve Aggie and be with Ivy tomorrow.

The men drank in silence while Patrick scanned the crowd, recognising a few faces from the pub in Hornsby, timber cutters, most likely here for the woodchopping, he guessed. His gaze landed on the bearded man who still stood on the verandah, laughing with a few others. 'Do you know many of them?'

Riley didn't bother following his gaze as he took out his tobacco pouch. 'Known most people up here all my life but not all I count as friends,' he told him. 'Smoke?'

'No thanks,' Patrick said. 'So, were you born up this way then?' he continued, curious as he glanced around at the town and considered what it must have been like to be raised there.

Riley rolled his smoke. 'Yes, a bit further up. Family had oyster farms.'

'Why aren't you still doing that?'

'They got killed off by an algae plague so we had to find other ways to make do,' Riley said, lighting a match.

'Oh, I see. So do you spend all your time making deliveries, then?'

Patrick didn't know why he was prying, especially considering the wary glance Riley was sending him, but he couldn't seem to help himself.

'Mostly,' Riley said.

'I suppose people need a lot of supplies. I didn't see too much farming going on,' Patrick observed, sipping his drink.

'Fishing and timber work are the main ways to make a quid up here,' Riley told him. 'It's tough land to farm, for the most part. People need more than they can grow.'

'And is it hard to get supplies?' He was pushing it now, Patrick knew.

Riley flicked his cigarette. 'Not if you know the right people.' He took a long draught of his beer. 'You seem to ask a lot of questions. What line of work are you in?'

'I'm studying law,' Patrick said and Riley nodded with a sudden smile.

'Should have guessed.'

Patrick grinned a little ruefully. 'Sorry about that. I didn't mean to cross-examine you, I was just trying to understand things, get some insight into what Ivy might have seen or experienced up here. She's ... very important to me,' he admitted.

Riley didn't meet his eye, simply sipping his drink. 'Yes, I can see that,' he said.

'The river life is far removed from what she's used to, let me tell you,' Patrick continued. 'She's lived a pretty sheltered existence.'

'And you haven't?' Riley looked at him directly and it was a challenge more than a question. Patrick felt a little self-conscious as he straightened his waistcoat.

'Not entirely,' he said, defensive at first, but Riley's stare wore him down. 'Well, probably, I suppose,' he had to acknowledge, 'although these past few days have ripped any shelter away, that's for sure.'

Riley dropped his gaze, appearing guilty now. 'I'm so sorry about Barney ...'

Patrick shook his head. 'How could you possibly expect him to forget such a thing?'

'Well, it was Barney, I guess I should have thought of another way.'

'Even so,' Patrick said, shaking his head, 'you weren't to know. It wasn't just fearing the worst, although that was a living hell.' He paused, finding it hard to say the words out loud for the first time. 'They put me under house arrest. I was the last one ... alone with her ... so ...'

Riley looked taken aback. 'Surely they weren't going to charge you?'

'If she couldn't be found, yes.'

Riley stared at him as he lowered his glass. 'I suppose they thought … well, where *were* you?' he said. 'Why did you leave Ivy alone? Especially to go swimming?'

'She wasn't swimming when I left her. She was up by the creek and she wanted more champagne so …' He trailed off, wondering how he'd ever thought it would be all right to leave her so vulnerable. He certainly would never do so again.

'I suppose you weren't to know,' Riley said, repeating Patrick's words back to him and glancing over at the men further along the verandah once more. They were getting drunker and louder and Patrick changed the subject, needing to piece the missing bits of the last few days together.

'So what was going on up here? How close to Hornsby did you get before you had to turn back?'

Riley drank again before answering. 'Only got about half an hour or so away from Fiona's. We took shelter in a cave when the storm hit and had to wait it out for a few hours. That's when I realised how sick she'd become.'

'Must have been worrying,' Patrick said, trying not to let his jealousy rise again at the thought of this man being alone with Ivy in a cave for hours on end.

'Very,' Riley admitted, 'but that wasn't the worst of it. The place we stopped in had some other visitors,' he said, nodding towards the bearded man and his cronies. 'Cost me my best bottle of rum to get them drunk enough to pass out and get Ivy away from there.'

'Didn't they see her?'

'No, luckily,' Riley said. 'Would have been bloody dangerous if they had.'

'Surely they wouldn't have harmed her in any way. I mean, she's a lady …' Patrick said, appalled.

Riley drained his drink. 'Women are worth more than gold up here. Lady or no, they're viewed in the same way. That's why

I couldn't leave Ivy alone and unconscious in the first place. I just couldn't. I'm so sorry for what you all went through but if I had my time over I'd do the same thing again.'

The two men looked across the table at one another, new understanding between them now, but Ivy sat between them too. For all Riley had told him it was what he *hadn't* said that niggled at Patrick the most, and it was there every time Riley uttered her name. Even though he hadn't known her long, this river man cared for her, more than he was letting on. Patrick knew it because he recognised it. He felt the same way.

'Speaking of which, I'd best get back to keeping an eye on things. Don't forget Barney's collecting you at eight tomorrow morning, if he bloody remembers,' Riley added with a rueful smile.

'Want me to write him a note?' Patrick said.

'I already have, for what it's worth.' Riley stood and put on his hat. 'Thanks for the drink, Patrick.' He reached out his hand and Patrick rose to shake it. Regardless of what Riley felt for Ivy, they all owed him more of a debt than Patrick had realised, protecting her the way he had.

'Thank you for everything you've done. We can never repay you but … thank you. And I swear, if there's anything we can ever do for you just name it and it's yours.'

'Hopefully I won't be in need of a budding lawyer any time soon,' Riley said.

'Maybe not, but my dad's a judge so …'

Riley let out a short laugh. 'Well, let's *definitely* hope I never have to call that favour in. See you in the morning, then.'

With a tilt of his hat he was gone and Patrick watched him unmoor his boat and stoke the fire to start the engine, sending him a last wave as he chugged away, and a few other men raised their hands.

Patrick put his hat on and turned to walk upstairs to take that longed-for rest but not before catching the bearded man's eye.

'See ya later, Riley,' he called but his gazed remained trained on Patrick, who knew one thing was for sure: Ivy wasn't the only Merriweather daughter who required protection up here tonight. But he'd need his wits about him to stop Frankie from getting in trouble, especially when she was determined she could 'bloody well' look after herself. Ivy may have tripped and fallen but, if he knew anything about Frankie, she was likely to run and launch herself straight into the middle of strife.

Twenty-One

The moon was rising once more, a little later and little less full than the night before, as if it had taken an afternoon nap, just like Frankie had herself. The room she was staying in was a pleasant one and the moonlight danced on the river and glinted among the treetops that stretched out on either side of the shoreline. It was entrancing but Frankie had woken up ravenous and the view wasn't doing anything to assuage her appetite. She freshened up and dressed quickly, deciding to go and knock on Patrick's door rather than wait for him to come to her or go downstairs by herself. It sounded like a big party was in full swing and as much as she loved socialising there was no way she was going down alone after seeing such rough men there earlier on. Besides, she wasn't in the mood to make friends after these past few emotional days. But she was hungry.

Frankie straightened her blue cotton blouse and skirt and headed out to Patrick's adjacent room, hoping he wasn't asleep, but he answered straight away.

'I was just going to come and get you,' he said, not appearing too pleased. It wasn't really the done thing for a single woman to knock on a bachelor's hotel room door.

'Oh well, here I am. Ready to eat? I'm starving,' she said brightly and she thought he looked set to say more but then he just sighed.

'Hold on,' he said, grabbing his wallet, and they set off.

They reached the bottom of the stairs and there seemed to be people everywhere but Patrick managed to gain the now flustered-looking Margie's attention to ask where they could eat.

'Restaurant's pretty full,' she told them above the noise, 'but when the band starts it should empty out. Can you wait half an hour?'

'Looks like we'll have to,' Patrick said.

'Have a drink in the ladies' parlour,' she suggested before bustling off and they made their way over to it. It was busy too but Patrick went to order some drinks and Frankie found a spare corner booth, which a couple had fortuitously vacated just as she went to walk by. It was a bit cosy for her liking but beggars couldn't be choosers and if Patrick looked wary as he approached then so be it. There was far too much ridiculous propriety in their society, as far as she was concerned, especially when it came to restrictions on what a young lady couldn't say or do. So what if they now had to sit close enough that their knees kept touching? He was practically engaged to her sister, for goodness' sake.

The wine was welcome and cool and she drank the first mouthful rather quickly.

'Not too fast there, Frankie,' he said and she made a face.

'Don't tell me you're turning into a bore.'

'You're the feminist. Aren't they supposed to support temperance?'

'I see nothing wrong with a man enjoying a drink so long as he can handle it,' Frankie said.

'Or woman?'

'Yes, or woman, and you can get off your high horse tonight. I think we both deserve a few drinks and a good meal after everything we've been through,' she added.

'I don't feel much like celebrating,' he said, although he drank his wine rather fast too.

'It's not celebrating so much as recovering. Anyway, we may as well do something to while away the time.'

'That's true,' Patrick said, 'although you're going to need to be very careful here, Frankie. There're some unsavoury types hanging around so don't stray away, all right?'

'I'm not a dog that goes straying,' Frankie said, getting annoyed with him now. 'Anyway, where would I go?'

'I'm just saying …'

'Unsavoury. Honestly, Patrick, you really need to stop being so pompous. There's perfectly nice people living up here too, I'm sure.'

'I'm not worried about the nice people, I'm worried about the not-so-nice ones. Riley told me there's good reason to worry too.' He went on to tell her about Ivy's dangerous near-encounter and Frankie's eyes grew round as she sipped on her wine.

'You don't really think they would've harmed her?'

'Riley thinks so, most definitely, and he'd know. So please, Frankie, don't give me any more reasons to worry tonight, all right?'

Frankie softened, realising she was being a bit hard on him after all he'd been carrying.

'Sorry I called you pompous,' she said, pulling a face.

To his credit he smiled. 'If that's the worst thing you ever call me I'll be surprised.' He looked towards the dining room. 'I can't hear the band yet but do you want to see if we can get some dinner?'

Frankie practically jumped up to get to the door and peer through the window but it was still full to the brim. Fortunately

Patrick hadn't left their spot so they could sit and have another drink while they waited.

'See if they've anything to snack on,' she said as he went back to the bar and he returned with a bowl of peanuts.

'Goodness knows where these came from but at least it's food,' he said, putting the glasses and bowl down.

'I know a man who may know a man,' she said cheekily and Patrick feigned surprise.

'I hope you're not suggesting our friend Mr Logan procured such ill-gotten exotic goods?'

'Suggesting but not complaining,' she returned, cracking the first shell and eating the nuts hungrily. 'Mmm, they're good.'

It was a quite a fun activity and it was just as well it did involve food because it took a good hour until they finally got a table. And three glasses of wine. Frankie felt quite tiddly and found herself giggling as Patrick regaled her with stories about their cricketing friends.

'How is this the first I'm ever hearing of it?' she asked after one rather hilarious story about Nick Johnson crouching down and splitting his pants in front of a large group of school girls.

'I'm pretty sure you'd be the last person he'd want to know,' he said and she felt suddenly awkward but was saved from answering as the waiter approached. 'Ah. Here's the food.'

It was local oyster soup served with crusty rolls, soon followed by whiting in butter sauce, and it was all very delicious. Frankie savoured every mouthful.

'Oh,' she groaned when she was done, leaning back and holding her full stomach. 'I could get used to river life if it was like this every day.'

'Yes, it's quite surprising to find all this here,' Patrick said, finishing up too and looking around them. 'I was beginning to think the whole area contained nothing but shacks and shady characters.'

'There you go again,' she said.

'It's not pompous if it's true,' he asserted. 'Anyway, I'm not looking down my nose at them. I actually feel sorry for the people up here, to be honest. I didn't realise how hard their lives were.'

'That's exactly what's wrong with this country, and no, no, I'm not just saying this to criticise you,' she said, halting his objection. 'Too many people stick their heads in the sand and pretend other people's problems don't exist, but they *do*, Patrick, especially when it comes to women. Why is it that you and I can live in fine homes and eat and drink whatever we like and have soft beds and nice clothes,' she said, gesturing at his outfit, 'yet most people up here live in squalor?'

Patrick sipped his wine, thoughtful now. 'It's the way of things, I suppose. Some are born lucky, some aren't.'

'No,' she said, shaking her head. 'That's a definite advantage but things stay this way because of the law. The people who suffer most can't change the very laws against them and that's woman-kind, Patrick. The property of men,' she said with disgust. 'Yet ironically we can't own property unless our spouse dies. We can't even open a bank account let alone stop husbands from beating their wives and stealing their dignity …' she paused as tears filled her eyes, waiting for him to argue, but he didn't. Instead he took her hand. She stared at in surprise. 'I … I'm sorry. I think it's just the wine.'

'Don't be sorry,' he said. 'I'm the one who should be. You've opened my eyes up here, Frankie, it all has. Ivy being in danger and the way she could have been treated, merely because she's a woman. I didn't know men could treat ladies that way, well, I mean, I suppose I did but I would have thought it was rare. Very few cases have ever come to light that I know of.'

'Then it's sadder still.'

He looked at her sombrely and nodded. 'Yes, it is.'

'But now that you know …'

'Indeed,' he said, releasing her hand and looking abashed he'd taken it. 'Now that I know I have an obligation to be less apathetic.'

'I'll hold you to that,' she said.

'I have absolutely no doubt that you will,' he said and she giggled, wiping the few tears away. 'Come on now, what say we have one more drink before we retire?'

'I thought you wanted to take it slow?'

'I wanted *you* to take it slow but I shouldn't have been so pompous, as I recall. Must work on that too.'

'I can hold you to two things then,' she said, and she couldn't help but giggle again as he raised his hand and called for the waiter in an affected voice.

They enjoyed their last drink with lighter talk of cricketing antics once more and he rose to escort her out. Frankie was definitely more than a bit tiddly now and she swayed slightly as they went but the band had started and Frankie couldn't resist pausing to look into the main room.

'Frankie …' Patrick began.

'I just want a quick look,' she said, watching as a woman sang above the playing of a very fast piano. 'Come on, we can stand over there,' she added, pointing to a space in the corner of the room.

'Oh, all right then,' he said and they sidled over.

Frankie had never heard music like this before. Her parents were always listening to orchestral music or brass bands on the gramophone, and she and her sisters enjoyed the current songs of the day, but this was different. It had a very rapid beat and the woman seemed to be having so much fun singing it that people dancing in the crowd were spontaneously whooping as it rollicked along. By the time it ended the woman was grinning broadly.

'Well, howdy folks,' she called out. 'I sure am glad y'all came on down to hear us play tonight. Hold on to y'belt buckles 'cos here's another one from my very own home state of Texas.'

'She's American,' Frankie said, loving the woman's accent.

'That's where ragtime music comes from,' Patrick told her. 'I've heard it recently in some of the nightclubs in town with the boys.'

She would have loved to hear more about what went on with the cricketing gang during *those* particular nights but the music was belting out again and this time she couldn't help but dance.

'Come on,' she said, grabbing Patrick's hand and he didn't resist, joining her on the dancefloor and taking her in his arms. The music was like a pulse, pumping through her veins and guiding her feet about, although she wasn't too sure what dance in particular they were doing. There was something wild and freeing about such lack of convention and Frankie could almost feel all the worry and angst she'd been carrying begin to fade, as if the music was lifting it straight off her and flinging it away.

Life is good, it seemed to say, as the fiddle flew and the piano tinkled at a merry pace, and so it was. Ivy was safe and there was hope in this new year now, for if she could convince someone like Patrick Earle to lose his apathy towards the Cause then everything she fought for was within grasp. It felt powerful to influence a man like him. It felt powerful to cast convention away and dance like this. It felt powerful to be a woman.

Patrick had his hands about her waist and she looked up at him, suddenly acutely aware of that fact, and her smile began to fade as another feeling surfaced, one she didn't and couldn't want.

'I … I think we should probably stop now …'

Patrick blinked as if coming out of some kind of a trance. 'Of course.'

He led her off the dance floor and out the side doors so they could avoid the crowd and, as they walked along the near-empty verandah, Frankie wanted nothing more than to get to her room. To forget whatever that feeling was before it took root and began to twist into her mind and become something to ponder, or fear. But there was a hand on her waist again and she was being spun about and it wasn't Patrick who held her, it was a man with a long beard.

'Well, well, there you are. I've been looking for you all night, pretty girl.'

'Get your filthy hands off me,' she said, pushing at him in outrage and a good dose of sudden terror as she smelt the rum and beer on his breath in the muted light.

'What do you think you're doing?' Patrick demanded but another man grabbed and held him and then there was a third, even more frightening looking than the other two, with pockmarked skin and bloodshot eyes where the moonlight landed. He came up close, shoving the bearded man away.

'I think I'll have this one, mate.'

'Hey, I saw her first.'

'Get away from her right now or I'll call the police,' Patrick demanded angrily.

They looked as one towards Patrick and began to laugh.

'Good luck over this ruckus,' the pockmarked man said. He put his arms around Frankie and she punched at his chest.

'Let bloody go,' she screamed, twisting about in terror, but he was strong.

'Hit me again and I'll hit you, young *lady*.' His tone had darkened and she didn't doubt he meant it.

'Lay a finger on her and I'll kill you,' Patrick said.

'Shut that poonce down, will ya, boys?'

The other two men laid on punches of their own but like most private school boys Patrick had been taught to box properly and he took them both on.

'This should be good,' the pockmarked man said, rocking as he looked around to watch, amused. Frankie noticed a bottle on a table and saw her chance. Without really thinking she picked it up, and smashed the man over his head with all her might.

He fell immediately to the ground and the other two looked around in surprise.

'Hey,' the bearded man said. 'What ...?' He didn't finish, however, as Patrick took his chance too, cracking a big upper cut right on his bearded chin. The man fell backwards onto a table and chairs with a crash.

The third man growled and launched himself but Patrick simply stepped aside and he fell straight down the stairs, landing in a groaning mess below.

'Come on,' Patrick said, grabbing her hand and running to reception.

'Is he dead?' Frankie said, turning back to see. 'Oh God, I think I've killed a man.'

They rushed inside and found Margie at the counter.

'There's been ... an altercation ...' Patrick panted.

'Oh lord, what now?' Maggie said, not as alarmed as either of them would have expected. She walked over to peer down the verandah. 'Humph, Donovan and his cronies. You just leave them to the police sergeant. I'll send word, not to worry.'

'But ... but he could be dead ...' Frankie said, shaking with shock now.

Margie peered again and shook her head. 'Nuh, he's moving.' Frankie dared to take a peek too and saw for herself that he was rolling about. 'You best make yourself scarce though. Angus,' she stopped a burly man walking by, 'get the sarge. Bloody Donovan and the boys have been at it again.'

'Right you are,' he said, hurrying off.

'Off you two go then,' she said. 'I'll keep an eye out until they get here.'

'But … but won't the police want a statement?' Frankie stammered.

Maggie gave a short derisive laugh. 'I think their records all speak for themselves. Besides, best keep your own noses clean. I'm sure you don't want no trouble with the law.'

'No,' Patrick said and Frankie realised it was very much the last thing he wanted. 'Thank you,' he said earnestly and Margie gave him a nod before turning back to keep watch. 'Any friend of Riley Logan's is a friend of mine.'

They made their way quickly upstairs to hide in the shadows of the upper verandah and listen to things unfold as police whistles sounded and drunken voices carried.

'We was set upon. Honest.'

'Must have been ten of 'em, sarge.'

But the police were having none of it. It didn't take them long to lead the men away into the night and the only noise that remained was the ragtime music as it wafted up towards Frankie and Patrick, muted now, but still a pulsing, vibrant sound. Frankie was shaking though, whether from adrenaline or alcohol or something else she couldn't be sure, and the music didn't have the same charm as before. It felt out of control, something she now knew to be either a very fun state to be in, or a very scary one.

'Are you all right?' Patrick said.

'I … I suppose. No-one has ever laid a … a finger on me before.'

'It's all right,' he soothed. 'The whole thing's over and you're safe and sound.' He gave her shoulder a reassuring hug. It was comforting but the awareness of earlier returned and she was glad when he dropped his arm. He touched his cheek gingerly.

'Are you hurt?'

'A bit, but not too badly,' Patrick said, moving his finger to his eye socket, which looked swollen and likely to blacken on the morrow, even in this faint light.

'I'm … I'm sorry … if we hadn't stayed to dance—'

'Don't be. It isn't your fault.' He cut her off. 'You can't help it if thugs like that prey on innocent women. I'm just glad we got away in one piece.'

'Yes, but if we'd gone straight to sleep like you suggested …'

'Then I would never have gained the very precious memory of you whacking a man over a head with a bottle,' he finished for her and she had to smile.

'I … I can't believe I did that.'

'I can,' he said, chuckling. 'Seriously though, don't feel bad about this. You should be proud you defended yourself down there.'

'But it was my fault.'

'It wasn't your fault. You can't help being a woman, Frankie.'

Frankie wrapped her arms around herself, those words sinking in as she stared out at the silvered night. 'No, that I can't.'

Patrick gave her a thoughtful glance. 'We'd best get some rest now, I'd say.'

'Yes, yes, we should,' she said but she felt very alone once she was back in her room and he'd made sure her verandah door was well locked before saying goodnight. Very alone and very vulnerable, which was a strange feeling and an unnerving one.

She dressed for bed, taking comfort in routine, but Patrick's words stayed with her like a mantra, long after she'd changed and lain down, unable to sleep as she gazed out at the moon. He was right, she couldn't help being a woman. And for the second time it was his words that made her feel the raw truth of that fact, more keenly than ever before in her life.

Twenty-Two

It was already heating up but Ivy was enjoying being above deck so much she didn't complain. The fresh air was invigorating and the day so lovely that a little warm sunshine was no great price to pay. Aggie was resting downstairs in the bunk, her shift a restless one, spent on the bench. Not that she grumbled, of course, but Riley had mentioned it. Riley was on watch now and likely exhausted himself, having slept on the hard wooden floor of the deck, but she was learning that he was a man who never seemed to complain. He never seemed to stop doing things for others either, or so she'd observed and heard from Fiona. That some of that good work seemed suspiciously illegal bothered her, though, and now that it was just the two of them, sitting and having tea in the morning sun as they waited for Frankie and Patrick, she decided to delve a bit, if he'd let her.

'You must have a lot of work to catch up on,' she began.

Riley looked up from his book and laid it aside. 'It's fine. I can catch up easily enough.'

Ivy tilted her head, wondering how to go about this, and Riley raised his eyebrows.

'What?'

'It's just … well, something's been making me rather curious, that's all.'

'How so?' he said, but there was a wariness there.

'Well, you seem such a good and generous man, I mean, obviously you are, but I can't help but get the feeling some of these deliveries you make aren't quite … above board.'

Riley sipped his tea before answering. 'No, they're not,' he admitted.

Ivy was taken aback at his honesty. 'But that can get you into serious trouble, surely.'

He sighed, putting his tea down too and taking out his tobacco pouch. 'It's hard for a girl like you to understand, I guess.'

'Try me,' she said and he raised his eyes to her challenge.

'People need medicine, things for the home … booze,' he admitted, 'but food especially. They'd likely starve if blokes like me didn't bring supplies up here. There are very few shops along the river, and they charge like wounded bulls anyway – people can't afford a lot of what they need. You can see how hard it is to farm this sandy soil, too, let alone tame the bushland.' He nodded over at Fiona's meagre garden. 'So if they can't live off the land either, what else is there to do?'

Ivy considered that. 'Why don't you open your own store? Charge what they can afford to pay.'

Riley rolled his cigarette. 'It's not as simple as that.'

'Why not?'

'Because of the cost of getting the supplies in the first place and transporting them up here, the time involved, let alone how long it would take to build a store in the right location …' He drifted off.

'You've thought about it, though, haven't you?' she guessed.

Riley lit his cigarette, watching her. 'Yeah,' he said. 'I have.'

'Surely you'd have enough contacts to get supplies at a decent price and there's so much timber and land, I can't see why you couldn't build a decent place.'

'True,' Riley said.

'So?' she said. 'What's stopping you?'

'I don't know.' He shrugged.

Ivy didn't believe that. 'Yes you do.'

He studied her closely, his gaze growing intense. 'I've never had someone I wanted to build a life like that with.'

There was something in the way he said it, wistful and bare, that made her feel he was speaking directly to her heart. It took her breath and for a single insane moment she wanted to tell him she'd be that person. She'd share in that life of helping others, a life that mattered. Suddenly she was aware of him as a man not six feet away, blue eyes boring into hers. A man who thought she looked like a sea princess, seizing this last stolen opportunity to convey the rest of what he couldn't, or wouldn't, say.

The moment was interrupted by the sound of a flock of wood ducks taking off nearby and Ivy pulled herself back to reality. She already had her future planned out, and a man to share it with, something she had very nearly lost these past few days. The last thing she should even have been thinking about was choosing anything or anyone else.

'What about you?' Riley asked, the spell broken as he flicked his cigarette away, stood and started coiling some nearby ropes. 'What's your dream then?'

Ivy shrugged. 'Oh, you know, marriage, children.'

'To Patrick?' he asked and the question hung heavily in the air.

Ivy hesitated, not really wanting to tell him, as silly as that was. 'Yes, if he asks me.'

Riley nodded, not meeting her eyes as he worked. 'I'm sure he will.'

Ivy wanted to ask why. Because Patrick had said as much? Because she was someone a man would be lucky to marry? Because Riley himself would marry her if he could? But such questions were impossible ones to ask and she stayed silent, confused and more than a little ashamed of where her thoughts were taking her this morning.

'What about other interests? Your sisters seem very active, out there in the world.'

He'd struck a nerve and she wondered if he knew it as she replied. 'I'm not really sure, although I do like to draw and paint.'

'An artist?' he said, eyebrows raised.

'Yes, although it doesn't seem very important now that I … well, after everything that's happened.'

'How so?'

'Frankie and Aggie do so much to try to better the lives of others and here I've been, all this time …' She shrugged, feeling ashamed about that now too.

'All this time? You can't be more than twenty, surely.'

'Eighteen the day this happened,' she said, pointing at the bandage on her head. 'It was my birthday.'

'Born on the first day of the year, eh? Well, I'd say that makes you an expert on new beginnings,' he said, tossing a rope aside and grabbing another. 'I reckon you just might find that you see things a bit differently now and you never know what that may bring about. Anything's possible.'

Ivy considered that as she stared out at the river, flowing in a gentle current beneath the clear blue sky. 'I suppose I've always thought my sisters were the clever ones and I'm just, I don't know, a decoration or something.'

'You seem clever to me.'

Ivy grimaced. 'Dad said to me that it's a form of intelligence to be able to really see the beauty in nature and appreciate it, you know, with my drawing and all, but that doesn't seem much now. Aside from that, my existence so far has been pretty meaningless, really, but I thought all that I wanted was a beautiful life, surrounded by beautiful things.'

'And now?' he asked and she glanced back over at Fiona's dilapidated home.

'I think I just want less ugliness in the world,' she told him, surprised at the depth of that new feeling. 'I've always tried to avoid it, to pretend it isn't there, but …'

Riley was still watching her and she met his gaze. 'I'm sorry you've had to see the things you've seen, that our lives are so … ugly to you.'

'No, no, it's not that. You and Fiona, you're part of the beauty in the world, the goodness. It's the other side of things,' she added as George emerged from the shack and slammed the door shut. They both watched as he stormed over to his boat and Ivy raised worried eyes back to Riley.

'She's promised me again he doesn't do it,' Riley told her quietly.

'But others do,' she said sadly. That knowledge was wedged in her mind since those drunken men had voiced their terrible sins, an ugliness she would never be able to erase now. 'I wish I could do something to help them all. To live a life that matters, as Frankie says, like she and Aggie do.'

'Anything's possible, Ivy,' he said again. 'I believe you could do anything if you really wanted to. You've a big heart and, yes, a clever mind, more than I think you realise. Look how easily you've managed to worm things out of me, things I've never told anyone else, you know.'

'Really?' she said, surprised.

'Really.' He had that look on his face again, the wistful, bare one that did things to her heart that it really shouldn't do. 'I believe in you.'

It brought tears to her eyes, hearing him say that.

'But that isn't the point, Ivy,' he added. 'You need to believe in yourself.'

She nodded, knowing he was right, and looking at his earnest expression, she couldn't help but tell him the same.

'So do you, Riley,' she said. 'For what it's worth, I believe in you too.'

Twenty-Three

'One, two, three, four …'

'No peeking,' Aggie called out, hiding behind the chicken coop with Tricia, who was giggling beside her.

'Seventeen …'

'Where'd the other numbers go?' she whispered to Tricia, who giggled again.

'She always cheats.'

'A hundred. Coming, ready or not!'

She came running on her little legs and looked around in confusion before spying them and dashing over.

'You have to tag us,' Tricia yelled, taking off with Aggie, and Annie chased them up and down the beach before Aggie ran behind Fiona, who was taking what seemed a rare break, reading the paper in the morning sun.

'Help!' Aggie yelped before being grabbed around the legs by Annie and surrendering. 'Oh, all right. You win.'

'My turn! My turn!' Tricia declared.

'I think you two should have a turn without me,' she said, collapsing on the sand, and Annie ran off as Tricia buried her face against the shack wall and began to count.

'One, two, three …'

'Where do they get the energy?' Aggie said and Fiona smiled.

'It's endless,' she said, putting the paper aside and picking up her mending instead. 'You've quite a bit yourself for someone who's likely been up half the night.'

'Oh, I slept in the chair well enough,' Aggie said, although she was rather weary.

'And there's nothing like a good night's chair sleep to give a person a spring in their step.'

Aggie smiled, lying back and leaning on her elbow to watch the girls play as Fiona sewed a cotton dress. 'Well, at least I wasn't up worrying for the first time this year.'

'Yes,' Fiona said, staring out at Ivy as she sat on deck, talking to Riley. 'It's been quite a start indeed.'

Aggie looked over at her. 'I don't really know how to thank you for what you've done, taking care of her so. I feel like you were being the big sister for me,' she added. 'I can't tell you what that means.'

'I know a fair bit about being a big sister,' Fiona told her, focusing on her sewing again. 'We never stop worrying about them is the problem. It's like having a grown-up child sometimes. Mind you, Riley looks after me too. Looks after all of us and that's a fact.'

'Seems to me you do a lot of looking after around here. It must be hard, isolated as you are, and with another on the way.'

Fiona paused in her mending to pat her stomach. 'Yes, it is I suppose, but that's a mother's lot in life.' She glanced over at her. 'Have you children of your own, then?'

Aggie felt that old empty ache return. 'No. No, we don't think we can, unfortunately,' she said, finding it strange and endlessly sad to admit it.

Fiona studied her, her expression one of pity. 'That's a terrible shame,' she said, nodding over at the twins. 'You would make a wonderful mother.'

Aggie looked at them too, wondering how it ever came to be that something as natural as having a child should be denied her. Even Fiona, for all her hardships, had this blessing at least, but Aggie could hardly begrudge her that. It seemed it was all she had.

The sound of an approaching boat echoed along the river, ending such thoughts, and Aggie stood to see Barney's vessel round the corner. He'd been employed by the Merriweathers as an escort for the day and was ferrying Frankie and Patrick back from the inn. Aggie turned to Fiona.

'Coming over to hear about their adventures?'

'No, I think I'll rest here a while longer,' Fiona said, stretching out her back and wincing. 'Anyway, what makes you think there's been adventures?'

'It's Frankie,' Aggie said with a sigh. 'There always is.'

'Dear God, what happened to you?' Ivy exclaimed as the others arrived.

'Bloody Donovan, Deano and Petey up to no good again,' Barney said, helping his passengers swap boats. 'Got locked up for their trouble though.'

'They attacked you?' Ivy said, horrified as she studied Patrick's injuries, which included a black eye and swollen lip.

'Tried to but we managed to beat them off,' he said, coming over to sit by her side where she lay propped up on the deck. He smiled at her reassuringly but it made him grimace. 'Ouch,' he said, touching his sore lip.

'What do you mean "we" …?' Ivy said. 'Don't tell me Frankie was involved?'

'I'm fine, don't worry,' Frankie said but Ivy had begun to cry.

'Oh no, oh, what happened?'

'Hush, I'm fine, Ivy,' Frankie soothed, sitting on her other side and giving her a hug. 'See? Not a scratch.'

'But what did they do?' she said, sniffing back tears.

'One of them grabbed me, then another, but Patrick punched the other one square in the jaw …'

'Beard,' Patrick corrected, trying to make light of things.

'Petey,' Riley said quietly, his anger evident.

'Then the other one took a swing but he fell headfirst down the stairs.'

'Locals are calling the spot Deano's Leap after him this morning,' Patrick said, still attempting levity but Ivy couldn't stop crying.

'But Frankie must have been so frightened …'

'Well, yes, but by then she'd smashed a bottle over the other man's head and he'd fallen to the ground so we got away.'

'You … you smashed a bottle over a man's head?' Aggie said, eyes wide.

'Donovan,' Barney confirmed with a grin now. 'How's that for a bit of justice, eh?'

'That's the same men, isn't it?' Ivy said, swiping at tears. 'The ones that were near the cave that day?'

'Yes,' Riley said. 'That's them.'

'Oh Frankie, I'm so sorry.' Ivy wept. 'And Patrick, your poor face.'

'I'm fine,' Patrick told her. 'They were too drunk to be a serious threat. Besides, Frankie wields a bottle like she wields a cricket bat. They never stood a chance.'

Frankie smiled at her, adding, 'I think I may have to play for the university, maybe dress as a man. Patrick could smuggle me in.'

But Ivy gripped at both their hands and it took some time to calm her down, as Barney and Riley muttered together over on his boat. It worried Ivy, that conversation, and she hoped they wouldn't retaliate against such dangerous men, but as much as she cared about Riley and his family, she also realised that this was his world, and a man's domain. It was no real place for a woman and certainly no place for her. Whatever startling thoughts had run through her mind earlier that day, she could never share in the life of Riley. It seemed a madness it had even occurred to her.

Barney and Riley agreed they could leave after lunch if Ivy was up to it and she readily said she was, desperate now to get home to her parents and her safe life on Rosemead Road, although she'd meant what she'd said to Riley earlier. She'd no longer be sitting idly by and inasmuch as she couldn't even consider a life up here, she'd be doing what she could to address the ugliness that scarred such worlds.

Frankie and Patrick took over watching her for a few hours, giving both her and Aggie a rest before the journey, but soon it was time for them to leave with Barney and for Ivy to pack up and say goodbye. It was heart-wrenching to say farewell to the girls and Fiona. Aggie had already tearfully done so but now it was Ivy's turn and the enormity of what this woman had done for her hung heavily in the air as Fiona stood in the water, her hands around her daughters. They were crying softly, their faces buried in their mother's skirts, but somehow Fiona still found time to mother Ivy one last time too.

'It's getting very hot,' she said, glancing up at the sun. 'Make sure you don't overheat and stay below deck.'

'You must be hot yourself,' Ivy said, looking at Fiona's too-warm dress that strained at her belly.

'I'll put on my mended cotton one in a moment.'

Ivy nodded, supposing she only had very few. 'Here,' she said, handing over an envelope, having secured what money she could from her sisters and Patrick to give to Fiona and help her as best she could. 'It isn't much but just in way of thanks.'

Fiona shook her head. 'No, I couldn't possibly …'

'Yes, you can and you will. Take it, Fiona, please. I owe you … I owe my life, I dare say.' Tears rolled down both their faces and Fiona nodded.

'God be with you, Ivy. And bless you for this.'

'I'll send more and I'll come back and visit, I promise.'

'No. Don't come back here, Ivy. It's not a place for someone like you.'

It wasn't a place for someone like Fiona and her daughters either but the words would only cause pain if spoken aloud.

'Goodbye,' she said simply instead.

Aggie was already below deck and, with Frankie and Patrick now gone, there was nothing for it but for Fiona to make her way back to the shack with the girls – three lone figures headed towards a broken-down dwelling, looking to lead broken-down lives.

Ivy dragged her gaze away and went downstairs. Aggie had already dozed off again in the chair and Ivy looked at her fondly, then around at the cabin that had seen so much over the past few days. She ran her hand across the bunk bed where she'd feared for her life more than once. A life she'd never take for granted again. It was then she noticed a dress in the corner, Fiona's, and she picked it up. Dresses were precious commodities up here, as Ivy had just witnessed, and Riley's sister had been generous to lend it to her. It would have to be returned for she'd need it soon enough.

Ivy went upstairs and looked over to Riley, who was busy drawing up the anchor. That would take a few minutes so rather than disturb him she carefully climbed over the side and made her way to shore. It was exerting but she had enough strength for this, she felt, especially considering how much Fiona had done for her. The twins were checking for eggs over at the coop and didn't notice her either so she could just slip in.

'Hello?' Ivy said, pushing open the door. 'Sorry, Fiona, I forgot I still had this—' but the words were halted by the sight before her. Fiona was getting changed, her back bare as she gingerly pulled the dress away, and Ivy stared in shock at the black-and-blue bruises across it. Fiona had turned at the sound but too late to cover herself and her eyes flew to Ivy's in terror.

'Fiona …?' Ivy said, looking in horror as she glimpsed bruises across her pregnant stomach and breasts too.

Fiona drew up her dress slowly with shaking fingers and her chin trembled as she spoke.

'Don't tell Riley.'

'But … but I …'

'Don't tell Riley, Ivy, please,' she pleaded, her eyes glittering with unshed tears. 'He'll kill him.'

Riley's voice sounded, traced with worry as he called Ivy's name.

'If George dies and Riley goes to gaol we'll have nothing at all and the twins could well starve,' Fiona whispered. 'This is a better fate than that.'

'*Ivy*,' Riley called.

'Go,' Fiona said. 'Go and forget you ever saw.'

Ivy backed away, stumbling in shock across the rocky beach as Riley jumped over the boat's side.

'What are you doing over there?' he said as he quickly approached. 'You're not well enough for that, for God's sake.' he said, coming to pick her up. She wrapped her arms around his neck as she'd done so many times now, burying her face against the warm comfort of him, as he gently got her back on board.

It was all she could do not to weep and beg him to fetch Fiona and the girls too but his sister stood at the doorway watching, her stance rigid with fear, and Ivy knew that it wasn't her choice to make.

And so the boat drew away, leaving Fiona to her wretched life. To her version of a better fate.

Part Four

Empty arms

Twenty-Four

Sydney University, March 1902

We want the right to vote.
We want the right to vote.

The refrain rang out across the university campus as they set off as one towards the city centre, only a few hundred strong but more would follow and join in until their numbers hopefully swelled to the point that office workers and passers-by would take notice. Certainly their voices were loud enough to draw attention and the vehemence of the impassioned women who marched made Ivy feel simultaneously impressed and intimidated. It was wonderful to be here, doing something for the Cause for the first time, but a bit frightening too. These women meant business and there was volatility in the air.

Frankie was in her element, of course, striding along with Aggie, and the three sisters held a placard that read 'Australia needs a mother'. It had been Barney's idea, surprisingly, and Ivy found the sentiment a simple and beautiful one, if bittersweet for poor Aggie. She carried it proudly though, chanting loudly with

Frankie and the others, a smile on her lips as she looked across at Ivy. Their own mother, Harriet, was on Ivy's other side, holding her arm protectively, still hovering over her youngest daughter even though she'd been home these past two months and had long recovered.

Yet that was a mother's lot: to worry and protect, and sometimes love to the point of self-sacrifice or suffering. Ivy knew it to be true now, sadly. This country needed womankind to have a voice, like one all-encompassing maternal figure. It needed that power so that they could change the way things were, for people like Fiona and her daughters. For them all.

She raised her chin high as they walked, chanting loudly too, before noticing Patrick waving from a classroom window as they passed. Nick Johnson and Greg King were there too, and they cheered the women on and clapped, which warmed Ivy's heart. There was hope in the support of these young men, a unification of the sexes that was their best chance to win the vote, and surely that would be soon. For every day counted to Ivy, now that she understood how precious being healthy and safe truly was, and how soul-destroying it was to live otherwise.

On and on they marched until they reached Town Hall where one woman stood upon the top step and read a fresh report aloud. Vida Goldstein was in America and had recently become the first Australian to visit the White House and meet the president in the Oval Room. It was remarkable and inspirational and Ivy hung on every word along with the rest of the crowd as the news sailed over George Street, history unfolding.

'The president is reported to have jumped up when Vida entered and he shook her hand with great enthusiasm saying: "I'm delighted to meet you. You're from Australia. I'm delighted to hear that".' She paused as spontaneous applause broke out before continuing. 'The president went on speak highly of the Australian people and how much he'd admired those he'd met during the Spanish–American war but said he was just as impressed by the fighting spirit of Australian women.' This received a great reaction from the crowd and the woman had to hold her hand up for a while to calm them down, although she was smiling too.

'Apparently the president is sympathetic to the Cause and very impressed with the inroads we have made. We are about to be the *first in the world* to have women able to stand for parliament and we're also poised for that next great leap: the female vote. His exact words to Vida were "I've got my eye on you down there in Australia".'

The crowd exploded with enthusiastic cheers and a band struck up the tune that had become their anthem.

Daughters of freedom, the truth marches on,
Yield not the battle till ye have won!

Ivy sang along with the rest, tears in her eyes as she linked arms with her sisters and mother. Please God, let it hurry and come to pass, but until then let her new plan to do what she could for Fiona and the girls find success that weekend. They may well be only three of the countless subjugated women who lived in that male-dominated river world, but they were three she knew. And helping them was one step Ivy could take towards a life that mattered.

Patrick had been impatient to see Ivy but when her whole family turned up at the restaurant for lunch after the rally it made him reconsider what he'd been planning to say. He'd been hoping to arrange the perfect romantic evening for Saturday night but it would be rather tricky with her sisters and mother listening in, and now her father and Robert were arriving too. Why not just invite the entire cricket team as well, he silently lamented, shaking his head as Nick and Greg did, indeed, walk in.

'Thought you were headed back home,' Patrick said.

'Ivy just saw us on the way to the train and invited us along,' Nick said, appearing very pleased about that.

'Well, this makes a party of things,' Frankie said, looking around at the widening throng.

'With everyone in town on the same day we decided to make this lunch a surprise for your birthday. A bit belated, but still,' Ivy said, smiling up at Frankie happily as she took her seat. No-one had felt much like celebrating another birthday so soon after the catastrophe of Ivy's picnic but her family had obviously made the spontaneous decision that today was the day. Patrick couldn't really begrudge her that as Frankie gaped at them all, obviously stunned.

'Aren't you going to say something?' Ivy said, giggling at her sister's response.

'I … I just, well, yes. How bloody marvellous!' she said with a wide grin.

A few other restaurant patrons gasped and muttered, a table of stuffy-looking gentleman drinking whisky nearby looking over at her in disdain.

'I say.'

'Not in public dear,' her mother muttered, but Nick and Greg just chuckled and Patrick had become so used to her impropriety by now it certainly didn't offend him, although he was glad his parents weren't here. The Merriweather family was becoming a hard sell to them these days as potential in-laws as it was.

Nick took a seat near Frankie, beating a disappointed-looking Greg. Frankie had been a hot topic of discussion between the two on the recent interstate cricket tour, irritatingly so at times.

Patrick knew both of them were keener than ever to gain her favour. She really did look very fetching as she took off her hat, Patrick had to admit, strands of blonde hair escaping from their pins and falling about her flushed, pretty face. She caught him staring and he felt immediately self-conscious, drawing his attention firmly back to where it should be: Ivy.

She looked gorgeous as well, of course, resplendent in a blue dress and green hat with sapphire satin ribbon about the rim.

'Blue and green today?' he queried as she took off her hat too and laid it aside, her red curls brilliant against the bright hue of the dress.

'Yes,' she said, brushing her hair back and touching the faint scar that lay at her temple lightly. 'I thought … well, I thought I'd wear the colours of the river.'

She didn't elaborate further but he could hazard a few guesses at the connection. Ivy had seen far more than he would have ever wished on her up there but, he supposed, in a way, having more of a conscience towards the poorer classes was a good lesson to learn. It had certainly affected him far more than he ever would have expected. Still, he didn't want to focus on such things today. He simply wanted to enjoy spending time with her and basking in her lovely, gentle personality. There'd been enough drama to last them all an age.

'You look very pretty,' he told her and her dimpled smile was quite a reward.

'So, tell me about the march,' Albert said as drinks were ordered and menus passed around. 'I was a bit too late to catch the end, unfortunately.'

'That Vida Goldstein,' Harriet said, 'honestly, if we ever have a female prime minister it really should be her.'

Nick made the unfortunate mistake of laughing, earning raised eyebrows from Frankie.

'Disagree, do you?'

'Oh, er … not at all. I just thought it was a joke.'

'And why would you think that?' Harriet asked.

'Well, I mean, don't get me wrong, I believe women should have the vote and all but I think one of you ever becoming prime minister is … unlikely.'

'Unlikely, perhaps, impossible, most certainly not,' Harriet told him and a few of the men at the table nearby audibly scoffed. Patrick groaned. It seemed this lunch was destined to have at least a few dramas, after all.

'I think perhaps I might have the beef,' Patrick said, intervening as smoothly as he could and the conversation was steered to the menu for the time being, although he suspected it would be short-lived. Sure enough it returned to Vida and her remarkable successes in America by the time the food arrived.

'Just imagine that: the very first Australian invited to the White House and it's a woman,' Greg said. 'Who would ever have thought such a thing.' Frankie opened her mouth to speak but he cut her off quickly, obviously recognising his mistake. 'Not that it's unimaginable … I mean it's great. Good on her,' he finished rather lamely and Ivy smiled over at him.

'Yes, good on her, indeed,' she said kindly and Patrick's heart swelled at how sweet she always was.

'I should think so,' Frankie said. 'It isn't every day that the President of the United States says he has his eye on the remarkable work of Australian women to one of our finest ambassadors – and in person no less, all the way on the other side of the world.'

'I don't think he actually said "remarkable work" but yes, it is amazing how he's recognised our efforts and singled her out,' Aggie said.

'It is remarkable,' Nick said. Frankie smiled at him for that comment and so he continued on, encouraged. 'A pity she'll have to give it all away when she marries.'

Patrick would have kicked him under the table if he could have reached but he was forced to try to fix that inflammatory comment with words instead.

'Completely unfair,' he agreed. 'Although perhaps she won't choose to marry. I've heard it said she's turned down several offers in favour of her work for the Cause.'

'She shouldn't have to marry *or* give her work away if she did. It's a disgusting state of affairs,' Frankie blustered. There were more glares and mutterings from the next table at her strident words.

'But surely …' Greg began. 'Oh, I suppose I'm just going to say the wrong thing again here, but if women all stop getting married and having children then that's an end to society. Actually, an end to the whole human race … isn't it?'

'Humph,' Frankie said but Ivy was kind once more.

'I don't think *most* women don't want marriage and children, just a few choose not to, which is up to them, I'd say. The majority of us still want to have families and homes so I don't think the human race is doomed quite yet.' Her father looked impressed at her short speech and her mother and Aggie were nodding with approval, but Frankie harrumphed again.

'I bloody won't be,' she asserted in a loud voice. 'Just let a man try to tell me what to do the rest of my days.'

Nick looked at her, shocked and crestfallen. 'You mean … you'll never even consider it?'

'Not in a million years,' she stated firmly.

'Just as well,' muttered one of the men at the table nearby and Nick turned towards him immediately.

'I beg your pardon?'

The man looked over at Frankie with disdain as he held his whisky aloft. 'I'm afraid, madam, you overestimate your charms if you think gentlemen would be lining up to marry a mannish bluestocking such as yourself.'

The other men at his table laughed but Nick stood up. 'How dare you address her so?'

'I dare as I please because I'm a gentleman myself and I have an obligation to protect our way of life,' he said loftily. 'I dread to think what would happen if harridans such as this young woman here were given any real power.'

'Harridan …?' Ivy gasped. The rest of the men in their party stood as one as the waiter lurked nervously by, but Patrick found himself moving in front of the offensive man first, and his blood was up.

'I think you owe this young lady an apology,' he said, heart racing hard in fury.

'Lady?' he scoffed. 'You use that word loosely.'

Patrick's fist curled but Frankie took over.

'And you, sir, are no gentleman.' She stood too, jaw raised in fury. 'In what terrible ways do you suppose we would alter your way of life if we were given the vote and held sway?'

The restaurant had stilled now and men and women alike watched the exchange. Patrick still itched to punch the arrogant man in the nose but Frankie was handling things with far more cool so he restrained himself and watched her go.

'You'd have us give away all the simple pleasures, for a start,' the man began, still slouched in his chair and nodding at his whisky.

'Not all feminists are interested in temperance,' she replied, lifting her own glass of wine. 'If an individual can hold their drink I see no harm in it. Go on, what else?' Frankie had him pinned with her flashing blue eyes and Patrick almost pitied the man now.

He shrugged. 'You'd disturb the natural order of things and take women out of the home. Infants can't care for themselves.'

'There's no reason why a woman can't work and be a mother too, especially once the children go to school. What other objections have you, then?'

The man sneered and Patrick suspected he was running out of ideas. 'My dear *lady*, when will you feminists accept that women simply don't have the mental capacity for rational thought as do men? We cannot have the laws of this country based on the emotional and sentimental rhetoric of the weaker sex.'

A few members of his party nodded at that. 'Hear, hear,' said one, but the rest of the room seemed to eagerly await what Frankie would say next.

'On the contrary, *sir*, emotion and sentiment underscore the very fabric of all decent society, and if you're suggesting women are stronger in these areas so be it. I'll take it as a compliment on our behalf, for without it there can be no compassion and no love for our fellow man, or woman,' she added. 'All Australians deserve to be protected and looked after in this new nation: men, women, rich and poor. And every single one of them deserves the right to vote and make this a country to be proud of … an Australia that cares.'

Ivy stood then, tears forming as she began to clap and it caught on around the room as women and, indeed, even a few men, stood and applauded Frankie's words. She looked around in surprise as their own table joined in, her parents and Aggie beaming at her with pride. But it was Patrick's eyes she sought as the arrogant party of men slunk out from the restaurant and, even though he couldn't fathom why she had looked for his reaction above all, it moved him that she did. More than it probably should.

Twenty-Five

Bobbin Head

It was a still morning and the river shone like polished glass. Ivy stared out at it thoughtfully, her sketchbook open as she traced a likeness of a wallaby, grazing nearby with a few others, her little joey peeking out and watching Ivy with interest. She worked in plain lead pencil, immersing herself in the process, hoping that it would calm her as it usually did, but it was a challenge. The occasional vessel arriving was an immediate and nerve-racking distraction but Riley Logan's boat was yet to appear. She wondered if Barney had delivered her note, considering his track record, but surely he would remember this time. She hoped, anyway.

Ivy wasn't sure which aspect of the day was making her the most nervous although returning here, just a bend in the river away from the scene of her ill-fated birthday, was certainly part of it. This area had a haunted feel about it now but even so it was a beautiful place, Ivy reflected, staring around at the hazy hillsides that glowed in warm autumn sunshine and slept in shadowed recesses in turn. The pelicans that sat upon the mooring poles were sweet too, even if trying to pat one wasn't a good idea, she thought with a smile, recalling the story Frankie had told her of being defecated upon.

The sound of an approaching boat lurched her stomach but it was a false alarm, just a small fishing trawler. Not Riley arriving at last. However, the knowledge that he would likely show soon forced her to admit that the largest part of her nerves centred on seeing him. Ivy didn't like facing that truth. It felt disloyal to Patrick to admit she'd missed Riley these past two months but she had, and that didn't mean she didn't still love Patrick, for she did. How could she not when he was such a handsome, attentive, intelligent man, and so good to her, coming to her side when she was in crisis, and brave too, fighting those men who'd attacked Frankie. He'd become part of the family now and she knew he would propose soon and she'd of course accept, and he'd prove to be a faithful and supportive husband.

There was no question she was in love with him but the niggling question also remained of why she missed Riley so. And why he so often came to mind.

Ivy put her pencil aside and stared at the bend in the river where his boat might soon appear, trying to understand what it was she had so missed. She missed the comfort of him, she supposed, his ever-dependable presence. Ivy had never felt so safe as when she was with him. She missed his smile too, and the way he looked when he confessed his deepest truths, like he trusted her implicitly, and maybe even more than that. Maybe that he'd grown to care for her too.

Perhaps it was merely that he'd rescued her so she had a developed a case of hero worship, but whatever it was she wished she didn't feel it. It was confusing and it wasn't fair to Patrick to even be considering such things. To be thinking about the words Riley had never spoken but had been written there all too clearly whenever she'd caught his gaze. In the gentle way he'd carried her. In the touch of the cloth as he'd soothed her skin. Ivy shook her head, banishing those last thoughts especially, knowing she shouldn't be seeing him again, but she had to. For Fiona's sake.

Another rumbling engine approached and she watched the spot as Riley's boat appeared at last. Ivy's heart leapt but she refused to acknowledge any further feelings, focusing on why she'd come instead. She stood as he edged closer to shore, trying not to notice how masculine he seemed as he moved about the boat, throwing ropes and dropping anchor. How welcome it was to see his smile. Such silly, romantic notions, she admonished herself, but she felt flustered as he waded over, just the same.

'Well, hello there,' he said, hands on his hips as he stopped before her, ankle deep in the water, pants rolled to the knee. 'You're looking very well.'

Ivy almost took that for flirtatious but then remembered the last time he'd seen her.

'Oh, yes, quite recovered. Just a small scar to remind me of my folly,' she said, lifting her hat so he could see it. He came closer to investigate and she sucked in her breath as he touched it lightly.

'No-one would notice, I don't think,' he said and Ivy nodded, feeling rather giddy and ridiculous as he smiled down at her.

'Hopefully not,' she said.

'Is that your sketchbook?' he said. She'd quite forgotten she still held it. 'May I?'

Ivy handed it to him and he flicked through with interest. 'You're really good,' he said. 'Seriously. I love this one,' he said, pausing at the one she'd just been doing of the wallaby.

'You … you can have it if you want,' she said, trying not to feel too elated that he liked them.

'Really? I mean, if you don't mind … thanks,' he said, grinning at her.

'I have some other things too,' she said, turning away to fetch what she'd brought, and begin explaining why she'd asked him to meet her. She had rehearsed in case she inadvertently revealed the truth about George beating Fiona. Yet it was difficult now that he was here and she'd had so long to fear for her.

'Barney told me Fiona had another little girl,' Ivy began.

'Yes, the girls wanted to call her Mermaid but Fiona's settled on Ivy.'

That halted Ivy in her tracks, especially the fond way he'd said it, and she had to swallow against sudden emotion before commenting.

'That's … so kind,' she managed. 'I've brought her some things, she and the girls. I thought it was the very least I could do. Just some material and books and toys, and some clothes and extra things for the baby.'

'I won't pretend to know what half that stuff is for but thank you. I'm sure they'll love everything,' he said, peering into the large box of supplies and scratching his head. 'If I can fit it on board. How did you get it down here?' he said, looking around.

'Barney helped me,' she said. 'I tied my horse to the back of the wagon so I'll just ride home.'

'Right,' he said, looking over at Shadow. 'Nice mount.'

'He's a good boy,' she told him, preparing to say the rest. 'Riley, do you remember when you told me about the idea of building a store up the river, one that sold things people could afford?' He nodded so she continued. 'Well, I was thinking that I could help you with it, I mean financially, if you added an extra room or two out the back.'

'What do you want them for? Planning on moving in?' he asked quite lightly, but he was watching her intensely now.

'I want to open a school.'

That surprised him. 'A school?'

'Yes. I'm planning to earn my teachers' licence and run a small school. To do something in life that matters, remember? And I was thinking that perhaps Fiona could help me run it, and the store with you. The girls could go to the school and we could all watch the baby.'

'Not sure if George would allow that,' Riley said. Ivy didn't tell him that was the most important part of her plan: to get Fiona away from George as much as possible. She couldn't help her to actually leave him. Husbands could take children away from their mother legally and at any time, and spousal desertion would certainly be grounds for George to do something that cruel. However, being at the school and store would mean Fiona had a lot of time away from his presence, which was something, at least. Not an end to his beatings, of course, but potentially less time to inflict them. It also would mean the girls got an education and the family had more access to supplies and fresh food. In all, a step up from their current difficult lives.

'He might if he could see the benefit of more food on the table and more access to supplies,' Ivy pointed out.

'True,' Riley said.

'I also thought … well, I thought it might be nice for you, fulfilling your dream and all,' she added and he smiled at her and rubbed his neck.

'Trying to help everyone have better lives in one fell swoop, I see,' he said.

'That's pretty much the plan,' she admitted. 'What do you think?'

'I think you and I have been thinking about the same things,' he told her. 'I've already got the land and started building.'

Ivy gaped at him before letting out an incredulous laugh. 'Truly?'

'Yep. Want to come and see?'

'I … yes, of course. When?'

'How about right now? It's only an hour and a bit upriver.'

Ivy checked at her watch and shook her head. 'Oh no, I'll be out too late and I have dinner reservations,' she said, remembering somewhat guiltily that she had plans to dine with Patrick that night. Perhaps she shouldn't be organising to go out on Riley's boat, but this was hardly a date. 'What if we went another day? Say next week sometime?'

'How's Tuesday?' he suggested. 'I was only planning on a large front room for the store and living area out the back but we could certainly expand on that easily enough. It's a good block, nice and flat and high enough to avoid the king tides and floods.'

'Does it flood much up there?'

'All the time,' he said. 'Surprised it didn't flood when you were there. Every other disaster seemed to happen.'

'I'll pack my umbrella, just in case.'

He grinned at her. 'Might be an idea. Right you are. I'll pick you up here at, say, ten in the morning?'

'Sounds perfect,' she said and stood back for him to place the drawing in the box and lift it up to load it onto the boat.

'Bloody hell, how much do baby things weigh?' he commented and she had to giggle. Soon they were on board, however, and Riley came back to shore. 'So I'd best be off. See you on Tuesday, ten o'clock, then?'

She nodded. 'I'll be then one standing under enormous rain-clouds holding an umbrella.'

He chuckled at that, backing away. 'It was good to see you.' He tipped his hat, his last look lingering as he started the boat and drove away before disappearing around the river's bend a minute or so later.

Ivy watched the *Hawkesbury Queen* until it had gone.

'It was good to see you too.'

Patrick couldn't seem to stop fidgeting and Ivy wondered again at his strange mood.

'How were classes today?' she asked, trying to make conversation.

'Hmm? Oh yes, fine, fine. Bit boring but, you know, that's law for you.'

He was twiddling with his fork and looking over at the door to the kitchen repeatedly, prompting her to ask, 'Patrick, what on earth's the matter?'

'Nothing,' he said quickly, sending her a reassuring smile. 'Not a thing. How was your day, anyway? Do anything interesting at all?'

'Actually, I did do something I'd been meaning to do for a while. I made up some gifts for Fiona and her children. Did I tell you she had the baby? A little girl. Called her Ivy, in fact. Isn't that so sweet?'

'It certainly is,' he said, taking her fingers in his own, 'the sweetest name of all.'

'I meant sweet of her,' she replied but she was blushing now.

'How will you get them to her? The gifts, I mean?' Patrick asked.

'I sent word and met up with Riley Logan down at Bobbin Head. They've probably already got them, in fact. Barney helped me get them down the track.'

Patrick frowned and withdrew his hand to sip his wine. 'I don't really think you should have anything more to do with the people you met up the river. I mean, sending gifts is one thing, but keeping in touch or going up there to see them wouldn't be a good idea.'

'Why ever not?' Ivy said. 'They took very good care of me and it's the least I can do.'

'Because it isn't safe, Ivy. You nearly died, for a start.'

'That's hardly the river's fault or the people—'

'And you nearly got attacked by drunk and dangerous men. Frankie and I *did* get attacked, as you know. It's no place for a beautiful young woman, Ivy. I won't allow it.'

'Allow …?' That word clogged in her throat and she glared at him. 'Excuse me, but I am not your … your *servant* to allow or disallow anything.'

'Of course, of course. Allow isn't the right word, I'm sorry,' he said, immediately contrite as he took her hand once more but his eyes still kept flicking to the kitchen.

'You don't seem very sorry,' she observed.

Patrick shook his head and gave her his full attention. 'I am, truly. I don't know why I put it that way. I guess it's a phrase I picked up from my father and it just … came out. I really meant that I don't want you to go. I'd be so worried if you were in danger again. Quite honestly I don't know if I could survive it twice, the fear of losing you.'

That softened her somewhat but she was still annoyed, possibly due to fact that he was right in many ways – it wasn't somewhere she should go to again, but if Riley was with her she knew she wouldn't be afraid. Not that she would be telling Patrick about her plans for Tuesday's jaunt, especially now, and it was suddenly clear that he would definitely be against her much larger plan to become a teacher and open a school up there. Not that he could stop her … unless …

'I understand,' she said, smiling a little now and deciding she'd better sound him out, partially at least. 'I did have something else I wanted to talk to you about. I … I've been thinking about studying.'

'Well, that's an excellent idea. What do you want to study? Art?'

'Actually, teaching.'

'You want to be a teacher?' he said, jaw dropping.

'Yes, I thought it would suit me. I love children and … whatever's wrong?'

'It's just that, well, I'm not sure you're aware but … married women aren't allowed to teach.'

'What?' She didn't know what to be more stunned about, that fact, which she indeed *hadn't* known, or the fact that he'd just suggested marriage. Or the fact that a waiter was walking out of the kitchen carrying a cake with candles and heading their way while a man playing Mozart on a fiddle seemed to be doing the same. The cake was placed before them, a ring box open at the centre containing a large diamond ring and Patrick looked a bit sick as he got down on one knee before her.

'Ivy Merriweather, will you do me the honour of becoming my wife?'

It was the moment she'd longed for and dreamed of until more recent, confusing times, never imagining she'd have any reason to even consider saying 'no', and his timing couldn't have been worse, proposing in the middle of their first-ever disagreement. Yet, looking into his handsome face and remembering how much she loved him, there was really only one answer to give.

'Yes,' she whispered, before clearing her throat and accepting more clearly. 'Yes, Patrick, I will marry you.'

Patrick gave a huge smile of relief as the rest of the restaurant patrons broke into spontaneous applause. The waiter and the fiddle player beamed but, as he rose to kiss her lips for the first time since her birthday, Ivy couldn't help but wonder what she was losing by gaining a husband, and what would matter in her life from now on.

Twenty-Six

'You won't be able to work here any more if you do this, you understand,' Sister Ursula said in her stern, intimidating way. 'Father Brown has turned a blind eye to the fact that you're married but he won't let you continue on as a mother who should be at home.'

'I do understand that,' Aggie told her, 'although I hope to still be able to help out from time to time, as the other mothers do.'

'Of course,' Sister Ursula said, 'that would be quite acceptable should you choose to do so. We will certainly miss your skills, I've no doubt.' That was quite a compliment coming from the nun and Aggie attempted a smile.

'Thank you, sister. So, how long do these things usually take?'

'Well, it depends on which child you choose and what Father has to say about things. You will need his approval, legalities aside.' She said it in a matter-of-a-fact way but there was an underlying edge of resentment there.

'Does that happen very often?' Aggie would have thought any parents willing to adopt would find it easy to do so. It wasn't a common occurrence.

'Not often, no,' Sister Ursula said, staring out the window with a sigh. 'I suppose now that you're leaving I can tell you that Eddie was offered a place with a childless couple out at Windsor last month but Father put a stop to it.'

'Why?' Aggie said, devastated for poor Eddie.

Sister Ursula sent her a glance. 'He said he didn't deserve the opportunity.'

'Oh no,' Aggie said, heart breaking for him.

'He won't be likely to have any more opportunities at ten years old,' Sister Ursula said, watching the children as they ran out for recess, Eddie leading the way. 'He would have enjoyed it, I think. They have a mill and a few a good milking cows …' She drifted off then pulled herself back to her senses. 'Anyway, what's done is done. You'll need to make your choice and we'll see what he says.'

'Of course,' Aggie said. 'I'll discuss things with my husband, he knows so many of the children already too.' She wondered how they'd ever choose. 'It will be a very difficult decision, I'm afraid.'

'Indeed,' Sister Ursula said, gazing out at the children once more. 'I don't know if I could ever decide myself.'

Aggie looked at the older woman, her face drawn with hardship beneath her habit, and wondered at the other choices she'd made in life, especially in taking up a religious vocation. To choose never to marry or have children for freedom and autonomy like Frankie was one thing, but to abstain because of God seemed extraordinary to Aggie.

'It's one of those times in life when you stand at a crossroads, I suppose, but sooner or later you have to choose a path,' Aggie reflected.

'Yes,' Sister Ursula said. 'I will pray for God to guide you, Aggie. Perhaps He will make this decision for you, somehow.'

Aggie wondered at that but as the nun said no more she considered herself excused and walked out, slowly coming to terms with the fact that she would soon have to make up her mind; with or without God's help. The decision seemed almost an impossible one. How to choose between children like baby Annabel or the irascible Eddie, if indeed she could get Father to allow it? How to favour one orphan over another?

It was overwhelming but Aggie was determined to do it. Since Ivy's return they all seemed to have been re-evaluating their lives. For Ivy's part it was marriage to Patrick and Aggie couldn't have been more pleased for her sister at that wonderful news when she'd told her that morning. He'd proven himself a loyal and good man and it would be a happy afternoon at Kuranda as they celebrated later that day.

Frankie had been much encouraged by the positive reception she'd received when she'd given her impromptu speech and was now talking about running for parliament once the federal bill was officially passed, which was bound to be soon, gauging by the papers.

And so Aggie had made a choice of her own: to be a mother after all. To fill her empty, aching arms with a parentless child, and to love and care for them with her entire being. It was finally really going to happen and she couldn't wait to tell Robert the news that Sister Ursula had given her approval for the process to start.

This New Year may have begun in turmoil but, two months on, all three Merriweather sisters were moving towards brighter futures, and on their own terms. Each following their own water, as Ivy and their father liked to say. For life seemed far briefer and more precious than it had before. The opportunity to embrace whatever happiness you could was too valuable a thing to ever squander. To give a child a loving family seemed the most logical path to take in the world, especially when they'd all come so close to losing one of their own.

'To the happy couple,' Albert toasted and glasses were raised all round.

'The happy couple,' they all echoed and Frankie joined them, trying to ignore the inner turmoil she felt at the news. She'd expected it, of course, they all had, even Patrick's mother, although she looked like she'd been sucking on lemons all afternoon, so pursed were her disapproving lips. Ivy would win her around though, Frankie was sure. She always managed to charm her way through life.

'For they are jolly good fellows,' John Hunter began to sing and they all joined in. Patrick and Ivy smiled, slightly embarrassed but obviously pleased too as the song eventually concluded.

Her sister was glowing, radiant and the picture of health in a new blue-and-white checked dress and matching wide white bonnet. She looked so much a part of the pretty gardens near the main pond at Kuranda that Frankie supposed she could sit for a portrait for a fashion magazine right there and then. Patrick looked handsome standing beside her in his white jacket and navy trousers, completing the overall effect. They truly appeared the ideal couple. Sipping champagne and eating the rather delicious cake Dossie had brought along only added to the picture perfect feel of the afternoon but Frankie was trying not to be too cynical. This was the life Ivy wanted and one Frankie most assuredly did not. *Good luck to them*, she said to herself, taking a large sip of her champagne.

'I think there's a bit of a chill in the air. Perhaps you should put on a shawl, dear,' Dossie was saying to Ivy. Ever since Ivy's accident and illness, Dossie had treated her like some kind of heroine in the tale of Dossie's own hypochondriac life. That there was someone to fuss over meant she could offer endless advice and quote Dr Pratt whenever possible, having attributed Ivy's 'miraculous healing' to the man. That the doctor had been elevated to Jesus-like status had Frankie rolling her eyes as Dossie added, 'The doctor said you must keep an even temperature at all times. You don't want to risk the shaking fever twice, you've been blessed as it is and no mistake.'

Frankie looked at her mother, expecting a smirk, but Harriet merely looked worried. It still hadn't quite left her, that haunted look, but hopefully it would with time, especially if good news kept arriving. Looking over at Aggie's animated face as she whispered near the citrus trees with Robert, Frankie hoped there was perhaps there was more on the way and she prayed for that miracle to occur above all.

'Whatcha doin'?' Pretty Boy asked Frankie, his head cocked at a quizzical angle as he sat on the back of the bench nearby, and Albert chuckled, wandering over to her side.

'Yes, what are you doing? You've been unusually quiet today.' Her father had recovered from Ivy's ordeal quite well by now, although his illness had lasted a good month after she'd come home and he'd had to keep his distance from her. But as much as Harriet looked constantly concerned, Albert had had a reflective air about him as he came to terms with the shock of nearly losing his darling Ivy.

Frankie shrugged. 'Oh, nothing. I'm just a bit tired really. Sat up half the night trying to finish that article on enfranchisement.'

'Douglas says they expect it could pass within the next month or two,' Albert muttered, glancing over his shoulder at the man, 'but don't let on I told you.'

Frankie broke into a grin. 'That's good to hear. He wouldn't be saying it lightly.'

'No, indeed. You'll have the federal vote before summer comes, I'd say, then the real fun begins.'

'How so?' she said, taking a forkful of cake.

'Well, it's a bit like a wedding, really. People focus a bit too much on the celebration and not quite enough on the marriage itself.' He paused and Frankie wondered if he was really using a metaphor or making a pointed comment as he looked over at Ivy and Patrick, but then he continued. 'There's been so much focus on women getting the vote that there doesn't seem to be much planning as to precisely what laws they want to challenge or who they want to vote for to achieve that end.'

'We want to challenge any laws that discriminate and vote for whoever supports that,' Frankie said. 'It seems rather straightforward to me.'

Albert sipped his champagne. 'If there's one thing I've learned about politics it's that nothing is ever straightforward. If they can find a way to make the process more complicated and convoluted they will, unless they see something in it for themselves,' Albert pointed out. 'Men will still be voting too, Frankie, and there are many who fear change. Don't expect too much in these early days, is all I'm saying, and remember to keep on reading everything you can about politicians if you seriously want to take them on.'

'I have been,' she said.

'Not just the laws and suggested reforms,' he explained. 'I mean read the men themselves. You're an astute judge of character and good at thinking on your feet, Frankie, but you need to understand why men *won't* want change, more than why women do.'

'Some men want change,' she said, looking over at Patrick. 'Some want to move forwards and take a chance on new beginnings.'

'Yes, when the change is welcome and expected. It's the unexpected that people don't like ... but life will hand you those sometimes.' Albert paused to watch a dragonfly land on one of the pond's lilies. 'Ah, a *Hemicordulia tau*. You're late to the ponds, young lady.'

He wandered off to watch the dragonfly and smoke his pipe, and Frankie pondered his words. It was true that men would resist changes to the law, they already were, of course, and her altercation with that horrid man at the restaurant illustrated just how many would view her: a harridan and a bluestocking, wanting to stop men from drinking and running their lives as they pleased. Trying to take women out of the home and tipping the balance of power away from their traditional male control.

Frankie looked at the happy couple once more, thinking there was nothing wrong with a woman wanting to be in the home as long as the man treated her as an equal, and as long as she could leave that home to make her mark in the world as she pleased. Their own mother was proof of that. It really came down to who you chose to marry and Frankie had to admit that Patrick had surprised her these past few months.

Despite his stuffy upbringing he'd accepted Frankie's criticisms and he'd been openly admiring of her passion for the Cause more than a few times now. Perhaps he'd keep on surprising her and make his own efforts towards real change.

Watching him now, however, she saw a man acting as was expected of him as he claimed the hand of her beautiful little sister who had long adored him. Yet there was nothing to disapprove of and everything to admire because Frankie now knew he was also capable of facing the unexpected with courage and humility, qualities she greatly esteemed. No, she didn't disapprove of this union, nor of Patrick himself. It was the admission that she didn't want to make that filled her with disapproval as she watched the lovely scene before her.

For there was only one word for what she was feeling and it dragged at her conscience, challenging her passions and all the vows she'd declared. Frankie was jealous of this sister she so loved and that felt horribly unworthy and disloyal, especially when she wanted nothing more than for Ivy to have a happy, healthy, wonderful life. It was everything Frankie could ever have wished for only two months ago, that she would live to see this come to pass, but envy festered today, much to her shame.

Patrick looked down at Ivy and smiled, his arm protective about her waist, and nothing could stop the memory of when his hands had held Frankie's waist that night and the wild ragtime had carried all concerns of the heart and mind away. When he'd been suddenly just a man to her and she'd been alive to that fact, deep to the core, as she stood in his arms. Drugged by something she hadn't known she would ever want when she'd declared an existence devoted only to the Cause. Realising she'd underestimated a very primal part of what it meant to be a woman.

Twenty-Seven

Hawkesbury River

She shouldn't be here. Ivy felt it with every fibre of her being but somehow she was and her stomach fluttered with excitement as Riley whistled away happily, breaking into occasional song as his boat chugged along.

> *Many years have passed since I strolled by the river,*
> *Arm in arm, with sweetheart Mary by my side*

She recognised it as the one he often whistled or sang and the whimsical tune suited the day perfectly – it was pristine, if cool, and the wind whipped at her hat as they went. She held onto it as she gazed about, taking in the little coves and beaches that dotted the shoreline, thinking how many places you could live along here, if life were just that bit easier.

Yet it soon would be, once Riley opened his store and people were closer to affordable supplies and other things they needed, like company. The new road down to Berowra would bring opportunity to them as well and Ivy could already see these isolated residents benefiting from having carriage access as well as a store further along. It would render this area less of a man's world as it drew civilisation together and provided the river dwellers between Hornsby and Wisemans Ferry with something sorely lacking: a community. Ivy had meant it when she'd said she couldn't live here the way it was but knowing that it was changing she wondered. Especially considering that Riley was changing with it.

Ivy tried not to think about the possibilities that came with this new, settled-down version of the man as she watched him work but his words from two months ago tugged at her heart. How he'd never found someone he wanted to build a life like that with, his expression so wistful and bare. It tore at her now, knowing she could never be a part of it, and she knew she'd have to tell him about her engagement to Patrick. How that meant she couldn't become a teacher and share even a portion of that life with him up here, but not yet. Just not yet.

It felt like one last guilty adventure, because even though she'd keep her vow and send Fiona and the girls money and supplies from time to time, she also knew it would be the last time she would actually come here. She couldn't continue to go up the river behind Patrick's back. It was bad enough she was doing it today but she hadn't been able to resist, and after having been engaged only three days, she didn't want to think too hard about the reasons why. She just wanted to enjoy this last hurrah with Riley after everything they'd been through. Surely she owed him that, having encouraged this dream of his in the first place, and surely there was no harm in it, regardless, she reasoned, but the diamond ring lay heavily on her finger inside her day glove.

Ivy decided to make the most of it and find out everything she could about Riley's life, if she couldn't actually be a part of it. Like filling in pages of a mental book she knew she'd revisit again and again in years to come.

'So where exactly was it that you grew up around here?' she said, interrupting his whistling.

'Fair way up,' Riley told her, sitting down at the wheel. 'It's a long river by the time you get all the way to Windsor. My family were oyster farming here before that, just around this corner at Greenman's Valley.'

'Why is it called that?' she said, curious, if a bit distracted by the way he so deftly manoeuvred the vessel.

'Not too sure you'd enjoy that story,' he told her, sending her a doubtful glance.

Ivy tucked her feet in, preparing for the tale. 'Well, now you have to tell it after a comment like that.'

Riley sighed. 'All right, but you can't say I didn't warn you.' He took out his cigarette pouch, balancing the wheel with his knee as he rolled a smoke, much to her fascination. 'It's named after an escaped convict who murdered a woman and her baby.'

'Why would he do such a thing?' she said, immediately horrified.

'I warned you …' he began.

'All right, all right, I'll try to be less shocked by whatever comes next, I promise. Go on.'

'Well,' Riley continued, 'and this next bit is pretty grue-some: he was caught and they sentenced him to die by drowning. They weighted down his body with rocks at low tide and watched till he died. Then they left him tied up with his hands and legs outstretched. No-one untied him and eventually his arms and legs turned green.'

Ivy tried hard to hide her revulsion. 'Oh,' she simply said and he chuckled.

'Sorry, but you really should see the look on your face. Any-way, there is a spooky end to the tale. Many people claim to have seen the ghost of the young mother walking along these shores, holding her baby.'

'Did you ever see it?' Ivy said, eyes round as she stared ahead at the haunted area.

'No, but my old da said he did one night. Swore it blind. He swore he knew the green man too. Apparently they worked together, sandstone quarrying along here for a while. Didn't have a hell of a lot of luck and it was bloody hard work, 'scuse the French. The mills weren't much better. Life was tough all round except for oyster farming, which was a pretty good existence, really. I thought, anyway. I always like to be on the water.'

'Yes, Fiona said that. Said your mother called it the life of Riley when she watched you out there, you looked so happy.'

'Yeah, she did like to say that,' he said, his expression both fond and tinged with sadness at the mention of her. He was silent for a moment and she prodded gently.

'Where did you say they're buried?'

Riley nodded upriver. 'On Bar Island, just further along up here, actually. Mum used to bring us down to attend church there sometimes, although it's closed now. I suppose it's rather a nice spot, as far as cemeteries go. I just wanted her to feel close to God and Dad would have just wanted to have been close to her.'

Ivy watched the emotions flicker across his face, feeling his pain. 'And what about you? Do you believe in God?'

'Not any more,' he said. 'I gave up on the idea when they both went so suddenly … what about you?'

Ivy tilted her head, looking over towards the widening mouth of Berowra Creek as they hit the Hawkesbury proper. 'It's hard not to believe in some kind of creator when the world can look as beautiful as that,' she said, gazing out at the approaching expanse of glittering blue and green water. It lapped against the carpeted hillside of the mainland and the island that sat like a glorious adornment at its centre, perfectly serene in its flow and attracting wildlife like the great artery of lifeblood it was. Wallabies grazed with their young along its shores while a pair of sea eagles soared above, and a school of tailor jumped up ahead, scattering diamond droplets in the sun in their haste to avoid whatever chased them below.

'Life just seems so miraculous to me now, although I suppose I always have seen it that way. There's beauty everywhere if you stop and notice, I think, but especially up here.' With you, she wanted to add, before banishing the disloyal thought, but the lingering knowledge remained that they shared this love, the two of them, each happiest taking in the detailed wonder of their natural environment.

'Funny you should say that at this moment,' he said. 'That's Bar Island, where they're buried.' He nodded over at the island as it rose before them and Ivy lifted her eyes towards its crest. It was like a monument itself.

'It couldn't be more fitting,' she told him.

They moved on in companionable silence after that, each watching the river world pass by and waving as they passed the occasional inhabitants.

'How much further?' she asked.

'Not too far,' he assured her.

'What's the name of it?'

'Well, officially it's around the corner from a place called Spencer near Singleton's Mill. I thought we'd give it our own name though. The School Shop or something?'

Ivy felt her guilt rise once more, knowing she should have told of her change in circumstances sooner, but surely she could steal just a little more time to enjoy this dream before it was gone.

Not twenty minutes later they arrived at a picturesque spot, the timber frame of the structure now clearly visible. It was low tide and the water was the colour of tea where it rippled and ran across the shallows, leaving a wide stretch of wet sand to spread before it in welcome. Ivy remembered Riley mentioning that the river often flooded, however, and sure enough the building sat well back and high above the water level, safe and secure. She was surprised just how much progress he'd made in so short a time. Riley dropped anchor and they waded towards it.

'Why, you've done so much,' she exclaimed. 'You must be close to putting in the walls.'

'Not too far off,' he told her, showing her around with a boyish enthusiasm. 'This is the main shop where we'll run a decent-sized counter, all the way along I think, and I've decided to build a storeroom as well as a living area out back. Might be time for me to stop sleeping among crates of supplies all the time,' he said, turning around to send her a quick grin. 'I haven't started on the schoolroom yet but I was thinking right here, at the rear, with an entry at the side near where the children could play on this grassy bit and down on the beach,' he said, pointing over to a wonderful area that would prove a dream playground should it ever come to pass. 'We'll need a jetty too, but that won't be too hard to make. And well, that's about it so far,' he said, pausing to look over at her nervously. 'What do you think?'

Ivy knew the time had come for the truth but looking at that expression she almost couldn't bear to utter the words, yet she'd been unfair to let him hope all day. She needed to come clean.

'Riley, I need to tell you something and I'm afraid it's going to affect things for you for a while.' His face fell and he looked worried now as she sat on the grass and patted the ground nearby. 'Maybe we should sit for you to hear this.'

Riley sat, looking wary as she began to try to explain without letting him down too fast. 'About this teaching idea, although I truly think you should still build a school here, it can't … it can't involve me.'

Riley stared. 'But it was your idea.'

'I know it was,' she said, feeling wretched, 'but I hadn't considered ... that is ... Riley, I can't become a teacher because it's against the law for married women to teach.'

He looked at her for a long moment. 'When are you planning to get married?'

'Soon,' she admitted, dropping her gaze away to avoid the pain in his eyes. 'Patrick and I got engaged three days ago.'

'Right,' he said and she flinched at the hurt she heard there. 'I see. It's just ... I mean, I just thought when you suggested this that you weren't thinking about marriage and kids right now. What ... whatever happened to all that "a life that matters" stuff you were talking about?'

'I can still live a life that matters, I just can't live it as a teacher ... and I can't live it here.'

'No,' he said. 'I don't suppose you can.'

He stood then and paced about, moving a few bits of timber and pausing every now and then to think. She waited, knowing she'd done the wrong thing by delaying this news and regretting it. She hadn't considered he'd take it so hard but in retrospect perhaps she should have. That there were feelings between them was obvious to him too, she was sure, but it could never be admitted. Especially not now.

'Why didn't you tell me sooner?' he asked after a while and she dragged guilty eyes to his.

And that much of an admission lay silent between them. Because, for a host of reasons she'd never say, the stark truth was she simply hadn't wanted to.

Riley made his way to Fiona's, not even thinking why he did it – his natural inclination was just to be around family. How different he'd felt journeying down the river this morning and how incredible it had been to share that ride to the building site with Ivy, letting her inside his heart once more, telling her things he'd never told a soul. That she'd let that closeness build to such heights only to slam him with the news that she would soon marry and be gone from his life, the wondrous hopeful dreaming of the past few days now dashed for good … it was difficult to fathom why such a kind girl could be so cruel. Yet he'd read the reason in her eyes: she'd wanted that one last day.

As to why he could only really guess. A secret little attraction because he'd rescued her perhaps? Or maybe she was just toying with him for sport. Who knew? That she'd wanted to teach and open the school he well believed, but to think it through so poorly … against the law or not, once a woman married very few he knew ever went to work. Spinsters like Margie down at the inn certainly, but motherhood tied most women to the home and even Riley had known a proposal was on the cards from Patrick, months ago. Riley had just been hoping things had cooled between them and that he stood a chance. He'd been hoping a lot of things, fool that he was.

The trip back to the bay to get her home had been a very different one and they'd barely spoken but she had said a few words that gave him pause before he left her on the shores of Bobbin Head and said goodbye for the last time.

'I know you are probably going to rethink things now but I do want to ask … well, not that I have any right to ask you for anything but, please, Riley,' she beseeched him, 'still get Fiona involved with the store. I worry about her being so isolated and lonely and it would do her so much good to have regular company.'

Her beautiful face had looked up at his, filled with that compassion that had tugged at his heart ever since that moment in the cave, and he'd nodded, hating that she affected him so but moved by her concern too.

'Goodbye, Ivy,' he'd said and turned to leave her, never looking back despite the sorrow in her words as they followed him.

'Goodbye, Riley. If I can ever repay you in any way, you know where I am.'

He knew where she was all right, Riley reflected grimly now. In a rich man's house getting ready to marry another wealthy gentleman, as a lady like her well should. Looking to spend the rest of her days the wife of a lawyer and the mother of his children, then just idle, he supposed, doing whatever mattered in such a world. Ill-suited to have even considered working with poor river children on the banks of the Hawkesbury with the likes of Riley.

Well, he hoped the comforts of such a life kept her satisfied and fulfilled for years to come, Riley thought, moving from heartbroken to just plain angry now.

He was approaching Fiona's place and the girls came out and waved.

'Mum's sick,' Tricia called as soon as he was within earshot.

'Yeah, she can't get up so we're cooking tea,' Annie said. 'Want some eggs, Uncle Riley?'

He wondered if those two ever got tired of eating eggs, especially considering how often they let cracked shells fall into the pan, but he didn't comment, concerned now for Fiona.

Riley dropped anchor and strode to shore, picking up the twins for a quick hug before lowering them to the ground to let them run off to the coop.

'Hello,' he said, peeking through the door.

'Riley,' Fiona said from where she lay with little Ivy. The baby was fast asleep and Riley regretted that he couldn't have a cuddle and let some of this anger over her namesake dissipate but Fiona looked pale and he went to investigate.

'What is it? What's wrong?'

'I'm just a bit exhausted from the baby is all,' Fiona said, 'and I tripped last night and fell over that damn box. The twins keep dragging it out,' she said, gasping as she shifted her back, 'and forget to put it back against the wall.'

The box of gifts from Ivy had proven extremely popular with the girls and they found it hard to resist exploring the contents that still lay within it over and again, especially the toys.

'I'll have to make you some shelves,' Riley said, checking her temperature, but it seemed normal. 'Or we get George to haul his lazy arse home and do something around here for a change.'

'Don't … bother …' she grunted.

'Let me have a look,' he began.

'No,' she said, eyes flying to his. 'I … I don't want to move the baby. Took me an age to get her to sleep.' Little Ivy did look to be out like a light, her perfectly angelic face tiny against Fiona's chest as she dozed. Riley relented, although his old fears over his sister and George niggled.

'Are you sure you don't want me to put her in her cot for you?' The baby's cot was in fact just a wooden crate nearby but it had a soft new blanket, thanks to Ivy's generosity.

'No,' Fiona said, 'leave her here with me.'

'What can I do for you then? What if I take the girls down to the inn for a feed and give you a break? Treat them to something other than eggs?'

'They'll probably still order them,' she said with a slight smile, 'but yes, that would so good of you, if you don't mind. I could really use some peace and quiet.'

'Will George be home tonight?' Riley asked, even though it was always anyone's guess.

'He said he was staying out with … a few mates.' Barney and his brother-in-law had ceased going fishing together these days. Even Barney'd had enough of late nights putting up with George's worsening drinking, especially when he needed to start so early at the orchards. Riley wondered at the identity of these new friends of his brother-in-law, hoping George hadn't started down an even darker road by hobnobbing with the likes of Donovan.

'Will you be all right on your own? Let me fetch you some tea and biscuits or something.'

'That would be lovely, Riley,' she said, closing her eyes. That she'd agreed to that worried Riley even further. Fiona rarely accepted anyone waiting on her. He made the tea and added a few biscuits to a plate, settling them next to her before packing the excited twins on the boat. Then he went back in one last time to check on Fiona before they set off.

'You're sure you'll be right by yourself, Fi? I can stay here if you prefer.'

'No, no, go. A good night's sleep would be heaven itself.' She reached her hand out weakly and he held it for a moment, looking down at his sister and her tiny child with tenderness yet concern. The need to question her further was tempting but she looked so tired he couldn't bring himself to badger her right now. Tomorrow he would though, most definitely. She shouldn't be as worn down as this.

Baby Ivy sighed in her sleep, a tiny contented sound and Riley smiled at them both instead.

'She looks just like you,' he said to Fiona, placing a kiss on his fingertips and touching them to each of their foreheads softy. 'Sleep tight.'

And so Riley left them alone in peace to head up to the inn to get the girls some dinner before docking the *Hawkesbury Queen* around a quiet bend and settling them in below deck. Then he did the only thing left to do of any comfort, sitting back to spend time with his closest companion the river and have a few stiff drinks of his own. To contemplate what life would look like on the morrow, now that all his plans had changed once more. Come what may, one thing was for sure: he'd be keeping Fiona's part in Ivy's plan alive, fulfilling the last favour she'd ever asked of him. The more he could get his sister and nieces away from George and over at the new store, the better, especially if George had begun running with Donovan and the rest. It was one thing to worry about one drunken husband, quite another that she be exposed to a whole brutal gang.

Twenty-Eight

'Riley! Riley! There he is …'

'Thank God. Riley!'

Riley awoke to the cries a little groggy. Not because he was hungover from the few drinks he'd had last night, but because of the poor sleep he'd endured, worrying about Fiona and brooding over Ivy as he dozed in the cabin chair. The twins were still fast asleep, wrapped up in each other's arms in the bunk, and Riley yawned and stretched before going above deck to see who it was calling him. He blinked at Barney and Margie in surprise.

'What is it?'

'We think you'd best go check on Fiona,' Barney said, panting and twisting his hat in his hands as Margie came up behind him. Riley went instantly on alert.

'Why? What's happened?'

'George turned up at the inn last night after you left, drunk with Donovan and those other fools,' Margie told him, still out of breath. 'I told Angus to get them to clear off, which they did, eventually, but …'

'I saw 'em as I passed by for work this morning and somethin' ain't sittin' right,' Barney said. 'They were heading away

257

from Fiona's and in a mighty bloody hurry and George was with 'em too.'

Riley stared, registering what this could mean.

'Why would George leave with them and not stay home after drinking all night?' Margie said, clearly agitated.

'I've been looking for you ever since,' Barney explained, 'then I saw Margie and she told me how drunk they were and that you were here—' Riley suddenly leapt into action, throwing instructions over his shoulder.

'Wake the girls and bring them on your boat, Barney, and Margie too if you can,' he said. 'Fiona wasn't well as it was.'

'What's wrong with her?' Margie said as Barney jumped on board the *Hawksbury Queen*.

'She couldn't get out of bed,' Riley said, cranking the anchor chain. 'Said she tripped over and she was just tired but …'

Margie looked at him worriedly as Barney came up on deck, passing the girls down to her, still half asleep.

'Uncle Riley?' muttered one, but he was throwing fuel in the fire box and preparing to start the boat with alacrity now, cursing himself as a hundred kinds of fool for not staying with Fiona like every instinct had told him to do.

'Follow me as soon as you can,' he said as he moved off, wishing the half-hour journey away so he could get to Fiona's side and find her safe. Please God, let her be safe.

He glanced back at the others as they made their way towards Barney's boat, the twins' faces tired and confused as they clutched Margie's hands. It wrenched at his heart and he drove the boat as hard and as fast as he could to get to their mother, trying not to imagine the worst. Trying to believe George would never let Fiona come to any serious harm and that he'd taken off in a hurry with Donovan and the others for any other reason. To get more whisky from one of their hidden caves. To get in a fight with some of the rough lads up at Windsor for sport. To be in a hurry simply because going fast was a lark.

The trip seemed to take an eternity but finally Fiona's shack came into view and Riley stopped the engine and dropped anchor as rapidly as possible before dragging his legs through the water in a rush to shore, staring at her door, dreading what lay closed behind it.

He pushed it open to the sound of baby Ivy's distressed cries from her makeshift cot and the terrifying sight of Fiona slumped on the bed at an odd angle, her blood staining the sheets in deep pools of crimson. So much. Too much.

Her night rail was torn against her half-naked flesh that was mottled with horrifying bruises, and Riley rushed to her side and turned her over to look into her face, but she was so pale it seemed barely any blood remained inside her. It crusted at her temple, in her hair, down her limp and bruised limbs, pooling between her legs. Her eyes tried to focus on him but one was blackened and so swollen she could barely open it. She managed to say his name, so faint it was little more than a breath.

'Riley.'

'Fiona,' he said, tears beginning to choke him. 'Oh my poor girl.' He looked at her broken form helplessly and could do no more than draw the sheet to cover her with one hand as he gently pushed back her bloodied hair with the other.

'Baby,' she whispered, and he reached over to pick up little Ivy. Her cries receded as he soothed her with one arm, holding Fiona's limp hand with the other, unable to place her in her mother's arms. She could longer seem to hold her.

'Take … my girls …' she said, looking from the baby to his face.

'No,' he said, 'please, don't say it …'

'Take my girls ... to Ivy. They deserve ... a better ... life ... than this.'

'No, you have to stay,' he begged, the tears running down his cheeks. 'We all need you. You can't—' He shook his head. 'You can't not be in this world. You can't.'

'I want ... you to go ... to her too.' She was fading with each word but still fighting to say them. 'I know ... you love ... her.'

'Fi,' he sobbed, as her breathing drew slower and fainter, her gaze resting on her baby.

'Love ... them ... Riley ...'

She stilled, his name her last word as her eyes stared sightlessly and he blinked through his tears in disbelief.

'No,' he said. 'No.'

He ignored the sound of the door opening behind him as he looked at the impossible sight of his sister's now lifeless form.

'Dear God.' Margie's voice carried. 'Keep them outside, Barney.'

She came forward and placed one hand one Riley's shoulder as he dissolved in racking sobs, hugging the baby close. 'She's ...'

'I know, love, I can see,' Margie said, her voice breaking. 'I can see.' She wept with him before leaning forward to close Fiona's eyelids with shaking fingers and offering a short prayer. 'Holy Mary, mother of God, pray for us sinners, now and at the hour of death, Amen.'

But Riley could only weep and hold little Ivy against his heart, as if to pour all the love he felt for his once strong, dependable, supportive sister into her child's tiny body. Fiona. His rock, his family. His closest friend.

'Let me ... let me clean her up before the twins say their good-byes, eh?' Margie asked gently, wiping at her eyes. 'Might be best you tell them, unless you'd rather it came from me.'

He nodded, taking one last look at his sister before standing. He took the baby outside to be met by the sight of the girls standing together, eyes wide as they held hands and waited. Barney stood back a few yards, cap in hand, sending Riley a devastated, sorrowful glance.

'Is Mum still sick?' Tricia asked. Riley went down on one knee before them, clasping the baby close.

'Why are you crying?' Annie said and they looked at him, fearful now.

'Mum has …' he began, but how to tell them? Then he remembered how Fiona had told him the news when their own mother had died, all those years ago. 'She's gone to the angels.'

They stared at him in shock.

'But why do they angels want her all the way up there?' Annie said, as tears began to well.

'We need her here to take care of us,' Tricia said, 'and baby Ivy needs her too. She'll be hungry soon and cry.' Her bottom lip quivered as she began to cry herself.

'Margie will find her some milk, don't worry about that. You need to be strong little mothers for Ivy now,' he said, his voice faltering at the words. 'Feed her and care for her just like Mum did, all right? Make her and the angels all very proud,' he added, barely able to speak now. 'And I'll look after you,' he whispered. 'Always.'

The twins fell into his arms and, as he held his three nieces tight, he made another silent promise: to take Fiona to Bar Island and lay her to rest next to their parents. Three graves in a row to stare out across the glittering water. The place that Ivy described as so beautiful it made you believe there surely must be a God.

Then he'd send these three precious lives who remained to Ivy Merriweather, adhering to their mother's dying wish, and he'd go to her himself eventually, too. Not because he believed they could be together and she would love him as well, but because that's what Fiona had asked him to do.

Margie came to the door and Riley stood. He handed her the baby as she ushered the girls in to take one last look at their beloved mother, and walked away to stare out at the river and make one more final, solemn vow. One that could well mean he risked never making it back to any of them, ever again, despite their mother's last request, but it was a risk he knew he had no choice but to take.

The sound of his nieces wails of sorrow rent the air and he looked over at Barney, whose grim expression revealed he could read the truth of things too. For there was no way Riley Logan could live out the rest of his days on this earth knowing that the men who raped and killed his sister lived on it too.

Twenty-Nine

'You can't choose them all,' Robert said gently for the third time that day. 'Just one to start with, Aggie, then maybe another in a year or so.'

They were staring out of the kitchen window of the orphanage, watching the children run around and play. They'd been there for nearly an hour but Aggie couldn't bring herself to make the choice.

'It's impossible,' she said again. 'If I pick one I'll hurt all the others.'

'They'll understand, surely,' he said.

'No, they won't. I wouldn't, if I were them,' Aggie returned and he sighed, rubbing his hand over his face.

'Darling, we can't adopt twenty-six children. We just can't. We've a three-bedroom cottage, for a start, and I don't know what the neighbours would say if we start pitching tents all over the garden.'

'It's a possibility,' she said. She realised she really was starting to go a bit mad over this because she was actually half serious.

'No,' he said firmly but with an amused smile now, 'it's not.'

'Maybe … maybe a baby would be best because they'd only ever know of us … or maybe a child who's longed for parents because they miss their own—' She broke off, wondering if she would ever be able to make this decision and wishing she could confide in her family so they could help her make it. She and Robert had decided to keep it a secret though, at least until they knew which child they would adopt. It was a hard enough decision to make just on their own, let alone with a whole other bunch of opinions thrown into the mix.

'I think I'd like to sleep on it,' she said. She'd been saying that all week and Robert sighed.

'All right, dear, but tomorrow we decide on this once and for all. I don't really want to have to wait until I'm old and grey before I get to hold my child.'

She smiled, wrapping her arms around him. 'I can't wait to see you do that, hold our child I mean, not so much be old and grey.'

'Tomorrow then?' he said, kissing the top of her head.

'Tomorrow,' she agreed.

They walked back to the wagon and as they drove away the children all ran over to wave, each face so adored Aggie could only hope that Sister Ursula's prayers would be answered. That God Himself would somehow make this decision for them.

The sun had set and Aggie was sitting with her sisters and mother in the parlour, drinking tea while Robert and her father chatted in the garden with Patrick and smoked their pipes. It was nice to have the men to converse with during dinner, of course, but now that it was over and it just the women, Aggie was sorely tempted to break her promise to Robert and confide in them about the adoption. If she didn't she was seriously beginning to doubt she could ever decide on her own, but Frankie was talking and she tried to distract herself with what her sister was saying.

'What I really need is to study law, blasted dean. They let women in to other faculties, it's so ridiculously unfair not to let us in to the one area of study that can help us gain representation. How am I supposed to argue about law if I don't understand it?'

'That Ada Evans is making her way through,' Harriet pointed out. 'What one woman can do, another can do.'

'Humph. If I could copy Ada, I would. Fortunately for her the dean was away when she snuck her way in and enrolled. I don't think he'll let that happen again for a long while.'

'Why don't you ask Patrick to help you?' Ivy suggested. 'He could tutor you, I suppose, make it part of his own studies.'

Frankie gaped at her. 'I'm … I'm not sure if he …' she spluttered. 'I mean …'

She was blushing all of a sudden and Aggie watched her, a suspicion that had been brewing of late growing. If she didn't know better, Aggie would have sworn her sister had developed feelings for Patrick Earle, as unlikely a development as that seemed. Of all the men they knew he would have been the last one she would have thought Frankie would be interested in a few months ago. Yet, after what they'd been through together and the proximity they'd shared up the river, and now having him there at Kuranda so regularly, well, Aggie could see how such a thing could have occurred. Rather typically disastrous of Frankie, though, to finally have romantic feelings for a man and it be one of the very few she could never possibly have.

'I think that's a marvellous idea,' Harriet said as she handed Pretty Boy a biscuit and he began to nibble away happily. 'Ah, here he is now. Patrick, how would you feel about having a study assistant?'

'How do you mean?' he said, as the men all came back in and Ivy poured him a cup of tea.

'Just that Frankie was saying she'd love to study law to help her stand for parliament but as she can't, perhaps it would be an idea that she help you study and pick up on things that way.'

'Oh, no, I'm sure you don't want me to burden you—' Frankie began.

'What burden? I think it's a grand idea,' Patrick said. 'I'd welcome someone to test me and help me summarise, especially. It's rather a lot to take in at the moment.'

'Ignoramus,' Pretty Boy commented. Patrick turned to look at him in feigned offence and everyone laughed. Everyone except Frankie, Aggie noted. She just looked a bit ill.

'Not quite an ignoramus, I hope, but I'd appreciate any assistance you could give me, truly,' Patrick said.

Patrick was in his final year at university and Aggie knew he found it challenging right now, especially after such a difficult start to the term. It did seem a very good suggestion, unless you suspected what Aggie suspected, in which case it was terrible one.

'Well, that's settled then,' Harriet said, pleased. 'Seems we're on a roll, solving two people's problems at once. Who else has a dilemma?'

Robert looked across at Aggie and she sent him a pleading glance.

'Oh, all right, tell them,' Robert conceded. 'I don't think you'll ever decide otherwise.'

'Tell us what?' Ivy asked, as they all looked from Robert to Aggie in confusion.

'Actually, we do have a dilemma. A rather nice one really,' she began, as Robert came around to stand behind her and she reached up and took his hand. 'We've decided ... well, we've decided to adopt.'

'Oh,' Harriet exclaimed, 'oh, my darling, I was so hoping you would!' She rushed over and Aggie found herself swept up in her mother's embrace as Albert pumped Robert's hand.

'Marvellous, just marvellous, my boy. What wonderful parents you'll make.' He was teary at his own words, and Frankie and Ivy had jumped up too to join them all together in one big, Merriweather family hug.

'Come on, you're a part of this family too,' Albert said to Patrick and he laughed and joined in, one arm around Ivy, the other around Albert, and there was so much happiness in the moment, Aggie was glad she'd told them this way.

'Ah, it feels so good that you know,' Aggie said as they slowly broke apart, but Harriet remained, seemingly unable to let Aggie go, she was so overcome with joy.

'I suspected and hoped but, oh, it's so wonderful. Our first grandchild. Is it to be a boy or a girl?'

Aggie looked at Robert and he sighed.

'Well, you see ...'

'That's the dilemma, isn't it?' Frankie guessed as she sat down and wiped her cheeks with her handkerchief. 'You can't decide.'

Aggie nodded. 'It's so hard after working at the orphanage. I love them all, and so does Robert. To single one out seems so unfair to the rest, and yet ...'

'... and yet we have to,' Robert finished for her.

'However will you make your choice?' Ivy asked and Aggie shrugged.

'Sister Ursula said perhaps God will decide for us, although I can't see how.'

'What if you put all their names in a hat?' Frankie suggested.

'Or narrowed it down to the most suited to you and we all take a vote?' Ivy said.

'Maybe choose one that looks most like you, so they never know they're adopted,' Patrick suggested, 'unless you don't think that matters anyway.'

'Of course it doesn't matter, as long as the child is loved,' Frankie said. 'Anyway, once Dossie finds out everyone's going to know. I doubt you could keep it a secret from the child even if you wanted to, unless you moved away. Which I won't let you do,' she added.

'Maybe you should choose a boy,' Harriet suggested, 'even up the sexes in this family.'

'Oh, but a little girl,' Albert said, fondly. 'Is there anything more wonderful?'

Robert was sending Aggie an 'I told you so' look and she had to smile at her family's enthusiasm, even if it was only making the decision more difficult.

'I think we …' she began, but she was interrupted by a knock at the door.

'Whoever can that be?' Harriet wondered.

'If it's Dossie she'll be telling you choose one that's never had a sniffle in their life and has good teeth,' Frankie warned, to everyone's amusement as Albert went to answer.

'Can I help you?' His voice carried from the entry hall.

'Is Miss Merriweather at home?'

The others quietened down.

'Which one?'

'Ivy.'

Ivy stood as Albert bade the woman to enter. As she came into view Aggie didn't know her, but both Patrick and Frankie seemed to, standing too.

'Margie?' said Patrick.

'I … I'm sorry to come unannounced like this but I have a message for you from Riley and … and something to deliver.' She looked very anxious and Aggie looked at Patrick and Frankie then back at Margie in confusion.

'Margie works at the inn, down at Wisemans. This is the lady who helped us,' Frankie explained.

'Oh, well, then you're most welcome in our home,' Albert said. 'Thank you for calling the authorities that night. You have our most sincere thanks.'

'Not at all, they had it comin' to them and no mistake, even more so now that—' She stopped abruptly, searching the faces in the room. 'Which one of you is Ivy?'

'I am,' Ivy said, watching the woman nervously. 'What … what message has Riley sent?'

Margie's nervous gaze jumped from one face to the other, her uncertainty apparent.

'It's all right, we're all family,' Albert said, but Patrick was frowning and Aggie wondered at the contents of the message. Riley was a single man, after all.

'There's … there's a letter.' Margie handed it over, looking close to tears, and the room was very tense as Ivy opened it, shaking now, and read aloud. '*Dear Ivy, It is with great sadness I must convey to you my sister Fiona's …*'

'Oh no,' Ivy gasped, dropping the letter to the floor and breaking into sobs. 'No, no …'

Margie put shaking fingers to her lips, crying too, and Aggie felt sick as she bent to pick it up. 'Don't … don't tell me …'

But Margie nodded and Aggie and Frankie broke down as well. Patrick went to Ivy and put his arm around her. 'Dear God,' was all he said, but he held her shoulders tight.

'The man's sister? The one who cared for you?' Harriet asked as a distraught Ivy wept. 'Oh, Ivy, oh I'm so sorry,' she said as she sat down next to her and took her hand, the room filled with the renting of combined grief. 'Read the rest, Aggie,' she said quietly after a moment. 'We may as well hear it all.'

But Aggie couldn't stop crying now, thinking of that capable, kind lady, caring for Ivy while heavily pregnant and with her little daughters by her side. Goodness knows what would become of them and her new baby now.

'I'll do it, dear,' Robert said and she handed over the letter, unable to speak.

Dear Ivy,

It is with great sadness I must convey to you my sister Fiona's passing. She was found too late after being severely beaten and Barney witnessed her husband George, Donovan, Deano and Petey all fleeing the scene of the crime. As you can imagine, I am working with the law to seek justice.

'Beaten ...?' Aggie gasped in horror but Ivy continued only to cry.

She was very fond of you, as I'm sure you know, having called the new baby after you: Ivy. On her deathbed she made the dying wish that I send you the most precious gifts she left behind, her three daughters.

Robert paused and Aggie looked across at Ivy's stunned, distraught face.

'She ... she left me ...?'

Legally, George still has rights over his children but the man will be always on the run or dead himself soon enough. As such, you and I will be their legal custodians until we decide what must be done. I will come to discuss things with you as soon as justice has been served but in the meantime I feel I must tell you her exact dying words: 'Take my girls to Ivy. They deserve a better life than this.'

Fiona deserved better too, as we both know. Please honour her last wishes by caring for them until I can get to you. Knowing your

kind heart and how supportive your family have been, I completely
trust that you will.

Riley Logan.

Aggie watched as Ivy slowly rose to her feet, her sobbing stalled as she stared at Margie. 'Where … where are they?'

Maggie crossed to the door and nodded. They all stood to watch the familiar figure of Barney walk in, the girls beside him. The twins looked around with frightened, grief-stricken faces and he held a tiny baby against his chest.

No-one seemed to know what to do but then Ivy knelt down and opened her arms and the girls ran over and buried their faces against her. Then Aggie did what seemed the most natural thing in the world and went over to Barney and held out her own and he filled her empty arms with the most beautiful child she had ever seen. A baby girl called Ivy, recently motherless, until right now. For no matter what happened from here on, Aggie knew she would be the one to love this child, cherish her for Fiona with every fibre of her being, and her twin daughters too, God willing. If that's what Ivy and Riley chose. Robert came and gazed down at the baby for the longest of moments before raising his eyes.

'God made the decision,' he whispered, as tears fell down his kind, dear face.

And as tragic as the reason was, she knew that they were parents now, at last.

Part Five

The natural law

Thirty

Smuggler's Ridge, NSW, 11 June 1902

The smoke from the fire was unlikely to be visible but Riley doused it just the same, despite the cold bite of the morning air. Every action had to be one of caution, every decision well thought through. He hadn't hunted down these bastards for these past three months only to lose the advantage now. A man could well disappear up here along the ridges that edged the old, disused convict road to become phantom-like within the deep, thick bushland and creek marshes below. But not if you were being tracked by a local, born and raised and with enough knowledge of this land from firsthand experience to know what to look for. He'd been fortunate enough to stumble on an Aboriginal elder too, a man he remembered from his youth who everyone simply called Pop due to his advanced age, even then. He was very old now but sprightly enough to be out foraging on his own that day and keen to help Riley, once he'd figured out what he was up to. It hadn't taken long.

'You lookin' for them bad blokes? That Donovan?' he'd asked.

Riley figured it could only be to his advantage to be honest and answer in the affirmative and he'd been proven right. Apparently Pop's granddaughter had been the wife Donovan had killed and Riley had spent a full day and night with the man as he gave him advice on what to look for and the all the likely places the fugitives would go.

For fugitives they were. The law may not have given Pop's family any justice but they couldn't ignore Margie and Barney being witnesses to events that fateful night, nor the state that poor Fiona had been found in. They were wanted men but the police had given up the search long ago, figuring the gang would eventually just show up, and, when they did, they'd be arrested on the spot. Every local station had sketches of them on the wall but Riley knew these men better. They'd have plenty of supplies stashed away in caves up here and they could hide out for a very long time. But they didn't deserve to live for a long time. They didn't deserve to live for a day.

That he was taking the law into his own hands bothered Riley not a whit, even though he'd never actually taken a man's life. He knew if he did kill them all no-one would ever be the wiser in such remote land. Certainly no-one would care if they lived or died. Riley didn't know of a single person who liked any of them, indeed they were despised. Especially Donovan. The river had always contained its own brand of local justice, each man a law unto himself, and if they did the wrong thing quite often it was dealt with outside the confines of the greater legal system. That was the way Riley had been raised and the way these men had been raised too. The natural law.

They'd be expecting him to come after them, and likely watching their backs, but every day that slipped by would see them slowly lowering their guards, until that longed-for moment arrived and Riley found them. Then justice could be served.

Riley packed up, tossing his billy tea away and rolling his swag, looking out at the partially cloudy day and wondering what the weather might do. It would affect the way these men behaved – if it poured rain they'd make camp and he could continue his search and get an advantage, but the disadvantage of losing their tracks, as he had yesterday, outweighed it. If it was sunny they'd hike along, just as he was, traversing Smuggler's Track and the bushland that stretched for miles around it. However they'd return to favoured spots sooner or later, Riley was betting, and he was developing a pretty good idea where those were.

The last tracks he'd found had led to the north-west, up here, and Riley set out to follow the main trail before breaking off down a thin gully towards a cave he knew of, guessing they'd be needing fresh supplies of whisky by now. The last two he'd found had been emptied out and there was no way these men would last a day without grog.

Riley walked along, briskly now, thinking about Fiona and churning with hatred as he scanned the track and looked for clues. Better that than he think about the other subject his mind always returned to: *Ivy*.

How it had come to pass that she be the one to raise the remaining three members of his family while he hunted for Fiona's killers seemed an impossible irony. It had him sleeping restlessly at night, especially when he considered the difficult mess they'd be in trying to share custodianship on his return. It seemed much simpler to focus on revenge, which was just as consuming yet far less complicated; singular and straightforward with only one person's actions and decisions to consider: his own.

Riley saw the spot where the smaller track broke off up ahead and approached carefully, scanning the ground for any possible human signs. There were wallaby tracks imprinted clearly enough, and little fairy wren marks in the soft mud near the puddles, but no tread of a boot that he could see. He decided to go on and check anyway. There was a storage cave down there he'd heard George speak of when he was drunk a few times and it was too close by not to investigate.

He could see Marramarra Creek through the trees as he went, a winding, snakelike waterway that twisted through the thick forest and scrub. It wound as though it searched for something, as if it too hunted for life, although it sought to give it, not to take it away. It was picturesque, Riley supposed, unable to prevent his mind from flicking back to Ivy. No matter what path she chose in life, he hoped she would always take the time to pause and sketch, and never lose that passion for appreciating what was beautiful in this world. Despite everything he kept the drawing of the wallaby carrying her joey folded up in his shirt pocket, a reminder of that fact. A sweetly maternal image to reassure him that his three nieces were safe with Ivy and away from the violent ugliness that had destroyed Fiona.

The image of his sister at the end of her life flashed through his mind then. It haunted him, that moment, and although he knew he should choose from a thousand other memories, that was the one that stayed. Like a bloody stain he couldn't wipe away. Indeed, it would remain until she was avenged, he knew. Until the blood of the men who raped and killed her stained the earth too, seeping into the dirt, their cruel bodies incapable of ever harming another woman again.

Riley continued on, fiercely focused now, every sense on alert as he watched for any movement and listened to each sound that came from the thickly forested surrounds. After three months on his own, save his short spell with Pop, Riley felt like a part of the bushland himself and he was highly attuned to the life-forms within it. The flicker of a honeyeater's wings, the scratch of a goanna as he moved further up a gum tree, the lament of a crow that echoed in sad resignation – more like a prophecy than a warning, as Riley walked towards an inevitable fate.

On he went, deeper and deeper into the valley folds that would lead him to a sandstone outcrop and several hollows below where the cave should be, all the while listening out for that one sound that would differentiate itself from all others. Evidence of the cleverest life form of all, the one that did the most despicable of things: humanity.

It took several hours of hiking to finally reach the outcrop and the sun had long been obscured by cloud, which made it difficult to guess the time but Riley figured it was well past lunch. Normally he'd have stopped to eat his usual fare of beans and damper but he was nearing the expanse of sandstone now and the prospect of climbing down to look for the cave was too tempting. He might even find a clue, or at the very least something else to eat.

It was a steep climb and at first he thought he'd started at the wrong end of the ridge, so thick was the scrub but then he noticed something unusual and crept along stealthily to get a closer look. It was a clean broken branch, too thick to have been caused by a wallaby or a goanna, and it was a recent break, judging by the fresh cream colour of the wood. A waft of smoke drifted towards Riley then and it was laced with the unmistakable scent of wallaby meat. It made his mouth water on top of all the adrenaline. Riley crept forwards, heart thumping hard, stilling suddenly as he heard the sound he'd been waiting for these past long months, rising up from below. Voices.

His heart drummed painfully against his ribcage and he moved with painstaking care not to give himself away with a crack of a twig or the scuff of his tread on a stone, following the drone until he could hear a man clearly yell.

'Look out, y'burning it, ya stupid bloody mongrel.'

It was Donovan. Riley parted the bush in front to peer through and there they were, the four wanted men, and they looked the part. All of them sported beards and they were filthy, the stench of them mixing with the wallaby meat on the breeze. Riley felt a surge of hatred so strong it was all he could do not to take his rifle and start shooting but he'd never get them all that way. And every single one of them had to pay for what they did to Fiona. The most logical thing to do was the hardest option: to sit and wait for his chance to pick them off, one by one. Still, he'd waited three months to avenge his sister. He could bide his time now.

'Get out of the way,' Donovan grunted, shoving Deano aside and turning the wallaby, which had been crudely cut up and skewered on a mangled contraption to dangle above the enormous fire. It was gruesome to behold but it smelt good just the same. Any meat probably would after living on beans and damper for so long.

'You've made the fire too bloody big again,' Deano complained, 'and that stupid skewering thing of yours brings it too close. Course it's gonna burn.'

'Hey, who took me whisky?' Petey bellowed as he searched the ground behind him.

'None of it's yours, is it? It's my bloody stash,' George said as he made his unsteady way towards the bushes next to the nearby cave to relieve himself. Riley's eyes narrowed as he watched him, this brother-in-law who was supposed to be Fiona's protector yet allowed these disgusting brutes to ravage and beat her in front of his own tiny baby. What kind of a man would ever do such a thing? And how could Riley have ever believed Fiona that he hadn't been hurting her all along? Riley wondered how it would feel when he killed him, if he'd feel satisfaction or relief or perhaps even ashamed that he'd been so poisoned by hatred he enjoyed it. Two wrongs never make a right, his father always taught him. He wasn't sure if he'd say that now.

Deano had sat down heavily to give Donovan a filthy look and he took out a bottle of his own, swigging from it.

'Hey, is that mine?' Petey said.

'Nuh.'

'It is mine. Give it over.'

'I said, it's not yours.' Deano's tone was menacing now.

'Give him the fucking thing,' Donovan growled as he turned the meat.

Deano glared at him. 'I'm gettin' pretty sick of you telling me what to do.'

'Yours is over here,' George said, finding a bottle where he stood and Deano went over to get it slowly, tossing Petey's on the ground.

'If you've broken that you'll pay,' Petey said.

'Touch me and I'll kill ya,' Deano told him. The bottle was intact, however, and the four drank in silence as Riley watched on. Maybe he wouldn't even have to shoot these men himself. They looked ready to do the job any minute, the tension of living a fugitive existence day in, day out in this remote bushland together obviously wearing thin. That they were starting to turn on each other was obvious judging by the cuts and bruises they sported: a black swollen eye on Deano, rough and bloodied bandages around Petey's leg and George's head, a gash that ran the length of Donovan's forearm. Insults and threats flew and it only got worse as the day wore on and they got drunker and meaner.

By sunset knives had been drawn by Deano and Donovan twice and Petey had begun cleaning his gun as George looked from one to the other, obviously frightened. He was in far deeper than he'd bargained for, befriending this scum – George was used to beating a woman, not fighting hardened men. Riley watched his fear without pity, thinking how terrified Fiona would have been all these years and especially that last terrible night. How afraid the little girls would have been too.

Donovan stood, slicing off more of the wallaby meat, half-eaten by now as the fire blazed.

'Thought we decided we were gonna salt that and take it with us tomorrow,' Deano said.

'You decided, which means I don't give a shit,' Donovan said, tearing at the meat and dangling his knife from his fingers with a nasty grin in the bright firelight. 'Got a problem with that?'

'Yeah, I got a problem with that,' Deano said, standing up and rocking unsteadily in his boots. 'I got a problem with all your bossy bullshit.'

'Why don't ya clear off then? No-one's holding a gun to ya head. Yet.' Donovan looked over at his own rifle and back at Deano, eyebrows raised.

'You better be careful what you say, Donovan. I can slit ya throat in the middle of the night and none of these blokes'd care.'

'That so?' Donovan said, looking at George and Petey.

Petey stopped cleaning his gun to glare back and answer. 'You're the one that got us into this shit.'

'Didn't see you sayin' no to a turn.'

Riley felt murderous rage of his own begin to pump in his veins at those words and he picked up his rifle, shouldering it; waiting for the moment to arrive when he'd take aim.

'What about you?' Donovan said to George.

'You … you didn't have to hit her so hard,' George stammered, staring at Donovan's knife. 'Now I got no wife and I can't see me kids and Riley … Riley's gonna kill us if he finds us.'

'Bah, he won't have the guts,' Donovan scoffed drunkenly, twirling his knife, 'but I tell ya what, if he turns up I reckon I'll knock him off too. Can't believe he had those fine women staying on his boat and didn't give us a go. Come to think about it, why the hell didn't you have a crack?'

'Couldn't get near 'em with Riley hanging around,' George muttered, his eyes still on Donovan's knife.

'Well, ya know what I think? I think you're a coward,' Donovan said, stumbling closer towards him.

'I'm not ...' George said, eyes round beneath the bandage on his head as Donovan waved the knife towards his face.

'Prove it then,' Donovan said, arms wide.

'H-how?'

'Little game I know called chicken,' Donovan said and Riley's blood turned cold as George blanched.

'I'd rather n-not.'

'Aw, come on. It's simple,' Donovan said. 'You just get a knife like this, see? And you throw it close as ya can at the other bloke's hand against the tree.'

'Think we're too drunk for that,' George said, looking sick.

'Chicken?' Donovan said, making clucking noises.

'Stop it,' George said, the fear getting to him. '*Stop it, you bloody bastard!*'

Donovan paused. 'Well, you're gonna have to play after saying something rude like that.' He grabbed the man and threw him against the tree, holding George's hand flat against it, palm out. George struggled but Donovan just slammed him back against it harder.

'Just let him do it,' Petey said. 'We won't hear the end of it until you do.'

George looked too terrified to respond, stilling now, his hand visibly shaking against the bark. Donovan made quite a show of taking ten paces and turning before lifting the knife and taking unsteady aim. Riley held his breath as it flew through the air, missing George's hand but spearing straight into his upper arm.

'Arrrgh!' George screamed, falling to his knees in agony. 'Get it out, get it out!'

Deano stood, glaring at Donovan. 'What the fuck did you do that for?'

'Help,' sobbed George as the blood ran.

'I missed,' Donovan said, arms akimbo again and grinning.

Deano knelt down and pulled the knife from George's arm. He screamed again and clutched at it as his shirtsleeve became increasingly soaked in red.

'Ya never think, that's your problem,' Deano said as the blood continued to pour. 'Now we got a badly injured man in the middle of bloody nowhere.'

'He'll be right.' Donovan shrugged.

'Looks pretty nasty,' Petey commented over George's yells of pain.

'Shit. You know, you really are the lowest arsehole I ever met,' Deano said, furious now. 'I reckon I should just haul George outta here, get back to town and tell the cops you're the one that murdered his missus and where you are.'

'Do that and it'll be the last thing you ever do,' Donovan said, his grin fading. He picked up his knife and held it tight. It dripped with blood as George writhed and cried. Riley gripped his gun nervously, unsure whether or not to act.

'Can't see how you're gonna stop me,' Deano said, taking out his knife and holding it up. The two men began to circle, stumbling as they went as George continued to sob.

'Shut up,' Donovan told him.

'I … I can't …' George cried out.

'Shut up or I'll make you,' Donovan yelled, his eyes trained on Deano, but George continued to cry.

'I warned you!' Donovan turned and threw his knife again, and this time it landed in the man's chest. George gave a final terrible grunt of pain before slumping lifelessly to the forest floor. Riley watched in shock as Deano launched himself on Donovan, seizing his chance.

Petey floundered to his feet. 'Get off, get off!' he shouted, trying to take aim. He pulled the trigger and a shot split the air, causing the men to break apart but then Donovan yanked the knife from George's chest. They immediately tussled again, blades held in each of their hands as they strained to keep the other's away. Petey threw his gun down and tried to pull Donovan off, but only succeeded in knocking Deano's blade away by mistake. Donovan swung around, burying his blade in Petey's throat. Deano watched in shock as Petey lurched then collapsed onto his back with a terrible gurgling sound, his head lolling to the side. A trickle of blood seeped from his mouth through his beard. Dead too.

Donovan didn't miss a beat, reaching down to pull the blade straight out of Petey. He turned back to Deano, who lay sprawled on the ground.

'Enough,' Deano said, staring at Petey in horror. 'Enough now, Donovan,' he repeated, shaking his head. 'We're ... we're the only ones left.'

'I'll decide when it's enough,' Donovan yelled, holding up the knife in manic triumph. 'You said you'd kill me in my sleep so yeah ... it's not enough yet, is it?'

Deano glanced over at his discarded knife and lunged for it but Donovan saw that coming. He threw his own blade once more and it landed straight in Deano's heart.

He let out a groan and Donovan wandered over to twist it cruelly, taking a third life and leaving Deano to lie with his eyes open, gazing sightlessly towards the sky. Riley watched grimly, sickened by the massacre he'd just witnessed, but Deano's dead eyes reminded him of the moment Fiona had passed away and he knew the moment for vengeance had finally arrived.

'You tried to mess with me and look what happened, eh? Look what happened,' Donovan yelled to the three bodies strewn near the fire. 'No-one threatens Donovan, see? No-one. King of the river, that's me. *King of the river!*'

Riley emerged from the bushes and cocked his rifle. Donovan spun around in surprise but it took a moment for him to focus on Riley.

'Ha,' he said, 'well I'll be. Managed to track us down at last, have ya?'

'You knew I'd come,' Riley said quietly.

Donovan looked about and spied Deano's knife. Riley followed his gaze. 'Don't think there's much point trying to get that while I'm holding this, do you?'

'Can't go down without a fight,' he said, lifting his fists. 'Think we should settle this man to man though, don't you?'

'You're not a man, you're a filthy animal, about to meet your maker. How does it feel knowing that, Donovan? Thinking about all the terrible, low-life things you've ever done.'

Donovan began to back away towards the blazing fire, staggering as he stared at the barrel of Riley's gun.

'No such thing as God, is there? All made-up stuff to scare people into living boring lives,' he said, but he was starting to sweat now as he drew ever closer to the flames.

'Guess you're about to find out,' Riley said, taking a step forwards. Donovan stumbled back a little more.

'It was an accident, I swear, I never meant for her to die ...'

'There are some things no-one can survive,' Riley said, lifting his gun to take aim.

'You wouldn't really kill me, would you?' Donovan said, desperately. 'Never heard of you doing it before. You'll end up in hell too, if you do.'

Riley hesitated, itching to pull the trigger but finding it hard to commit the ultimate crime. To end a life, even one as evil as

Donovan's. Ivy's face drifted into his mind then, beautiful and kind, and her words came back to him, about there being a God. He lowered the gun slightly. But surely even God would forgive this sin, an act of justice. A life for a life.

Donovan began to grin and held up his hands. 'You wouldn't shoot an unarmed man.' But the action caused him to stumble once more and this time he fell backwards, straight into the great fire. 'Argh,' he screamed, '*help!*' He struggled to stand but he'd become entangled in his own skewers and the carcass of the wallaby as his clothes caught on fire. '*Help me!*' he screamed but Riley merely watched for a moment before turning and walking away. Donovan's terrible cries filled the night.

He may never know whether or not he'd have pulled that trigger but he did know he wouldn't be reaching in to pull Donovan, the murdering, raping, self-proclaimed king of the river, from the fiery hell of his own creation. For who was Riley to interfere with the natural law?

The screaming faded into the night as Donovan's life fed the fire, until only the voice of the river lands remained, a rhythmically calming song of a thousand parts, calling Riley to the water to begin the long trip home. It gleamed before him in silvery tones, a narrow silken road to lead him to the greater Hawkesbury gateway, then on to his nieces and the rest of his life. Satisfied that his sister had been avenged and by her murderer's own hands, and with the relief that he didn't have blood on his own, after all. Well may Ivy Merriweather belong to another man but Riley's life was entwined with hers nonetheless, due to Fiona's wishes. Whatever friendship they would share he was glad he could do it as a decent man and not a killer, the ugliest aspects of river life left behind while he journeyed to her beautiful world.

Thirty-One

Town Hall, Sydney, 12 June 1902

They waited together, armed linked as the crowd sang.

Daughters of freedom, the truth marches on,
Yield not the battle till ye have won!

The lyrics brought tears to Frankie's eyes, thinking of poor Fiona and the daughters she'd left behind in her battle to survive. A brutal fate that could well have been Frankie's own, meted out by the very same men. Ivy's too. Still, today marked the first important step towards change, the one they'd all been fighting for, so long and so hard. After all the rallying, writing, speech-making and petition signing, the fight to give women the vote, and consequently the power at last to hold some influence over the laws they were expected to live under, was drawing to a close. Australia would be only the second country in the world to do so, after New Zealand, and the first in the world to let women stand for parliament.

Frankie fully intended to be one of those women, although it could well take a long time and much more campaigning yet. Her father had been right about expecting legislative change to be slow. The world of law was a man's one and getting anything new passed would be a complicated and convoluted undertaking. Studying with Patrick had taught her that much. Yet this was the start and, as men had their final say and made it official, women across the country awaited the announcement expectantly.

Ivy and Aggie stood beside Frankie with their mother, although it hadn't been easy dragging them all away from the twins and the baby. This was too important a moment to miss, however, one to go down in the history books, and Robert and Albert hadn't minded looking after the girls. Frankie felt they stood there on behalf of every woman over the centuries who'd longed for power over their own lives and the millions who still did, worldwide. That it was happening right there in the newest country in the world, Australia, filled her with overwhelming gratitude and the deepest of pride. Her throat clogged with both emotions as the speaker took to the podium and the large crowd surrounding Town Hall steps quietened down to listen.

'Ladies and gentlemen, we expect word any minute now but while we wait to see if the act is passed, as we all so desperately hope it shall be, we can read to you direct quotes from esteemed members of parliament on the matter.'

'This should be interesting,' Harriet muttered.

'Straight from the House of Representatives, Sir Edward Baddon has stated: *A bachelor will have his one vote. The married man, happy in his family, whose wife's vote is one which he can command – and most men, I think, can command their wives' votes …*' There was much derisive laughter and booing before she continued. '*… will have two votes; whilst the man who is unhappily married, and whose wife as* *a matter of certainty and principle and established policy will vote in the opposite way to that in which he does, will have no vote at all.'*

'How does that work?' Aggie said. 'He still gets his vote – they both do.'

'Good luck debating with that moron, Frankie,' Harriet said and Frankie had to chuckle. It was good to see her mother almost back to her old self.

'Sir William Lyne, who introduced the bill, has said: *not only is it just to accord women the vote, it is in the best interest of the entire community.'*

There was much cheering and applause for that comment and the speaker held up her hand. 'One more, one more,' she said. 'Senator Richard O'Connor: *I see no reason in the world why we should continue to impose laws which have to be obeyed by the women of the community without giving them some voice in the election of the member who makes those laws.'*

There was an enormous ovation at those fine words and Frankie had to wipe away a tear as she hugged Ivy close.

'It's changing, Ivy girl. It's changing at last.'

Ivy nodded, too choked up to speak as they held each other tightly. Then a messenger ran over to the speaker. She took the telegram in her hand and scanned the few words before smiling broadly and reading them aloud.

'It has just been passed by the new nation of Australia that all citizens over the age of twenty-one years are afforded voting rights to elect federal government,' she paused, 'including women.'

The centre of the city of Sydney erupted as people cheered and cried in the streets and Frankie embraced her mother and sisters, unable to contain herself as she openly wept too. It felt as if they'd been handed a lifeline in a treacherous sea and, even though they'd need to fight many currents and waves until they made it to shore, there was no way they'd ever let it go.

The celebrations lasted a long while but they finally decided to head back home to the children and share the news with them and the men. Harriet managed to buy the last newspaper from the stand so she could walk in holding up the headlines.

It was a merry ride on the train as she read out loud from it, but she paused at one point, frowning.

'Listen to this: *native men and women are of course excluded from voting at federal or state level, however it is expected that the fight for universal state voting for non-coloured women continue.* What's this "of course" business? Frankie, there's one of your first debates, right there.'

'I'm afraid changing that will take a very long time,' she said, knowing the plight of Indigenous people was a terrible one from her recent reading. 'They have practically no rights at all. I'd alter all of the injustices against them, if I could.'

'What other laws would you change?' Aggie asked her.

Frankie considered that. 'Well, I think we all know the first one, that it be illegal for men to beat their wives,' she said, and each of them nodded sadly, 'but I suppose the marital rights law would be the second. Then the right to own property without having to be a widow to do so ... and to have a bank account, after that. To have proper independence.'

'Hear, hear,' Harriet agreed. 'What would you change, Ivy?'

'Me? Well, I recently found out that married women aren't allowed to be teachers so I'd change that one.'

'Married women aren't allowed to work in most professions,' Frankie told her, 'although menial jobs and factory work seem to be accepted by the powers that be.'

Ivy shook her head. 'Yes, but you'd think that teaching ... anyway, it seems most unfair to me. I was actually considering about becoming a teacher until Patrick told me that.'

'Were you really?' Harriet said. 'What a shame, then. I think you would have made a marvellous teacher.'

'Really?' Ivy said, looking pleased. 'Well, that's nice to hear, at least.'

'What about you, Aggie?' Harriet asked her.

'I think unwed pregnant women should be able to have somewhere to go that doesn't involve giving their baby up,' she said, 'and maybe ... well, maybe even be priests if they so want. I think Sister Ursula understands true Christianity far more than Father Brown ever would. She'd never turn some poor girl away.'

'She seems a bit scary to me,' Ivy said.

'Yes, she is, but she's a kind woman underneath that. Priests have too much power for men like Father Brown to wield it.'

'It's all about power, isn't it?' Frankie said. 'The power to make laws, the power to control their spouses, the power to work, have a profession, own property, power over money. They've had all of it, up until now.'

'Yes, still, we've won one of the most important fights today, the power to vote; *the right that covered all other rights*, as Vida Goldstein said,' Harriet said, folding the paper.

'And we'll be able to stand for election, which will give us the chance to have our say firsthand,' Frankie said, grinning with excitement the prospect.

Ivy looked at her in wonder. 'Imagine that.'

'A world first!' Harriet crowed happily.

'We need to get elected first,' Aggie reminded them.

'We can and we will,' Harriet predicted. 'We can achieve anything our hearts desire if we have enough passion and determination, and you all have that in droves,' she said, nodding at them with pride. 'What a wonderful day to be a woman, girls. A wonderful day indeed.'

And so it was, Frankie acknowledged, sitting back to stare out the train window and knowing she'd remember it for as long as she lived. A day to tell her own daughter about, if she'd ever have one, but just because her marriage to the Cause was no longer needed, that didn't mean she was free to consider such things. Her political fighting had just begun, which meant there still wasn't room for a husband and babies. That choice, to raise a family and build a home, was for women like Ivy. With a man like Patrick Earle to love you.

'*Daughters of freedom, the truth marches on,*' Harriet sang loudly, holding the newspaper aloft and leading the way into the house. '*Yield not the battle till ye have won!*'

Tricia and Annie came running out from the back room where they'd been playing with Albert, their little faces filled with excitement. 'Hooray! Nanny won the vote!'

'We all won it – including the two of you, my cherubs,' she told them as they hugged her. The twins adored their adopted grandmother and Harriet had been a big part of their recovering from losing their mother, and, indeed, their entire way of life in one day. They adored Albert, their new Pop, too and loved staying at Kuranda, although there were times when the grief struck them, as was to be expected. Tricia was prone to sudden bouts of tears and Annie could sometimes be found hiding and withdrawn, yet they were still very young. Frankie knew Aggie hoped they would forget the pain altogether as time wore on, but that came with its own price. It also made them all sad to think how little they would probably remember of Fiona.

This was a happy occasion, however, and the twins had clapped and wrapped their arms around the three sisters in turn. Aggie sat and they perched themselves on her knees. 'Did you make a cake?'

'Uh-huh,' they both said.

'Did you leave eggshells in it?'

'Uh-huh,' they both said again, giggling now.

'It's got green icing,' Robert told them, walking in with Albert, who was carrying the baby, 'heaven knows why. Good news then?'

Harriet held the paper aloft. 'Freedom!'

'Hooray,' Albert said, as little Ivy looked over at Aggie. She let the twins run off to finish their baking and fetched the infant from Albert. Robert came to her side and she gave him a kiss on the cheek.

'A very special day – so glad we could be there to hear it like that,' Aggie said. 'Thank you for looking after them.'

'You never need to thank me,' Robert said, reaching up to stroke the baby's cheek. She smiled her adorable smile at him and Frankie knew that Riley Logan would have a hard time of it if he wanted to take these children away from them. That they were Aggie and Robert's now seemed the most natural thing in the world, a blessing that had come out of tragedy, and they were the most doting and loving parents Frankie had ever seen.

'Tea!' declared Harriet as she marched to the kitchen. Everyone dispersed, leaving Frankie to pick up a doll that one of the girls had dropped, reflecting on how different this house was now. Dossie had commented that Fiona's children were very fortunate to have landed on the Merriweather's doorstep but Frankie knew they were the fortunate ones. It had changed all their lives for the better, having such beautiful young souls around them after so much turmoil and tragedy. Aggie had a shine about her now and Harriet had lost her haunted look. And Albert was too busy chuckling at the twins' antics as he worked to appear quite so preoccupied.

Ivy had purpose too, helping to look after them and planning her impending wedding, now only a few days away. In all, Frankie thought, her entire family was moving on with a far more chaotic, love-filled life. Although it was still underscored by tragedy, there was something about the children's attitudes that affected them all and Kuranda was bursting with the joy that can come from such a big extended family.

Frankie absolutely adored the girls too but she was so busy with her writing and study that she hadn't spent as much time with them as everyone else. Even the usually hard-working Robert had taken to stepping out of the office early and going in late. The only other person as busy as she was seemed to be Patrick, and a good share of his time was spent with her, alone. She'd wager he actually spent more time with her than he did with Ivy but Frankie couldn't say no to studying with him when her whole career centred on politics now. It was unavoidable and relentless. And it was torturous.

For somehow, somewhere along the line, Patrick Earle had managed to do the impossible: have her develop feelings for him. At first she'd thought it was only that he made her aware that she was a flesh-and-blood woman but it was so much more than that now. *Feelings.* What a confusing and volatile state of emotions that word encompassed and, oh, how she'd tried to ignore them, but as soon as Patrick was near, or even if he came to mind, they seemed to ignite of their own volition and take over. She reeled from one to the other: excitement, joy, despair, frustration. Anger, hope, attraction. No, it was more than attraction, if she were brutally honest with herself. It was desire.

Frankie had never really felt it before, not like this. Thinking you may want a man to kiss you was attraction. Feeling every nerve of her body go on alert whenever he sat close, knowing if he touched her she'd find it almost impossible to resist, was something else altogether. It made her feel out of control, which Frankie hated, and disloyal to Ivy, which she hated even more. Worst of all, it left her horribly, shamefully, more and more jealous.

How on earth she'd managed to go from that disturbing moment of feminine awareness on the dancefloor at the inn to developing full-blown feelings for her sister's very soon-to-be husband was beyond her, and yet she had. It clung to her wherever she went, even on a day like today; his face never far from mind, his name popping into her head with frustrating regularity.

Would you like a cup of tea? *Patrick.*

What time are you leaving for the train? *Patrick.*

There's a knock at the door. *Patrick.*

Then there really was a knock at the door and she went to open it, staring him straight in the face. *Patrick.*

'Hello,' Patrick said. 'I heard the news. Figured you'd be celebrating.'

'Hello,' Frankie said. 'Come in, come in.'

Patrick entered, wondering why she wasn't happier. She'd been moody of late, exasperatingly so at times, but today he'd certainly expected an exuberant, elated Frankie, not a subdued one. He was disappointed. 'I figured you'd be ecstatic.'

'I am,' she said, smiling now, but it seemed a bit forced. 'Everyone's fetching tea and cake.'

'Oh, what kind of cake?'

'Green.'

Patrick chuckled, following her to the kitchen and trying not to ponder Frankie's odd reaction. He tried not to notice that she was wearing her new white blouse again too but with less success. The sheerness of the material hinted at what lay beneath as she walked in front, allowing him a moment to take in tempting details of her unobserved before forcing his gaze away. It was hard enough trying to ignore such tantalising glimpses sitting next to her as they studied, let alone here, in Ivy's home. Especially when Frankie leant to turn a page or reach for a book and he could see the clear imprint of lace against her skin. He was determined not to dwell on her that day, however – thinking about Ivy's sister instead of Ivy was starting to become far too much of a habit. It was just as well he'd soon be finished his degree and a married man, for surely it was just the constant proximity to Frankie that was making his imagination run wild.

'Hello, all. What great news, eh?' he said, refocusing his attention as they entered the kitchen to a sea of happy faces. That was more like it. 'Green cake today, I hear. Anyone found some shell yet?'

'Pop's got a bet on it,' Annie said, waving at Patrick happily from her chair, her face smeared with icing. 'Said whoever finds bits can have a penny.'

'How much are you out of pocket so far?'

'That makes thruppence,' Albert said, finding another one and investigating it with his spectacles.

'Hmm,' Patrick said. He sent Ivy a smile and thanked Harriet as she poured him a cup of tea. 'Well, I'd best eat up then. So, how was town?'

'Wonderful,' Ivy told him. 'You should have heard what some of the politicians had to say. You tell it, Frankie. You'll recall it better than me.'

'Oh, that reminds me,' said Patrick, turning to Frankie. 'I ran into Mr Forsyth on the way here and he said to ask you if you could write a report for the paper.'

'How ironically perfect,' Harriet said with a satisfied chuckle but Frankie merely poured her tea.

'Jumping on the bandwagon now, is he? We'll see.'

'I would have thought—' Patrick began. 'Well, anyway, at least tell me. I'm dying to hear what happened.'

'Me too,' Robert chimed in.

'Oh, no, let Mum tell it,' Frankie said, tapping her spoon. 'I'm not sure if I quite … remember.' That seemed out of character too and Patrick stared at her, confused.

'That's not like you. I heard you recite constitutional law off by heart for a full half-hour yesterday, and that was boring stuff.'

'I don't feel like it,' she said shortly and Ivy frowned at her.

'All right. No need to get huffy,' Patrick said lightly but she was beginning to annoy him. Again.

'Who's huffy?' Frankie shot back but Aggie intervened.

'It's been such an exciting day. You tell it, Mum.'

Harriet didn't seem to notice anything amiss and went on to tell them all that had transpired. Patrick shoved his annoyance with Frankie aside to listen and he was soon swept up with the story, booing and cheering with the others, including the twins, even though they really couldn't understand what the politicians meant.

The buoyant mood of the rest of the family overtook him and he found himself looking around the room, reminding himself how lucky he was. Aggie sat in the corner giving the baby her bottle and she and Robert looked so happy Patrick couldn't help but smile. Meanwhile Albert was patting Ivy's hand and gazing fondly at Harriet as she told the tale. This was such a close-knit family to be marrying into, far more so than his own. Despite everything they'd been through – Ivy's disappearance, the fear and horror at the thought of losing her, inheriting the care of three infants after the tragic death of their mother – the Merriweathers had found a way to make things work. Patrick was proud to become one of them.

He'd just have to make sure he got past this attraction he was feeling for Frankie pretty damn fast, he told himself firmly, not including Ivy's increasingly maddening sister in his gaze. He certainly didn't want to be carrying *that* for a lifetime. Fortunately, in his experience, this physical type of connection with a woman usually fizzled out in time, just a natural biological urge that passed, so long as other emotions didn't get on the way. It wouldn't do any good to start considering it to be anything more when he so clearly loved Ivy.

The impromptu tea party finished up and Patrick saw a perfect opportunity to spend some time alone with Ivy before studying with her frustrating sister this afternoon, and he knew exactly the way he wanted to spend it. There would be nothing like a good kissing session with his fiancée to curb any lust he might be feeling towards someone else. They hadn't been doing too much of it, really, in fact things had never really been as heated as that first time on her birthday. Initially that was because he didn't think she was well recovered enough, physically or emotionally, but then lately it was more because they were only having a short engagement and he had wanted to save it all up for the honeymoon, only two days away.

That didn't seem a very good reason that day, however, it being misty and cold and pretty much perfect weather for cosying up with a woman, so Patrick suggested they go down to the shed to feed Shadow so he could get her alone.

'Just let me get my shawl,' she said, fetching it and wrapping it about her. She looked lovely in the deep green hue, as always.

Shadow was glad to see them, and even gladder to be fed, and he munched happily while Patrick turned to put his arms around Ivy, feeling a bit self-conscious as he did.

'Oh,' she said, but nothing more, and he bent down and kissed her. It was a nice kiss, pleasant and explorative, but it lacked the heated passion they'd shared in the forest and he wondered how much the champagne had to do with things on that day. He pulled back to look in her pretty face.

'You know, you really are so beautiful,' he told her, and she was, so he kissed her again but then it was her turn to pull back.

'Perhaps we shouldn't really, I mean, the wedding is so close now ...'

She was right, of course, but it didn't feel natural that they not feel eager to share stolen moments of passion beforehand. Maybe tomorrow night on the eve of the big day, when they went to Nick Johnson's dinner party and had some champagne. That may calm down what he suspected were just pre-wedding jitters and help things along. But, as they made their way back to the house and he went home to get organised to study and await Frankie's arrival, the unnerving knowledge that they hadn't fired each other's blood remained. The three hours ahead he'd spend alone with Frankie suddenly seeming a very, very long time.

Frankie was trying to get ready but Ivy obviously wanted to ask her something.

'Spit it out, Ivy, for goodness' sake,' Frankie said, her guilty conscience causing to her sound cross.

Ivy gaped at first but then she blurted the words in a rush. 'Why don't you like Patrick?'

Frankie stared at her in shock. That was pretty much the last thing she'd expected her to say. 'I ... I do like him. I like him very much.'

'No, you don't. You're funny with him and you always have been. I mean, I thought you got on rather well when we were up the river but since then ... you've gone all prickly around him again.'

'I'm not prickly around him.'

'Yes, you are,' Ivy corrected her. 'You just were, in fact.'

Frankie hadn't realised she'd been so obviously irritated with Patrick and frowned.

'I don't want to argue you with you about it, Frankie,' Ivy continued. 'I meant what I said when I told you I never want to fight again, I just want to know why so I can try to understand how to help the two of you get along.'

'I do like him,' Frankie said again. 'I mean, look at all the time we spend together studying. I couldn't stand to do that otherwise.'

'That's different. You have something in common to focus on then, don't you? But without it, you really seem, I don't know, annoyed with him all the time.'

'We just … we clash, I suppose,' Frankie said, looking for a plausible way to explain it. 'We're too alike perhaps.'

Ivy considered that. 'Yes, I suppose you are, really.'

'We're both competitive, and interested in law and sport,' Frankie said, latching on to those facts, 'and we're both rather outgoing, I'd say.'

Ivy studied her. 'Yes, but it's also because you think he's pompous. You've said so before.'

Frankie sighed. 'Not so much any more. He's come a long way since he's been with you. I think you've rubbed off on him.'

'I think it was just, you know, what he went through,' Ivy said thoughtfully, flushing as she added, 'with the police.'

'You need to let any blame you feel over that go, Ivy. It was an accident and just one of those things. You can't go marrying the man if you're going to feel remorseful and therefore beholden for the rest of your life.'

'You … you don't want me to marry, do you? You think it's a waste of a life not to work or study.'

She looked sad about that and Frankie took her shoulders. 'No,' she said gently. 'I don't think that. I think it's a wonderful choice for you and that you'll be very happy with Patrick and that the girls will love whatever siblings or cousins … or however that's going to work, that you give them,' she said, and Ivy smiled. 'I'm happy for you, truly.'

Ivy nodded. 'All right then. I'm sorry to have questioned you so, it's just that your opinion is very important to me. I don't think I could marry a man that you didn't like.'

'I don't think I could stand to *let* you marry a man that I didn't like,' Frankie said and Ivy smiled again. She gave her a hug.

'Thanks for the chat, Frankie.'

'Any time, Ivy girl,' she said, watching her leave with mixed emotions, 'and I do like Patrick. I like him very much.'

Ivy nodded and smiled again before walking out and Frankie stared after her.

Very much, indeed.

'Don't forget you've a final fitting for your suit in the morning,' his mother said as she lay down the refreshments tray. She looked unimpressed at serving them, but their maid was sick. Patrick couldn't help but compare her to Harriet Merriweather, who seemed to revel in making the tea for her family and guests and had no servants at all.

'Yes, I know,' Patrick said.

'Father Brown asked that we drop off the church donation too, so you may as well do so while you're at it.'

'All right,' he said, picking up the teapot to pour. 'Tea?' he asked Frankie.

'Yes please.'

'How long are you studying for this afternoon?' Sybil said. She avoided even looking at Frankie, who Patrick knew she heartily disliked, telling him more than once that she found the notion of him studying with 'that woman' preposterous.

'Until about seven. I've my last exam first thing.'

Sybil tutted. 'Ridiculous state of affairs, sitting an exam the day before your wedding.'

'I couldn't very well ask them to postpone it on my account. Fortunately it's only the one exam on Constitutional Law, which Frankie knows more about than I do.'

'Indeed?' Sybil Earle said, still not looking at Frankie. 'Can't see why that should be of interest to you now you've secured the vote, which is what you suffragettes were after, as I understand it.'

'We are after far more than that,' Frankie said, 'and we're hoping to secure parliamentary representation now that we're eligible; change some of the laws ourselves.'

'Well,' Sybil said with a sniff. 'Call me old-fashioned but I still say a woman's place is in the home.'

'A woman's place is wherever she feels fulfilled,' Frankie said clearly, unintimidated by his mother's coldness. 'Why should they be the ones forced behind closed doors to a life of domesticity?'

'Because that's the natural way of things,' Sybil said, turning to look at her for once. 'All the law-making in the world won't change that fact. Natural laws need to be obeyed first and foremost and it's the women who have the children.'

'Not if they choose not to,' Frankie said.

Sybil looked scandalised. 'Why on earth would anyone choose to be a spinster?'

'Spinsters get to live a life of their own choosing, not one dictated by their husbands. They have freedoms a married woman isn't afforded, like being able to work and have a profession.'

'But they never marry and have a family! I still say it's unnatural and no self-respecting woman should wish it upon themselves,' Sybil asserted, looking down her nose at Frankie.

'On the contrary, I think it shows marked self-respect to choose it,' Frankie said coolly. 'I most certainly intend to.'

Sybil stared at her. 'Well,' she said again, her words clipped, 'it's your choice, I suppose. I'll leave you to your studies then.'

She exited, nose high in the air. Patrick picked up his teacup with amusement but he was thoughtful too, and still wary of Frankie's mood today.

'You've got your work cut out for you, convincing people like my mother about women's rights,' he said, taking a sip and choosing his comments carefully. 'They'll hold fast to the "natural way of things" argument for many years to come, I'm afraid.'

'Should be a law against that,' Frankie said, taking her tea as well and sitting back with a flick of her long plait.

Patrick studied her for a moment, unable to help thinking how gorgeous she was when impassioned and how it did seem a shame that she'd never marry, regardless the dangerous direction of such musings.

'What?' she said, eyebrows raised. He couldn't resist commenting, despite himself.

'Don't you ever think about what you'll truly be giving up and wonder if you'll be missing out … I mean romance wise?'

Frankie studied her cup, avoiding his gaze. 'Sometimes,' she admitted.

That piqued his curiosity. 'Who's caught your eye? Nick?' he said, feeling jealous at the thought.

Frankie flicked him a glance. 'None of your business. Anyway, it wouldn't be worth it if it meant I'd be chained to the home.'

'It doesn't have to be that way though, does it? I mean, if the man supported your freedoms, like you father does with your mother. She lives a pretty fulfilled life out of the home.'

'Not as fulfilled as it should be,' Frankie said, 'but yes, he would never stand in her way, it's just the law that limits her endeavours.'

Patrick placed his cup down, considering that. 'I wouldn't stand in my wife's way if she wanted to go out into the world and forge a career. I'd support her in any way I could, even in something as difficult as trying to change the laws herself.'

Frankie looked over, watching him now. 'I'm sure Ivy will be very glad to hear that, should she ever choose to join me.'

Patrick stared back. He'd quite forgotten about Ivy somewhere along the line in this conversation and felt rather taken aback and ashamed.

'Yes, well, I'll have to make sure I tell her so,' he said, sitting up straight and clearing his throat. 'Anyway, where were we?'

Frankie put down her cup and drew her notes over. 'The proposed Act 43, to consolidate enactments relating to usury, interest, and to certain instruments and contracts.'

'There should be five subheadings,' Patrick began as he stood up to focus his thoughts on where they should be, starting to pace. 'No, four. Bills of loading, usury … no, oh, God, I'm never going to remember this one.'

'It's actually an easy acronym,' Frankie said, tapping her notes. She was always suggesting acronyms for recollecting facts. Patrick actually found it very useful and goodness knows he needed all the help he could get with this exam. Constitutional Law definitely wasn't his strongest subject and it seemed to be hers. He hadn't been just flattering Frankie when he said that to his mother before.

'Go on then,' he said.

'Bug Merriweather. B. U. G. MW.'

Patrick stared at her then chuckled in surprise. 'Well, that's simple enough, I suppose. B. U. G. MW. Bills of loading, Usury and interest, Guarantees and … Memorandum in Writing!' he finished, pleased. 'Hey, that *is* a really easy one. Thanks.'

'You're welcome,' she said, looking pleased herself. 'Now elaborate on each.'

Patrick groaned but he was soon away, his confidence restored by his recollection of the subheadings and his mind firmly on the job at hand. It took about an hour to recite everything though, and by that time he was definitely ready for a break. Not only because he was mentally drained but because he'd sat down and it had been her turn to pace, her body moving back and forth in front of him in endless parade. It was warm and cosy in the small room too, and without her coat he had to endure the sight of her body in that damn blouse over and again.

It was starting to make him edgy and, after the unexpectedly personal conversation they'd shared and the rather poor attempt he'd made at sparking things between himself and Ivy earlier, he was also getting annoyed with Frankie again, as unfair as that was.

'Relating to …?'

'I'm too tired,' he complained.

'Come on, it's not that hard.'

'Frankie, stop pushing me,' he warned as she stopped directly in front of him.

'Relating to …?'

'*I don't bloody know.*'

Frankie gaped. 'Well, you don't have to be so rude about it.'

Patrick stood up too. 'You always go too far.'

'Hey, you're the one that gets the degree and all the glory.'

'You're getting a free education out of it,' he pointed out.

'… that no-one will ever recognise!'

'That's not my bloody fault!'

'Stop bloody swearing at me!'

'You stop swearing at *me*!'

He glared at her and she glared back, both of them breathing hard and both of them furious. Suddenly, before he even knew what he was doing, he pulled her into his arms and kissed her. She pulled back with a gasp and he thought she might slap him but then she fell straight back in and started kissing him too. Patrick felt a white-hot rush of desire shoot through him. There was nothing merely pleasant or explorative about this experience, it was pure, all-consuming lust and he could feel every inch of her womanly body pressed against him, until all of a sudden she pushed away.

'No, no, we can't … oh God … we can't …'

She held her fingers to her mouth and the movement drew his stare to her lips, wanting them back on his desperately, but sense was slowly returning now as she backed along the wall.

'We can't do this … my God, what were we thinking … Ivy …'

She shook her head, tears in her eyes, before running from the room. He stared at the flung-open door as she exited, wanting to go after her. Knowing he shouldn't. Then his mother walked past in the hallway, registering the sound of the front door slamming before meeting Patrick's eyes with raised, disapproving eyebrows.

'Finishing early?'

Patrick nodded as his mother walked on, thinking his marriage may well now be finished too, before it had even begun.

Thirty-Two

Aggie sat in her parents' bay window, staring out at the gardens below where the twins raced about and her father strolled with his notebook. It had only been six months since she'd she sat there with her sisters on Christmas Eve, thinking she'd never have a child. Never feel that depth of love other lucky women got to feel. Looking down at baby Ivy, her heart swelled with that precious maternal love, so powerful it felt like it could burst, as the infant kicked her chubby legs and smiled at her. She was such a pretty little thing. In fact Ivy and the twins were the most beautiful children in the world, as far as Aggie was concerned, but her protective instinct filled her with fear too, for what if Riley Logan took the girls away from them?

Surely he wouldn't, he *couldn't* do such a thing. They were her children now, hers and Robert's. Ivy knew it, she could see it in her sister's understanding expression as she let them look after the three girls here at Kuranda full time. Aggie and Robert had moved in from the moment baby Ivy and the twins had arrived, the idea of separating the children from Ivy unthinkable until Riley returned and the official decision regarding custody was made. But what if Riley wanted to raise them himself, up on that

309

river? Worse still, what if George somehow got away with murder and came back to claim his children?

It kept her awake at night, even though she should be exhausted after caring for them all day long and getting up to feed the baby in the wee hours. Yet nothing on earth felt as powerful as this need for her and Robert to keep these children and make them their daughters.

There was a knock on the door and Ivy poked her head through. 'Is she asleep?'

'No, wide awake and in a very happy mood,' Aggie said, looking down at her lovingly as Ivy came over to do the same.

'Look at that face. Aren't you just the sweetest? Yes, you are,' she cooed. Baby Ivy gurgled and smiled and looked altogether so gorgeous both women laughed.

'She agrees, as well she should,' Ivy said, lowering herself onto the other side of the seat. 'I could sit and watch her day.'

'I pretty much do when I'm not running after her scallywag sisters,' Aggie admitted. 'Magnificent time-wasters, babies. I've hardly left the house for weeks.'

'What has Sister Ursula to say about things?'

Aggie shrugged. 'She expected me to stop work anyway. Robert told me she simply said "God works in mysterious ways" and left it at that.'

Ivy nodded, watching her thoughtfully for a moment. 'He does indeed. Aggie … Aggie, I hope you get to keep her. I mean, when Riley comes, we'd have to agree, but I'll do everything I can to hand over my guardianship and have you adopt them.'

Aggie looked at her, her heart filled with gratitude. 'Thank you,' she whispered as the baby curled her hand around her finger. 'I know you will.'

They gazed at her a while longer then Ivy spoke again. 'I would still want to see them all the time, and Riley too, as Fiona wanted;

I'm thinking the twins could spend lots of nights with me, or him, especially at this age. They're such social little souls and I think it would make everyone happy, and the girls, to share them around a bit.'

'Yes, that would certainly be important, that you both remain a big part of their lives,' Aggie agreed, although fearfully.

'Riley is a good man and he'll want what's best for them,' Ivy reassured her, 'but we'll have to wait and see.'

'Yes,' Aggie said, 'I guess we will.' There was nothing else to say about it, but as Aggie looked at her much-loved sister she couldn't help but reach over and squeeze Ivy's hand. 'Thank you again for doing this for us. It's ... everything, as you know.'

Ivy smiled. 'It just seems so natural and right that it be you. I mean, you know I'd take them full time with Patrick if you didn't. He said he'd be willing. But I'll see them all the time anyway ... and we'll hopefully be starting a family soon,' she added, looking guilty. 'You know, if that's how it happens for us.'

'I can't see why it wouldn't,' Aggie said. 'You've never had the problems I've had in that ... area.'

'Yes, I know, but ...' She trailed off, blushing, and Aggie frowned, realising there was more to it.

'What is it?'

'Oh, nothing ...'

She looked embarrassed and Aggie understood.

'You're worried about the bedroom, aren't you, on your wedding night?'

Ivy's eyes flew to Aggie's and she gaped at her but then nodded. 'Yes ... yes, I am a bit.'

'What is it you're worried about?'

'Well, I mean, I don't know, it's just that Patrick and I, we started off ... wonderfully on my birthday. I mean, just kissing, and it felt so incredible, but since then ...'

Aggie considered that. 'I suppose he's had a lot on his mind,' she said, picking up the yawning baby and wrapping her in her blanket to cradle her close. 'Especially when all the drama occurred and he was so worried about you. He probably felt like you needed to be handled with kid gloves for a long while.'

'Yes, I thought that too, only …'

'Only what?' Aggie prompted, absently stroking the baby's back as her eyes began to close.

'Only today he … he started kissing me again and I don't know, it didn't feel the same.'

Aggie frowned, slightly worried about that. 'Well, I guess on your birthday you'd had quite a bit of champagne. Maybe you need some Dutch courage to get things going once more? I know we always get a bit amorous when we have a tipple or two,' she confided and Ivy blushed again, then nodded.

'Oh,' she said. 'That's an idea.'

'You've got Nick Johnson's party tomorrow night before the big day. Why don't you have a few glasses and see if you don't enjoy a goodnight kiss after that? I'm betting anything you will. Patrick's a very handsome man, after all,' she added.

'Yes, he is.'

'We really do like him, Robert and I,' Aggie added. 'He'll be a wonderful brother-in-law.'

'I'm sure he will,' Ivy said, sighing. 'I just wish Frankie thought that too. She says she likes him but I don't think she does, the way she always gets annoyed at him all the time. Haven't you noticed?'

Aggie chose her words carefully. 'I think worrying about Frankie not liking Patrick is the last thing you should concern yourself with.'

'You really think so?' she said doubtfully.

'I really do.'

❖

He'd washed and shaved and wore a new shirt and breeches but Riley Logan still felt very nervous as he sat on his borrowed horse outside Ivy Merriweather's home. It was impressive and intimidating, as were most houses along here, but hers was the most beautiful. As it bloody would be, he thought with a sigh, feeling unworthy of visiting her. She seemed like a princess living in a castle and he just a commoner, gazing at her from afar. Yet he wasn't here to court her, he reminded himself, he was here to see his nieces and decide what was best for them, although the idea of Ivy raising them with Patrick was a difficult one to conceive.

It had to be sorted out, however, and he was looking forward to seeing them. This was the longest he'd ever gone without visiting the twins and he supposed the baby would look very different now. Suddenly he couldn't wait, and he dismounted and tied the horse to the front post, going through the gate to knock on the door.

Riley wiped his palms on his trousers nervously as the sound of footsteps approached and children's voices could be heard. The door opened and an older man wearing spectacles looked out.

'Can I help you?'

'Yes, I wonder if Ivy is home at all? I'm ...'

'Uncle Riley!' Tricia cried and Annie came running too. They nearly bowled him over, climbing up for hugs, and he held them tight.

'There now,' he said as they both buried their heads against him and began to cry.

'We missed you,' Annie said, clinging hard.

'I missed you too, little poppets,' he said, kissing the tops of their heads. He lowered them down and each twin held one of his legs as he introduced himself to the man.

'I'm Riley Logan,' he said, stretching out his hand.

'Albert Merriweather,' the man said, tears in his eyes too. 'And I must start by saying thank you … thank you for saving my daughter. We owe you the biggest debt of gratitude …' He took off his spectacles to dab at his eyes with his handkerchief.

'It was my greatest pleasure,' Riley replied sincerely. The greatest of his life, in fact. 'Is she …?'

'Of course, of course,' he said. 'Do come in. Ivy!' he called. 'Oh, and you'll want to see the baby but Aggie and my wife have just taken her out for a walk. Let me go tell them you're here.'

'I can wait …'

'No, no, they won't be far away,' Albert said, grabbing his coat. 'Back in a moment.'

He left and Riley heard the tread of footsteps, looking up to see Ivy come into view, slowly descending the staircase. He gazed at her, entranced by the vision she made. The window behind made an ethereal backdrop as the light caught her glorious red hair, and she looked like an angel, silhouetted by the glow and dressed in yellow, eyes widening in her beautiful face as she spied him.

'Riley,' she said softly, pausing momentarily before doing something most unexpected and running down the stairs to embrace him.

He put his arms around her, stunned to be doing so, holding her soft form against his chest for the briefest of sweet seconds before she drew away, too soon.

'Oh, oh, I'm so sorry,' she said, beginning to cry. 'I just haven't seen you since … since …' She looked down at the twins who were still clinging to Riley's legs and didn't finish but he understood. 'Did you … are those men …'

'She's been avenged,' he told her quietly. 'By each other in the end, but I saw it with my own eyes.'

'Is Daddy coming here too?' Tricia asked, perhaps picking up more than Riley had supposed she would. Riley looked down at her then back at Ivy, who simply shrugged. He thought now was as good a time as any.

Riley knelt down in front of them. They stood together, holding each other's hands, and Ivy rested her own on each of their shoulders.

'Has Daddy gone to the angels too?' Annie asked.

'No, he's a bad man,' Tricia said, 'he'd go to the other horrible place.'

It shocked Riley to hear such a thing come out of his four-year-old niece's mouth and it made him phrase what he said about George carefully.

'I didn't realise you felt that way … and I didn't know Mummy was so unhappy,' he said, 'and I'm sorry for that. But Daddy has gone away now, to wherever God has decided to take him, and Ivy and I are going to help look after you.'

'Are you gonna get married?' Annie asked hopefully, and he wished more than anything on earth right now that he could say yes.

'Nuh, Ivy's marrying Patrick on Saturday, remember? We're flower girls,' Tricia said, and the news cut at Riley's heart. He forced himself to continue.

'That's right. We will work it all out for you, though, and the most important thing to know is that we love you, with all our hearts,' Riley told them. 'And we are going to make your lives very, very happy.'

'We like it here with Aggie and Robert,' Tricia told him. 'They let us make cakes all the time and we have a pop and a nanny.'

'And a Frankie,' Annie added.

'Do you now?' Riley said, glancing up at Ivy with a smile. 'Well, that's very special, isn't it?'

'Come and see our room,' Annie said, tugging at his hand. 'We've got lots of toys and it's like being princesses, only we don't sleep for a hundred years. Pop says we're early birds.'

'Without worms though,' Tricia added and Riley chuckled, patting her head and standing.

'I'll come see in a minute. I just want to have a word with Ivy first.'

'All right, we'll make you a cake. A blue one,' Annie decided.

'Why blue?' he asked but they'd run off.

He looked questioningly at Ivy but she just smiled at him, still with tears in her lovely eyes. 'You handled that very well.'

Riley sighed, rubbing his neck. 'I can't believe how little they cared, but then again ...' He paused, still staring at her and unable to halt the next words. 'You're looking very well.'

Her dimples darted as she replied softly. 'So are you.'

Something shifted inside him and he reached up one finger to graze her cheek, despite the news of her impending marriage, and the dimple faded beneath his touch. Another emotion passed across her face and Riley recognised it, feeling it too. Unbelievably, it was longing.

But the sound of footsteps approaching interrupted the moment and Riley turned to see Aggie arrive, holding the baby, her parents behind her with the pram. And, as his eyes caught Ivy's sister's, he witnessed another reaction on this emotionally charged afternoon. One of pure fear.

He was here. He was here and he could take her children away. Aggie truly liked Riley Logan but right now he was the last person she could ever wish to see. Her hold tightened on baby Ivy as she nodded and made herself greet him.

'Hello, Riley.'

'Aggie,' he said with a smile. 'Good to see you again.' He looked a bit confused though and she supposed her true feelings at seeing him there showed.

'This is my wife, Harriet,' her father said and her mother's reaction to meeting Riley was transparently worshipful.

'You saved our girl,' she said, clasping his hands in her own. 'I can never, ever thank you enough.' Then she hugged him and Riley looked over at Ivy, rather embarrassed.

'Anyone would have done the same,' he said.

'Not necessarily,' Albert said. 'We thank God every day it was a decent man like you.'

Ivy was looking rather shame-faced now but Riley merely praised her as Harriet let him go, wiping her cheeks.

'Ivy deserved no less and was a very brave patient. It was an honour to care for her.'

He said it with tenderness and Ivy gave him a look that made Aggie wonder, but there was too much terror coursing through her to think about what it meant. She clutched the baby with trembling hands, knowing she needed to show her to him and wishing little Ivy wasn't quite so adorable now that her uncle had arrived with the power to take her away.

'Hey,' he said gently as Aggie regretfully handed her over. The baby blinked up at him and he held her with care. 'How's our little one been?' Then he reached up and took her tiny hand in his and she smiled at him. Tears filled his eyes as he half-laughed, half-cried at the sight. 'You've got your mother's smile,' he told her and Aggie realised that she did. The family resemblance felt like a threat, however, and Aggie resisted the urge to take the baby from him and run a hundred miles.

'She's such a good baby,' Harriet told him. 'Never a moment's bother. Mine cried half the night, especially Frankie.'

No, Aggie wanted to say. Tell him she's difficult, that she wails all night long and he'd never get a minute's peace.

'She was an easy baby right from the start, Fiona said,' Riley told them, still gazing at her. 'Fortunately.'

There was so much sadness in his voice that Aggie felt for him but she still itched to take the baby out of his arms as the twins came running back in.

'Uncle Riley's here, Nanny,' Tricia told Harriet, hugging his leg. 'We're making a blue cake.'

'Well, that sounds a treat,' she said. 'Come on in and sit down, Riley. Would you like a cup of tea?'

'I'd love one,' he said, still holding the baby and looking about awkwardly.

'Allow me,' Aggie said, putting out her arms quickly, and it felt like heaven as he handed baby Ivy back and she held her close.

They all moved into the lounge room where Pretty Boy sat on his tree. He looked at Riley curiously. 'Pretty Boy,' he said and Riley looked taken aback but then he started to chuckle.

'Well, I've been called many things but never that.'

The others laughed too but Aggie seemed incapable of it, as she sat with the baby, rigid on the edge of her chair.

'Can you put the cake on for us, Nanny?' Annie asked.

'Of course,' she said and the trio moved off to the kitchen to get it baking and make the tea.

'So,' Albert said, 'how long are you in town for?'

It was a simple question but a loaded one and Aggie awaited the answer with bated breath.

'I'm not really sure,' Riley said. 'I need to understand what's been going on with the girls first and discuss things with Ivy. It's kind of an odd situation, and I'm sorry for the position we've put you all in,' he added.

'No, no, don't apologise,' Albert said. 'Having three little girls in our home once more has been an absolute delight.'

'Well, that's good to hear,' he said. 'I knew from what Ivy had told me about you all that this was a safe and happy place to send them, although it was a huge thing to ask. I don't know what

Fiona was thinking really when she said we both should care for them,' he glanced at Ivy, 'but I think she just knew they'd be loved. Those were her last words, anyway. Love them, she said.'

Aggie hugged the baby. Fiona certainly got her wish.

Ivy nodded at him. 'They are definitely getting plenty of that,' she told him.

Riley paused to gaze at Ivy, and Aggie read something in it again, despite her own fears, starting to wonder if Fiona had chosen these two people to care for her children together for more than one reason.

'What are you planning to do?' Albert said as Harriet returned with the tea tray. Her mother stood frozen as they all waited to hear the answer to that life-changing question.

'Well, first of all, you should know that George, Fiona's husband, is now dead.' He said it without emotion and Aggie let that news soak in. She felt rather emotionless about it herself. A man like that didn't deserve pity and certainly didn't deserve his three precious daughters. She'd doubted the outlawed George was an obstacle in her and Robert's quest to keep the girls, regardless, but it was good to know he never would be.

'I'd say we're sorry for your loss, however ...' Albert said, and Riley glanced at him grimly.

'He's a loss to no-one,' Riley said, and Albert nodded.

'Indeed.'

'So that leaves us where?' Albert said.

'Well, that depends. What do you want to do, Ivy?'

Ivy looked over at Aggie and smiled at her and Aggie felt a surge of love for her sister as she replied. 'From the moment they arrived the children have been drawn to Aggie and Robert and I think that, well, the truth is ...'

Aggie closed her eyes, took a deep breath for courage and spoke up. 'I can't have children of my own,' she said, opening them once more and clasping baby Ivy against her. 'Robert and I, we love them so,' she admitted as tears begin to choke her words. 'We want them to be ours.'

Riley looked at her, nodding slowly as he took that in. 'But I still want to be in their lives.'

'You can be. We all can, in fact,' Ivy said. 'Aggie and Robert are just down the road so they'll not be too far from the river and you … and Patrick and I too. We're moving in here while we build our house so … so the children will have so much love in their lives, just like Fiona wanted.'

'I suppose it could work,' he said as Aggie silently begged him to agree. 'But it's not exactly what Fiona asked for. She wanted them to be with you and … and with me.'

Ivy stared over at him and there was so much emotion there Aggie feared the very worst: that her sister secretly loved this man and they would raise the three girls together, as his dying sister had requested. As a family.

'It … can't work that way though, can it?' Ivy said.

Riley stared back and for one terrifying moment Aggie thought he would say that it could.

'No,' he said. 'I suppose it can't.'

'They will be very happy, having so many people care for them,' Albert said, 'but we would never keep them away from you, understand. They're yours to visit whenever you wish it, or to visit you. We'd respect your sister's wishes, of course.'

Riley nodded. 'Yes, I'm sure you will, and I suppose this is the best outcome for them. A dream life, really, having so many people spoiling them,' he said, looking at Ivy one last time before uttering his verdict. 'I agree.'

Aggie nearly collapsed, so great was her relief, and Harriet managed to put down the tea tray to put her arm around her.

'Thank you for this,' Harriet choked as Aggie leant against her, the baby held close. 'First you save our daughter's life and now you give us grandchildren to love and Aggie … Aggie and Robert this chance to have a family.' She shook her head, looking over at him with tearful gratitude. 'You've changed all our lives forever, Riley Logan.'

Riley smiled at her, looking back at Ivy once more. 'And you've forever changed mine.'

'I can ask our friend Douglas to draw up the adoption papers and make it legal,' Albert said. 'Should only take a few weeks. Are you planning to stay nearby?'

'Most likely down on the boat,' Riley said. 'I hadn't really thought about it, to be honest. I was in too much of a hurry just to get here.'

'You must stay with us, at least until after the wedding,' Harriet said, recollecting herself now and beginning to pour the tea. 'We've an extra bed in the annex we'd be happy for you to have and you can spend some time with the girls.'

'I'm not invited,' he hedged but Harriet waved his objection away.

'Of course you are. You're part of the family now.'

Riley's eyes were on Ivy as he slowly agreed. 'I guess I can, then.'

And the look Ivy sent him meant Aggie couldn't completely relax and believe the girls would truly be her daughters, knowing she wouldn't rest easy until those adoption papers arrived and were signed. For love was a powerful thing, never more so than when dying wishes were made. Aggie hoped desperately that Douglas Earle would draw up the legal documents fast and that his son kissed her sister properly after drinking champagne tomorrow night. She needed this wedding to go ahead and their marriage to last.

Thirty-Three

Happy birthday to you,
Happy birthday to you,
Happy birthday, dear Nick,
Happy birthday to you!

Frankie sang along but without her usual gusto. She was devoid of any feelings other than guilt as she watched Ivy float about, as beautiful and colourful as ever in her new, bright blue dress. Patrick watched her too, but every now and then he sent Frankie a look and it seared through her whenever he did. She was aware of where he was even without looking, so intense was the weight of his presence. However she thought she could endure this night she'd never know. Still, Nick had begged her to come and she'd felt it would be too mean not to show, even though it felt like torture.

'Champagne?' Nick asked her, back by her side after cutting the cake to applause. He'd been hovering about all evening and Frankie suspected he was beginning to try to woo her in earnest, little knowing he couldn't have picked a worse possible evening to do so.

'Yes, please,' she said, partly to get rid of him for a minute and partly because she could use a drink. The two she'd already had were simply making her feel worse, churning in her remorse-filled gut as she tried to think about anything else but Patrick and Ivy and the terrible thing she'd done. But it was no use. The memory replayed in her mind over and over again. She couldn't believe he'd suddenly kissed her in such a way and she couldn't believe she'd kissed him back, and with so much passion. Her greatest fear – that she'd give in to her feelings without restraint if the moment arrived – had come true. She felt way out of control of herself, giving in to the feelings he'd been firing in her with such thoughtless abandon.

She felt like a fraud too – all her declarations of never needing or wanting a man in her life seemed a mockery. How could she be so weak as to capitulate so easily when the moment of truth arrived? And how could she devote her life to politics and freeing the binds that tied women down if she was going to give in to men she desired so easily? Next time she could end up married and unable to work, or, worse still, embroiled in an illicit affair. That she was in danger of that very possibility with Patrick terrified and sickened her. It should be easy to simply say that it was just a one-off but a mighty force had been awakened within her. Powerful and drugging. It frightened Frankie that it had completely stolen her morality and reason at first touch. The natural law overruling her, after all.

'Here you are,' said Nick, handing her the champagne. She looked at him properly. He was a good-looking young man, tall and broad-shouldered, and rather amusing when he wanted to be. Frankie wondered if his touch would have the same effect on her or if it was just Patrick that ignited it. She wondered if she should experiment and let Nick kiss her tonight to try to find out but that could be inviting a whole other world of strife into her life, especially if she did feel the same burning passion that she'd felt with Patrick. Nick was single and there wouldn't be any reason to break away from his embrace, except the obvious one – that she didn't want a man in her life. To toy with him so seemed most unfair.

'Thanks,' Frankie said, accepting the champagne and taking a sip.

'Cake should be passed around soon,' he said.

'That's nice,' she replied, distracted by the sight of Patrick crossing the room to talk to Aggie and Robert, ridiculously handsome in his new evening suit.

'I meant to say you look lovely tonight,' Nick said and she turned to him again, trying to keep her focus away from Patrick.

'Thank you,' she said. Her dress was new as well. The three sisters had gone shopping for bridesmaid dresses a few weeks ago and bought three evening dresses while they were at it, in anticipation of this party. It was red and had been made to hug her figure, and Frankie had regretted the choice when she put it on tonight. Her mother had twisted and pinned her thick blonde hair in a French chignon too, leaving her neck and shoulders bare, and Frankie felt altogether far too on display.

'Did you get any nice presents for your birthday?' she said, changing the direction of the conversation.

'A new cricket bat, want to see?'

'I'd love to,' Frankie said. Anything to get away from Patrick.

'It's just in the study,' he said, leading her down the hall.

Nick pushed open the door and she saw that it was a large room with an extensive library of books and several artworks on display. Nick's father was a wealthy businessman and Frankie stroked the huge timber desk at the study's centre in awe.

'What a wonderful space to think,' she said, taking in the fireplace and bay window with interest.

'Yes, isn't it? I'm lucky enough to do most of my studying in here,' he said. 'Speaking of which, Patrick tells me you two have been hitting the books together. I wouldn't mind a study partner too, if you had the time.'

Frankie could feel the colour rise to her face and looked away to hide it, wondering when Patrick had mentioned it. Surely not tonight?

'I might do,' she hedged, drinking her champagne.

Nick noticed, raising his eyebrows. 'Thirsty?'

She glanced at her now-empty glass in surprise. 'I must have been.'

'I'll get you another in a moment. Now, where'd Mum hide that bat?' he said, opening the cupboard to look. 'Puts things away so fast I don't have any time to … oh, here it is.'

Nick drew it out and Frankie inspected it with appreciation. 'What a beauty,' she said. It was a wonderful bat but she couldn't help but feel that he seemed rather indulged and immature all of a sudden. A rich young man with expensive toys his mother puts away for him. In fairness, life hadn't dealt him any harsh lessons in maturity as yet, she supposed. Not like herself. Or Patrick.

'Properly oiled willow, all the way from England. I should be able to whack a few fours with this, I hope.'

'I should think so,' she said, investigating it for a moment longer before he put it back in the cupboard with care. He turned around and she looked to the door but he took her hand, surprising her.

'Frankie,' he began, his expression earnest. 'I know you say you never want a man in your life and I realise how independent you are, but I've rather liked you for an awful long time and I was just wondering … well, seeing as it's my birthday, if you might reconsider … and … and …'

Then for the second time in as many days a man caught her off guard and kissed her. She went to pull back but reconsidered, deciding she may as well let the experiment occur at this point. It felt nice and not unenjoyable, but there was no flooding passion, by any means. No heat searing through her veins that blocked all common sense. Nick grew bolder, putting his arms around her and drawing her close and she could appreciate that he was quite muscular and attractive but still there was no urgent reaction to him. There was a reaction behind him, however, and Frankie opened her eyes to stare straight into Patrick's angry gaze. She pulled back, aghast.

'What do you think you're doing?'

Nick swung around in surprise. 'Patrick. Sorry, mate. Your er ... future sister-in-law and I were just ... well, actually I was kissing her, as you probably saw,' he said, sending him a rueful grin. 'We probably should head back in to the party now, though.'

'Yes, they're asking for you,' Patrick said, his tone even, but Frankie saw the anger still flashing in his eyes. 'You go ahead Nick. Frankie, a word with you, please.'

'Don't keep her too long,' Nick said, smiling at Frankie, and she tried to smile too but it was an effort.

He left and Patrick glared at her. 'What do you think you're doing?' he demanded again.

Frankie felt mortified but his attitude was making her angry too. 'Kissing Nick Johnson,' she said. 'Do you have a problem with that?'

'Yes,' he said, still glaring.

'Well, I don't see why you should. He's a single man, I'm a single woman – there's no law against it, is there?'

'I would have thought you'd have been feeling a bit too upset to be kissing someone else after ... after what happened yesterday,' he said, lowering his voice.

'You're the one who seems upset,' she said, sticking out her chin.

'You're damn right I'm upset,' he said in quiet fury. 'I was up half the night, feeling like the world's biggest cad and thinking you'd be feeling wretched too, and I was going to apologise but now ...'

'Now what?'

'Now it seems like you don't care.'

Frankie swallowed hard. 'Of course I care,' she admitted. 'I was up half the night as well.'

'Then why did you think kissing Nick Johnson was going to fix anything?' he said, looking hurt rather than furious.

'I suppose I ... I just wanted to see ...'

Patrick moved closer and her heart began to beat wildly. 'See what?'

'If ... if ...'

'If it felt like that with other men?' he guessed.

'Yes,' she whispered, staring at his mouth.

'Does it?' He looked at her like he was barely controlling himself, and she knew they were playing a very dangerous game, yet she couldn't seem to stop herself.

'No.'

His eyes burnt into hers but she dragged her gaze away and moved towards the door.

'I can't do this, Patrick ... we can't do this to Ivy ...'

'I don't know if I can go through with it,' he said and she stopped still. 'I think ... I think I'm—'

'*No*,' she said desperately, turning back to face him, halting his words. 'You can't say it. It's just a phase. It will fade away. I've chosen not to have a man in my life and that's my prerogative and Ivy ... Ivy will be your beautiful wife come tomorrow.'

'But—'

'You need to forget anything ever happened between us, Patrick – I'm not a woman who will ever marry and have children anyway. You chose the right sister in Ivy,' she said, trying not to cry, thinking of her younger sister's sweet face. 'Be a good husband to her,' she finished, turning to leave the room.

The party was in full swing and Ivy was laughing at something Nick was saying as he and a few of the other cricketers stood around the gramophone with Robert. Dessert had been served, and the table was surrounded while quite a few couples danced nearby, but Frankie avoided them all, skirting around the edge of the room to fetch her coat and just go home. Yet there was one person she couldn't avoid as Aggie's gaze found her, flicking over to where Patrick emerged from the hallway, then back again. Frankie knew her sister could see what was going on, as clearly as if Frankie had told her. Aggie knew Frankie's heart too well not to see when it was breaking.

Thirty-Four

Ivy had drunk a few glasses of champagne, as Aggie had suggested, but Patrick didn't seem in a very amorous mood as his carriage driver took them home. He seemed preoccupied and when she took his hand he looked at it in a strange way. She persevered anyway, needing to feel the way she'd felt on her birthday to know she was truly doing the right thing in getting married tomorrow.

She reached up to cup his cheek and kissed him and he kissed her back but it was the same as a few days ago in the stable: nice but lacking that wonderful feeling they'd shared before. She drew back to look at him, confused.

'Is something wrong?' she said.

'No,' he told her, 'everything's fine. I'm just a bit tired, is all.'

He put his arm around her and she snuggled in against him but even with her very limited knowledge of such things Ivy knew something wasn't right. Two people who were getting married on the morrow should be eager to kiss one another, and madly in love, and it worried her. She wanted a husband, he obviously wanted a wife, and they liked each other. What was missing between them?

Yet, even as she thought the words she knew the answer. *What's missing is the way Riley makes you feel.*

She tried desperately to push that truth away but once Patrick had dropped her off with only a perfunctory goodnight kiss she couldn't seem to halt it.

Everyone was in bed when she went into the house but Ivy knew she wouldn't be able to sleep so she headed out to the ponds, strolling about them restlessly, huddled in her coat. Wondering if Riley was up, despite herself. She drew closer to the annex, unable to resist being nearer to him and suddenly there he was, wide awake and rolling a cigarette as he leant against the annex door, but he was really watching her.

'How was the party?'

'Good,' she said, coming closer, 'how was your night?'

'Had a great time playing with the kids, then it was pretty much the same as usual,' he said, 'just keeping company with the moon and reading awhile.'

Ivy nodded. She would have preferred to be here than at the party, listening to his rumbling voice paint pictures of wondrous tales from days gone by. It surprised her, realising that she'd changed from the social butterfly she used to be to someone who was happier with the gentler comforts of home.

Riley stepped away from the door, pocketing his unlit cigarette as he moved towards her.

'So what did you get up to? Eating cake and drinking champagne?'

'Yes,' she said, tracing his features with her eyes, drinking him in. How wonderful it was to have him here at Kuranda in flesh and blood, no longer just a memory.

'Dancing?' he said and she shook her head.

'Patrick said he didn't feel like it.'

'Seems a shame to get all dressed up in your finery and never get to dance.'

She smiled up at him. 'Is that an invitation?'

Riley smiled back. 'It is now.'

He took her in his arms, never taking his eyes from hers, and slowly began to lead her around. She remembered this safe, warm place, as she leant her cheek against his chest. The gentle comfort of him. *Home.* The word floated through her mind as he began to hum softly under his breath, the same tune he often whistled or sang, and it reverberated against her ear.

'What's that song of yours?' she mumbled against him.

'It's American,' he told her, 'it's about a man who lives on the Wabash River.'

'Sing it to me?' she asked and he softly began.

Many years have passed since I strolled by the river,
Arm in arm, with sweetheart Mary by my side,

He stopped dancing, and she drew back, her eyes moving up to his, and he was gazing at her with intensity.

It was there I tried to tell her that I loved her,
It was there I begged of her to be my bride.

Ivy reached up, unable to resist kissing his mouth from where those beautiful words escaped. Riley pulled her against him, wrapping his arms around her and kissing her back. There was nothing unrestrained about this kiss and Ivy felt passion leap for the second time in her life, only this time it was even more consuming, like she wanted to crawl inside him, so much did she want this. So much did she love him. Her heart exploded with the fact and she drew back, the reality of that sinking in.

'I ... I can't ... do this. I'm getting married to Patrick tomorrow,' she said, shocked that she'd completely put that out of her mind. 'I ... I could never do that to him ... not after all I put him through before.'

'I love you,' Riley said, pushing her hair back from her face and cupping her cheek. 'Fiona knew it. It was her other dying wish, that I go to you and love you. That's why she wanted us to share the children, to keep the people she cared for the most together and for me to find happiness ... with you.'

Ivy began to cry at those words. 'But I can't do this to Patrick. It's too cruel.' She sobbed, backing away and shaking her head. '... and it's too late. I'm sorry, Riley, sorrier than you'll ever know.'

And with that she ran back to the house and up to her room to cry away the ache in her heart, broken by the knowledge that she'd found passion once more, but it came wrapped up in love for the wrong man. A man she believed in and a man who believed in her, but from whom she was wretchedly destined to forever be parted.

Thirty-Five

Aggie stared out the window to where the lone figure of Riley Logan stood, head bowed in the moonlight, and she clutched baby Ivy tight. Fear flooded through her as she considered what she'd just witnessed and what it could mean. For Ivy did love Riley Logan, she'd read it clearly in the way they had just danced and held each other and kissed, and in the wretchedness of Ivy's sobs as she ran from him. Ivy was too kind a girl to break things off with Patrick on the eve of their wedding day. But she didn't know what Aggie knew, that Frankie had feelings for Patrick and, if the look on his face had been anything to go by that night, he had feelings for her too.

Still, this wedding would go ahead. Ivy and Frankie were both blindly unwilling to hurt each other, yet ultimately they were making decisions that would leave them wretchedly unhappy. Aggie could well foresee it. And poor Riley Logan would be left alone in the process. There was really only one person who could put a stop to all this and that was Aggie herself, the single soul that knew the truth of it all, reading the turmoil going on with her sisters as clearly as if their stories lay before her in an open book.

But her own happiness lay in the balance in all this too, for if Riley married Ivy instead, the legal custodians of her children would be together, just as their dying mother had probably planned. That they would take them and raise them together seemed too logical and voided Aggie and Robert's need to adopt the three girls, for it was the power of Fiona's wishes that would hold the most sway. That love was sure to influence Riley's decision above all others, despite what Ivy might say.

Yes, sisterly love was a powerful thing and it was holding them all in its grip now as sibling loyalty made prisoners of them all, yet looking over at her sleeping husband's contented face and at the baby that rested in her arms, Aggie knew it had fierce competition. For the love a man and a woman shared was a force to be reckoned with too. And a parent's love likely more powerful still.

Well should it be a celebration of romantic love in the church tomorrow at Ivy and Patrick's wedding but in reality it looked set to be the scene of all forms of love going to war. In a year when a woman's right to vote was the most important topic of the day it seemed a woman's right to love would be the greatest fight of all.

Thirty-Six

Our Lady of the Rosary Church, Sydney, 14 June 1902

Sister Ursula began playing the 'Wedding March' and the congregation rose as one as the little twins walked down the aisle, adorable in their matching pink dresses, followed by Frankie and Aggie, also in pink. Ivy tried desperately to calm the nerves coursing through her body but it was no use.

'You ready, Ivy girl?' her father asked and she looked at his dear face, fighting the urge to blurt the truth: that she couldn't possibly marry Patrick Earle today. That she loved Riley Logan, with all her heart. He was her home and she belonged with him, building a life on the river where there were moments so beautiful you simply had to believe there was a God.

But it wasn't a river version of God joining her to Patrick today, it was a Catholic one. The service was being celebrated in his family's faith, at his mother's insistence, and it was too late for Ivy to take Him on as she stared out at the packed church. It was too late to change her mind, lest she hurt this man who had been through so much because of her. He deserved her loyalty on this day. And what God would join together, Catholic or otherwise, neither man, nor woman, could legally divide.

Ivy nodded at her father and he led her down the aisle to smiles from the assembled throng, but Ivy searched each face desperately, finding the one she most wanted, yet dreaded to see. He sat by himself, towards the back, and she caught his eye in the briefest of moments, reading burning love there and a last-minute plea that she change her mind.

Yet, as she dragged her eyes away and looked to the end of the aisle, Patrick met her gaze too, nervous and wide-eyed as he watched her approach. She knew she couldn't leave him at that altar any more than she could tell her father what she truly felt, and so she kept putting one foot in front of the other, helpless to avert her fate.

Sister Ursula changed the tune mid-song, as Harriet had suggested weeks ago, and the words filled Ivy's mind.

Daughters of freedom, the truth marches on,
Yield not the battle till ye have won!

And so Harriet's three daughters made their way down the aisle on this cold winter's day, yet there was no truth marching with the bride, for the battle for true love was well yielded. Indeed over before it had barely begun.

She reached the end of the aisle and could see Father Brown glaring at Sister Ursula as she finished playing the anthem but the old nun glared defiantly back at him. Ivy registered that at least one woman in this church had won a small victory today.

Father Brown turned to Albert then, his loud voice booming.

'Who gives this man to this woman in holy matrimony?'

'I do,' her father said and Ivy felt the finality of the situation descend over her as he took her hand and placed it in Patrick's.

He looked slightly sick too but tried to smile and she tried to return it as they turned to face the priest and the Latin Mass began. Ivy looked over to her sisters as they stood beside her, her last bastion of hope. Her protectors. But only God Himself could save Ivy's broken heart now.

Frankie was drawing on the deepest strength she possessed: the love she felt for her family, especially for her younger sister Ivy as she glowed in bridal white like the angel she was. It was the only thing that stopped her running from this place and away from the terrible truth: that she was in love with the man Ivy was marrying. For 'feelings' had ceased to be the word she applied to what coursed through her. All the emotions she felt for him had become that one, great, all-encompassing force. He'd almost uttered the word himself last night but she'd stopped him, for it could never be admitted by either of them now.

Yet it was true. She loved him, as maddening and argumentative as he could be.

They fired each other's blood in more ways than one yet he'd admired her for her mind first, long before their bodies had a played a part in it, to the point he would support her, she knew, if she was the one who married him that day. He'd listened to her and he'd changed, a respect not many men she knew afforded women. A man she once considered pompous and incapable of supporting the feminist cause was now a man who would help a wife have a career and fight for reform. He'd come a long way that year, showing a depth of character she would never have supposed he possessed, and a loyalty unsurpassed as he stood honouring his vow to Ivy. Doing what was right, despite how he felt.

Frankie knew she would go away while they honeymooned and not return for quite a long time, perhaps visit her great-uncle

Frank in Queensland or go to Melbourne and perhaps try to meet with Vida Goldstein, who was returning from her American tour. Begin her spinsterish political life in earnest, knowing the only man she ever would have compromised it for would never be hers. The one who still would have let her pursue her passions, indeed support them as they studied and lobbied together, and who would have helped her find a way to navigate it all as a married woman. They could have journeyed through their careers together, fulfilling aspirations. Lifting one another up. He was a rare such man, as she'd realised too late. But she was duty bound by her love for her sister, and she was destined to be his sister too.

The priest droned on, binding Ivy to this man, like a spell they'd never be able to break. Latin words, like so many others found in law. But this was God's law, and the law of nature – the primal fact that men and women were drawn together and joined by the flesh – ruled on. The decision irreversible once vows were made in these holy walls.

Frankie lifted her gaze to Aggie, knowing she was the only one who would ever suspect the truth. There was no censure as her sister returned her look, only understanding, and something else Frankie struggled to read. But then the big moment arrived as the priest reverted to English and Frankie braced herself to watch the life-changing moment that would seal all their fates as Ivy finally became what Frankie had never have thought she wanted for herself and indeed, would never be: Patrick Earle's wife.

Aggie struggled as she watched it all unfold. There were so many people to love that it was impossible to choose what was right when her heart overflowed with it all: sisterly love one moment, maternal love the next. Beside her, Frankie's eyes were huge and round, like she watched a funeral service rather than a marriage. At their pew, the twins were transfixed, and baby Ivy cooed and smiled on Robert's lap, bringing all of Aggie's mothering instincts to the fore. And then there was her love for her husband as he sat distracted from the ceremony, gazing at their soon-to-be daughters adoringly.

Everyone she loved most was caught in this web and Aggie was the only one who could untangle them but, oh the risk, she agonised, looking over at the baby once more. She was standing now, her little legs flexing in her stockings as she tried to find her balance. It reminded Aggie of something, one of her earliest memories, of her father calling from the lounge room all those years ago. 'She's walking!'

Aggie's gaze was drawn to that baby, now a grown-up bride, as she took yet another momentous step. Somehow Aggie found the courage to look at Ivy's expression properly for the first time, finding her sister's eyes trained on Father Brown's face as he intoned, '... a decision to be made reverently, solemnly and in the eyes of God ...'

But Ivy's eyes were filled with terror and something that broke Aggie's heart: a terrible aching sadness. Something that her sister would now live with for the rest of her days, married to a man she didn't love while the one she did watched on, tied to her by a dying woman's words.

'... what God joins together, man must not divide ...'

Baby Ivy gurgled happily and Aggie felt a tear inside as she desperately tried to choose between those warring loves.

Father Brown cleared his throat. 'If there is anyone here who knows of any reason why this man and woman should not be joined together ...'

The love she felt as a wife, as a mother, as a sister ...

'... let them speak now or forever hold their peace.'

Aggie's eyes flew from the baby then back to Ivy and all Aggie saw was the little girl in her sister once more, the one she'd so achingly nearly lost not six months ago.

'Then, by the power invested in me …'

'I object.'

Thirty-Seven

There were gasps around the church and Aggie's heart beat hard, heat flooding through her with the shock that she'd been the one to say it.

Father Brown paused and stared over at her, astounded at first then demanding, 'On what grounds?'

Aggie sought desperately for the right words but realised the truth must simply march on. 'This man and woman don't love each other, they each love someone else.'

There were more gasps and Sybil Earle could be clearly heard. 'Of all the outrageous things … Patrick, refute this nonsense at once.'

But Patrick was turning towards Ivy and they both gaped at one another.

'You love someone else?' Ivy said, eyes huge.

Patrick hesitated before answering. 'Yes,' he admitted as the room erupted further. 'Yes, I'm sorry but … but it's true. I do. And … and you?'

Ivy nodded, tears glistening in her eyes. 'I do too.'

She looked down the aisle towards the back of the church where Riley Logan was slowly standing. Scandalised muttering from the congregation rose as he began to walk towards her, and Ivy ran down the altar steps. Riley began to run too, then she launched herself in his arms as he spun her around, both laughing yet crying too. Lowering her to the ground, he lifted her veil, his expression rapturous and reverently adoring as he kissed her.

'I love you,' she wept.

'I love you too.'

'Well, I'll be,' Harriet said.

'A common man like that over my Patrick …?' Sybil said, clearly furious, but Ivy and Riley didn't care. They were still kissing, then held each other close.

'Marry me?' Riley said.

And Ivy smiled through her tears as she looked up at him, her face incandescent with pure joy. 'Yes.'

The crowded church was filled with shocked whispers and exclamations as they watched, but soon eyes began to turn back to Patrick.

'And … and what about you then?' the priest spluttered. 'Who is the woman you profess to love?'

But Patrick was already staring at Frankie, his expression filled with desperate heartache. 'One who won't wed me, I'm afraid.'

Frankie stared back, still appearing stunned, but her face slowly lit into a glorious, tear-filled smile. 'Oh, I don't know,' she said, eyes glittering. 'It's customary in these situations for the groom to marry the bridesmaid.'

Patrick gazed at her in disbelief before he broke into a smile too, one filled with love, and he moved over to stand before her. 'Well, I'd best act on that decision immediately before you realise you've just broken your own law.'

'Some rules are made to be broken,' she said as he took her in his arms and kissed her. Sybil Earle collapsed in a faint.

'Frankie ...?' Harriet could be heard saying in amazement, turning to Albert, but he could only shrug. Aggie watched her parents shake their heads and begin to laugh, adding to the chaos in the church, and Father Brown looked around in consternation, red-faced.

'Sit down now, all of you,' he boomed loudly. 'This is a church, I'll have you remember.'

But the place was in complete uproar as the two couples continued to kiss and he threw his hands in the air and walked out. Aggie was left alone by the altar, her eyes trained on Robert. They were the only two people not moving or commenting as the twins ran down the aisle to Ivy and Riley at the back of the church. Aggie slowly followed them and Robert joined her, handing her the baby. She cradled little Ivy fearfully as they reached them. Ivy and Riley had drawn apart as the twins hugged their legs with excitement and Ivy looked at Aggie tearfully, her face shining with happiness as a bride's should. Ivy took her sister's hand.

'Thank you,' she whispered. 'I don't know how you ever knew, but thank you,' and Riley put his arm around Ivy, nodding, his expression reflecting hers.

'We can never ever repay you for this ...' he said but Aggie just looked at him with more terror and longing than she'd ever felt in her life.

'Yes ... yes, you can, in fact,' she managed to say as the twins stood between them all and she held the baby close.

Ivy and Riley gazed at one another, understanding dawning, and he looked back to Aggie and simply smiled. 'This doesn't change things for you. They'll all still be part of our lives and loved by us, as Fiona wanted, but it's you who deserves to have them in your home,' he added, tilting his head thoughtfully. 'I'm now realising that's one of the most courageous things I've ever seen, Aggie, considering what you thought you could lose.'

'We will all love them,' Ivy said, 'but they'll still be your daughters.'

Aggie began to cry as the terror melted away, and Robert held her shoulders, tearfully offering his thanks.

The twins gazed at them and Robert reached down and picked them up, one in each arm, and Aggie could finally believe that she had, at last, her own family.

'Does this mean we get to live with you?' Tricia asked and Aggie nodded. Tricia smiled at her, snuggling into Robert's neck contentedly and Aggie's heart swelled as Annie spoke.

'Do we still get wedding cake?' she said hopefully.

Aggie had to laugh then too but it was actually a very good question.

'We need a double wedding first,' Riley said. 'Where's that priest got himself to?' he wondered, looking around.

'He's run off to douse himself in holy water, I dare say,' Harriet said, coming over with Albert.

They paused in front of Ivy and Albert shook his head. 'Ah, my darling girl,' he said, 'what can I say? You look so happy.'

'I am. Truly,' Ivy told them both, beaming. 'I just can't believe Frankie too …'

Harriet nodded. 'Yes, let's get that odious priest back here to make this all official before any more of you change your mind. Dossie's over there giving Sybil Earle smelling salts as it is.'

Her parents set off to fetch him with Robert and Riley, the twins tagging excitedly along, leaving the two sisters alone. Aggie looked over at her sister and then down at her baby, Ivy's name-sake, feeling more complete and at peace now than she'd ever felt in her life.

'What made you decide, in the end?' Ivy said, thoughtful.

'Remembering my earliest memory, your first steps,' she said, holding the little infant's feet in her palm. 'This isn't my first baby Ivy, don't forget.'

Ivy smiled, a grateful, love-filled one, but Frankie was approaching and Patrick could be heard trying to calm his distraught mother down.

'Well, I'm sorry you don't want me to marry "that woman" but I'm afraid you're just going to have to get used to the idea ...'

The three sisters took one look at each other and embraced, happy tears falling, then Frankie pulled back to look at Ivy, doubt in her expression. 'I ... I hope you really are all right with this. I didn't mean ... it just happened ... I'm sorry ...'

'No,' Ivy said, 'never be sorry. I'm the happiest woman in the world that this has happened and that it's happening for you too. Mind you ... well, I can't believe I thought you didn't even like him ... and I definitely thought you'd never marry, not after all you said about it.'

'Me either,' Frankie said. 'I seem to have accidently fallen over the idea, which seems appropriate, for me.'

'But what about your political career?'

Frankie grinned. 'If anyone thinks a pesky ring on my finger is going to stop me from making a lot of noise they've got another think coming.'

'Patrick will support you, you know. He's changed a lot in his views,' Ivy said.

'Yes, he won't hold me back, I know. I wouldn't be saying yes otherwise, believe me.' She looked to Aggie. 'Thank you,' she whispered, her gaze moving down to baby Ivy. 'I can imagine how hard it must have been for you to speak up ... that is ... now that Ivy and Riley will be together ...'

'Nothing will change, as far as the children are concerned,' Ivy told her. 'This is the way it was always meant to be.'

Frankie stared from one to the other. 'So … so we all get what we want then?' she said in amazement, a happy laugh escaping as she clutched at both their hands.

'Looks that way,' Aggie told her joyfully, squeezing Frankie's fingers. 'Well, everyone except Sybil,' she added as the woman continued to complain.

'Yes, what a mother-in-law I'm inheriting. I think we best get a move on before she faints again,' Frankie said, rolling her eyes. 'Where is that bloody priest anyway?' she added too loudly and the woman gasped once more.

'Good Lord above, have mercy.'

The three Merriweather girls chuckled as the priest did, indeed, turn back up with the others and the two brides made their wedding march together not long after. Radiantly happy as they did so, not just as daughters of freedom but as sisters of freedom now, their battle for love finally won.

Thirty-Eight

Wahroonga, NSW, Christmas Day 1902

It was a beautiful home, sprawling and elegant, yet the three Merriweather girls had spent most of the day running around after children. The family hosting the party for the orphanage was generous and had laid out an enormous spread, and there was even to be a Nativity play this evening before the little ones were lavished with presents from under the enormous tree. It was far more than Aggie and her helpers had been able to give them in the past but this new guard of volunteers were very wealthy. They were kind women too and Aggie had been glad to relinquish her role to them and was grateful the Merriweathers had been extended an invitation today. It was a sort of thank you for all the years their family had been involved with the Sisters of Mercy and it was a special day, a final official farewell.

Frankie had only just returned from a trip to Melbourne with Patrick and they'd all sorts of adventures to report, including hearing Vida Goldstein speak *and* meeting the prime minister at a horse race. Frankie had walked straight up to him and introduced herself as 'a degreeless budding lawyer'. According to Patrick the man had impersonated a fish at the time.

Baby Ivy was fast asleep after running about on her chubby legs half the day, having given her proud parents an early Christmas present by taking her first steps earlier this week. Aggie still got weepy every time she spoke about it.

Looking out the window, the three sisters could finally rest for a while as the children ran about on the lawn below. Ivy watched on, patting her rounding stomach and commenting, 'Do they ever run out of energy?'

'Only when they're asleep,' Aggie said, laughing at the sight of the twins who were ostensibly competing in a boiled-egg-and-spoon race but in reality had paused to eat them. 'You'll be fine, don't worry. I know you'll make a wonderful mother. Look how much they all adore you as their aunt. Besides, you'll have Eddie with you to help out and that boy never runs out of steam.' Ivy and Riley had taken Eddie on as a shop apprentice in their brand-new store, and Father Brown hadn't been able to object to an actual position for the now-turned eleven-year-old. The twins adored him when they visited and he'd taken to river life like he was born to it. Riley said he was the hardest working lad he'd ever encountered, confirming Aggie's suspicion that his mischief-making was largely due to boredom.

'Is he still staying out of trouble?' Frankie asked.

'Not entirely,' Ivy said with a grin. 'He may or may not have been responsible for a sign found nailed to Windybank's wharf.'

'What did it say?' asked Frankie gleefully.

'Welcome to Windy Bum's,' Ivy said to Frankie's great amusement.

A waiter was walking by as afternoon refreshments were served and Frankie signalled to him, still chuckling as she passed some champagne along.

'What shall we drink to? A merry Christmas?' Ivy said.

'I think we're already having one of those,' Aggie replied. What with the neighbourhood carols last night and this wonderful Christmas Day, it would be a difficult holiday to top in future years. 'What's on the political agenda in 1903, Frankie?'

'Well, let me see. There's talk of a federal election come December. I very much hope to see some bills passed as a result of pressure on policy leading up to that. The first female vote is bound to have quite a bit of influence. Well, we're hoping anyway.'

'That sounds promising,' Aggie said.

'Yes, so long as the rich and influential don't swap too many envelopes along the way. It's a grubby game politics, or so I'm finding.'

They watched as some of the children of the wealthy new volunteers mingled with Eddie, the orphans and the twins, and Aggie marvelled at how differently young children could view each other compared to adults.

'They don't seem to know or care who is rich or poor or where each other have come from,' she said, watching her adopted daughters, 'or how much suffrage has changed all their fates.'

'The boys seem to be letting the girls play sport today, which is a start,' Frankie said. 'Perhaps some of the events of this year are already beginning to rub off.'

'Perhaps,' Aggie said. 'I just wonder how much the girls can achieve now, if they will make big inroads in their lifetime and have their time in parliament. It's still such a male-dominated world.'

'They need to not let that dissuade them,' Frankie said. 'For every closed door they find they need to knock on it again; to stay in the race and not keep letting the men draw too far ahead. It's all about perseverance, I'm finding. Not giving in.'

The others considered that. 'Do you think they'll find the world a kinder place in the end?' Ivy wondered as she touched her hand to the window pane.

'I like to think so,' Frankie said, watching too as Tricia's voice rang out.

'Eddie!' she called.

'Wait for us,' Annie added and Eddie paused in his running with the other boys.

'Come on, slow coaches,' he called back, looking over impatiently at the cricket game forming.

The twins chased after him hard, grabbing the hands of two other little girls as they went.

'They'll have their turn to speak out and make it so, soon enough,' Frankie said. 'Their own choices to make and a world to build.'

'Yes,' Ivy said softly, 'I suppose it's up to them.'

The sun beat down as the children raced on, Eddie no longer waiting for the twins.

'Eddie!' Annie cried again.

And Ivy heard the impatience edged with fondness as Eddie called back over his shoulder.

'You need to keep up with us, girls.'

Author's Note

This characters and events in this book are fictional however it is based on real events in history. Despite the enormous early successes of suffragettes in Australia, it took many years for laws to be changed and for representation to be attained. As such, I have included a timeline, letting events speak for themselves, but with much gratitude and admiration for the brave and passionate souls that fought for equality and all those who still do, to this day.

Yield not the battle till ye have won.

- 1890: First working women's trade union established
- 1891: Age of consent raised from 13 years to 16 years
- 1891: 'Monster petition' signed by 30,000 people supporting the right for women to vote in Victoria
- 1894: Blind children are given the right to an education
- 1895: Women are given the right to stand for election in South Australia
- 1902: Non-Indigenous women are given the right to vote and stand for election in federal parliament

- 1902: Ada Evans graduates from Sydney University with a law degree but, despite continuous lobbying, she is not admitted to the bar until 1921 and never practises
- 1903: Vida Goldstein stands for federal election but is unsuccessful
- 1903: Marie Curie becomes the first woman to receive a Nobel Prize (Physics)
- 1902–1914: Australian women visit the UK and USA in support of international suffrage, including Vida Goldstein on a sold-out tour. Muriel Matters chains herself to the divisive House of Commons grille in London. It is permanently removed.
- 1918: British women are given the right to vote
- 1920: American women are given the right to vote
- 1921: Edith Cowan becomes the first woman elected to Australian parliament and introduces the Women's Legal Status Act, allowing women to legally be considered 'persons' and therefore able to practise law
- 1943: Enid Lyons becomes the first Australian woman to be elected to the House of Representatives
- 1956: The marriage bar is lifted, allowing married women to remain teachers
- 1961: Contraceptive pill is allowed to married women
- 1962: Indigenous Australians are given the right to vote
- 1965: Merle Thornton and Rosalie Bogner chain themselves to the bar in the Regatta Hotel in Brisbane, demanding that women be allowed to drink in public bars
- 1966: Married women are allowed to work in the Commonwealth Service
- 1967: Indigenous Australians are recognised as citizens

- 1969: Abortion is made legal but only to women whose mental and physical wellbeing is considered to be in danger
- 1971: Bank of NSW grants women loans without a male guarantor
- 1972: Commonwealth government passes the right to equal pay
- 1972: Contraceptive pill becomes widely available
- 1972: Single mother's benefit is introduced
- 1972: Paid maternity leave is introduced
- 1975: First women's refuges are funded
- 1975: Women gain the right to file for no-fault divorce
- 1975: Racial discrimination act is passed
- 1975: Rape in marriage is outlawed in South Australia
- 1977: Employment on the basis of marital status or gender is outlawed
- 1979: Margaret Thatcher becomes Britain's first female Prime Minister
- 1983: Australia ratifies the convention on the elimination of all forms of discrimination against women
- 2008: Abortion is decriminalised in Victoria
- 2010: Julia Gillard is elected Australia's first woman Prime Minister
- 2016: Hillary Clinton becomes America's first woman to receive a presidential nomination
- 2016: Pakistani activist for female education Malala Yousafzai becomes the world's youngest ever recipient of the Nobel Peace Prize
- 2017: Same sex marriage is legalised in Australia
- 2019: Abortion is decriminalised in NSW
- 2019: Climate Activist Greta Thunberg becomes *Time Magazine*'s youngest ever Person of the Year

- 2020: Jacinda Ardern becomes the first woman to be re-elected as New Zealand's Prime Minister
- 2020: Kamala Harris becomes the first female Vice President of the United States of America

Acknowledgements

Embarking on a novel with such an important theme can be very daunting so before I give you all a few insights into the stories behind the story, I would firstly like to thank those who believed in, and supported me, on this journey. My wonderful agent, Helen Breitwieser, my amazing publishing team at HarperCollins: Jo Mackay and Nicola Robinson, my editor Annabel Blay (what would I do without your cleverness and insight?), and my publicists, Jo Munroe and Natika Palka.

I'd also like to thank my ever-kind husband, Anthony, for being my rock and helping me in my research, and my sons, Jimmy and Jack, for their understanding nods as I wailed over phrasing and for coming along on research days. You make me laugh and love every moment. Thank you also to Theresa Meury and Zoe Blockley for listening to me rave on about the events of days gone by, and to Guy Whitington for being my male literary sounding board. When it comes to authordom, the value of true friendship can certainly be measured in patience.

As one of three sisters, it was a great pleasure to write about the Merriweather girls. Like Aggie, my sister Linda is a nurturing, loving type and mothers us all, and Gen, although far from being a tomboy, embraces every opportunity in life with great enthusiasm and determination, much like Frankie. For my part, I suppose I'm a romantic idealist like Ivy, and I do love to sketch and dream away, especially along the Hawkesbury. The riverlands wind along at the end of my street and some of this novel was written at that beautiful location.

I am eternally grateful that I have these two by my side, my greatest supporters, and that we have our dear mum, Dorn, to thank for our belief in each other and, indeed, womankind. We were always encouraged to chase our dreams and to never consider our gender as a disadvantage. On the contrary, she and all of my wonderful aunts revelled in claiming every advantage that came with each new law passed, each inroad made. Education, in particular, was highly esteemed by these intelligent women who were initially denied tertiary opportunities. Thank you for inspiring me by example and for your wisdom and strength in so many, many other ways. Thank you also to our matriarch, Gladys Clancy, my nana, who led the way by example. You inspire my every day.

Those of you who have read my previous novels would know by now that I love to weave real life into my tales and *Sisters of Freedom* is no exception.

To start with, Kuranda is a real home. My sister owned it and lived there for several years, and the current owners, Jo Anne and Bryan Moffat, have kindly given their permission and allowed me to use it as the setting for the Merriweather family home. It is true that it was built at the turn of the century and was celebrated for its design. I've tried to capture the charm of the place, which holds warm and wonderful memories and does, indeed, have historical significance due to its original inhabitants.

In the early twentieth century, Kuranda was owned by Robin Tillyard, a celebrated entomologist. Robin was married to Pattie, a graduate of Cambridge who was denied her degree. She worked with her husband, illustrating his books, and she was also a suffragist. The couple had four daughters, Patience, Faith, Hope and Honour. All four girls excelled at sport and pursued studies of their own. Patience gained a scholarship to Canberra University, Faith gained her masters and became an entomologist, Hope drove ambulances in the First World War and studied painting and Honour was a champion swimmer who studied nutrition. She also became an active member of the New Zealand Federation of University Women.

The Tillyards moved to Canberra after living at Kuranda and were well known and respected. Pattie became deeply involved in community work and argued 'there ought to be a woman on every governing body'. She became known as the grand dame of Canberra society and established the Australian National University Tillyard prize in 1940. A statue was erected in her name.

It was their years at early Hornsby that most fascinated me, though. I often stood at the base of the stairs at Kuranda imagining these passionate young women holding on to their hats and flying down the stairs to join their parents in the adventures of the day. There's a feeling of purpose in that beautiful home, a sense of excitement in its architecture and grace. Some places simply hold on to the spirit of the past.

Finally, Pretty Boy was our bird growing up and we all adored him. He was the cheekiest individual imaginable and my mother did walk around with him on her shoulder, although only at home. My brother, too. (PB had favourites and did peck my dad for clipping his wings.) My Uncle Frank gave him to us and he had my Aunt Gladys's voice, saying how pretty he was to anyone who walked by.

Somehow I feel he captures the spirit of those early feminists who didn't allow their clipped wings to hold them back in life and spoke the truth fearlessly, boldly and to all who'd listen. They taught us all to fly, in the end. Long may their legacy soar.

Don't miss ...

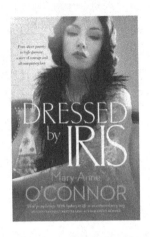

DRESSED
by IRIS

by

Mary-Anne
O'CONNOR

Available Now

talk about it

Let's talk about books.

Join the conversation:

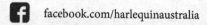 facebook.com/harlequinaustralia

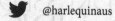 @harlequinaus

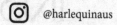 @harlequinaus

harpercollins.com.au/hq

If you love reading and want to know about our
authors and titles, then let's talk about it.